A

DROP

OF

HAUNTED

BLOOD

Rory North

Chapter One
Swords, Stones, and Potted Plants

Felix glared at the racoon perched on top of the trash can. "Listen, buddy," he said. "I respect you. But if you don't let me throw this bag in there, we're going to have a problem." He took a slow step forward. The raccoon didn't budge.

"Seriously, my sister has a sword. Don't make me get her." Felix doubted Helena would be eager to use her weapon on local wildlife, but that was the only comforting thought he could come up with. Thick gray clouds obscured the first rays of morning sun, and the lights from his house weren't doing much to illuminate the end of the driveway where the trash can waited for pickup. He couldn't help but feel a little uneasy.

The raccoon's head tipped to the side. Did it understand that it was being threatened? What were the chances it had rabies? The last thing Felix needed was a trip to the hospital. But he was already running behind, and if he missed the bus again this week, Mom would definitely stop letting him stay out late with the tennis team.

"All right. You asked for it." Felix lifted the trash bag and swung. The raccoon hissed and flashed its upsettingly large fangs before leaping off the can and into the bushes lining the edge of the driveway. Felix stumbled forward. He crashed into the trash can, and the whole thing tipped over, spilling bags onto the cement.

There was a decent chance Mom was watching from the kitchen window, so he bit back a string of curses as he righted the can and shoved the bags back inside. He added this morning's trash on top, slammed the lid shut, and turned around. The raccoon sat on its hind legs ten feet away, eyes on him.

"The hell is your problem?" Felix had never had particularly strong feelings about raccoons, but this same unnaturally large one had been out here every morning for the past week.

The raccoon blinked. Felix shuddered.

When he walked back into the kitchen, Helena looked up from the textbook she was reading and crammed another bite of cereal into her mouth. As usual, she'd gotten up early enough to be ready long before everyone else was even awake. The dirty blonde hair she'd gotten from Dad was pulled up in a ponytail, and she wore a bright blue shirt with her university's logo on it. Her longsword lay unsheathed across the counter in front of her. Felix could already hear Mom's lecture about leaving weapons there.

Helena swallowed. "You okay?" She asked, brow furrowing.

"I'm fine," Felix told her. He rested his arms on the counter and leaned forward so that he could see his face reflected in the sword's shiny blade. "That raccoon was out there again."

May walked into the room as the words were leaving his mouth. "Aw, are you still scared of that raccoon?" she teased.

Felix groaned. "I'm not scared of it. I just don't want rabies!" His reflection's green eyes narrowed. "And it was your turn to take out the trash, anyway."

"Then why'd you do it?" May asked.

"You were taking one of your long ass showers, and the bus is going to be here in five minutes!"

"I'm not going to school today," May said. She tucked a piece of her chin-length dark brown hair—she shared the color with both Mom and her twin—behind her ear. "Neither is Ezra."

Felix looked up. "What? Why not?"

"We have a doctor's appointment."

"Why don't I have one?"

"It's a twin thing."

Helena rolled her eyes. "It's not a twin thing. She and Ezra need a few booster shots before they go to college this fall." She closed the textbook she'd been reading, and Felix's brain hurt just seeing the words "Advanced Physics" on the cover. "May, we should go look for that raccoon later today and make sure it's not—" She hesitated. "Make sure it doesn't have rabies."

May folded her arms. "You think it could be...sick?"

"Probably not, but I want to be sure."

Great. They were having one of their weird little conversations again. Felix lowered his chin to his arms and glared at Helena's sword. This close, he could see the tiny geometric symbols carved into the metal and around the teal-colored grip. When he'd asked Helena what they meant years ago, she'd mumbled something about buying it secondhand.

"Should we get Mom to help?" May asked.

Helena shook her head. "No, I think we can handle it ourselves."

Mom entered the kitchen a moment later. Ezra trailed behind. "Ezra, where did you put my phone?" Mom stopped in her tracks when she saw Felix. "Felix, your hair!"

Felix ran a hand through the mess of light brown hair he hadn't touched since waking up. "Uh..." Mom usually didn't pay close enough attention in the morning to catch when he hadn't brushed his hair.

"Come here."

The distant rattle of the school bus reached them. "That's the bus. I have to go." Felix started backing toward the front door.

"Helena can drop you off on her way to class." Mom's stern gaze moved to the kitchen, where Helena was already grabbing her sword off the counter.

Despite being an early riser, Helena tended to run late, too. Better not to risk it. Felix grabbed his green baseball cap off the dining table as he passed it. "I'll just wear this all day. Look, it matches my hoodie."

"I thought I asked you to stop leaving hats lying around."

"That's why I'm taking it!" Felix continued to inch backward toward the front of the house.

Before Mom could respond, Ezra picked up one of his plants off the counter—something with white flowers Felix could never remember the name of—and looked up. "Did someone rearrange these? This one's supposed to get more light."

"Sorry, Ezra, I moved them while I was cooking last night." Mom turned her attention back to Felix, absentmindedly twisting one of the silver rings on her hand as she did. She usually did that when she was anticipating something. What was going to happen when he left for school? What secret conversation was the rest of his family going to have without him?

May decided now would be a great time to chime in. "How come Ezra gets to keep his plants around the house, but I have to keep my rock collection in my room?"

"Not now, May."

The bus was almost to the stop outside, judging by the roar of its engine. Felix waved as he pushed open the front door. "Bye, love you!"

Mom sighed. "Love you." A smile crossed her face. "Good luck on your history test!"

Oops. Felix had forgotten about that. "Uh, yeah, thanks!" He'd have to cram during lunch. The door clicked shut behind him, and he set off down the driveway.

Dad stood next to the mailbox, clutching a few envelopes in his hands and staring intently at something in the distance. "Bye Dad, love you!" Felix called as he passed.

That snapped Dad out of whatever trance he'd been in. "Hey, Felix," he said as he turned. "You have tennis practice today, right?"

Felix nodded. "I'll be back around dinner."

Dad looked a little surprised at that. "Not staying out late with the team?"

"Nope. Got homework." Felix felt a twinge of annoyance at the question. Did everyone else want him out of the house today?

He reached the bus just as the last kid—besides him—was scrambling on. Felix hurried on after them, nodded at the bus driver, and made his way to the very back row where Jace waited.

"Wow, you actually made it today," Jace said, lifting his backpack so Felix could sit down.

"Yeah, well, I almost had to fight that raccoon again." Felix sank into the seat next to the window and threw one last glance at his house, where Dad was walking inside. Felix's gaze darted back to the sidewalk, and he frowned.

"Maybe you should try locking up your trash can," Jace suggested.

Felix barely heard him, too focused on the unfamiliar man standing at the end of his driveway, his back turned to the bus. His slicked back blonde hair, white suit pants, and matching white jacket with gold embroidered edges seemed excessive for the suburbs. Especially at seven in the morning.

"Who's that?" Felix asked.

Jace glanced around the bus. "Who?"

The man looked back over his shoulder. His eyes glowed like a wild animal's in the low light.

"What the hell?" Felix blurted.

"Huh?"

"Did you see that guy's eyes?"

Jace leaned past Felix to peer out the window, but the bus was pulling away from the curb, and the man had turned back around. "That guy in front of your house?"

"Yeah. His eyes were glowing."

"Are you sure you weren't seeing things?" Jace asked. "It's still kinda dark."

Felix shifted uncomfortably in his seat. "I don't know. He seemed sketchy."

"You think he's going to rob your house?"

"No. Probably not. I'm sure it's fine." Trying to shake off his concern, Felix added, "He's probably just one of my parents' weird friends."

"I mean to be fair, your family's kind of weird too."

"What? No they're not."

"Your sister carries around a sword."

Okay. Fair point.

Jace continued. "If he's one of their friends, wouldn't you recognize him?"

Felix shook his head. "No, I don't really know any of them that well." His parents' friends only seemed to visit when he was going to bed, or leaving for tennis or school. This guy could've been one of them, he supposed. Maybe Felix had briefly met him already and forgotten about it.

Even with that rationalization, he was still unsettled. His anxiety persisted through the bus ride, but when he arrived at school, it was overwhelmed by the stress of the history test. Felix took every spare moment he had to review his messy notes and before long, he'd all but forgotten the strange man standing in front of his house.

The test left him feeling less than great, but he still had hope that he'd get away with a decent score. There were only a couple months left of school, anyway, and his grades were high enough to carry him through a few iffy exams.

Once school was out, Felix didn't have much time to think about his grades or the strange man before tennis practice was in full swing.

It was past five by the time the team wrapped up. Jace approached Felix as he squeezed his racket into his backpack. "Hey, wanna get burgers and shakes?" Jace asked. "It's discount night for our school. I think the rest of the team is going."

"Sorry. I promised my parents I'd be home for dinner tonight," Felix told him. "And I still have to finish that stats assignment."

"No worries," Ian chimed in as he walked by. "I can drop you off at your house on our way."

Felix nodded at him. "Thanks."

Fifteen minutes later, Ian was pulling up along the street in front of Felix's house. Felix grabbed his backpack, waved goodbye to the others in the car, and stepped out onto the sidewalk.

The moment the car door shut behind him, a chill ran down his spine. The house was unusually silent for this time in the evening. Most of the lights were off, too. Felix tried to shake his apprehension, but there was something in the air that made him feel like his blood was humming. Ian's car sped off, and Felix forced himself to move forward.

To his relief, as he approached the porch, the door creaked open, and Mom appeared in the entryway. Some part of him thought it was strange that the door had already been ajar, but the thought only lingered a moment. He waved. "Hey!"

Mom stood in the shadows out of reach of the setting sun, making her face impossible to see in any detail. Felix blinked, and she was gone.

He paused. "Mom?" he called again.

A light breeze pushed the door open a few more inches. The quiet that followed was broken only by the distant chirping of birds. Then, another gust. Felix stood frozen.

"Hey, dork," came a voice from behind him. May's voice.

Felix whirled around. "How did you get behind me?"

May tossed a pale blue-gray stone into the air. "You can see me, then." It landed in her palm, and her fist closed around it.

"Why wouldn't I be able to see you?"

May held up her free hand and flicked his forehead.

"Ow!" Felix clapped a hand to the spot. "What was that for?"

"I can touch you, too." May placed the hand on her hip. "I probably shouldn't be the one telling you this. Go find Mom. Or maybe Helena? She must be around, somewhere. We're all still getting the hang of things."

"Can't you just tell me what's going on?" Felix pleaded. The buzzing sensation in his veins was growing. Despite the fact that his sister looked perfectly calm, every part of his brain screamed that something was wrong.

May sighed. "Okay, don't freak out. But I'm dead."

Felix stared at her blankly. "What?"

"I'm a ghost."

Felix...should have had a stronger reaction to that, he thought dimly. But it was impossible to process the statement fully. To really believe it. Not sure he could stand much longer on his shaking legs, he dropped to a sitting position in the damp grass. "If you're dead, why are you talking to me?" he asked. Then, feeling a faint flicker of hope, he asked, "Is this a weird prank?"

"Yeah, go inside and see what happened. You won't think it's a prank, then." May considered for a moment. "On second thought, maybe don't do that. You've never seen a dead body before, have you?"

"Have you?" Felix asked incredulously.

May shrugged. "Yeah. Lots of times."

Felix stared up at her. The sun wasn't hitting her quite right. Air shimmered around her, and for a moment he thought he could see the street on the other side of her form.

There had been more than he'd realized, hadn't there? More secrets. More missing pieces. He asked the question he'd been wanting to ask for years. "What are you guys hiding from me?"

May grimaced. "A lot of things," she answered. "But we were going to tell you eventually!"

"Tell me what?"

"About our abilities." May held up a hand. "Which I'm not sure if I can use anymore. I can feel the pull, but...everything feels different when you're dead."

Felix shook his head. His eyes stung. "You can't be dead. Why aren't you sad?"

"Well, I've had time to adjust." May scratched her head. "I think it's been about an hour? I don't know, time's weird now."

"Be serious for once!" The first tears found their way out of Felix's eyes. "What the hell am I supposed to do?"

"I don't know, go ask Mom! If you can see me, you should be able to see her, too."

Felix felt like he'd been swallowed by an ocean. Like he was a stone dropped in a choppy sea. And there was an uncomfortable building pressure in his head. "Mom—is she—?"

"All of us are dead," May said plainly. Why was she so calm? None of this made any sense. "Honestly, we always knew something like this might happen. We sort of planned for it, actually. But I guess we should have prepared you, too. Sorry." She hesitated a moment. "There's supposed to be a way to put our souls back in our bodies, but I don't know how it works. Or if it's actually possible like Mom and Dad said."

Her shoulders sagged as she continued. "And sorry we're not exactly in mourning. We're still trying to figure some stuff out. Helena's pissed. She killed the guy, but he'd already gotten her pretty bad. And the rest of us." A faraway look crept into her gaze. "He's one of the most dangerous people we know of. It's a miracle we lasted as long as we did."

"Some guy came into the house and killed you," Felix said blankly. Had he seen the killer that morning? Could he have stopped this?

"Felix, this wasn't some random attack." May knelt down so that she was eye level with him. "We thought we'd have time to tell you what we were protecting."

"Tell me now, then!"

"I can't. Mom and Dad kept things from the rest of us, too." May's tone turned surprisingly bitter. Her gaze moved to the house behind Felix. "All I know is that there's some kind of magical war, and I'm not sure we know which side is the right one."

Magic? War? "You can't be serious."

"I hate to dump this all on you at once, but yeah. Our family has magical abilities. And now we're ghosts."

"Our family...except for me, right?"

"We all manifested our abilities around ten years old. When it happened, Mom and Dad would tell us everything. And it just...never happened for you." May grimaced. "We were getting ready to tell you everything, anyway, but knowing about magic when you don't have any can be dangerous. We wanted to keep you safe as long as possible."

A foggy memory surfaced in Felix's mind. Something about Ezra coming home from elementary school one day with vines tangled in his hair. How after that day, he would participate in the occasional secretive conversations the rest of the family had.

The pressure in Felix's head worsened. Something trickled down his face, below his nose. May frowned. Felix touched a finger to the skin above his lips, and when he pulled it away, he found it stained with blood.

Before he could speak, May reached out a hand, brow furrowing deeper. "Maybe you do have something."

Felix sniffed. "What?"

Her hand met his. There was a blinding flash of bright blue light. Felix closed his eyes and flung up his other hand to shield his face.

When he opened his eyes, May was gone.

"May?" Felix jumped to his feet. "Hello?"

Of course she'd leave him without any real explanation. Felix looked down and spotted the rock she'd been holding laying in the grass. He picked it up and ran a thumb over the markings carved into it, not unlike the ones on Helena's sword. He slid it into his pocket.

The world spun fast enough to put Felix on the verge of throwing up, but he couldn't stay out here. He sprinted up to the open front door. "Guys? Anyone?" His voice strained.

When he stepped inside, his backpack slipped off his shoulder and clattered to the floor. The body in the middle of the entryway, spilling blood onto the hardwood, was a man he didn't recognize.

Wait, no, he did. It was the man who'd stood in the driveway that morning, after all. The man's eyes were open, but they weren't glowing like they had been. Plain, hazel eyes stared blankly up at the ceiling. Empty.

Helena's sword was stuck in his chest.

Felix dared to take one step forward, and then another. He gingerly reached out a trembling hand to touch the hilt of the sword.

Helena was suddenly in front of him, manifesting from thin air. Her hands moved to rest on top of his. "Felix," she said softly. "Can you see me?"

"Of—of course I can see you," Felix stammered.

Helena lifted her eyes from their hands to meet his gaze. "I probably shouldn't be the one to explain everything," she said. "You need to find Mom."

"Where is she?"

"Felix, all of us are—" Helena closed her eyes and took a deep breath. "Do you feel anything out of the ordinary?"

"It's kind of hard to tell!" Felix exclaimed. "I have no idea what's going on or why there's a dead guy laying on our floor!"

"I know. I'm sorry. But if there ever were a time for you to find your ability, it would be now."

"Ability?" Felix's hand tightened around the sword's hilt. "May said that too. What does that mean?"

"Maybe we were right, and you don't have one. But I always hoped—" Helena's eyes opened. "Wait, you talked to May?"

"Yeah, she explained that you guys were ghosts, then touched my hand and disappeared. There was a bright light. My nose was bleeding." Felix's eyes widened. "Wait, did she...leave for good? Did I do something wrong?"

"No. You haven't done anything wrong." Helena studied his face, her head tipping to the side. "I'm going to try something, okay? Whatever happens, you need to go find Mom."

She lifted her hand and placed it on his shoulder. Felix squinted as another bright light flooded the entryway, replacing the evening gold with shades of blue-green. As quickly as she'd appeared, Helena was gone. Chest tight, Felix took a hesitant step forward, unable to keep himself from swaying.

It was then that he saw Helena's body, lying ten feet from the man's, her arm outstretched. "Helena?" Felix choked. *It's okay. It has to be. I was just talking to her.* He frantically looked around, taking in more blood as he did. "Hello? Is anyone else here?"

He stumbled past the man and Helena, growing dizzier by the second. One of his hands flew to his pocket and searched for his phone, but he couldn't find it. Had he left it in his backpack? Where was his backpack?

The next room he entered was the kitchen, and everything was a blur from there. There was a flash of dark blue light. A flash of dark green light. That was the last thing he remembered before he opened his eyes and found himself lying on his back, staring up at the ceiling.

A man leaned into view. "You dead, too?"

Chapter Two
Bright Guardians

Felix shot up into a sitting position and stared at the man standing over him. "Who the hell are you? How did you get in my house?"

"You left the front door open," the man said blankly. He looked younger than Felix had initially thought. Mid-twenties, maybe? It was hard to be sure, thanks to the black mask pulled up from around his neck to cover the bottom half of his face. The only feature offering any hint of expression were his stern honey brown eyes. His jet-black hair was just long enough to be held back in a ponytail, save for the short pieces hanging around his light face.

He wasn't alone. The woman next to him gently elbowed him in the side. "Maybe I should talk to him, Archer." She and the man were dressed in similar outfits that Felix guessed were a uniform. Black boots, black pants, black jackets. The man—Archer, apparently—wore a deep red shirt under his jacket, while the woman's shirt was a bright yellow, a striking contrast to her dark brown skin and tight coils of black hair.

Archer shot her a sideways glance. "What makes you say that?"

The woman didn't answer. She cleared her throat and flashed Felix a sad smile. "Are you Felix Carver?"

"How do you know my name?" Felix asked.

"We're from the Bright Guardians." When Felix's only response was an empty stare, the woman frowned. "You haven't heard of us, have you?"

"Your family didn't tell you anything about us?" Archer asked. "Our records say you don't have an ability, but we assumed you at least knew about us."

"No idea what that is." Felix's heart was going to explode. "I'm sorry, I have no idea what's happening. Do you know my family? Or where the rest of them are?" Maybe he should have clarified that he was asking about their ghosts, not their bodies, but his thoughts were far from organized.

The woman lifted her gaze, expression darkening. "Did you not see...?"

"Kendra," Archer cut her off. "He's radiating magical energy. We need to get him out of here."

"Yeah, I can feel it," Kendra replied. "What about Gideon's body?"

"Even if some part of his soul is sticking around, he won't be able to leave the house on his own. Let's get Felix outside, and I'll come back and kill whatever's left of him."

"My ability would be better for tracking his ghost."

"Fine," Archer said. "I'll babysit the kid. But we need to take a look at the bodies, too. Before police get here." He shot Felix a questioning look. "You haven't called anyone yet, have you?"

Felix shook his head. The motion triggered a ringing in his ears. "Hey, uh, I think I might need to go to the hospital or something."

Kendra looked worried, but Archer seemed unconcerned as he folded his arms. Black leather gloves hid his hands. "He's in shock, I'm sure," he said.

"I think it's more than that," Kendra said. "Some kind of magic is affecting him."

"Then we'll deal with it back at the castle. It's not our area of expertise."

Castle? Felix didn't know of any castles here in Washington.

A crash came from the next room. Archer and Kendra whirled around. Archer had a dagger in his hand now, leaving Felix to marvel at how quickly he'd drawn the weapon.

Ezra stumbled into the kitchen, clutching a potted plant of all things. "Relax, it's just my brother," Felix said as he stood up. Archer and Kendra exchanged glances. Kendra's dark eyes widened with concern.

Ezra was the first person to look genuinely upset. In fact, he looked like he'd been crying, and his brown hair was disheveled. "Felix, I'm so sorry."

Kendra spoke as if Ezra hadn't said anything at all. "Felix, your brother's...dead. I'm sorry."

"Yeah, but he's right there." Felix frowned. "Didn't you just hear what he said?"

"Felix, I think you're the only one who can see my ghost." Ezra set the plant on the counter, making Archer and Kendra jump as if it had appeared out of nowhere. "This is our fault. We should have told you about the Bright Guardians sooner. But we wanted to keep you safe as long as we could."

"Well, it's not surprising there are ghosts here," Archer said. "But it's strange he can see them when we can't."

Ignoring the comment, Felix moved toward Ezra. "Where are Mom and Dad?"

Ezra rested a hand on Felix's shoulder. This time, there was no flash, though that buzzing sensation was returning. "I think you need to do with me what you did with them," Ezra said. "I don't know exactly what happened, but your ability seems to involve ghosts."

"What do you mean?" Felix asked. "I haven't seen Mom and Dad yet."

"Yeah, you did. When you came in here."

Felix's brow furrowed. "I don't really remember coming in." Wait, had he seen them? He had the vague impression he'd tried to hug them, touched them, and then there'd been those lights...

"It did happen quickly," Ezra murmured.

"He's overwhelmed," Kendra said. "Let's get him out of here."

"Wait!" Felix grabbed his brother's arm. "Ezra, why isn't the same light-flashy-thing happening with you?"

"You probably need a secondary material to channel your magic. Mom and Helena need metal, and I need dirt. But I don't know what you were using with everyone else." Ezra's hands were shaking, Felix realized. Could ghosts have panic attacks?

"I don't remember much," Felix said. "My nose started bleeding while I was talking to May, and there was a bright light—"

Ezra's face lit up. "Blood."

"What?"

"Felix, your blood. That could be what activates your ability." Ezra leaned forward to squint at Felix's face. "Your nose stopped bleeding, so we'll have to try something else."

"Care to explain your brother's side of the conversation?" Archer asked.

"Uh, yeah, in a sec." Felix glanced back at Archer. "Hey, could I borrow that dagger?"

Archer's eyes narrowed. "Absolutely not."

Felix's gaze darted across the kitchen counter and landed on the knife block. "Okay, fine." He hurried toward it. He really hoped he was understanding Ezra correctly.

Alarmed, Kendra took a step forward. "Felix!"

"Wait." Archer held up a gloved hand. The concern didn't leave Kendra's expression, but she didn't move to stop Felix, either.

Felix yanked a random knife from the block and pricked his thumb on the tip of the blade. A single drop of blood welled on his skin. "Is that enough?" he asked, looking back at Ezra.

Ezra managed to look even paler than he already had. "Let's find out." He walked forward to stand in front of Felix.

"What's going to happen to you?" Felix asked.

"I don't know, but I think everyone else is still...here. With you." Ezra reached out a hand toward Felix. "I can feel them."

As soon as his fingers grazed Felix's shoulder, there was a flash of bright green light. Ezra's dark hair, green eyes, shaking hands—it was all gone in a heartbeat.

Felix flicked his gaze to Archer and Kendra. "You guys saw that, right?"

"The bright flash of light and the outline of a boy?" Archer asked. "Yes."

A new voice spoke. "Is it my turn, now?"

Felix, Archer, and Kendra turned in unison as a man entered the kitchen. "You," Felix hissed. His grip tightened around the kitchen knife as he pointed it at the man who'd killed his family. "Please tell me you guys can see him."

The man grinned.

"Yeah, we can see this one." Archer twirled his dagger around in his hand. "Gideon Pollock. I warned you you'd end up dead, didn't I?"

Gideon laughed. "That little knife's not going to do you much good."

Archer's eyes narrowed. "You think you can ignore banishing sigils? You're a ghost, Gideon. Bound by the laws of magic."

"And you of all people should know that some ghosts are more powerful than others." Gideon lifted an eyebrow. "You had a hard time getting rid of that old friend of yours, didn't you?"

"Archer—" Kendra warned.

Archer lunged forward, dagger swinging. Gideon dodged the blade, laughing as he did. A second dagger appeared in Archer's other hand, with a black and red handle that matched the first. He stabbed at Gideon's abdomen. Gideon disappeared before the blade reached him and reappeared behind Archer.

Kendra moved forward now, holding up her empty hands. "Felix, open that window. The screen, too."

Felix dropped the kitchen knife and hurried to the window over the sink. He struggled with the latch for a moment before getting it open, then shoved against the screen's frame with all the strength he could muster. The moment the screen popped free, something darted past him. A butterfly. Three more followed, and he could just make out strange markings in the patterns on their wings.

Archer attacked again. Gideon vanished and rematerialized at his right. Claws appeared at Gideon's fingertips as he swiped a hand at Archer's face, forcing Archer to duck. Archer retaliated a moment later, and this time his blade grazed Gideon's neck. Gideon flickered a few times before disappearing.

Kendra lowered her hands. More butterflies had entered the kitchen now, and they flapped in slow circles over her head. "Is it too much to hope that banished him?"

Gideon answered her question by reappearing behind her. "I'll admit, that stung. But I'm still holding on."

The butterflies Kendra had summoned flitted around Gideon's head. Gideon glared at them and flickered out of view. His disembodied voice echoed around the kitchen. "Your insect friends are going to have to move faster than that if you want to trap me."

"He's gotten a handle on being a ghost remarkably quickly," Archer said. He returned his daggers to his sides, then reached behind his back and drew a sword from its scabbard. Symbols etched into the metal reminded Felix of Helena's blade, though these ones were larger and more detailed. A red metal rose was embedded in the black pommel, and the matching red grip came to a stop beneath the small but intricate black crossguard.

More of Helena's sword admiration had rubbed off on Felix than he'd realized, he thought as he bent down to pick up the kitchen knife he'd dropped. As his hand neared the metal, his stomach turned, and an odd sensation in his chest made him feel like something was trying to break free. A crackling sound cut through the air around him.

Felix was distracted by the reappearance of Gideon mere feet from where he stood. Gideon smashed a fist against the wall to his left. The cupboards flew open, and dishes slid off the shelves and rained down on Archer, who lifted an arm to shield his head as he continued his approach. Plates and bowls shattered on the ground.

"I think this might be better than being alive!" Gideon exclaimed. He vanished again.

A swarm of bees came in through the window. Felix yelped in surprise and ducked. The bees flew over his head in a tight formation and moved toward a spot in front of the fridge.

"You can't hide from me, Gideon," Kendra said. The bees took on a roughly human outline. Archer raced forward and swung his weapon through their formation.

Drop the knife and grab my sword!

The exclamation took Felix by surprise. He could hear Helena's voice, but he couldn't see her. "Helena?" He straightened up and turned in a circle. "Where are you?"

I'm seeing what you're seeing, Felix.

"What? How?"

I don't know, Helena said. *The last thing I remember is talking to you in the entryway. But I think I can still use my magic. Let me kill that guy!*

"He's already dead."

Then we're going to kill him again. Grab my sword.

Felix raced past the ongoing fight between Gideon, Archer, and Kendra. "Felix!" Kendra barely got his name out before she was dodging an attack from Gideon's clawed hands. She'd drawn a dagger of her own, too, but the swarm of bees—whose stripes formed strange patterns—formed a shield in front of her that was apparently enough to deter Gideon.

Ignoring her concern, Felix returned to the hallway where Gideon's body still lay. He grabbed the handle of Helena's sword, doing his best to avoid looking directly at the corpse. As he pulled the weapon free, a surge of energy flooded his veins.

"Wait, I don't know how to use a sword!" Felix lifted the weapon. This was going to be much harder to swing than a tennis racket.

Come on, both hands on the grip, Helena told him. *All you have to do is hit him, and the sigils will do the rest. Hopefully. We may need to dump some holy water on him.*

"Holy water?" Felix asked. "Since when are we religious?"

We're not, but that stuff kills ghosts!

"They're already dead!"

You know what I mean!

Felix didn't, but he adjusted his grip on the sword and headed back to the kitchen. He'd failed a lot today, but maybe he could do one thing right.

Archer looked Felix up and down as he reentered the kitchen. "Stay back. That sword's not going to work on him."

"Let us handle this," Kendra added.

Helena huffed. *They think I wouldn't use a weapon with sigils on it?*

"Helena says the sword's got sigils," Felix said. "Whatever that means."

"They might not be strong enough for Gideon," Archer replied.

"Guess we'll see." Felix's hand tightened around the sword's hilt. "Helena, you got anything else to add?"

Yeah. This.

Bright blue-green electricity jumped up and down Felix's arms. The sight sent a brief panic through him, but there was no pain and seemingly no damage to his skin. So, after taking a steadying breath, he charged toward Gideon.

"Well, that's interesting," Gideon said. He reached back and grabbed the toaster sitting on the counter behind him. In one swift motion, he yanked it free from the wall and chucked it at Felix.

Felix didn't move out of the way fast enough. The toaster smacked into his forehead. He gasped in pain as he stumbled sideways into a wall, the lightning on his skin dying out in a shower of sparks. He lifted a hand to his face and found fresh blood trickling from a gash. When he moved his gaze to where Gideon had been, the man was gone.

Archer and Kendra hurried to Felix. "Gideon's strong enough to pick up material objects," Archer said. "Not for long, but long enough to do some damage."

"Felix should leave," Kendra replied with a nod. "We can't keep an eye on him and Gideon."

"I agree."

Kendra lowered her voice. "I have sigil-marked insects around the house. I can close the perimeter until we have him trapped in one place. But I have to bring them in slowly, so the circle doesn't get disrupted."

Felix climbed to his feet. "Can you control insects or something?" he asked.

"That's part of it." Kendra rested a hand on his shoulder. "Felix, go outside. I promise we can handle him. I'm sure your parents kept holy water around here somewhere—"

Gideon appeared behind Kendra and Archer. His eyes met Felix's. A smirk crossed his face.

Anger boiled Felix's blood. He lifted the sword and darted forward between Kendra and Archer. The blade moved through Gideon's form. He flickered. Disappeared.

And then he was back, laughing again. "That *really* hurt. But it still wasn't enough. Maybe if you'd used Archer's sword."

Felix let Helena's sword clatter to the ground. The lightning was back, jumping between his fingers and casting a teal glow across the kitchen. "I'm getting rid of you one way or another!" He lunged at Gideon with his bare hands.

Felix collided with Gideon, whose form was solid to his touch. Electricity jumped from his hands to Gideon's ghost as they staggered through the kitchen, making the man hiss in pain. *Good.* Felix grabbed Gideon's shoulders. "Why did you kill them?" he demanded.

A blinding flash of white light knocked Felix onto his back.

It took Felix a moment to get air back in his lungs. Gasping, he sat up. Gideon was gone. Felix scanned the kitchen, waiting for the man to reappear, but his family's killer was nowhere to be found.

Archer returned his sword to its scabbard. "I wouldn't dare hope that was a real banishment."

Kendra helped Felix to his feet. "That lightning wasn't yours, I'm guessing," she said.

"I think that was my sister." Felix tipped his head back. "Helena? Can you hear me?"

Nothing. He was alone again.

"You're carrying their ghosts," Archer said. Eyes narrowing, he added, "And you've got Gideon, too."

"Huh?"

Archer lifted a hand to pull down his mask, exposing the lower half of his slim face. "We've known for most of recorded history that ghosts can be contained inside of objects," he said. "But outside of active possession, as far as we know, no living being has ever held a ghost inside of them. Let alone multiple."

"He has an ability after all," Kendra said, sounding a little awed.

"And he can use the abilities of the ghosts he's holding." Archer pinched the bridge of his nose. "This is a nightmare."

"Nightmare?" Felix asked. "Why?"

"You have access to six different abilities, you haven't trained to use any of them, and you're carrying the soul of a dangerous magician in a way that's never been done before," Archer said. "We have no idea how long you can hold him, if he's conscious, or if he's capable of breaking free."

"Archer, now's not the time," Kendra said. "Let's get him to the castle."

"Right," Archer muttered. "The King's Council needs to hear this as soon as possible."

Kendra hesitated. "Sure. Felix, go get a bag and some changes of clothes. If you need to come back later, we can arrange that, but pack light for now."

A bee followed Felix to his bedroom. He didn't say anything, but he had a feeling Kendra was somehow using it to keep an eye on him. He did his best to keep his outward appearance calm, but his internal monologue was mostly just screaming at this point. *Ghosts! I fought a ghost! With magic!*

Maybe he was still in shock, but he couldn't say he was completely fazed by the existence of ghosts, or other mild supernatural phenomena. Maybe it was his family's weirdness that he'd picked up on—no matter how hard they tried to hide it—but deep down he'd always thought there might be something more to them. To the world.

Actually seeing it with his own two eyes, though? Unreal. And wielding the magic was something else entirely. A small part of him was convinced this was all a dream he was going to wake up from.

He wished it was just a dream.

After packing up the essentials, Felix wandered in and out of his family's bedrooms. At first, he thought he was just stalling, but as he stood in the middle of his parents' room, something compelled him to open the bottom drawer of their nightstand.

Dad's leatherbound journal. Felix ran a hand across the forest green cover before opening it. He was surprised to find the entire thing was written in a language he didn't recognize, though the letters themselves were from the alphabet he knew. As he slid it into his backpack, he spotted one of Mom's silver rings sitting next to where the journal had been in the drawer.

Strange, he swore she'd been wearing that one this morning. It was her favorite. He picked it up and examined the flames engraved around the band.

It was too small to fit him, so he searched Mom's jewelry box for a plain silver chain, slid the ring on, and hooked it around his neck. The cool metal slid underneath his shirt and rested against his chest.

Ezra's plants had found their way onto just about every shelf and table in the house. Felix picked one—a cactus that he figured was the least likely to die in his care—and carried it with him. He also checked his pocket to confirm he still had the stone May had left behind in the front yard.

On the way back to the kitchen, he paused next to Gideon's body. Being near it made his nausea return, but something caught his eye. He forced himself to kneel down and take a closer look at the gold necklace that glinted in the low light.

Several items were attached to the chain: an animal fang, a large dark brown feather, and what looked like a fragment of bone. Frowning, Felix lifted the chain to get a closer look. It must have snapped at some point during the fight, because it came free from Gideon's neck easily.

"Felix?" Kendra called from the next room. "Are you ready to leave?"

Felix hastily shoved the necklace into his hoodie pocket and stood up as she walked into the entryway. "Yeah."

Kendra held out Helena's sword to him, which she'd found the scabbard for. "You should keep this with you."

Felix nodded as he took it. "What about...my family?"

"Don't worry, they'll be taken care of. Other Guardians are already on the way to handle all of this." Kendra placed a hand behind Felix's shoulder and steered him away from Gideon's body. "Right now, we're going to get you somewhere safe."

Chapter Three
A Pocket Dimension Full of Sunshine

Felix found himself in the backseat of a surprisingly plain black car. He wasn't sure what he'd expected magicians to drive, but as he buckled his seat belt, he supposed it made sense for them to blend in.

Kendra drove while Archer brooded in the passenger seat. His black mask covered his face again, and he still wore his gloves as he inspected his blades.

After a few minutes on the road, Felix cleared his throat. "So, how far to this castle?"

"Drive's about an hour," Archer said.

"Maybe we could explain what's happening to him," Kendra suggested.

Felix yawned. Archer threw a glance back at him. "Assuming he doesn't pass out, you're welcome to explain whatever you'd like."

"I'd like to know what's happening." Even as the words left Felix's mouth, he realized it was pointless. He'd been fighting to keep his eyes open since the moment he sat down. He leaned against the car window and tried to focus on the passing greenery.

The next thing he knew, he was blinking sleep out of his eyes as they pulled off a freeway exit. He recognized the area, and he was still pretty sure there were no castles nearby. Then Kendra took a sharp turn off the road into the trees, making Felix's heart rate spike.

Except they were still driving on pavement. The new road hadn't been visible until they were on it. Trees formed a tunnel overhead, and after a few moments, the evening light shifted from the cloudy gray they'd been driving under to a brighter sunset.

Felix pressed his hands against the window as they emerged from the tunnel. The road ahead twisted and turned over rolling green hills, leading up to a towering castle of white stone and pale blue roofs. Forest surrounded the property on all sides.

"Whoa," Felix breathed.

A small smile touched Kendra's lips in the rear-view mirror. "Welcome to Bright Castle."

The car rolled to a stop in a small lot shaded by a variety of fruit trees, where a few other cars were already parked. From there, it was a short walk up a grassy hill to the entrance of the castle.

"Where are we?" Felix asked as he climbed out of the car. "Geographically, I mean."

"Pocket dimension." Archer closed his door and didn't elaborate further. Well, that was good enough an explanation for Felix, for now.

Felix took it all in as they walked to the castle's massive front doors, the same shade of blue as the tower roofs. Hawks circled in the sky far above. Patches of trees were scattered across the hills, and Felix caught a glimpse of a pond in the distance before they stepped inside.

"Let's get him to the throne room before people start asking questions," Archer said.

Felix adjusted his backpack. "Is it okay that I'm just carrying this sword?" Even with the blade in its scabbard, he worried that someone would freak out.

"Don't worry. No one will think much of it," Kendra assured him.

The three walked down several long hallways, all with shiny white floors, blue and gray wallpaper, and silver detailing. They passed quite a few portraits on the walls, some of which depicted people wielding elements or standing next to animals. Many wore more old-fashioned clothing, while others appeared modern. A few people in the paintings wore the same uniforms as Kendra and Archer.

They passed a handful of real people, too, wearing either the same uniform or formal suits. A few looked at Felix with interest, but averted their gaze when Archer shot them a glare.

Felix, Archer, and Kendra finally came to a stop next to a set of dark blue double doors. A woman stood on one side, and a man on the other. They both wore entirely black suits, save for their silvery shirts.

"Tell King Atticus I'm here," Archer said. The woman nodded and disappeared through one of the doors. After a quick glance at Felix, the man followed.

"I'm going to talk to a king?" Frowning, Felix added, "What's he the king of, anyway?"

"The Brightlands," Kendra said. "They're mostly gone, now. All that remains is this castle and the property around it."

"But the Bright Guardians are stronger than ever, and our king leads us," Archer added. "Along with his council."

"Huh. Weird," Felix said.

"Weird?" Kendra raised an eyebrow.

"I don't know. It just seems like a weird system to have." Felix shrugged. "Isn't the concept of a monarchy a little outdated?"

A new voice spoke. "The kid has a point."

Felix whirled around. A man had crept up on the three without making a sound. He leaned back against the wall opposite them with his arms folded, but it was clear he was the tallest. Unlike the others, his black uniform jacket was zipped up to the high collar. As his head tipped to the side, Felix noticed that his black hair—which was a little longer than Felix's—had an iridescent sheen to it.

"He doesn't know anything about how the King's Council works," Archer said to the man. "And you should watch what you say about them. You know you're on thin ice."

The man snorted. "The ice I'm on is as thin as the Earth's crust."

"What are you doing here, Sebastian?" Kendra asked, her tone far more polite than Archer's.

Sebastian shrugged his broad shoulders. "I heard what happened. Thought I'd drop by and introduce myself." He waved to Felix. "Sebastian Armitage. Nice to meet you."

"Uh, Felix Carver." Felix waved back.

"You're wasting your time," Archer said. "The king only wants to speak to us."

"Funny, I heard this was an open meeting," Sebastian replied.

"Open meeting?" Archer glanced at Kendra.

Kendra folded her arms and tapped a finger against the sleeve of her jacket. "He's right. The throne room's crowded." She frowned. "Word spread fast."

Sebastian clicked his tongue. "You shouldn't be keeping spies in the throne room, Kendra."

"Like you said, open meeting. And the ant chose to go in there of its own accord." Kendra lifted an eyebrow. "Seems like someone snuck food into a meeting again."

Sebastian reached into his jacket pocket and took out an open granola bar. "I don't know what you're talking about." He took a bite.

"Disgusting," Archer muttered.

Kendra looked to the doors. "I wonder why the king decided on an open meeting. I thought he'd want to speak to us privately, first."

"I'll talk to him." Archer grabbed one of the door handles. "Wait here. I don't want everyone swarming Felix."

"I'll come, too!" Sebastian said, ducking in behind Archer before the door closed. Whatever Archer's response was, Felix doubted it was enthusiastic.

"They don't seem to like each other," Felix said.

"They don't," Kendra said. "It's very annoying."

"Whose side are you on?" Was that rude to ask?

Kendra shrugged. "Neither. Archer hates Sebastian for something that isn't his fault, and Sebastian hates Archer for being a stickler for the rules." Her arms dropped to her sides. "And they both think the other can't be trusted."

Felix lifted an eyebrow. "Am I allowed to know about this thing that isn't Sebastian's fault?"

"You'll learn more about it eventually," Kendra said. "The Bright Guardians have a complicated history. Eight years ago there was an...uprising of sorts. Sebastian's family was involved, and he's the only one who sided with us. But a lot of people still don't trust him. Including the council."

One of the doors opened. "The king's not in there yet," Archer said. "He's waiting for the three of us in the rear chamber. After we explain what happened, there's going to be an open meeting to discuss what we should do with Felix."

Felix and Kendra followed Archer through the doorway. They passed through a huge room illuminated by silver chandeliers hanging from the ceiling far above. At the front of the room, atop a raised platform, stood a tall silver throne with dark blue cushioning. A semicircle of tiered seating filled the opposite end of the room, with a gap in the middle to accommodate the doors.

Most of the people in the room were standing. Whatever conversations they had been having faltered as Archer and Kendra led Felix forward. All eyes were on Felix, but no one said a word to him. His gaze darted from face to face anxiously. Some offered him a smile, while others looked concerned or upset.

He, Archer, and Kendra circled around the throne to another blue door behind it, this one protected by five guards. They all stepped aside save for one, who opened the door before clearing the path. Sebastian, who appeared to have been unsuccessfully attempting to chat with the guards, gave Felix a thumbs up as he passed.

If that was supposed to make Felix feel better, it didn't work. His insides were still in knots, and his heart had been racing for so long he thought he might actually collapse.

The rear chamber was essentially a small office. Shelves filled with books covered the walls to the left and right, and a desk opposite the door held a couple more stacks. The man behind the desk looked up when they entered. Waves of auburn brown hair framed his face, stopping just short of his bearded jaw. His pale amber eyes rested on Felix for a long moment before his attention moved to Archer.

Archer crossed the room, lowered his mask, and dropped to one knee. "King Atticus," he said as he bowed his head. The king rose to his feet. He was younger than Felix expected. In fact, he couldn't have been much older than Archer and Kendra.

"That's him?" Felix whispered.

Kendra nodded.

"Should I bow or whatever?"

"You don't have to do that," Kendra replied quietly. She nodded toward Archer. "Archer just happens to be the King's Hand."

"Does that mean he's important?"

"Very."

Archer rose to his feet and told his and Kendra's side of the story. After explaining how Gideon had disappeared in a flash of light, he looked to Felix. "Apparently, something similar happened with all the other members of his family."

"Yeah," Felix said. He cleared his throat. "Uh, yes. I found my sisters first, and then I guess my parents, but I don't really remember that part. And like Archer said, he and Kendra saw the same thing happen with my brother."

King Atticus studied Felix, his head tipping slightly to the side. "Can you hear or see any of the ghosts now?" His voice was a bit high-pitched, with the faintest hint of an accent that was vaguely European. There was a clear air of authority to it, though.

Felix shook his head. "The only one I spoke to after taking them in was Helena, and I didn't hear anything from her after the fight with Gideon ended." He paused. "She also mentioned she couldn't remember anything between our two conversations."

"That's promising, though we should still be careful what we let him see and hear, in case Gideon is somehow listening." King Atticus turned to Archer. "The fact that he's carrying Gideon's soul has me concerned. But if he's capable of using the ghosts' abilities, he could turn the tide for us."

"Someone will have to train him," Archer said. "And he'll need a lot of help one-on-one."

"Most of the teachers have their hands full already, but at least one must be willing." King Atticus circled the desk and started toward the door. "Still, I'd like the rest of the council to agree to it before I finalize my decision."

His clothing resembled the other Guardians' uniforms, but with elaborate silver detailing along the cuffs and bottom edge of the jacket. The white shirt he wore underneath had a high neck that was also embroidered with silver, and he wore white dress shoes instead of black boots. He paused next to the chamber door to pick up a silver crown resting on a pedestal that Felix had missed when they'd entered. Jewels in a variety of colors circled the crown, sparkling in the light as the king lifted it to his head.

Felix, Kendra, and Archer followed the king back into the throne room. The crowd quickly surged into the tiered seating, with the exception of eight who instead formed lines of four on either side of the throne. While the rest of the crowd wore a mix of uniforms and suits and even some more casual clothes, these eight all wore black suits, each with a different color of shirt buttoned up underneath.

Archer led Felix to the center of the floor as the king took his throne. Kendra waved a quick goodbye before joining the others in the seats. Felix nervously glanced up at Archer, who was lifting his mask over his face again.

Felix wiped his sweaty palms on his jeans. A lot of people were watching him. *Anyone there?* he thought to himself. *I could use some encouragement.* Would the others even be able to hear his thoughts, or would he need to talk out loud? He thought he felt something stir in his chest but didn't get much time to dwell on it.

"This is Felix Carver," King Atticus announced to the room. "His parents, Thomas and Alice Carver, were semi-active Bright Guardians who were killed by Gideon Pollock earlier today, along with their other children. It's unclear what Gideon wanted with them, but he also died in the fight.

"However, all of their souls have remained here on this plane of existence. And Felix, who was formerly thought to have no magical ability, has seemingly bound their souls to his blood."

Murmurs rippled through the crowd. After a moment, King Atticus held up a hand, and the room fell back into silence. He briefly ran through the series of events that Archer had relayed to him minutes earlier.

"In addition to carrying their ghosts, Felix is able to use their abilities." The king let the words hang in the air for a moment before continuing. "If he were properly trained and in complete control of these spirits, he could be a powerful Guardian. Someone we need on our side." His head turned toward the Guardians standing to the left of his throne.

A man with short black hair who looked to be in his forties stepped forward. The shirt under his black suit jacket was gold and shimmered as he moved. "Are the ghosts in his blood still conscious?" he asked. "Gideon was powerful. Even in death, he shouldn't be underestimated."

"So far, it seems that they aren't aware of what is happening outside," King Atticus replied. "Though, Felix was able to have a conversation with one of his sisters."

The man gestured toward Felix with his hand, offering a glimpse at a wooden ring wrapped around one of his fingers. "I'm not certain it's safe to let him walk around just yet, then. Everything you've said about his ability seems to be speculation."

"Abraham has a point," a woman chimed in. Her long, graying hair was pulled up in a loose bun on top of her head, a similar shade to the gray of her shirt. "Even just training him could be dangerous."

King Atticus considered her statement for a moment. "Are you suggesting we lock him up?"

Abraham spoke again. "I hate to say it, but it might be best to keep him in a cell for now." Despite his preface, the man didn't seem very upset by the thought of throwing Felix in a cell. In fact, Felix swore he saw the edge of the man's mouth turn up in a faint smile. "And if Gideon is in there somewhere, this could be our chance to interrogate him."

A man with buzzed hair and a white shirt under his suit jacket stepped forward. "Do you hear yourselves? We can't throw a kid in the dungeon. He just lost his family!"

Felix couldn't keep an audible sigh of relief from slipping through his lips.

"And what would you propose we do, Michael?" the woman asked.

"Keep an eye on him. He's in a castle surrounded by Bright Guardians. Even if Gideon is in there somewhere, he doesn't stand a chance against all of us."

Abraham snorted. "Too much of a risk. Gideon could do untold amounts of damage before he was stopped." He looked at Archer. "He was a damn powerful ghost, wasn't he?"

Archer's only response was a nod.

Sebastian, who sat in the front row of the audience, spoke up. "Don't forget that Felix is carrying five other ghosts, as well. The Carvers are on our side."

The woman pursed her lips. "Only council members should be speaking right now, *Armitage*."

"Sebastian's right," Michael said. "If it's possible for Gideon to get out, that means it's possible for the other Carvers, too. If Felix communicates with them, we could get a better idea of what they're capable of."

"That's fine, if we can confirm that," the woman replied. She turned to Felix. "But right now, can you say with confidence that Gideon isn't a threat?"

Felix swallowed. "I—I'm not—"

"Give the boy a break, Eliza," a new woman spoke. "He doesn't know much more than we do."

"He doesn't know anything about the Bright Guardians, apparently," The first woman—Eliza—said, eyes narrowing.

The second woman wore a dark purple headscarf that covered most of her long black hair and matched her shirt. She looked at least twenty years younger than Eliza. "I don't think that's relevant to the issue at hand," she said. She glanced at the audience as she spoke, and light glinted off her narrow glasses.

"Would any other council members like to add anything?" King Atticus asked.

The remaining four spoke up to simply state their agreements. Two men took the side of Eliza and Abraham and suggested locking

Felix up, while the other two members felt that Felix could be trained with relative safety.

King Atticus lifted his chin. "Archer?"

"The council's concerns are valid," Archer said.

Felix's heart sank. If Archer was the King's Hand, whatever that entailed, his opinion was probably more important than the rest of the council's. And he *had* called the entire situation a nightmare.

"But," Archer continued. "I think the best possible outcome is worth the risks. If Felix can learn to wield all of these abilities, he could help us destroy what's left of the Uprising."

Relief washed over Felix.

After a moment, Archer added, "And if anything goes wrong, we can always lock him up later."

Ah. Great. Felix looked out at the crowd, wondering what they were thinking. Did the majority agree that he should be locked up? Or would they be on board with training him?

"And what if Gideon is somehow able to take control of Felix?" Eliza asked. Abraham shot her an unreadable glance. She returned his gaze for the briefest of moments.

"I'll do whatever it takes to rid the world of Gideon once and for all," Archer said with a cold determination. "Him and the other members of the Uprising."

"I've made my decision," King Atticus said. "Kendra Ford, please escort Felix to one of the empty rooms in the southwest tower."

"Wait, what's going to happen to me?" Felix asked as Archer led him to meet Kendra in the middle of the room.

"Not now, Felix," Kendra said under her breath. "But trust me, you're going to be fine."

Chapter Four
First Night

The sun had gone down during the meeting, leaving the world outside the castle windows dark. Felix slowed and peered through one, marveling at how many stars glittered in the sky. Were they real stars? Or an illusion over the pocket dimension?

"Since I'm leading you to a room and not a dungeon, I think the king is going to assign someone to train you," Kendra said.

Felix jogged to catch up to her. "You think that'll be hard to do?"

"Maybe. You do pose a challenge. But with everything that's on the line, I'm sure at least a few teachers will be up to it."

Felix wasn't convinced Kendra believed what she was saying but nodded anyway.

"How are you feeling?" Kendra asked.

"Awful," Felix admitted. "I'm exhausted. And—" He wasn't sure what to think about his family. They were dead, but they weren't really gone, right? Then again, he hadn't heard a word from them since leaving his house. What if the Guardians were wrong about his ability?

"I can't promise you'll feel better in the morning. But I'll do everything I can to help you, okay? And so will plenty of other Guardians here. Most of us...have dealt with loss, to some degree." Kendra sighed. "I know a few of the council members didn't seem to care about you, but I promise everyone's just trying to do what's best for the Brightlands. It's been hard for us, recently. We've lost a lot of family and friends."

"Is there some kind of war going on?" Felix asked, recalling what May had said to him. *All I know is that there's some kind of magical war, and I'm not sure we know which side is the right one.*

"The past few years have been quiet, but we're pretty sure the Guardian Uprising was just the beginning. The people responsible will be back. They failed eight years ago, but we didn't defeat them, either." Kendra hesitated. "Don't go around talking about all this, okay? They generally don't like to tell students much about it until they've graduated from the academy."

"Academy?"

"Bright Academy. It's our training program."

"Do you guys just throw the word 'Bright' in front of everything?"

Kendra chuckled. "I guess so."

A few more turns brought them into one of the towers. Felix tipped his head back to stare at the staircase spiraling upwards. "I know this is a castle, but is there by chance an elevator?"

Kendra strolled up to the wall next to the staircase and lifted a painting of a forest, revealing a panel of buttons. "The Brightland family is a big fan of aesthetics, so some of the more convenient features of the castle are hidden." She hit a button marked with an up arrow, and a faint chime came through the wall. A hairline crack appeared in the wallpaper, and a moment later, an elevator door slid open.

Inside the elevator, Kendra hit the button for the ninth floor.

"Hey," Felix said as he watched the door close. "How did you and Archer know my family was attacked? You were at my house right after it happened."

"Your father called us when Gideon showed up," Kendra said. Her expression darkened. "We came as fast as we could, but—not fast enough. I'm sorry."

Felix drew out the chain around his neck and fiddled with Mom's ring until they came to a stop. Outside the elevator, the stairs continued up for at least a few more floors. A hallway circled the outside of the staircase, lined with doors.

"Are these all bedrooms?" Felix asked.

"Dormitories, yes, technically," Kendra said. "You're the only person on this floor, though."

"Oh."

Kendra walked to the door opposite the elevator and turned the handle. It swung open. "Go ahead and get settled. I'll be right back with the key."

The room was impressive, in Felix's eyes. He had his own bathroom, a walk-in closet, a desk, and a nightstand next to the queen-sized bed. Deep blue velvet curtains covered the window. He wasn't yet convinced he wasn't going to be held prisoner, but if they kept him in here, maybe it wouldn't be so bad.

He set Helena's sword on the desk, tossed his backpack on the floor, and collapsed onto the bed on his back. He stared blankly at the ceiling, not quite ready to let himself think about any of the day's events.

A faint buzzing sound came from his backpack. Felix rolled over, leaned off the bed, and dug around until he found his phone. He had a text from Jace. *Hey, your house was on the news but no one seems to know what happened. Are you okay?*

"Felix?" Kendra knocked on the door.

"Come in!" Felix called. He dropped the phone back into the bag, making a mental note to respond later. Once he figured out *how* to respond.

Kendra stepped inside, a silver key in one hand and a small bag in the other. "Mind if I just set this on the desk?"

"Go ahead." Felix sat up. "Any word from the council?"

"I don't know what they decided, but I saw Archer coming up the stairs when I stepped off the elevator," Kendra said. She left the door open a few inches and moved to stand next to the bed. "He should be here any second. Here, I brought a first aid kit so that you can clean up that gash on your forehead."

Felix reached up to take the bag from her. "Archer takes the stairs?"

"When he's not in a hurry."

Felix set the bag on the sheets and turned so that his legs were hanging off the edge of the bed. "So, what's going to happen to my house and stuff?"

"We'll try to get that sorted out tonight. We also wanted to know if you have any family living nearby."

Felix shook his head. "My mom's an only child, her parents live in Texas, and my dad's family lives out east." He paused. "Are they Guardians, too?"

"I can double check the records for you. It's possible they left the Brightlands to do their own work. And if only one of your dad's parents was a magician, not all of his siblings may have inherited an ability."

"Have you ever heard of a kid with two magical parents not inheriting an ability?" Felix asked. "My family seemed pretty ready to believe I didn't have one."

"It's rare, but it has happened."

The door swung open. "Bad news," Archer said.

Kendra turned around. "What's wrong? What are they going to do to Felix?"

"Nothing, for now. He's going to be fine." Archer took a few steps into the room and sighed. "The problem is the person who's been assigned to train him."

"Oh, boy," Kendra muttered. "Should I take a guess?"

"Sebastian was the only one who volunteered."

"And the council really agreed to that?" Kendra sounded genuinely surprised.

"They sure did." Sebastian stepped out from behind Archer and entered the room. Glancing around, he added, "Ooh, this is a nice one."

"So, what, I'm a student now?" Felix asked.

"Not officially." Sebastian held up a finger. "You'll live here and train, but you're on probation until we have a better grasp on how your ability works. No missions, no classes, no combat with other students."

"What about my high school?" Felix asked.

"We'll sort that out soon," Sebastian said. "Don't worry about it right now."

"And the council really picked you to train him?" Kendra asked, still skeptical.

"I'm definitely the last person they wanted for the job." Sebastian shrugged. "Unfortunately, no one else was interested. Everyone's got their hands full with their current classes." With a smile, he added. "And besides, even they have to admit I'm a pretty good teacher. Lucky for Felix I took the semester off to focus on our other...special case."

Archer glared at him. "Maybe I should train Felix."

"But you're *sooo* busy with your job as the King's Hand."

"Which includes supervising training," Archer said. "You can expect me to check in regularly."

"Fine by me."

Felix cleared his throat. "What about the council members who, uh, wanted me locked up?"

"They have to accept the King's final decision," Sebastian replied. "At the end of the day, it's not a democracy."

"The king does take their thoughts into account," Archer added.

"Sure, sure, whatever."

Archer scowled.

"Still, be careful around the council members," Sebastian continued. "I doubt you'll run into them much, but they'll probably want to check in on your training, too."

"And there are eight of them?" Felix asked.

Sebastian nodded. "The two council members who supported you were Michael Beck and Sadia Malik. The two assholes—"

"Watch it," Archer muttered.

"—were Eliza Abernathy and Abraham Caldwell."

"All right, all right, we don't need to explain our entire political system to him right now," Kendra said, waving a hand in Sebastian's direction. "Felix, I'm sure you have a lot of questions, but is there anything else we can answer for you right now?"

Felix had no idea where to begin. His gaze shifted from Kendra to Sebastian to Archer and back to Kendra. "I guess I'll save most of it for tomorrow. But...can I ask about your guys' abilities?" He hesitated a moment. "I was mainly curious about Archer's mask."

Kendra glanced at Archer, who nodded. "Sure," Kendra said. "Archer's got poison magic. He can make poison from his blood, and there's usually a little poison in the air he breathes out. He can control it just fine, but the mask has been enchanted to absorb the poison so that he doesn't have to think about it."

Archer held up a hand. "And I wear the gloves because poison can leach into my skin."

"Yeah, and don't drink from his drinks, either," Sebastian added.

"I warned you to stop stealing my coffee."

Felix looked at Kendra. "And you can...control insects?"

"And see what they're seeing. They don't think the way we do, but I can communicate with them to a degree by essentially forming a hivemind," she explained. "My magic also lets me mark them with sigils."

"And Sebastian?" Felix asked.

"You'll see at training tomorrow," Sebastian said. "If you're up for it, that is. I know you've been through a lot, but the sooner you can prove yourself to the king and his council, the better."

Jumping into training so soon sounded like torture, but the implied warning about the council made Felix nod anyway. "I'll be ready tomorrow."

"Excellent." Sebastian clapped his hands together. "You'll get to meet my other student."

With that, he stepped out of the room and disappeared.

"I don't like it," Archer said. "It's almost as if he's...collecting the weird cases."

"I'd hardly call two a collection," Kendra replied.

"Who's his other student?" Felix asked.

Archer and Kendra exchanged a look. "Like he said, you'll meet her tomorrow," Kendra said after a moment.

"She's also not allowed on missions right now," Archer added. "Though her probation's probably going to last longer than yours."

"We don't know that," Kendra muttered.

"I did say 'probably,' didn't I?" Archer headed for the door.

"Oh, one last thing," Felix said, making Kendra pause, though Archer continued through the doorway. "Do you know what the rest of my family's abilities are? All I know is that Helena has some kind of lightning magic."

"I'll have to check the records," Kendra told him. "Like the king mentioned, your parents were only semi-active. Oh, we'll also make sure you get a tour of the castle tomorrow morning. If you get hungry in the meantime, there's a small kitchen stocked with food on the fifth floor of this tower, next to the staircase landing. I'm afraid we missed the big scheduled dinner."

"Thanks." Felix picked up the first aid kid and opened it. "What time should I be up tomorrow?"

"If you want hot breakfast, ten a.m. at the latest. They start serving food at seven. You don't have any allergies, do you? Dietary restrictions?"

Felix shook his head.

"Great," Kendra said. "In that case, the dining hall is near the throne room. If you can find your way back to that general area, all you have to do is follow everyone else. Otherwise, you're on your own. Sebastian will probably want to get started before noon, though."

"Sounds good."

"Good night, Felix." Kendra stepped out of the room and closed the door, leaving Felix to fumble around in the bag until he located some disinfectant and a box of bandages.

Felix moved to the bathroom to assess the damage. In addition to the gash and patches of dried blood, bruises had begun to form along his jaw, shoulders, and arms. Judging by the soreness, he suspected his back would be similarly bruised. They really let him see the king like this?

The sting of the disinfectant made Felix wince, but he pushed through the pain until he had the wound clean enough to avoid infection. Hopefully. The bandages turned out to be of the glittery variety. Felix picked out a green one and pressed it to his forehead.

Movement overhead caught his attention. He glanced up and spotted a small black spider crawling across the ceiling toward the vent. He shuddered but decided to let the creature be. For all he knew, it could be a magical spider.

Exhausted as he was, Felix wanted to try one more thing before he went to bed. If he could talk to his family again, even one person, then maybe spending the night alone in an unfamiliar place wouldn't be so bad. But if he had to fall asleep not knowing whether they were okay...

Felix sank to the floor next to the bed and closed his eyes. "Anyone in there? Mom? Dad?"

Nothing.

What was it Ezra had said? Something about Felix needing his blood to channel his power? Felix held up his hand and examined the finger he'd pricked earlier. A small scab had formed. He scratched at it until blood welled on his skin, and a single drop fell onto the white carpet. Oops.

Before Felix could worry much about the carpeting, the air above the blood shimmered and took the shape of a figure.

"Helena!" Felix exclaimed. "You're here!"

Helena looked around. "Where are we?"

"Uh, Bright Castle."

"Ah. Figures they'd pick you up," Helena said as she sat down next to him.

"Did you ever come here?" Felix asked.

"Sometimes. Mom and Dad didn't sign us up as official students, but we'd pop into training sessions or classes when they came to talk to other Guardians. They taught us everything else themselves." Helena studied Felix's face. "How are you holding up?"

"Better, now. Do you know where everyone else is?"

"They're in there with me. But I don't think they're conscious the way I am."

"What? Why not?"

"I don't know. Maybe because you used my ability?" Helena shrugged. "I can sense their energy in there, though. I guess I could try to wake them."

"'In there?' You mean in my blood?"

"Not exactly," Helena said. "There are...a lot of conflicting theories about the nature of the soul. Despite all of the magic revolving around it, we don't know much." Her gaze moved to the other side of the room, and Felix realized she was staring at her sword on his desk. "But there is a physical space you can access. That's where we are."

"You can see them in...my soul?" Felix asked.

"I can sense them. Once they awaken, I'm sure I'll be able to see them, too."

"And you can see what I'm seeing?"

"No, not always. Sometimes I can feel you calling for us. I can move into your mind the way I did at our house." Helena's expression darkened. "Which is why you need to be careful. Gideon's in there somewhere, too. And if we can get into your head, then he must be able to, too."

"But I could keep him contained, right?"

"I hope so." Helena sighed. "You shouldn't have taken him in."

"I didn't mean to. I—I panicked." Felix glanced down at the floor. "Helena, I had no idea what was happening. One minute I'm coming home from tennis, and the next—"

"I know, I'm sorry." Helena leaned over and wrapped her arms around him. "We have a lot to explain to you."

"Yeah, you do." He hadn't meant for that to sound as bitter as it did.

If Helena noticed, she didn't address it. "We were planning to tell you about all of this...eventually. Mom and Dad waited for our abilities to manifest before telling us. It's safer that way."

Felix sighed. "I get it." Part of him thought maybe that danger would have been worth it, to know what the rest of the family had been up to. But it didn't really matter anymore, did it?

"You should get some sleep. Tomorrow, we can figure out how to reach the others. Okay?"

Felix nodded, suddenly finding himself holding back tears. "Okay."

Helena was somewhat transparent, now, and fading further with each passing second. "I think your blood loses its power as it dries."

"Oh." Felix pushed himself to his feet. "See you tomorrow, then."

And then Helena was gone.

Chapter Five
Probation Pals

Talking to Helena didn't help as much as Felix had hoped. Once she was gone, all he had to keep him company was the weight in his chest. He'd been left alone with more questions than answers and no idea who he could really trust.

After a long, restless night of stumbling through his house in his dreams, he was awoken a final time by gentle rain on his window. Gray light spilled into the room through a gap in the curtains. Felix dragged himself out of bed and threw on a pair of jeans, a t-shirt, and his sneakers. Before heading to breakfast, he forced himself to type out a reply to Jace's text from the night before. *I'm okay, I'm with some family. I'll explain more when I can.*

Felix was miraculously able to find his way to the dining hall, which looked to him like a glorified school cafeteria. Sure, there were chandeliers overhead, and the tables had fancy tablecloths, but it was still just a big room of tables packed with people carrying trays of food.

A line formed at the front of the hall, a mix of adults and kids dressed in everything from suits to pajamas. Good. Maybe Felix could avoid drawing attention to himself. He slipped into line at the back.

He was given a tray and the opportunity to pick from the wide variety of food set out. After settling on a scramble of eggs, cheese, peppers, and bacon, along with a mix of berries, Felix found an empty table in the corner of the hall to sit at and pick at his food.

He was lost in thought for what could have been minutes or hours, for all he knew, before someone spoke to him. "Hey, kid, how you holding up?"

Felix glanced up as Sebastian slid into a chair across from him. "Okay, I guess," he replied. "I talked to my sister last night."

"Really?"

"Yeah. I was able to summon her ghost for a few minutes."

Sebastian rubbed his chin. "Interesting. You like your room?"

"Yeah." Felix stabbed a piece of egg and held it up. "I mean, it's really nice." The bite went into his mouth, and he was briefly grateful that the food here was delicious. Hopefully, that would make getting used to his new home a little easier.

"So, you're not too bothered that the king didn't really give you a choice?"

"Hm?"

"There was never any question about whether or not you would be staying at the castle," Sebastian said. "It was just a matter of whether they were going to put you in a dorm or a cell."

Felix swallowed and frowned. "Well, I don't have any family nearby. I don't really have anywhere else to go."

"Sure. But the king didn't ask."

"Guess not." Felix took another bite of eggs. He wondered how much he should let himself trust Sebastian. Kendra seemed to, but Archer certainly didn't. Then again, Archer hadn't exactly been the most supportive during the council meeting. Could Felix trust *him*?

After studying Felix for a long moment, Sebastian changed the subject. "Archer is insistent on supervising our first session, but he's in meetings until two. In the meantime, you'll get a tour of the place and meet your one and only classmate." His gaze moved to something behind Felix. "Oh, there's Kendra. Kendra!" He waved a hand.

Kendra approached the table and stopped next to Sebastian. "Still want me to take him to the library?"

"That'd be great. I talked to Arisa this morning. She said she could show him around." Sebastian stretched his arms out. "I have a few other things to take care of in the meantime. Let Arisa know that Archer and I will meet them in the east courtyard at two."

Felix quickly shoveled the last of his food into his mouth and rose to his feet. "Cool. Let's go."

Sebastian smiled as he stood up. A moment later, his expression fell, and he cleared his throat. "Oh, one last thing. The Guardians have set up a funeral for your family. It's tomorrow morning, at a cemetery near your house."

"I'll take you," Kendra added.

Felix's stomach dropped. That soon? "Oh. Okay. Thanks." He felt like he'd been plunged into an ice bath. "I think I'll need to stop by my house first, if that's all right."

"Of course," Kendra said. "Anything you need."

It's not like they're really gone, he reminded himself as he and Kendra left the dining hall. All he needed was a little practice, and he'd be able to summon them at any time.

"Are you a fan of books?" Kendra asked.

"Uh, some of them," Felix answered.

Kendra chuckled. "The library's one of the big draws for some of the students. It spans five floors. My fiancée's the head librarian. Which reminds me, do you know sign language by chance?"

"A little bit, actually. I took a few years of ASL in middle school. It was my dad's idea." Felix paused. "He was really into books."

"Makes sense," Kendra said. "Hana's deaf, so the regular patrons tend to pick up sign language."

Felix's lack of confidence in his memory must have shown on his face, because Kendra added, "If you wanted to brush up on it, I'm sure Arisa would be happy to help. She's Hana's younger sister. And Hana can read lips pretty well, if needed, and she'll talk if she's worried you won't understand what she's signing."

They turned a corner and walked halfway down the next hall. Two open doors led into the first floor of the library. Felix turned in a slow circle as he followed Kendra inside, taking in the stairs that led to the upper levels and the seemingly endless shelves packed with books.

The woman sitting behind the front desk was reading something on her computer monitor. She had a pixie cut of black hair and appeared to be Japanese. Unlike the other Guardians Felix had seen, she wore a simple black dress, though a black uniform jacket hung on the chair behind her. She looked up as Kendra and Felix reached the desk. Her face lit up.

Kendra grinned. "Felix, this is Hana Tamura," she said. She signed something to Hana.

Hana smiled and waved at him. Turning to Kendra, she lifted her hands and responded with something that started with, "Yes." Felix didn't recognize much beyond that.

Kendra nodded. "Arisa's probably on the third floor," she told Felix. "Follow me."

Felix and Kendra went up a couple flights of stairs and entered a maze of shelves. "Arisa!" Kendra called out in a half-whisper. "You over here?"

Felix looked around, admiring the colorful assortment of books. He wasn't the world's biggest bookworm, but he had to admit the place was impressive.

As he and Kendra entered an aisle, a girl popped out from behind a shelf at the other end. She bore a strong resemblance to Hana, sharing her round face, soft features, and dark eyes. Her black hair stopped just above her shoulders. "Hey, Kendra."

"Hi, Arisa," Kendra said. "It sounds like Sebastian already explained the situation with Felix."

Arisa looked Felix up and down as she walked toward the two. She was dressed about as casually as he was, in jeans and an orange-and-black flannel. "Yeah, Sebastian told me all about him." As she lifted a hand to tuck her hair behind her ear, the light caught a plain silver band around her wrist. There was a matching one on her other arm. Each bracelet held a single smooth orange gemstone.

"Nice to meet you," Felix said.

"Nice to meet you, too."

"Your bracelets are cool."

Kendra tensed. Arisa let out a cold laugh. "Thanks, they're cursed."

"Huh?"

Kendra cleared her throat. "Arisa has a—"

Arisa waved her hand. "I can explain it." She pointed at the bracelet on her right wrist. "This was found in a boarded-up room in the basement, along with a bunch of other artifacts. The historians were sorting through everything and identifying them, and they figured out the bracelet was a power amplifier. I tried it on—"

"After you were told not to touch anything," Kendra added.

Arisa rolled her eyes. "—and it wouldn't come off. The pieces of the latch fused together. Turns out it's cursed. I have more power now, but if I use it, I...it hurts me. Among other things." Her gaze flickered to Kendra. She raised her other hand to show Felix the second bracelet, which looked identical. "So, they made this counterbalance for me. I can still use some of the extra power, but this prevents me from using enough to cause problems."

"Our historians are trying to figure out how to break the cursed bracelet," Kendra said. "All curses have a way to be undone. It's just a matter of time until they find an answer."

"I'm on probation until then," Arisa said. "Which is stupid, considering I'm stronger now."

"We don't know the full extent of the curse—"

"But I'm still allowed to train. I don't get—oh, hang on." Arisa bent down and picked up an orange teddy bear off the floor, which Felix swore hadn't been there before. As she set it on her shoulder, its head turned to look at him.

"Whoa!" Felix took a step back in surprise. "That thing moved."

"This *thing* has a name." Arisa lifted her chin. "Clementine, this is Felix."

"Can it talk?"

"No, she can't talk."

"Arisa has the ability to animate inanimate objects," Kendra explained.

"Oh, cool!" Felix exclaimed.

Arisa looked pretty smug at that. "Thank you." She folded her arms. "But you apparently have multiple abilities, so I think you have me beat."

"Well, that's assuming I can figure out how to use them." Felix rubbed the back of his neck. "I'm still not sure how—"

Kendra's phone buzzed, cutting Felix off. "Sorry," she said as she pulled it from her pocket. Felix spotted Archer's name on the screen before Kendra answered it and held it up to her ear. "Hello?"

Whatever Archer had to say put a concerned expression on Kendra's face. After a few moments, she asked, "Do we know where it is now?" There was a pause. She sighed. "Yeah, I can track it down. I'll meet you by the north staircase." She hung up.

"Everything okay?" Felix asked.

"A group of students managed to summon a poltergeist."

Arisa frowned. "I thought the castle wards made that impossible."

"It is. We're not sure how they got it in, but it's already wrecked three rooms and now they've lost track of it." Kendra tapped her phone screen and began typing. "Arisa, could you go ahead and show Felix around the castle?"

"Uh, what about the poltergeist?" Felix asked.

Arisa laughed. "They're not too dangerous, just destructive."

"They can be dangerous," Kendra said sternly. "But they usually don't wander, and this one was summoned in the upper levels on the north side of the castle, far from anywhere you two should be. Stay away from that area and you'll be fine." She looked up from her phone long enough to shoot Arisa a warning look. "Seriously, don't go looking for it. If you hear or see any signs of it, go in the opposite direction."

"Sure thing," Arisa said. She set a hand on Clementine's head. "I'll just show Felix all the important stuff. Secret passages into the kitchens, the closets with the cool weapons, and that weird patch of mold on the third floor."

Felix wasn't sure Kendra fully heard Arisa. "Thanks, Arisa!" she said, eyes back on her phone as she walked away.

"Is that normal around here?" Felix asked. "The poltergeist summoning, I mean?"

Arisa led him to the library stairs. "Not inside the castle, but stuff pops up on the grounds sometimes. Never really anything to be concerned about, though. The wards at the edge of the Brightlands are kind of weak, but the ones protecting the castle itself are supposed to be nearly unbreakable," she explained. "It's a real challenge to summon anything interesting inside them. Kids do dare each other to try a lot, but if these ones actually succeeded, they must be pretty powerful. Or smart. They're going to be in a lot of trouble, though."

They passed the front desk. Arisa waved to Hana, and Hana smiled and waved back.

"Kendra said you could help me brush up on my sign language," Felix said. "I remember a little from middle school, but not much."

"Sure," Arisa said. "I have a lot of free time, anyway, since they took me out of my regular classes." Her face lit up. "Oh, I know some Japanese Sign Language, too, if you're interested in learning that."

"I should probably get caught up on American first," Felix said. "But maybe after that." He'd never had much success learning other languages, but he was willing to give it a try.

The two stepped out of the library. "The lower south portion of the castle is devoted to the Bright Academy," Arisa told Felix. "It's where the training yards and classrooms are located, and most of the student dormitories are in that area, too."

"Are there a lot of students here?" Felix asked.

Arisa led the way down the hall, toward the south end of the castle. "Depends on what you mean by a lot. There's around a hundred students right now. Parents usually send their kids to live here when they turn fourteen," she explained. "If they don't already live here, that is. A lot of families of active Guardians stay at the castle full time." She fiddled with one of the buttons of her flannel. "Like my parents. When I became a student, all that really changed was that I got to move into my own dorm."

"What makes a Guardian active? The king said my family was semi-active."

"Depends on how regularly you go on missions and attend meetings."

Felix's brow furrowed. "Missions?"

"We use our magic to deal with monsters and spirits. Sometimes a mission is just investigating civilian deaths to determine if the cause was magical. Once the cause is identified, more Guardians are called in to deal with whatever's responsible."

"They let students go on those?"

"Yeah. It's a good way to learn," Arisa said with a shrug. "New students only go on easy missions, though. Violent ghosts, some monsters, the occasional weak demon."

Felix considered asking Arisa to elaborate on what kinds of monsters the Guardians dealt with but decided against it. Just the word "demon" was enough to make him shudder. "So, if most kids start training at fourteen, I guess I'm a little behind on the student thing?"

"How old are you?" Arisa asked.

"Sixteen."

"Eh, you'll be fine. There's not a strict timeline for students. Most people graduate and are made full Guardians around twenty, but it varies." Arisa absentmindedly reached up to pat Clementine's head. "I've been on probation for months now, so I'm probably going to wind up graduating a little later, too."

The bear's face shifted in a way that reminded Felix of a dog being petted. He still couldn't decide if he found the bear creepy or cute, but despite his initial misgivings, he found himself mostly leaning toward cute. Mostly.

"What about you?" Felix asked. "How old are you, I mean?"

"Seventeen," Arisa answered as they turned a corner. She stopped. "That big white door in the middle of the hallway leads to the courtyard where we'll be training with Sebastian later today. It's not one of the typical training yards, but it's big enough to work for us." She pointed to a smaller blue door on the other side. "That's a weapon storage room. There are a bunch around the castle in case of emergency. They keep them locked, but I know how to get in."

Before Felix could question that, Arisa continued down the hall at a brisk walking place. He hurried to catch up.

Around the next corner, Arisa showed him a door hidden behind a tapestry that did, in fact, lead into secret passages. "Allegedly, there's a way out of the castle through them, but the basement is a maze and I'm not interested in getting lost," she said as she let the tapestry fall back into place. The tapestry displayed a map labeled "The Brightlands." Felix assumed it was whatever land Kendra had referred to yesterday that was now gone, given the vast landscape dotted with lakes and villages and even a small mountain range.

"I mostly use the tunnels to get into the kitchens where they keep the good snacks," Arisa continued. "Or to get around without running into other students."

"What's wrong with the other students?" Felix asked.

"Most of them are fine. They just try to avoid me. But they can't avoid me if I avoid them first." Arisa tapped the side of her head. "It's the ones that *don't* want to avoid you that you gotta look out for."

"Why?"

"Because they're usually assholes."

Arisa led Felix up a few floors and showed him a balcony overlooking a small courtyard occupied by a garden, a dining room about a quarter the size of the main dining hall, and a ballroom. And, as promised, she took him to a dusty classroom where a patch of dark mold had overtaken a corner of the ceiling.

"Why haven't they gotten rid of it?" Felix asked, hating every second he spent staring at it.

"No idea," Arisa said. "I think everyone is hoping someone else will do it."

"Isn't there cleaning staff or something?"

"Nah. They hired a witch years ago to put spells on the castle that keep it clean. Mostly. Every once in a while, a mess makes it through, and it always takes forever for someone to finally give in and clean it."

"Why a witch?" Felix asked as they returned to the hallway. "Guardians have magic."

"We have our innate abilities, and we know how to draw some sigils. But no one around here knows spellwork or potions or any of that." Arisa sighed. "Sometimes I wonder if a witch would be able to figure out my curse faster than the Guardians, but they avoid working with outsiders as much as possible."

Their next and final stop, according to Arisa, was the central courtyard. It was the largest one, and rather than a place for training, it was filled with stone pathways that wound around trees and benches and even a fountain spilling into a pond of fish. A few other Guardians and students milled about, enjoying the sun that had broken through the morning's rain clouds.

The real showstopper, though, was the silver statue at the courtyard's center, the top of which reached the fifth-floor windows. It depicted someone in armor similar to that of a medieval knight. In their right hand was a longsword with a wide blade.

"This is the Silver Paladin," Arisa said. "She had the ability to transform any metal into silver and manipulate it."

"What did she do to get such a big statue?" Felix asked.

Before Arisa could answer, approaching footsteps reached Felix's ears. He turned his head as four kids walked up to him and Arisa. Arisa groaned.

"Do you know them?" Felix asked, his voice low.

"These are the assholes I was talking about," Arisa muttered in reply.

The four kids all wore the same uniform Felix had seen many of the adult Guardians wearing. The first boy to speak wore a reddish-orange shirt with his. His black hair was cropped close to his head, and his light skin had a faint hint of a tan, which was no small feat coming out of winter in western Washington. "So, you're Felix Carver?"

"Yep. That's me." Felix shoved his hands in his pockets. "And you are?"

"Jack Caldwell."

"Caldwell?" Felix asked, heart skipping a beat. "Like the guy on the council? Abraham Caldwell?"

Jack laughed. "Yeah, that would be my dad."

It was then that Felix noticed the band of dark wood on Jack's right ring finger, similar to the ring his father wore. Felix threw a quick glance at Arisa, who was fidgeting with her counterbalance bracelet. Clementine stared at the kids from Arisa's shoulder, managing an expression that was a shockingly good glare, for a stuffed bear.

Felix turned his attention back to Jack. "Your dad seemed to think it would be better if I were locked up in a cell."

"Well, he's got far more experience than either of us." Jack shrugged. "But who am I to say? Congrats on winning the king's favor, though."

"Thanks," Felix said, even though Jack sounded far from genuine.

"So, what are two kids on probation doing here in the central courtyard?" Jack asked.

"Avoiding poltergeists, I guess."

Something flashed across Jack's expression, but it was gone before Felix could figure out what emotion it was.

"I'm giving him a tour of the castle," Arisa said coldly.

Jack shook his head, a grin crossing his face. "Arisa's hardly the one who should be giving you a tour." He pointed toward the statue. "Noah, tell him about the Silver Paladin."

Jack was accompanied by two girls and another boy. One of the girls was short and pale, with long blonde hair pulled back in a braid, while the other was more muscular with dark brown curls that stopped just past her shoulders. The boy had short waves of blonde hair and bore similar features to the first girl, enough for Felix to assume they were siblings.

The boy—Noah—nodded and looked up at the statue. "In 1955, a powerful group of werewolves called the Supermoon Wolves were able to amass enough strength to break through the wards and attack the castle."

"I know all this," Arisa muttered.

Noah ignored the comment. "The Silver Paladin led the fight against them and was single-handedly responsible for killing most of them, saving the last of the Brightlands and earning her title. If it weren't for her—uh, where are you going?"

Arisa had her hand around Felix's wrist and was dragging him away from the statue. "I just remembered that I left a sink running."

"What? Where?" Jack asked.

"In your mom's room!" Arisa yelled back. If Jack had a response to that, Felix didn't hear it.

Once they were back inside the castle, Felix asked, "They really hate you just because of your curse?"

Arisa let go of his wrist as they entered another hallway. "Nah, they were already kind of mean before that. They're mean to other kids, too, but the others put up with it because Jack's dad is so important. The kids who are really good at putting up with him get the privilege of being his friends."

A portrait on the wall just ahead of them fell from its place and crashed to the floor. The frame shattered.

"Whoa!" Felix took a step back as splintered wood rained across the floor.

Arisa's eyes widened. "I think that's the poltergeist."

The chandelier directly overhead exploded. Felix and Arisa jumped out of the way to avoid the ensuing shower of glass. Up and down the hall, other chandeliers followed, plunging them into darkness.

Chapter Six
And to Your Left, You'll See a Poltergeist

Arisa's voice cut through the darkness. "I don't suppose any of your abilities could help with this."

Felix looked around the hall, but it was no use. The world was black. "I still don't know what all of my family's powers are. Or how to use them. But maybe I can ask Helena." He closed his eyes and tried calling out to her. "Helena, can you hear me?"

Helena's voice answered in his mind. *Is something wrong?*

Felix breathed a small sigh of relief. "Yeah, there's a poltergeist around here somewhere. Does anyone happen to have any magical light powers?"

No, but Mom has fire, Helena replied. *Do you have any metal on you?*

Felix's hand moved to the chain around his neck. "I'm wearing Mom's ring."

Perfect. I can't help you with that, though. Try calling out to her.

"But I still don't know how I got your power to work!"

Well, you'll have to try. You don't need to talk out loud when I'm in here by the way, Helena told him.

Felix frowned. *Can you hear this?*

Yes.

A crash came from behind Felix. Whatever caused it couldn't have been more than twenty feet away.

"Felix?" Arisa asked. "You got anything?" She sounded calmer than Felix felt, but he thought he detected a slight tremble to her voice.

"Hang on." As the words left Felix's mouth, he felt Helena's presence leave him. He turned his thoughts to his mom, recalling the sound of her voice and the way her mouth turned when she was concerned. *Mom, can you hear me?*

Nothing.

And then, a new presence.

Felix?

Within seconds, Felix had tears in his eyes. With the lump in his throat, he was grateful Helena had explained he didn't need to speak to communicate. *Mom!*

Felix! What's going on? Mom's voice asked, her tone frantic. *Why are you in the dark?*

Poltergeist took out the lights, Felix explained. *Helena said you might be able to help.*

Hold out your hand.

Felix obliged, struggling to stop the hand from shaking. He felt the pull of something deep within. The moment he let it take over, vibrant blue fire sparked to life in his palm.

At the edge of the light, Arisa's head snapped toward him. "Whoa," she breathed. She lifted her gaze to meet Felix's. "Can you make it a little bigger?"

Add more fire slowly, Mom instructed. *Be careful.*

Felix concentrated on the sensation of warmth in his hand and pushed it further. The circle of blue light around them expanded to the walls.

What happened? Mom asked. *Your dad and I were talking and then you walked in and grabbed us. Where did he go?*

Another painting fell from the wall. Instead of dropping the ground, this one shot through the air at Felix and Arisa. They darted in different directions to avoid it. "Uh, I'll have to explain later," Felix choked out. "Or maybe Helena can tell you."

"Keep that light up," Arisa said. "I'll handle the poltergeist."

"What?"

"Trust me." Arisa reached into the pockets of her jeans and pulled out several pieces of paper, all marked with sigils. They folded themselves into cranes in her hands and took to the air. "Clementine, watch my back."

The bear hopped from her shoulder to the floor. Felix's gaze darted anxiously around the circle of light as he braced for the next attack. The cranes, meanwhile, moved in a slow circle in the air above Arisa. After a few moments, one of the cranes refolded itself into a plane and shot out of the circle, into the darkness.

"There!" Arisa turned in the direction it had gone. The remaining cranes flew past her and formed a new, wider ring at the edge of the light. Something invisible hissed at the center. The cranes narrowed their circle.

The faintest outline of a figure appeared in the middle of the cranes. "Let me out," a raspy voice growled.

Arisa laughed. "Yeah, good luck breaking through those sigils." She turned to Felix, and her expression softened. "You okay?"

Felix wiped his tears off his face with his sleeve. "Yeah, I'm fine." The fire in his hand flickered. He took a deep breath. "What now?"

A swarm of bees came around the corner. Felix turned and expanded the fire light. Kendra emerged from the darkness, following the swarm. When she saw Arisa and Felix, her eyes widened. "Did you two run into the poltergeist?" she asked as she hurried over to them.

"Run into it?" Arisa laughed and pointed. "We caught it."

"Well, Arisa caught it," Felix said. "I'm just the light."

"We walked into it on accident," Arisa quickly added. "And it killed the lights, so we couldn't run away easily. We were mostly focused on defending ourselves."

"Good." Kendra rested a hand on Arisa's shoulder. "Do you have anything you can use to banish it?"

"No, I only had the trapping sigils on me."

"That's okay." Kendra reached into her jacket and drew out a tall metal flask. "This should be enough." Uncapping it, she walked up to the poltergeist. The poltergeist hissed louder in response. With one swift motion, Kendra dumped the flask's contents onto the spirit.

Kendra's bees flew off in different directions. A violent gust of wind scattered Arisa's paper cranes and extinguished Felix's fire. He scrambled to reignite it, letting that strange pull in his chest surface again. Blue light fell over a perfectly calm hallway.

"Looks like that did the trick." Kendra recapped the flask and returned it to her jacket.

"Holy water?" Felix asked.

"Yep."

"Was it actually blessed by a priest, or whatever?"

Kendra shook her head. "Nah. We use a special set of sigils to convert water to holy water."

Arisa picked up her scraps of paper off the ground. Most were torn in half, and some had been reduced to nothing more than shreds. "Guess I'll have to draw up some more."

"That just seemed like a really violent ghost," Felix said.

"That's basically what a poltergeist is," Kendra explained. "They no longer have their human memories, but we don't know much besides that. Some people think they arise from a human soul being fragmented. Or that they come from people who have been trapped on earth so long they forgot why they were here in the first place." She walked forward. "Let's get out of here. I'll find someone to repair the lights."

Arisa picked up Clementine and held the bear in her arms as she and Felix followed Kendra. When they finally found a section of hallway lit by undamaged chandeliers, Kendra pulled out her phone, tapped the screen, and held it up to her ear. "Yeah, I found it. It's gone. Can you meet me by the throne room in five minutes?"

Felix willed the fire burning in his hand to vanish. When that didn't work, he focused on the tugging sensation in his chest and tried suppressing it. The blue flames flickered, then vanished. Felix studied the palm of his hand. There was no sign that the fire had ever been there at all. Like with Helena's lightning, he'd been able to sense it, but it hadn't hurt.

He couldn't recall when exactly Mom's presence had left, but she'd slipped away at some point during the encounter with the poltergeist. Felix wondered if she'd found Helena's spirit. Could they be talking to each other right now?

"Great. Bye." Kendra hung up her phone. "You two try to stay out of trouble until your training session, okay? Oh, and Arisa, don't forget you'll need to change into your uniform before then."

Arisa groaned. "Ugh. Fine."

"Do I get a uniform?" Felix asked.

"Yes," Kendra answered. "Sebastian said he'd take you to get yours after lunch. I'll see you two later, okay?"

The two exchanged goodbyes with Kendra, and she walked away. Arisa turned to Felix. "So, where are they keeping you prisoner?"

"Huh?"

"That was a joke," Arisa said. "Where's your room?"

"Oh. Southwest tower."

"You must have a nice view of the pond, then."

"I didn't notice," Felix told her. "I haven't even opened the curtains, yet."

"Well, can I take a look?" Arisa asked. "My room's along the southern wall. The most interesting thing I can see is the road leading up to the front of the castle."

"Sure! I should probably practice finding my way back there, anyway," Felix said.

That might have been the smartest thing he'd said all day. When they reached the next intersection, Felix turned left, and Arisa stopped.

"West is the other way," she said.

"Oh. Right." Felix turned around and let her lead the way to the tower.

When they entered his dorm, Arisa set Clementine on the desk and spent nearly a minute circling the edge of the room. "Hm," she finally said.

"What is it?" Felix asked.

Arisa walked to the center of the room and rested a hand on her hip. "I think it's smaller than mine."

"What?"

"That's a good thing! I have seniority."

"Barely!" Felix sat down on his bed.

Arisa moved to the window, pushed the curtains aside, and stared out at the castle yard. Though the sky above had turned from gray to blue, it looked like light rain was still falling over the forest at the edge of the hills. Fog hung over the trees. "Aw, you have to lean to see the pond," Arisa said. "It's still nice, though."

Felix's gaze moved to his backpack. "Do you know much about Gideon Pollock?" he asked.

"A little." Arisa turned around. "I know he left during the Guardian Uprising. He's one of the more notorious traitors."

"Do you know what his ability was?"

Arisa thought for a moment. "I'm pretty sure he could shapeshift into animals. But he needed a piece of them in order to transform. Similar to how you need metal to channel your mom's fire," she said. "Pretty much all abilities rely on a channeling material to work, unless the ability acts on an object like mine does. The things I animate are my channeling material, essentially."

"Animals," Felix muttered, barely hearing the rest of Arisa's explanation. He jumped to his feet, grabbed the hoodie he'd been wearing yesterday off the nightstand, and pulled out the necklace he'd taken from Gideon's body.

Arisa's expression darkened at the sight. "Where did you get that?" The unease in her voice suggested she already knew.

Felix walked over to her. He pointed at the fang hanging from the necklace. "Do you think this could have belonged to a raccoon?"

"Huh? Ew, I don't know." Arisa took a step back. "Why don't you use your dad's ability to figure it out?"

"What's my dad's ability?"

"No one's told you about your family's abilities yet?"

Felix shook his head. "Kendra said she was going to check the records for me, but I don't think she's had time yet. Do you know?"

"I don't know about the rest, but your dad's Thomas Carver, right?" Arisa asked.

"Yeah."

"He came to the library a lot. Mainly for the artifacts on the upper level, but he checked out a lot of books, too. Hana told me his ability was psychometry."

"Oh, cool," Felix said. "Uh, what is that?"

Arisa turned her head. Her eyes moved to the world outside the window. "The way I understand it, you can see an object's history. See memories that took place around it."

"So, I could see where this fang came from?" Felix lifted the necklace to examine the fang again.

"Yeah. And...you'd be able to see everything that happened to the person wearing that necklace." Arisa looked at him. "Anything they did." There was a warning hidden in her words.

"Right." Felix lowered his hand.

"I mean, you might be able to learn something useful from it," Arisa added with a slight shrug. "Maybe you could summon your dad and have him help?"

At the thought of his dad, Felix felt a new presence awaken inside of him. He focused on in, drawing it to the surface, setting it free. *Dad?* he tried.

It took a moment for Dad to respond. *Felix. Are you okay?*

I'm fine. Felix ran through a quick explanation of everything that had happened.

I'm glad you're okay, Dad said once he finished.

Yeah. Felix's hand tightened around the gold chain in his hand. Out loud, he said, "Arisa said that with your ability, I could see the history of this thing."

Is that Gideon's necklace?

"Uh, yes."

Put that away somewhere safe. I don't want you looking at it anytime soon.

"But I wanted to see—"

You're not ready.

As desperate as Felix was to know why Gideon killed his family, part of him was relieved. This wasn't something he really wanted to deal with right now. Not emotionally, anyway. Having Dad tell him to set it aside made him feel better about hiding the necklace away. Felix crossed the room to his desk and dropped it in one of the drawers.

I'll help you learn to use my ability, Dad assured him. *But it's going to take time.*

Felix nodded, finding himself holding back tears again. *I'll talk to you soon, then.*

"So, you can hear them talking to you in your head?" Arisa asked.

Felix waited for Dad's presence to fade away before he turned around to face her. "When I call on them, yeah," he replied. "I was also able to summon Helena's ghost, but I needed a drop of my blood for that."

Arisa's eyebrows lifted. "Do you think other people could see their ghosts when you summon them?"

"Maybe," Felix said. "But Kendra and Archer couldn't see them at my house."

"Well, ghosts who are in control of their forms can generally choose when they want to be seen."

"Oh. Gideon could do that," Felix recalled.

Arisa nodded. "And a magician's going to make a more powerful ghost than an ordinary person. Especially someone like him."

A knock at the door made Felix jump. He hurried to open it and found Sebastian waiting on the other side.

"Hey, kid." Sebastian leaned to the side and peered past Felix. "Oh, good, Arisa's here too." Gaze moving back to Felix, he said, "I'm supposed to get you a student uniform."

Felix blinked. "Even though I'm not technically a student?"

"Correct."

Arisa sighed and stepped away from the window. "Guess that means I should go get changed."

"Personally, I think we should be allowed to train in pajamas, but I don't make the rules around here. So, yes, uniforms all around. However..." Sebastian leaned against the doorway and held up a hand. "The uniform thing is going to have to be postponed, sadly, since that poltergeist shattered all the windows in the north wing of the fourth floor. Where we store our extra uniforms. We can't walk around there until they get the glass cleaned up."

"Lucky you," Arisa said, shooting Felix a jealous look.

"Well, I don't want Felix having an unfair advantage, so for today only, it's going to be casual wear all around." Sebastian slid his hands into the pockets of his jacket. "Except me."

"Unfair advantage? I'm new!" Felix protested. "I don't know anything!"

Arisa stuck her tongue out. "Sucks to suck, newbie."

"Ouch."

"Oh, yeah, she's real competitive," Sebastian said. "Thought I'd warn you in advance."

"Hey, Seb, is there any more news about the poltergeist?" Arisa asked. "I want to know how those kids were able to summon one through the wards."

Sebastian lifted an eyebrow. "Why, so you can do the same?"

"I would never!" Arisa held a hand to her chest and put on an exaggerated act of concern. "I'm just worried for Felix's safety. He could have been hurt if I weren't there."

Sebastian chuckled. "We're not sure, yet. Archer's questioning the kids now."

"Rest in peace," Arisa muttered.

"You two should go get lunch." Sebastian straightened up and stepped back from Felix's doorway. "Can't train on an empty stomach," he added before walking away.

Arisa crossed the room. Picking Clementine up from the desk, she asked, "Ready to eat?"

"Definitely," Felix replied.

"I was talking to Clementine."

"She can eat?"

"Oh, not food. I have to recharge her every once in a while with my magical energy." Arisa set Clementine on her shoulder. "It's easier on a full stomach."

The two took the elevator to the first floor and joined other groups of Guardians headed to lunch.

"Do you think Archer's yelling at those kids right now?" Felix asked.

Arisa laughed. "Archer doesn't really yell. That would be less scary than his death glare, though." They passed through the doors of the dining hall. "He'll probably just give them a terrifying lecture and put them on partial probation for a couple weeks. It's basically like being grounded."

"I mean, what did they think would happen?" Felix asked as they stepped into line.

"My guess is that they thought they'd be able to banish it before anyone knew they'd even summoned it," Arisa replied.

"Huh." Felix grabbed a tray. "Well, I'm just glad I have someone to eat with now. If that's all right, I mean."

"Sure. Beats eating in the library with Hana and Kendra. Not that I don't love them, but they're mostly talking about wedding planning stuff right now, and I could use a break." Arisa blew out a breath of air. "I had no idea picking out colors was so stressful."

Felix laughed, for a moment. But Arisa's mention of a wedding reminded him that he had a funeral to attend tomorrow. His face fell as he picked a chicken sandwich off the platter in front of him.

Arisa looked up from the fruit options and frowned. "Hey, you okay?"

"Yeah, I'm okay." Felix's hands tightened around his tray. "Just nervous about training, I guess. I don't know what to expect."

"There's nothing to worry about. Sebastian's the nicest teacher we could get," Arisa moved to the basket of rolls waiting at the end of the buffet line. "He won't blame you if you don't get the hang of it right away."

"That's good to know." The two stepped away from the line and headed toward an empty table at the edge of the hall.

"Then again," Arisa said. "Archer's going to be watching today. Oh, damn it, now I'm anxious too."

Great, Felix thought as he sat down. Now he was actually nervous.

Chapter Seven
Bear With Me

When Felix and Arisa arrived at the training yard, Sebastian was already waiting. To Felix's surprise, so was Kendra.

"You're watching us, too?" Arisa asked.

Felix looked around the courtyard as he set his bag and Helena's sword on the ground. It was big enough to hold a few tennis courts, but the ground was nothing but dirt. Castle windows peered down at them on all sides, and he wondered what the chances were anyone else was watching.

"Yes," Kendra told Arisa. "Although I'm more concerned about Seb and Archer than you two." She shot Sebastian a sideways glance as she rested a hand on her hip.

Sebastian held up his hands. "I'm pretty sure I'm not the problem here."

The door behind him swung open, and Archer entered the yard, adjusting his mask as he walked. His hair was pulled up the same way it had been yesterday.

Sebastian turned around and waved. "Hey, Archie!"

"It's like you want to be stabbed," Archer said. His hand dropped to his side as he joined the group. "Now, what do you have planned?"

"Felix is going to awaken the rest of his family," Sebastian said. "Then, I'm going to have him and Arisa run through a practice fight."

Archer folded his arms. "They're banned from combat."

Sebastian held up a finger. "They're banned from combat with non-probationary students. They can train with each other."

"Is that true?" Felix glanced at Kendra.

Kendra shrugged. "I don't see why not. It's Archer's call, though."

Archer sighed. "I suppose the practice would be good," he said. "Even if they won't be going out in the field anytime soon."

"Ah, they won't be going on *missions* anytime soon," Sebastian corrected.

"I don't like where this is going."

"We can discuss it later." Sebastian clapped his hands together. "Felix. Your family?"

"Right. The only ones I haven't talked to yet are the twins." Felix turned his thoughts to May and Ezra. For a moment, he thought he could hear Ezra running through a dozen panicked what-if scenarios, and May calling him a dumbass.

No, wait, that was actually May. *What took you so long, dumbass? I've been half-conscious for what feels like hours.*

"Sorry, May," Felix said. "This whole thing is still kind of confusing."

A second presence joined. *What happened? How long has it been?* Even Ezra's mental voice had a tremor to it.

Hey, it's okay, Felix assured him. *It hasn't even been a day.* Wow. It really had been less than a day, hadn't it? So much had happened.

Hang on, Helena's yelling at me, May said.

"Yeah, okay, you two can leave, for now," Felix said aloud. "I'm just trying to learn how to use your abilities."

Archer watched with a cold expression that made Felix feel like he was already doing something wrong. Thankfully, Sebastian was the first to speak. "Great! Sounds like we're ready to start."

"I think so." Felix shook out his hands.

"I don't want you to overwhelm yourself by trying too much at once, so we'll start with what you already know. Your lightning and fire both require metal, anyway."

Felix spent the next five minutes alternating between summoning electricity and flames. It turned out the hardest part wasn't making them appear, but rather keeping them where he wanted them. The fire kept to his palm when first created, but when Felix tried to wrap it around his entire fist at Sebastian's instruction, it tried to spread up his arm. The lightning was worse, eager to run off in every direction it could.

"You feel the pull of the ability, right?" Sebastian asked.

Felix nodded.

"Don't just let it out. You have to keep it on a leash."

Felix opened his hand and brought back the fire. Instead of letting it burn on its own, he concentrated on holding onto the spark in his chest.

"Now, try again. Surround your hand with it and make a fist," Sebastian directed.

Felix only let the fire expand a few inches at a time, stopping it whenever he feared he might lose control. Finally, his entire hand was enveloped in blue. He closed his fist.

Sebastian held up an open hand. "All right, punch me."

"But—"

"I promise you won't hurt me."

Felix took a few steps forward and pulled his arm back. After a moment's hesitation, he threw his fist. He hit something much more firm than a hand. A thin layer of bright light had shielded Sebastian's palm. Solid light.

"Not bad," Sebastian said. "You've still got the fire under control."

"Maybe you should teach him how to throw a punch, first," Archer called from the sideline.

"We'll get there."

Felix held up his hand and watched the flames dance. "Yeah, I think I'm getting the hang of it."

Sebastian backed up. "Good. Now hit this with a bolt of your lightning." He kicked a small rock toward Felix.

Felix focused on the rock, took aim, and drew out Helena's ability. His first attempt missed the rock by ten feet. He grimaced.

"Try again," Sebastian encouraged.

Felix concentrated harder, trying to visualize the lightning striking the rock. He released another bolt, letting it jump from his fingers. It hit the ground even farther from the rock.

"You're too focused on where you want the lightning to go, rather than the lightning itself," Sebastian said. "Keep control of it as it moves. You can't just give it a destination. You have to guide it through the air."

Felix turned his head. Arisa sat in the dirt a few feet from where Kendra and Archer stood, making animated stones roll around in circles. Kendra was unreadable, but she offered a small smile when Felix looked at her. Archer didn't react to Felix's gaze.

"Okay." Felix returned his attention forward, took a deep breath, and unleashed another arc of lightning. Still not a hit, but much closer. He only missed the rock by about a foot this time.

"Much better," Sebastian said. "Give it a few more tries, and we'll start the practice fight."

Three more tries later, Felix finally struck the rock. But while his subsequent attempts were close, he only managed the one hit. His jaw clenched as he readied more electricity.

Sebastian walked forward and picked up the rock. "That's enough. You're getting impatient. We'll give it another try later."

"But I was so close to hitting it again!"

"Your frustration is making you slip. You need to switch gears." Sebastian turned his head. "Arisa!"

Arisa jumped to her feet. "Finally!"

"Are you sure it's safe for us to fight?" Felix asked. "What if I hurt her?"

"I'll be fine," Arisa assured him with a smirk.

"If you keep your lightning and fire at the same level you've been practicing at, it won't hurt much if you hit her," Sebastian said. "Guardians are naturally more resistant to each other's magic than an ordinary human or monster would be."

"Okay." Felix lifted his hands.

"Hold on." Sebastian pointed at the ground. A line of white light cut across the dirt, spreading into a rectangle around Felix and Arisa. "The goal is to get your opponent out of the rectangle without stepping out yourself," he explained.

Felix closed his hands into fists and let them catch fire. "Wait," he said, looking at Arisa. "How are you going to attack—?"

Clementine jumped from Arisa's shoulder and launched herself at Felix. His fire flickered out as he jumped to the right to dodge.

Felix glanced at Sebastian. "She can use the bear to fight?"

"The bear's a product of her magic, so yes," Sebastian replied.

Felix whirled around as Clementine straightened up. She raised her arms and walked toward him. Two tiny blades emerged from slits in her paws.

Felix yelped in surprise. "There are *knives* in the bear's hands!?"

Clementine jumped into the air and swung at him. He leaned back. The blade sliced through the air inches from his face. He lifted a hand and unleashed a bolt of lightning that flung Clementine to the ground a few inches from the edge of the rectangle.

"Remember, you need to get Arisa out of the box," Sebastian said.

Felix turned and charged at Arisa, hands blazing. Her palms were pressed together in front of her. Before he could swing, she opened them. A dozen pieces of paper fluttered into the air, taking on the form of paper planes. One by one, they flew at Felix's face.

He attempted to torch them before they could reach him. He had a success rate of about one in three. The ones he missed either flew past him or grazed the skin on the sides of his face, leaving him with a few stinging paper cuts.

"Hope you have more of those sparkly bandages," Arisa said.

Felix pressed a hand to his forehead. He'd all but forgotten the bandage he'd put on last night. "I sure do," he shot back.

The planes returned to circle his head. He reached out with a fiery hand to grab one out of the air. Before he could reach it, the paper refolded itself, transforming from a plane into a crane. With a push of its wings, it dodged Felix's grasp and launched itself at his face.

Felix ducked. Something crashed into him, knocking him flat on his back. When he looked up, he found Clementine standing over him, pointing a knife at his face.

"How are you so strong?" he asked through gritted teeth.

"Careful how much energy you channel into her, Arisa," Sebastian warned.

Felix knocked Clementine off of him with a jolt of electricity. As he jumped to his feet, she swung at his ankles with her knives. He kicked her aside, and then actually felt a twinge of guilt. "Sorry!" he exclaimed.

Clementine flew over the edge of the rectangle. "The bear's out of the box," Sebastian said, shooting Arisa a look. She nodded.

Felix felt a presence enter his mind. No, a few. His family was watching. He didn't have time to focus on them, though. He let electricity run across his fists and threw a punch. Arisa dodged and retaliated with a blow of her own. Her fist met his chest and sent him staggering backward. He tried again, and this time, she caught his fist with her hand.

The electricity transformed into fire. Arisa's jaw clenched, but she kept her hold and swung her other arm. Felix jerked his head back to avoid the blow. It was an easy one to dodge. In fact, Arisa's punch missed him by a foot or so.

Then her foot swept his ankle, and he was falling.

Felix hit his back hard enough to knock the air from his lungs. It took him a moment to suck in a new breath. As he regained his senses, he realized his hand was burning.

"Ow." Felix shook the last of his flames off his hand as he sat up.

Arisa was holding her hand, too. Felix jumped to his feet when he saw her grimace. "I'm so sorry, did I burn you?" he asked.

"It's not that bad," Arisa insisted. "I can keep going."

Sebastian glanced at Felix. "How about you? Are you okay?"

Felix inspected his skin. "My burn's not bad, either," he said. "But how did I burn myself? It's my magic!"

Archer spoke up. "You're only immune to the fire as long as you're in control. For the most part, you'll prevent it from hurting you on instinct. But you could slip up if you lose focus."

Another thing to worry about. Great. Felix turned to Arisa. "Want to keep going?"

"Ready when you are," Arisa answered.

Felix dropped into a fighting stance. Before he could make a move, Arisa's paper planes returned with a vengeance. He flung up his hands to shield his face. Instead of reaching for his fire or lightning, Felix found himself drawn to the pull of a new ability.

Anyone in here want to help me out? Felix asked his family. The planes switched directions and began circling him with alarming speed. The circle tightened with each passing second.

Hm. Ezra was quiet for a moment, and Felix got the sense that he was thinking. Finally, he said, *I don't like this dirt.*

Felix lowered his arms, ducked out of the circle of planes, and took a step back. *What's wrong with the dirt?*

It's not good. Ezra sighed. *But it'll do. Okay, ready?*

"Ready for what?" The words slipped out of Felix's mouth as he jumped out of the way of another onslaught of paper. The new pull in his chest strengthened. Ezra wouldn't encourage him to use something as dangerous as fire or lightning, right?

After a moment's hesitation, Felix unleashed Ezra's magic.

A vine burst from the ground beneath Arisa and knocked her off her feet. The planes shifted direction again. Felix raised his hand, ready to hit them with fire, but another vine shot up from the earth to knock the first plane out of the air. Then, it twisted to hit the next. One by one, the planes went down.

Fire and lightning are powerful, but they're soulless, Ezra said. *The plants will work with you.* With that, his presence slipped away.

Something moved behind Felix. Arisa had crept up on him. Before he could react, she grabbed his arm and twisted it. Felix yelped in pain and took a step back in an attempt to escape her hold. Arisa lifted her foot and shoved it into his chest. He stumbled out of the rectangle.

"Ow!" Felix exclaimed as he hit the dirt.

Sebastian clapped. "Good job, Felix!"

Frowning, Felix replied, "But I lost."

"So? You used three abilities in combat, including one you've never touched before. That was impressive," Sebastian said. "The plants were your brother, right? Ezra?"

"Yeah, that was Ezra."

Arisa walked over to Felix and extended a hand to help him up. "Sebastian's right, that was good." As he rose to his feet, she added, "I'm used to those matches lasting longer, though."

Sebastian slammed a fist into his open palm. "Wanna see a real fight, Felix?"

"Uh, sure," Felix said.

"Archer, you in?"

"Sure." Archer strolled forward, pulling his mask down as he moved. He slid off his gloves and tossed them onto the dirt before taking the last step into the rectangle.

Sebastian entered the rectangle from the other side. "Kendra, count us down." He unzipped his jacket and shrugged it off, revealing a tight long-sleeved shirt underneath in a vibrant shade of blue that matched his eyes.

Kendra rolled her eyes as Felix and Arisa moved to stand next to her. "All right," she said. "Three, two, one, start."

Chapter Eight
Best Enemies

Archer moved first, drawing a dagger with striking speed and swiping at Sebastian's face. A square shield of light appeared in the air to block the weapon. A moment later, it was gone. Sebastian held up a hand. A beam of light materialized in front of his palm and took on the shape of a dagger. Sebastian grabbed it out of the air and swung at Archer, who dodged easily.

Felix glanced at Kendra. "So, Sebastian's ability is...?"

"Light magic," Kendra said. "He can temporarily convert light into solid objects. Or into energy to use in attacks."

It was hard to keep up with the action. Sebastian and Archer's strikes all seemed to miss each other by the narrowest of gaps, but when they each took a step back for a moment of air, Felix noticed a few thin gashes. Most were on their hands, but Sebastian had one down the side of his face.

Arisa noticed Felix's concern. "This is normal for practice fights," she said. "Nothing to worry about. There are a few Guardians with healing abilities at the castle."

"And items with healing properties, too," Kendra added. "In fact, the skin under your bandage should be completely healed up by now. You'd never even know the cut was there."

Felix reached up to peel off the bandage. Sure enough, when he touched the skin underneath, it was perfectly smooth. He noticed for the first time faint sigils printed on the underside of the bandage.

Sebastian and Archer were moving at full speed again, delivering blows in a blur. Lowering his voice, Felix asked, "Who do you think would win in a real fight between them?"

Kendra blew out a breath of air. "In terms of raw magical energy, Sebastian's unmatched. But Archer's got much more discipline. He's learned to channel some of his magical energy into speed and physical strength."

"Sebastian's the most powerful?"

"*One* of the most powerful. It's hard to compare Guardians directly, though. Different environments favor different abilities. Plus, raw power's only half the battle," Kendra said. "Learning to use your magic in clever ways is the real trick. You can beat someone stronger than you if you know what you're doing."

Kendra was right. Archer was unbelievably fast. Still, Sebastian managed to dodge most of his blows seemingly without much effort.

Archer slowed down and spun his dagger in his hand. Instead of going for another strike, he hooked his foot around Sebastian's ankle and sent him stumbling toward the edge of the rectangle. But Before Sebastian could step out of the box, the lines of light shifted a few feet, keeping him in. Archer was now standing outside.

"See? I win," Sebastian said.

"Isn't that cheating?" Felix asked.

"No," Sebastian said, in the same moment that Archer said, "Yes."

Archer stepped back in and swung again. While Sebastian ducked, Archer's other hand drew a second dagger from his side. His thumb slid along the edge of the blade as he brought it forward. He tossed it into the air, caught it by the handle, and stepped forward to slice through Sebastian's shirt and graze his shoulder.

"Ah." Sebastian pressed a hand to the wound and took a step back. "Poison."

"Not much," Archer replied, voice cold. "You should be able to handle it."

"Good way to slow me down, though." Sebastian lifted his light dagger.

Felix heard the door leading inside swing open behind him. Before he could turn to see who had come to join them, shadows swallowed the training yard. The sudden darkness sent his heart racing.

"Fighting again, boys?" an unfamiliar voice asked.

"Who is that?" Felix whispered, his eyes searching the black for any sign of movement.

"Relax," Arisa replied. "It's Hana."

The darkness retreated into an orb that hovered over their heads. Hana flicked her wrist, and the orb separated into tendrils of pure black that melted into the natural shadow beneath the southern wall.

Hana smiled and waved. "Hello, Felix!" she called aloud. Felix waved back before glancing at Arisa.

"Her ability is similar to Sebastian's, but she uses shadow instead of light," Arisa explained.

Kendra walked forward to meet Hana. Arisa's eyes were on the two of them as their hands moved intently. Whatever conversation they were having in sign language put a concerned expression on her face.

Felix glanced back at Sebastian and Archer. Archer already had his mask back up and was pulling his gloves on. Sebastian shrugged on his jacket as he walked up to Felix.

"He was definitely breathing poison during the fight," Sebastian said. "I'd steer clear of the air around the rectangle for a few minutes."

"Are you okay?" Felix asked.

"Sure, just a little lightheaded. I'll be fine in a few minutes." Sebastian zipped up his jacket. "Archer has perfect control over his ability."

Arisa nudged Felix in the arm. "I have to go," she said.

"Is everything okay?" Felix asked, his gaze darting briefly to Kendra and Hana. "I caught something about parents at the start of their conversation."

"Yeah, my parents just got back from a mission. They've been gone for a few days. Hana and I are going to see them." Arisa waved. "I'll see you later."

"See ya."

Kendra kissed Hana and signed goodbye to her before strolling over to Felix, Sebastian, and Archer. "I'm off to handle the last few details of the sale," she said.

"Great. Call me if you need anything else from me," Sebastian told her.

As Kendra walked off, Felix looked to Sebastian. "Sale?"

"Kendra will explain tomorrow," Sebastian said. "Now, we should probably go get you a uniform." He turned. "Archer, you coming with?"

"I suppose I should make sure he gets what he needs," Archer said.

"You think I could screw up getting the kid a couple of uniforms?"

"I wouldn't put anything past you."

Felix grabbed his bag and sword, and the three entered the castle. They took several flights of stairs up to the fourth floor. Felix did his best to hide how out of breath he was when they reached the top. He was in decent shape from tennis, but the match with Arisa had worn him out quickly. And the fact that had hadn't slept well the night before was catching up with him.

"What color are you thinking?" Sebastian asked as they neared the end of a hallway.

Felix considered for a moment. "Do the colors mean anything?"

"Not really. Guardians get to pick their own. Some people go with a color related to their power." Sebastian shrugged. "I just like blue. It brings out my eyes."

Archer rolled his eyes at that.

"You don't have to stick to one color, either," Sebastian added as they entered a long room occupied by racks of clothing. He gestured to the overwhelming selection. "Help yourself. It's organized by size. Shoes are at the back."

Archer paused next to Sebastian. "You'll need a formal suit, too. I'd recommend wearing it to any future council meetings you attend."

Felix wandered the aisles, selecting uniform and suit jackets—and pants—in his size. After a couple minutes of deliberation, he picked out button-ups and plain shirts in a few different shades of green and blue. Finally, he grabbed a pair of black boots and a pair of black dress shoes.

"I don't have to pay for all this, do I?" Felix asked as he balanced the shoes on top of his stack of clothes.

"Nope," Sebastian replied. He folded his arms, thought for a moment, then added, "Go ahead and take the rest of the day for yourself. You, Kendra, and Archer are leaving at eight tomorrow morning."

"Archer's coming too?" Felix mentally winced. He hoped it didn't sound like he didn't want Archer to come. He didn't, but he didn't want Archer to know that.

"I won't be following you around. I'm only going to supervise, since the funeral's being held by Guardians," Archer said. "Kendra's still going to be the one accompanying you." He started toward the door. "I have a meeting, but I'll see you in the morning."

Archer paused in the middle of the doorway. "Oh, and Felix?"

"Yeah?" Felix asked.

"Probably best not to take any ghosts to the funeral."

With that, Archer was gone.

"Has he always been that terrifying?" Felix asked.

Sebastian lifted an eyebrow. "You're scared of him?"

"I feel like he wants to murder me."

"A lot of people think that. But he won't bite. Archer's the King's Hand for a reason." Sebastian headed for the door. "He's one of the best."

Felix followed Sebastian into the hall, balancing his belongings precariously in his arms. "Better than you?"

Sebastian laughed. "Hard to say. Now, I have a question for you."

"Yeah?"

"What do you want to get out of training? Do you want to be a Bright Guardian?"

Felix stopped. "Honestly, I just...I want to know why Gideon attacked my family. I mean, it doesn't seem like they were super important Guardians."

"We don't know why he targeted them, yet." Sebastian paused and turned to face Felix. "But I can tell you that Gideon wasn't acting on his own. He works for someone who's trying to destroy our entire organization."

"Who?"

"I don't want to throw too much information at you at once."

"Well, it's the Uprising, right?"

Sebastian continued walking. Felix rushed to catch up.

"Yes. Though, they've started calling themselves the Moonlit Army, in recent years," Sebastian said. Quieter, he added, "Apparently, their leader has developed a flair for the dramatic."

"I want to help stop them, then," Felix said.

"It's not going to be easy," Sebastian replied. "Even without an army standing against us, the Bright Guardians have always had it rough. Taking on monsters and demons and spirits isn't the most pleasant day job."

"Yeah, I figured. That training session was a little more...dangerous than I expected."

"Guardians have a skewed sense of safety compared to ordinary people. And we're not used to outsiders." Sebastian shot Felix a hesitant glance. "If you're going to be here, you'll have to accept that. This is a place where it's normal to send teenagers out to fight monsters."

If Helena and May and Ezra could handle this life, then Felix would, too. He lifted his chin. "I'll do whatever it takes."

"Then I'll do whatever I can to help you."

Felix shifted the pile of clothes and adjusted his grip on the sword. "Is there someone who can train me to use my sister's sword? Helena gave me a couple of pointers once when we were bored, but I'm really not that good with it."

Sebastian rubbed his chin. "I don't really use swords. Archer's good with them, but he's pretty busy, and he's not really the teaching type anyway." He thought for a moment. "Honestly, Hana might be your best bet. She's excellent."

"The librarian?"

"She fights, too. And she's really good," Sebastian said. "She was at the top of her class growing up. I mean, you saw her in the training yard."

"I guess if she can counteract your power, she must be good."

Before Sebastian could respond to that, Felix stopped and groaned. They'd reached the door to the southwest tower, where a spider was perched on the handle. "Is this place always full of spiders?" Felix asked.

Sebastian's expression darkened for a brief moment. Then, he chuckled. "It's okay, they won't hurt you. And they keep out more annoying bugs."

"I guess." The spider scuttled off as Felix reached for the handle.

"Any other burning questions about the Guardians I can answer for you?"

Felix did have a couple, actually. "Do you need another material to channel your ability? Like how my mom and sister need metal?"

"Nope. Neither does Hana, actually."

"Why not?"

"We're not sure," Sebastian said. He lifted the small painting of a bird that hid the elevator call button and pressed it. "We all know the ins and outs of how to use our abilities, but it's not easy to study *why* they work the way they do. Every other magician I know of does require a secondary material to channel their magic. That, or their power acts on an object, in which case the object channels their magic instead."

Right. Arisa had said something along those lines earlier. The elevator door opened, and the two stepped inside. "Also, what's up with your hair?" Felix asked. "Is that part of your ability?"

Sebastian absentmindedly ran a hand through his hair as he answered, emphasizing its iridescence. "Oh, sort of. It's rare, but some Guardians have random physical quirks."

A minute later, they were stepping off the elevator onto the ninth floor. "One last thing about that uniform," Sebastian said as they stopped in front of Felix's door. "The material has sigils sewn into it. They make it resistant to magic and sharp objects, but it's inevitable that it'll get torn up eventually. Help yourself to that room anytime you need new clothes."

As he rubbed his arm where Archer had cut him earlier, Sebastian added, "They have mild healing properties, too, so you'll want to make sure you're wearing some that are in good shape."

"Got it," Felix said with a nod. He said goodbye and stepped into his room. As he dumped his pile of new clothing on the bed, he wondered just how much more dangerous things were going to get for him.

Chapter Nine
Haunted Funeral

They got lucky with the weather. Saturday morning was the only sunny one in Felix's hometown this week, surrounded by a string of rainy days on either side.

Even knowing that his family was just a thought away, the fact that Felix was at their funeral was harder to face than he'd expected. The multitude of neighbors and family friends offering condolences only made him feel worse. Kendra gave him a small, reassuring smile whenever he glanced at her, but she couldn't entirely hide the sadness in her gaze.

Felix had chosen to wear one of the suits from his house to the funeral, but as he looked around the cemetery, he recognized a few Bright Guardians in their formal attire. How many Guardians had his parents been friends with? Some of them looked familiar, but he couldn't name a single one.

Do you recognize any of these people? He sent the thought off to his family, wondering if anyone would respond. Hoping someone would respond.

To Felix's relief, Helena entered his mind. *Only a couple. Where are Mom and Dad?* Felix asked.

Talking. After a moment's hesitation, Helena added, *I think there's some stuff they're not telling the rest of us.*

Do you think you could stick around for a while? Felix asked.

I'll do my best, Helena promised. *It takes a lot of energy to come up here. We still get tired. Though I think it's your magical energy we're burning through now, rather than ours.*

Felix wanted to ask what it was like being bound to his soul, but Kendra spoke before he got the chance. "Felix," she said. "Is that one of your friends?"

Felix turned as Jace approached them. "Jace," he greeted, flooded with relief at the sight of his friend. "Sorry I didn't get back to you, I had a busy day yesterday—"

"Hey, man, I completely understand," Jace said. "I'm so sorry. I just can't believe—" He trailed off and shook his head.

Felix wished he could explain to Jace that his family was still with him. Maybe one day he'd be able to. But Kendra had warned that even if Jace did believe the real story, getting too involved with the magical community could put him in danger. If Felix wanted to keep hanging out with him, he needed to avoid mixing in his new life with the Guardians.

Jace rested a hand on Felix's shoulder. "Just let me know if there's any way I can help you, okay?"

"Well, one of these days, it'd be nice just to play tennis with the team again." Felix looked at Kendra.

"That should be doable," Kendra said. "Maybe we can pick a weekend."

"Who's this?" Jace asked, shooting Kendra a confused glance.

"She's one of the, uh, teachers at my new school," Felix said.

Jace frowned. "So, you're not coming back to Maple Point?"

"No. It's…complicated." Felix did his best to explain his new life at Bright Academy without revealing that he was actually training to use magic.

After that, he only had a few more minutes to catch up with Jace before Kendra gently interrupted to let them know it was time to sit down.

To Felix's relief, Helena's presence stuck with him for most of the ordeal. May and Ezra chimed in on occasion, too. May had a surprising amount of snark for her own funeral, mostly directed at the decor. Ezra balanced out her comments with compliments for the speakers, which included a couple of their neighbors, along with a Guardian named Michael Beck who had apparently been close to their parents.

Wait, I recognize him, Felix realized. *He's on the King's Council.* Michael was one of the council members who had vouched for him in the debate.

Oh, yeah, he's cool I guess, May said. *Hey Felix, you should summon us like you did with Helena. That would be really funny.*

I can't do that, Felix told her.

Aw, come on! I've always wanted to haunt my own funeral.

Helena jumped back in. *May, knock it off. This is serious. We're dead, remember?*

I don't feel dead.

Hey, Ezra said. *I want to hear Michael's eulogy. He always brought me plants from the castle when he visited.*

Felix, thankfully, managed to keep a straight face through his siblings' arguments.

Once the funeral was over, instead of heading back to the car, Kendra led Felix to where Michael was deep in conversation with a few other Guardians. When he noticed Kendra approaching, he stepped away from them to talk to her.

"Is everything good to go?" Michael asked.

"Just about." Kendra rested a hand on Felix's shoulder. "Felix, Michael and a few other Guardians offered to pay off your house. Once you're ready to leave the castle in a few years, we'll sign it over to you and you can move back in. Or sell it, if you want."

"Wait, seriously?" Felix asked. That was a lot of money to spend on a kid they barely knew, even if they were friends with his parents.

"Don't worry about it," Michael said. "You've been through enough already. We just wanted to help however we could."

"Who else helped pay for it?" Felix asked. "Anyone I know?"

"The Tamuras, Sadia Malik—she's the other council member who supported training you at the meeting—oh, and Sebastian chipped in quite a bit, too."

"Where do Bright Guardians get money?" Felix asked. "Does someone pay you all to hunt monsters?"

"Unfortunately, no," Kendra said. "The council does pay Guardians to go on missions, but most of those funds come from other Guardians who have sources of wealth outside of the Brightlands." She folded her arms. "Some of us take paying jobs from civilians who have issues with monsters, but that's rare. People with supernatural problems usually turn to witches or psychics first, since we keep our organization out of the public eye."

"Of course, they run into a lot of fakes that way," Michael added. "Most people have no idea where to look for help when they run into real magic for the first time."

"Why not make the Bright Guardians public?" Felix asked. "Offer to help people?"

"That would cause even more problems," Kendra explained. "It's best if people who haven't dealt with monsters don't know they exist. And we're not the only ones fighting them, anyway. There are witches, exorcists, other groups of magicians, even human hunters who've trained with weapons."

Movement caught Felix's eye, and he turned as Archer approached the group. A few non-Guardians gave him weird looks, undoubtedly wondering about his mask, but he ignored them.

"Archer, could you take Felix to the car?" Kendra asked. "I'll be there in a minute. I'm just going to go over one last thing with Michael."

Felix groaned internally. He had a feeling that "one minute" would wind up being closer to ten.

"Sure," Archer said.

"Oh, and Felix, we're transferring your records from your high school to Bright Academy," Kendra said. "At least, the version of it that exists to the public. All you have to do is take some online courses to fulfill general education requirements, and we'll give you a diploma when you turn eighteen."

"Can't send you into the real world without basic knowledge," Michael added with a small smile. "Even if you decide to become a full-time Guardian."

Kendra nodded and continued. "Since it's almost summer, we'll just have you take the rest of the year off and pick up classes again this fall. That will give you time to adjust to your training schedule."

"Thanks," Felix said. What a relief. He couldn't even begin to imagine trying to do something like math right now.

He and Archer walked to where Kendra had parked on the street. "You're holding up better than I thought you would," Archer commented when they reached the car.

"I mean, it's not like they're really gone," Felix said. "It's hard to mourn someone who's cracking jokes in your head."

Archer opened his door. "Don't forget that ghosts are ghosts, Felix. They may be in your blood now, but they can't stay forever."

The words didn't have Archer's usual iciness, but they weren't warm, either. When Felix glanced at his face, his gaze was somewhere far away.

Felix climbed into the back seat next to the boxes of belongings he'd grabbed from his house on the way to the funeral. "I know," he said. Did he? There hadn't been much discussion about what would happen to Felix long term, other than a few vague allusions to him eventually becoming a Guardian. Could he keep his family's ghosts with him indefinitely? Would they even want that?

He wasn't sure he could bring himself to ask.

Felix leaned against the window and rested his chin in his hand. His expectations had been correct. It took Kendra eight minutes to return to the car.

On the drive back to the castle, Felix finally got a better explanation for its location that somehow both was and wasn't in the middle of a forest in western Washington.

"One of the early members of the Brightland family had the ability to create pocket dimensions," Kendra said. "She used her power to build another realm for us to live in. With the help of other Guardians, the Brightlands were constructed with a vast forest, farmland, a lake, and an entire city where Guardians lived.

"Unfortunately, the wards we used back then weren't nearly as powerful as today's," Kendra continued as she pulled off the freeway. "Maybe it was because they had more ground to cover. Regardless, monsters and spirits were often able to break through. A particularly powerful family of demons used their hellfire to burn away most of the pocket dimension before they were defeated."

"Now, if you travel too far into the forest around the castle, you'll hit a barrier," Archer added.

"In the early 1900s, another Guardian was born with the same ability," Kendra said. "He tried expanding our dimension in hopes of restoring the former lands, but he wasn't able to do much before his death. I think he extended the barrier by about half a mile, in total."

"How common is it for Guardians have the same ability?" Felix asked. "Could someone else with that power come along and add more to the pocket dimension?"

"It's possible. Abilities are somewhat random," Kendra replied. "Guardians often pass down abilities similar to their own to their children, but unusual ones still pop up in kids all the time. Elemental abilities are probably the most common, but there's a lot of variation within that category." She sighed. "Unfortunately, this dimension building ability seems to be one of the rarest."

The conversation died out after that, and what little remained of the drive back to the castle was quiet. When they arrived, Kendra helped Felix carry his boxes up to his room and explained his new schedule to him.

"You and Arisa will meet with Sebastian every weekday from ten to noon and two to five," Kendra explained. "He'll decide what to do with each session, but I assume it will be a mix of practicing your abilities, training with weapons, combat, and learning about sigils and wards. Hana also told me she'd be happy to give you some sword fighting lessons starting next week."

"Cool." Felix sat down on top of one of his boxes.

Kendra paused by the door. "Also, I believe Sebastian's trying to get permission for some kind of field trip, so be prepared to spend a day on that."

"Field trip?" Felix asked. "Are we allowed to do that?"

"If King Atticus lets him," Kendra said. "Sebastian's not the most trusted Guardian, but he can be surprisingly persuasive."

"Does the king distrust him as much as Archer does?"

"I don't think so. But I'm not entirely sure what the king thinks these days," Kendra replied. Her gaze went distant. "King Atticus is hard to read, and I don't talk to him much."

She left after that. Felix moved to the window and peered out at the castle yard. Arisa had been right about the view being nice. It was hard to appreciate right now, though. He swept his gaze over the trees and wondered just how far it was to the barrier. Archer hadn't explicitly said it was forbidden to go to it, and Felix was curious what the edge of a pocket dimension was like.

He held up his hand and examined the burn he'd given himself during training yesterday. He could have put one of those healing bandages over it, but the thought kept slipping his mind when he was actually in his room. Besides, he still felt bad that he'd hurt Arisa, too. Maybe if he kept the burn around a little longer, it would remind him to be more careful in the future.

Chapter Ten
An Unexpected Field Trip

Thursday morning, Felix and Arisa barely had time to finish their breakfast before Sebastian showed up, clapping his hands together.

"I got the king's permission to take you kids to Everett," Sebastian announced, as if the two would understand why that mattered.

"What's in Everett?" Felix asked. The city wasn't far from where he lived—well, used to live—but he had never been except to drive through it.

"The site of a demon killing," Sebastian said. "The demons were weak, but there were two of them, which is unusual."

"Even weak demons are really rare, though." Arisa looked to where Clementine sat on the table. The bear nodded in agreement.

"They're supposed to be." Sebastian rested his arms on the back of one of the table's many empty chairs and leaned forward. "There was actually a more powerful demon just south of Seattle, but the king didn't want us going that far. That one was killed a couple weeks ago, so the site's probably stale, anyway."

"Uh, is this safe?" Felix asked.

"Perfectly safe. The demons are gone," Sebastian said. "All that's left is a trace of their magical energy, and that'll fade over the next few weeks. But this is a great opportunity to learn about handling demons, even if you won't be running into them anytime soon."

"Will we be gone all day?" Arisa asked.

Sebastian shook his head. "There's a party of sorts for the Guardians tonight. We'll come back in the afternoon so that I can get ready for that."

"A party?" Felix perked up. "Are we invited?"

"Sorry, it's for graduated Guardians only," Sebastian replied. "We'll be discussing missions and whatnot, anyway. You'd be bored."

"Is it here at the castle?" Arisa asked.

"Nope. Some rich Guardian's house." Sebastian straightened up. "Guy named Ernest Abernathy. He throws these parties all the time. I think he just likes having people around to gossip with."

Felix frowned. "Abernathy? As in Eliza Abernathy? From the council?"

"Yeah, she's his cousin. The Abernathys kind of suck as people, but they are rich, so I enjoy stealing their food." Sebastian stretched out his arms. "Anyway, I don't anticipate any trouble today, but bring weapons just in case. Standard protocol. I'll meet you at the front of the castle in half an hour."

Once Sebastian was gone, Arisa leaned forward toward Felix. "Everett is where my parents were last week."

"What were they doing?" Felix picked up his glass of orange juice.

"They were also looking for a demon." Arisa shook her head. "It's weird. Like Seb said, demons are supposed to be really rare. Even the weak ones."

"Hm." Felix finished the last of his juice. "Do you think we should be scared?"

"Not as long as we're with Sebastian. I just feel like there has to be a reason this is happening."

They dropped off their empty trays and went their separate ways to get ready. On his way out of the dining hall, Felix found himself staring at a group of students that passed by him. The kids laughed with each other as they carried their food to their table.

The Bright Academy students tended to steer clear of Felix, or at the very least pretend they didn't see him. He wondered if it was because of his family's deaths, or because of Gideon's soul. He also wondered if under different circumstances, or if he weren't on probation, he'd be friends with any of them.

After picking out a green shirt and changing into his uniform, Felix grabbed Helena's sword, even though he still had little practice with it. He also wore Mom's ring around his neck, as usual, and brought along Gideon's necklace, though he kept that in a plastic bag shoved way down in the bottom of his backpack.

He also brought May's sigil-marked rock. Over the past few days of training, Sebastian had only had Felix focus on using Helena's lightning, as well as some careful practice with daggers. Felix had yet to touch May's ability—whatever it was—and he hadn't had a chance to ask what the sigils meant, either. Well, he probably could have squeezed in, but he felt like he'd bombarded the adults with too many questions already.

Felix met up with Arisa and Sebastian at the front of the castle, and they walked to the parking lot. Sebastian led them to a sleek, dark blue car.

"Ooh, this is nice," Felix said. He circled to the other side of the car and jumped when he saw Archer waiting.

"King Atticus said he approved a field trip," Archer said.

If Sebastian was startled by Archer's sudden appearance, he didn't show it. "You surprised?"

"I wasn't expecting him to let you take them anywhere so soon, but it sounds safe enough," Archer replied. "Though it's a little early to start teaching Felix about demons."

"Maybe, but I don't want to waste such a good opportunity." Sebastian opened his door.

"I'll be in Everett this morning, too," Archer said. "I have to follow up on a few details in the Tamuras' mission report."

"This isn't you asking for a ride, is it?" Sebastian asked with a smirk.

Archer turned around. "No. Just letting you know I'll be nearby if anything happens." He walked off without another word. Felix wasn't sure if that was an offer of help if they needed it, or a warning. Either way, Sebastian was completely unfazed as he climbed into the driver's seat.

Felix and Arisa slid into the back. "Oh, I'm a bit late on this, but I've been meaning to thank you," Felix said as he pulled his seat belt into place. "I heard you helped buy my house for me." He only seemed to remember that fact after their training sessions had ended.

"Ah, it's no trouble," Sebastian told him as he started the car. "I have a bunch of extra money lying around, since my parents thought it would be a good idea to run off and leave everything behind."

"Huh?"

"Don't worry about it."

Felix glanced at Arisa, who shrugged. "No idea," she mouthed as she buckled Clementine into the center seat. The uniform shirt she wore was the same shade of orange as the bear.

Arisa and Felix spent the drive going over words in ASL, while Sebastian occasionally dropped fun statements such as "I killed a wraith in that town over there when I was a teenager," and, "That mini golf place is actually run by a vampire. Nice guy," and, "Hey, I almost got turned *into* a vampire in that creepy warehouse!"

Their destination in Everett was a rundown building a short walk from where Sebastian parked the car. The faded letters above the front doors indicated it used to be a grocery store.

"This place shut down a few months ago but boarding it up wasn't enough to keep people from sneaking in," Sebastian said as the three approached the store. "The Guardians who killed the demons are pretty sure they were already on Earth and found their way here to prey on people. They weren't summoned inside the building."

"Did people die?" Felix asked.

"Yeah. Demons don't mess around. I think the total was three deaths."

Felix's chest tightened. Three people. How many deaths had he seen in the news that were actually the result of monsters like this?

Sebastian pointed out sigils that had been spray painted on the building's walls. "The authorities will assume teens did this graffiti, but it's the work of Guardians," he said. "Once they knew the demons were killing people inside, they put these sigils around to trap them."

They circled to a rear door at the back of the building, where Sebastian lifted a hand. A beam of light burst from his palm and struck the handle. There was a crack, and the door swung open.

"Are we allowed to be here?" Felix asked.

"We shouldn't run into any trouble. If the police show up, I'll handle it." Sebastian stepped into the darkness.

An orb of light appeared above Sebastian's hand as Felix and Arisa followed him in. It drifted up toward the ceiling and expanded, illuminating the store's interior. The entire building had been cleared of shelves, leaving a massive open space inside. The three walked to the center.

"Okay, you two stand here and close your eyes." Sebastian pointed at a spot on the floor.

Felix stood with his back to Arisa and squeezed his eyes shut. He felt Clementine's fur graze his neck as Arisa shifted her weight. "Now what?" Felix asked.

"See if you can feel anything," Sebastian said. "One of the biggest challenges as a Guardian is learning to sense magical energy, but it's also one of the most important things to learn."

"I can feel it," Arisa said.

"What? How?" Felix opened his eyes and turned to look at her.

"It takes focus," Sebastian said. "And time. I'd be surprised if you got it right away."

Arisa's eyes opened. "I've only done it a few times before, and that was always with other Guardians." She made a face. "The energy here feels...bad."

"That's demons for you," Sebastian said. "As you get better at it, you'll be able to identify what produced the energy you're sensing. It's very important to know what you're dealing with before you walk into a fight." He clapped his hands together. "Now, let's talk about killing demons."

Felix shifted nervously. He wasn't sure if it was magical energy or just nerves, but he was starting to sense something off about the empty building. "Maybe Archer had a point," he said. "Shouldn't I start smaller? I still don't really understand how ghosts work."

"I'll find you a ghost as soon as I can, but I didn't have time to track one down this week. We'll talk more about them at our first formal lesson," Sebastian told him. "And most vampires and werewolves around here are law-abiding citizens."

"What?"

Sebastian rubbed his chin. "There are rumors that a witch nearby is serial killing people with curses, but witches are tricky, so we'll let a more experienced Guardian handle that. And I wouldn't want to pit you against a siren yet, either—"

"Sirens?"

"—all the big obvious monsters like dragons went extinct centuries ago—"

"*Dragons?*"

"—and most of the other creatures around here are likely native, rather than brought over from Europe. But the Native magicians handle those—"

"All right, all right!" Felix threw his hands in the air. "Tell me about demons."

Sebastian launched right into a lecture. "Demons come in a variety of forms, some more powerful than others," he said. "They're rare, but they occasionally turn up to hunt and kill people. They're fast, strong, and regenerate quickly when injured."

"Don't demons make deals with people?" Felix asked. "Or is that not real?"

"Ah, those are the extra rare ones," Sebastian said. "Powerful demons are more sophisticated. Rather than chasing people down, they take on human forms and trick people into giving up their souls. Makes them harder to find, too."

Arisa yawned. "So, what? They'll still burn up if you drench them in holy water or hit them with powerful enough sigils, right?"

"That's the same way Kendra and Archer were trying to get rid of Gideon," Felix remembered. "Does the same stuff that gets rid of ghosts work on demons, too?"

"Sort of," Sebastian answered.

"Are demons worse than ghosts?" Felix asked.

"Worse is a complicated term, but yes."

"Ah."

"Ghosts are easy to banish," Sebastian said. "For starters, salt is usually enough to keep them away from you. One spray of holy water, or a touch from an object marked with banishing sigils, and they'll be gone for good. If you have them trapped, you could also draw banishing sigils around them." He snapped his fingers. "Arisa, what does it take to get rid of a demon?"

"Demons are also killed by holy water, but it takes more. Stronger ones have to be completely drenched, otherwise they'll eventually heal their burns," Arisa answered. "If you're going to use weapons with sigils, you need a lot of sigils, and they have to be strong."

Felix folded his arms. "So, you just draw sigils on blades, and they can suddenly kill demons?"

"Bit of an oversimplification, but yes," Sebastian said. "The process of creating sigils takes a lot of time and magical energy, though. You won't be able to just slap some on a sword and be ready to go."

"So, that stuff in the movies about chanting in Latin to exorcise demons isn't real?"

"Nah, that's real. Exorcisms are for demons that are possessing people, though, and they don't outright kill the demon," Sebastian replied. "We magicians aren't the only ones fighting monsters. Others have come up with their own methods of dealing with them, and we use what works for us."

"You said there are a lot of law-abiding vampires and werewolves. Are there any demons like that? Maybe the kind that have human forms?" Felix shook his head. "Sorry, I have a lot of questions."

Sebastian chuckled. "It's understandable. And I'm happy to answer all of them." He paused. "But I've never heard of anyone meeting a good demon."

"Cool," Felix said. "Now, can I ask an existential question?"

Sebastian raised an eyebrow. "Go for it."

"We've got demons and holy water," Felix said. "Doesn't that mean there's a heaven and hell?"

"Ha, yeah, you think that we'd have life's big questions answered, wouldn't you?" Sebastian shrugged. "Unfortunately, the answer is just a 'maybe.' Demons are infamously tight-lipped about where they really come from."

Arisa nudged Felix in the side with her elbow. "Don't get too wrapped up in it," she told him. "You look like you're going to give yourself a headache."

"Okay," Felix said. "How do you make holy water, then?"

"That's just the common term for it," Sebastian said. "You can make it with spells, for example specific prayers. We use sigils, though. There's a sigil set that uses magical energy to convert regular water to holy water."

Felix sighed. "So, I don't just have to learn how to use my abilities. I also have to memorize a bunch of sigils? And all the different ways to kill monsters?"

"Pretty much," Arisa said sympathetically.

"Once you're strong enough, most monsters can be killed with your magic, too. It just takes a lot of energy. Besides that, a lot of the classic stuff applies." Sebastian began counting off on his fingers. "Salt hurts ghosts, silver kills werewolves, iron kills fairies... Hm, vampires are tricky, but if you can keep 'em out in the sun long enough they'll eventually burn up—"

"Should I be writing this down?" Felix asked.

"Oh, and beheading! That's good for a lot of things that can otherwise regenerate." Sebastian lowered his hands. "Or complete obliteration. But even if you can't kill something with your magic alone, you will be able to hurt it. In fact, you should do that first to weaken it before you move in with water or sigils."

"So, would garlic salt repel both vampires and ghosts?" Felix asked.

"I—" Sebastian paused. "Huh. Let me get back to you on that."

Sebastian's phone buzzed. He pulled it from his jacket, unlocked it, and frowned at the screen. "Hm."

"Is something wrong?" Felix asked.

Sebastian brought the orb from overhead back down to his hand. The light made every color of the rainbow shine in his dark hair as it descended. "I have to check something out nearby. Here." He reached into his other pocket, pulled out his wallet, and removed a twenty-dollar bill. "Go get yourselves some ice cream or something."

Arisa eagerly snatched the bill from his hand.

"We'll come back in a little bit to practice energy sensing again," Sebastian continued. "And I want Felix to try something after."

"Uh, sure," Felix said.

The three exited the abandoned grocery store together. Sebastian left Felix and Arisa at the street corner next to the building. Once he was out of earshot, Arisa turned to Felix. "I think we're close to the building my parents were checking out last week," she said. She pulled out her phone and opened the map app.

"Weren't your parents looking for an active demon?" Felix asked.

"Yep." Arisa looked up. "Two blocks from here."

"Great. How about we go look for ice cream in the opposite direction?" Felix asked. "Oh, or maybe a coffee shop. I could go for an iced coffee."

Arisa waved her phone in his face. "Or we could see some real action."

"That sounds like a bad idea," Felix said.

"Okay, this might sound crazy, but I think Sebastian wants us to check it out," Arisa said. "Why else would he bring us here?"

"To practice sensing demon energy?" Felix suggested. "Like he said? Everything he told us in the grocery store seemed pretty reasonable. Why send us to face a live demon alone?"

"He doesn't have the most conventional teaching methods."

Felix hesitated. "Even if he did want us to go, can we...trust Sebastian?"

"Why wouldn't we?"

"Archer doesn't seem to."

Arisa shrugged. "Archer has trust issues. Sebastian takes the worst of it, but Archer doesn't really have faith in anyone. Other than the king." She placed a hand on Felix's shoulder and lowered her voice. "Look, I know you're new to this, but I actually went on a few missions before they put me on probation."

"Did you ever run into any demons?" Felix asked.

"Well, no, just a few ghosts and an escaped pet griffin. But how much more of a challenge could a weak demon be? I have a couple bottles of holy water and papers marked with sigils, and you have your sword!"

"My sister's sword," Felix corrected. "And if this demon were really so weak, wouldn't the other Guardians have killed it already? Your parents could have dealt with it while they were here, right?"

"They didn't kill anything. They told me they were having a hard time tracking it down," Arisa replied. "When Guardians show up, demons hide. We have an advantage because we're young, so we don't look like much of a threat."

"But we're not much of a threat."

Arisa ignored the comment. "Also, in the library, I found a method of luring out demons that are already on this plane of existence that most Guardians don't know about. All you need are weaker versions of sigils used in summoning rituals."

Felix still wasn't convinced.

Arisa sighed. "Okay, Felix, look at it like this: Gideon killed your family. You don't know how to banish his ghost yet." She held up a finger.

"Uh huh," Felix said.

Arisa raised a second finger. "Gideon was working for someone. The leader of the Uprising. If you want to be allowed to fight them, you have to prove yourself to the council."

"Uh huh."

The hand dropped. "Defeating a demon would show that you're gaining control of your powers!"

"I guess that's true," Felix said. Who knew how long it would take him to gain the council's trust at the rate he was going? "But what are you hoping to accomplish?"

"I want to go on missions again. I've barely been able to leave the castle since they put me on probation." Arisa sighed and adjusted the bracelet on her right wrist. After a moment, she shook her head and met Felix's eyes. "I have a plan. Trust me, there's a way to do this without putting ourselves in danger. I think."

Felix turned in the direction of the supposed demon. "Okay," he said after a moment. "Let's check it out." He glanced back at Arisa. "But I'm not making any promises about going inside."

"It's a start." Arisa grinned. "Let's go."

Chapter Eleven
The Demon-Killing Demon

Felix wasn't sure how much faith to put in Arisa. She carried herself with a lot of confidence. All he could do was hope it wasn't misplaced. He still didn't buy that Sebastian actually wanted them to be here, but maybe this was his chance to prove he was worthy of training with the Guardians.

"This is the place," Arisa said, stopping in front of a small office building. "Since the Guardians are pretty sure the demon is in this building, they put up wards around it. It traps the demon inside and prevents ordinary people from going in." She held up a hand. As she moved it forward, the air shimmered. "If we can lure the demon out, we could kill it here at the edge without putting ourselves in danger."

"What about the people who work here?" Felix asked.

"The Guardians in charge of the case probably came up with a story to keep them out. Black mold or a bug infestation or something."

"And wards are sort of like sigils?"

"Not exactly," Arisa said. "You can make wards with spells, but like with pretty much everything else, we Guardians make them from sigils. If you searched the property carefully, you'd be able to find the sigils used to form the wards." She knelt down and opened her bag. "Now, let's do this."

Her hands moved into the backpack and pulled out a few pieces of paper covered in sigils, along with a small dagger. After setting them on the sidewalk, she picked up Clementine and set her inside the bag. "Hang out in here for a little bit, okay?" She zipped it up.

Felix elected to set Helena's sword and his bag on the ground too, for the time being. "Were you planning to do this the whole time?" he asked as Arisa arranged the pieces of paper in a circle.

"I thought there might be an opportunity." Arisa slid one of the papers a few inches to the left, grabbed the dagger, and rose to her feet. "Okay, they won't work until we activate them. I brought a lighter, but it would work even better if you used your mom's fire—"

One of the building's doors swung open. A boy stepped out.

Felix frowned. "Is that a demon? I thought they'd be scarier."

"Well, some of them can take on human forms to trick people, but this might just be some kid." Arisa squinted. She hid her dagger behind her back. "Unless..."

The boy jogged toward them. He looked about their age, but he was several inches taller than Felix. His clothes were surprisingly warm, given the weather. He wore a backpack, ripped black jeans, a dark purple sweatshirt, and hid his hair under a red beanie. Most of it, anyway. A few pieces of straight black hair peeked out on his left side, nearly reaching his shoulders. The hair poking out on the boy's right nearly matched, but it was pale lavender in color instead.

"What are you guys?" the boy asked when he reached them. "Witches? Sorcerers? Magicians?"

"Bright Guardians," Arisa told him.

"Magicians, then."

"Yeah."

"Wait, I thought the Bright Guardians were a secret organization," Felix said.

"Only to the public," Arisa replied. "The local magic community knows about us."

"If by local you mean the entire Pacific Northwest, then sure," the boy said. He tipped his head back, letting the sun fall across his light brown skin. "So, can you take these wards down? I'm trapped in here with a bunch of demons. Not exactly fun."

A jolt of alarm coursed through Felix. "Wait, a *bunch* of demons?"

His question was ignored. Arisa put her free hand on her hip. "If you're not a demon, you should be able to leave."

The boy hesitated a moment before reaching his hand out. His fingers grazed the invisible barrier. He yelped in pain and jumped back.

"I knew it!" Arisa pointed her dagger at him. "He's a demon. Let's kill him and—"

"Wait!" The boy held up his hands. "Listen, I'm not—all the other demons here are trying to kill me."

Despite the barrier, Felix took a nervous step back from the boy. "Why's that?"

"Because I've been trying to kill them." The boy grimaced and rubbed his forehead, where a horizontal scar cut across the skin a few inches above the center of his eyes. "I thought there were only three in the building. But there turned out to be a dozen more that were somehow masking their magical energy."

"A demon killing other demons?" Arisa asked skeptically.

"I'm not a demon," the boy insisted. "I mean, I'm not like the other demons. I was born a human."

"Nice try, but you're thinking of vampires. Demons can't turn humans into demons."

"Well, at least one of them can." He sighed. "Seriously, you can look me up. My name is Mason Briggs. I was a normal human up until a few months ago." After a moment, he added, "Well, technically I was a witch, but I wasn't born with innate magic."

"I don't believe it," Arisa said. "I've never heard of that happening before."

"Doesn't mean it can't."

"Why are you killing other demons?" Felix asked.

"Because they're killing people! And I'm strong enough to stop them." Mason held up a hand. "Do you want to watch me kill them to prove I'm on your side?"

"That sounds like a trap," Arisa said.

Felix glanced at her. "You don't think we can trust him?"

"Definitely not." Arisa sighed. "But if he is telling the truth, I guess we shouldn't let him get killed, either."

"Wait, I have an idea." Felix turned to Mason. "What have you been using to kill demons?"

"This." Mason drew a large dagger from under his sweatshirt. The blade was engraved with sigils.

"Whoa, where'd you get that?" Arisa asked as Felix took the blade from him.

"My parents."

The sigils on the blade were different from the ones the Guardians used. They were made up of more circles and loops, with few hard angles like the ones on Helena's sword. Felix ran his thumb over the dark purple handle.

"No holy water?" Arisa asked.

"I'd rather not carry around something that burns me." Mason folded his arms. "Even if it's not enough to kill me, it hurts like hell to touch."

Felix held up the dagger so that sunlight glinted off the blade. "You said you've been killing demons with this?"

"Yes."

"Let's see if he's telling the truth." Felix sat down on the sidewalk and closed his eyes.

"Uh, what's he doing?" Mason asked.

"Psychometry," Arisa said. "I think."

Dad, Felix thought. *I need your help.*

Dad arrived quickly. *You want to try psychometry?* he asked.

Felix held the blade out in front of his face and opened one eye. *Yeah. How do I do it?*

It's going to be difficult finding a specific event on your first go, if that's what you're hoping for.

I have to try, Felix told him.

Well, it's hard to put into words, but I'll do my best. Focus on the object and the pull of my ability. You'll be able to feel its history living inside of it.

Felix let the pull in his chest take over. Before he could attempt to guide it in any way, he was sucked into darkness.

He stood in the middle of a void, hands suddenly empty. He turned around and found an unfamiliar man nearby holding the dagger. As soon as Felix's eyes landed on him, the man swung at the air in front of him. A transparent figure materialized long enough to crumble to dust as the blade passed through it.

The man swung again. This time, the being that appeared was a demon. At least, Felix assumed it was. Pale gray skin over muscled limbs, spiraling black horns, clawed hands. A second demon followed, one with deep purple skin and short horns and glowing yellow eyes.

As the weapon cut down monster after monster, Felix got the feeling he'd gone back too far. *Dad? You still here?*

"I'm with you." Dad's voice didn't come from inside Felix's head, but from his right.

Felix's head snapped toward him. His eyes widened. "How are you here?"

"You brought both of our souls into the object's memory," Dad said. He smiled. "This is good, for a first try."

Felix beamed. "Thanks." He turned his attention back to the man. "But I think I went back too far. I need to find that guy I met. Mason."

"You can use mental tricks to navigate the timeline," Dad told him. "For example, imagine winding up a stopwatch."

"I've never done that before."

"Okay, uh, how about scrolling through your tweeter feed?"

"It's Tw—never mind. I'll try that." Felix closed his eyes and imagined that the story in front of him was something he could touch and move. Not a phone screen, like Dad had suggested, but more along the lines of a giant tapestry. He imagined it sliding past him.

"You're going backwards," Dad told him. "The man's moving in reverse."

Felix imagined the tapestry sliding the other way.

"Good. Try going a little faster."

Felix pushed time even farther forward, until he felt Dad's hand touch his shoulder. "I think this is what you want," Dad said. Felix opened his eyes.

"Take this to protect yourself while we're gone." The man who'd been using the dagger to fight handed it to a younger version of Mason with short, completely black hair, who materialized from the darkness as he took the weapon.

A woman emerged from the void next to him. She took Mason's hand. "Whatever you do, wherever you go, we'll always be proud of you. Just promise me one thing."

Tears brimmed Mason's eyes. He nodded. "Anything."

"If we fail, you have to get the Ironwood Wand back," the woman said. "I know it's too much for us to ask of you, but it's too dangerous to let that thief keep it. You need to protect it, okay?"

"I'll get it back," Mason promised.

The man and woman disappeared, leaving Mason to stare at the weapon in his hand.

"I need to go farther forward," Felix said.

"Try keeping your eyes open this time, so you can see where you are," Dad told him.

Felix moved the timeline forward again. Mason became a blur. Felix slowed down and stopped when he saw Mason running, dagger in hand, throwing terrified glances backward. He looked much closer to his current age. Asphalt appeared beneath his feet as he ran out into a dark street. And then—

"—hit and run," a nurse said as she stepped out of the darkness. "I'm sorry, the police said the chances of finding the driver are slim."

Mason sat in a hospital bed, hooked up to IVs and covered in bandages. "How long—" His voice came out hoarse. He sucked in a deep breath. "How long have I been out?"

"A week." The nurse lowered her voice. "It's a miracle you're awake right now. The doctors thought you were gone for good. I was able to get you out of the coma, but you don't have long. You have a decision to make."

"What?"

The nurse held up the dagger. "You hunt monsters?"

"Hey, that's mine!" Mason reached for the weapon, but the nurse easily moved it out of his reach.

"I know." The nurse examined the blade. "What do you kill? Vampires? Spirits? Demons?"

"Anything that gets in my way." Mason coughed, pressing his hand to his mouth as he did. When he pulled it away, blood stained his skin. His eyes went wide with panic. "What's happening to me?"

"You're dying." The nurse set the dagger on the table by his bed. "I can save you, but you might not want to be saved."

"Of course I want to be saved!"

"There's a catch."

"I don't care what it is," Mason said. "I made a promise. I have to see it through."

The nurse leaned forward. Her irises turned red, and her pupils narrowed to slits. "I'm a demon," she said plainly.

Mason recoiled. "What the hell are you doing in a hospital?"

"Hiding. Listen, boy. I have the power to save your life with my blood, but you'll be transformed into a demon."

"That's impossible," Mason said.

"It's true."

Mason shook his head. "I know what demon blood does to humans. You're trying to turn me into a mindless, bloodthirsty monster."

Before the nurse could respond, Mason broke into another coughing fit. One of the monitors beeped rapidly. Mason pressed a hand to his chest and sucked in a deep breath.

"I rarely make this offer," the nurse continued. "It's not easy for us, blending in. Other monsters have found ways to fit into society without drawing attention to themselves. But demonic power is hard to hide." Her expression darkened. "And unlike with vampires or werewolves, hunters tend to assume that every demon deserves to be killed."

Mason wiped blood from his mouth with his arm.

"You only have a few minutes left," the nurse said. "You can feel it, can't you?"

The fear on Mason's face was plain. He turned his wide eyes to the dagger, then back to the nurse. "You can't bring back people who are already dead, can you?"

The nurse shook her head. "No. But would you really want to doom your loved ones to the fate of a demon?"

"No," Mason said, his tone bitter. "But like I said, I have a promise to keep." He closed his eyes. "Do whatever it takes to save me."

Felix pushed even further down the timeline. Demons burst from the void around Mason and swiped at him with sharp claws. One by one, he cut them down with the dagger, moving with superhuman speed. His hair was longer now, and half of it had turned lavender. Short, dark purple horns protruded from his head. A black stripe circled each horn near the base, with a white stripe just above it. The scar Felix noticed earlier had appeared on his forehead.

One particularly large demon survived the first strike and growled at Mason. Mason hissed, exposing sharp fangs. His brown eyes flashed purple as he swung again and turned the demon to dust.

Felix's eyes shot open. The transition from standing in the void to sitting on the ground was disorienting, and it took him a moment to find his senses.

"Did you see anything?" Arisa asked.

Felix climbed to his feet and reached back through the barrier to return the dagger to Mason. "We can trust him," he said, his eyes meeting Mason's.

"Thank you," Mason said.

Felix squinted at Mason's teeth as he spoke. No fangs. Did they only come out when he fought?

Mason looked back at the building. "By my count, there are ten more demons inside. They're all weak. Easy to kill. But that also means they're good at keeping hidden. The Guardians are going to have a hard time finding them."

"What if we went in?" Arisa asked.

"They'd pounce on you in a heartbeat."

"Perfect!"

"No! Not perfect." Mason waved his dagger as he spoke. "You two clearly aren't fully fledged Guardians. You can't take on ten demons."

"Right. And how old are you?"

"Sixteen," Mason said. "But I've been training my entire life—"

"What do you think, Felix?" Arisa asked, cutting Mason off.

Felix picked up Helena's sword and slid it out of its scabbard. "Well, Mason made it look like striking down weak demons was pretty easy."

"Let me see that sword," Mason said.

Felix handed it over. Mason grabbed the handle, careful not to touch the blade, and examined the sigils running up and down the metal. He didn't look impressed.

"You know how to use this?" Mason asked.

"Uh, kind of?"

Mason scowled. "That doesn't sound promising." He held it back out to Felix. "The sigils on it will be fine for these demons, but you should really have it strengthened. I see a few places where I could fortify it."

"So, are we going in?" Arisa asked.

"He did say there are ten demons," Felix said. "We were expecting one."

"We were also expecting it would just be the two of us. He's got tons of experience killing demons!" Arisa glanced at Mason. "Right?"

Mason nodded.

Felix gave the sword a few test swings. Mason had looked pretty proficient in the dagger's memory. "Yeah, I bet the three of us together could handle this."

"If you insist," Mason said.

Arisa drew some pieces of paper from her pocket. They came to life in her hands, folded themselves into airplanes, and circled the air around her and Felix. "These will warn us if any demons get close." She eyed Mason. "I think I can keep them from picking up your magic, but try to avoid touching them."

Mason nodded and turned around. "Follow me. They're all hanging out on the same floor."

Arisa caught up to Mason on his right, while Felix moved to his left. "So," Arisa said. "How exactly were you turned into a demon?"

"I was in an accident. One of the nurses at the hospital was a demon with the ability to transform humans with her blood. It was the only way to save my life."

"Her blood?" Arisa asked, surprised. "Demon blood is supposed to give humans demon sickness."

"I was terrified that would happen to me," Mason said. "But I turned into this instead."

"What's demon sickness?" Felix asked.

Mason shot him a sideways glance. "It sends you into a murderous rage. You didn't know that?"

"He's new to the magic world," Arisa explained. "He didn't know he had an ability until last week."

"Really? It took you that long to figure out you had psychometry?" Mason asked as they stepped inside the office building.

"That's not really my ability." Felix quickly explained everything that had happened in the past week while Mason led the way to a staircase.

"I've never heard of an ability like that," Mason said. After a moment, he added, "But I'm sorry for your loss."

"Yours too." Felix hadn't caught exactly what had happened to the people in Mason's memory—Mason's parents, he assumed—but he suspected it had something to do with the wand he was after.

Mason's gaze lowered. "I didn't want to come back," he said. "Not as a demon. But I promised my parents I'd find something that was stolen from them."

"The Ironwood Wand?" Felix asked. He quickly added, "I didn't see much besides you killing demons, but I did hear that."

"It's an extremely powerful wand," Mason said, nodding. "My grandmother made it herself from ironwood she collected in the

Arizona desert. Up until her death, she said it was a mistake. She hadn't expected to create something so powerful." His tone turned bitter. "I guess she was right, since it got my parents killed. And me."

"Where is it now?" Arisa asked.

"A man stole it from us. When my parents tried to steal it back, he killed them."

Felix glanced around as they stepped out of the stairwell onto the fourth floor of the building. "Sounds like we're both after revenge, then." Seeing a place that should have been busy so empty was eerie, but he felt oddly calm given the circumstances.

"Guess so," Mason replied as the three set off down the hallway. "You might have it worse, though. One man is nothing compared to an army of magicians."

One of Arisa's paper airplanes burst into orange flames and dropped to the ground. Arisa lifted her dagger. "Something's nearby," she hissed. Felix's calm evaporated in a heartbeat.

A raspy voice spoke behind them. "So, the demon killer is back."

The three whirled around as a demon emerged from one of the open doorways. It stood over six feet tall, with skin a shade of deep emerald, and a thin tail ending in a black arrow-shaped tip that swung back and forth behind it. The black horns on its head resembled an antelope's.

"Oh, you brought friends?" The demon chuckled as it swept its gold eyes over them.

"It can't pass through my circle of sigils," Arisa told Felix. "Sorry, Mason, you're on your own."

Mason adjusted his grip on his dagger. "That's fine."

"Such confidence." Two leathery black wings stretched out behind the demon.

"It's got wings," Mason warned.

"I can see that," Arisa shot back.

"That means it's more powerful than the others I saw here."

The demon lunged forward with outstretched claws. Mason easily dodged, stepped behind the demon, and swiped at the back of its neck with his dagger. He grazed the demon's skin, drawing gold blood to the surface.

It wasn't enough to kill the demon. The demon hissed and swung at Mason again. It struck the side of Mason's head and sent him flying into the wall.

"Mason!" Arisa exclaimed.

Felix lifted Helena's sword. "Helena, can you hear me? I've got a demon to kill."

I've got something better than a sword, May said.

"May?" Felix frowned. "No offense, but I think Helena's going to be the best bet here—"

No, trust me, my ability's going to be way better. Take out a water bottle.

"What?" Felix watched Mason jump to his feet in time to dodge another attack from the demon.

You brought water, right? May asked.

"Yes, but I don't see how that's going to be helpful. It's not holy water."

Doesn't matter, take it out. And my rock. The one with the sigils on it.

No time to argue. May knew what she was doing. Probably. Felix set down the sword and reached into his bag.

Arisa sent a few of her paper planes flying at the demon. While it was distracted, Mason managed to deal another blow, leaving a gash on the demon's upper arm. The demon lifted its hands. Green flames appeared in its palms, shooting up high enough to torch the paper planes assaulting its face.

Felix pulled out his water bottle and May's rock. "Okay, what's your ability and how do I use it?"

Just throw the rock in the water bottle.

Felix did as he was told. Arisa shot him a weird look. "What the hell are you doing?" she asked.

"I don't know," Felix replied.

The demon swung its arm. Mason stepped back far enough to avoid its claws, but they snagged his beanie and ripped it off his head, exposing the purple horns Felix had seen in the dagger's memory. The movement also exposed Mason's pointed ears.

"May, could we hurry this up?" Felix asked.

Ten more seconds, May replied.

"Ten more seconds?"

With another swipe of its hand, the demon knocked Mason's dagger out of his grasp. Arisa sent three more planes at its face to distract it, but it burned them away easily.

Okay, May said. *Drink all of the water in the bottle.*

"It's almost full!" Felix exclaimed as he held it up.

Just do it!

Black claws appeared at the tips of Mason's fingers as he launched himself at the demon. He slashed at its face, leaving thin gashes, before hitting the ground and rolling to avoid the demon's flaming hands.

"You might be bigger," Mason hissed between breaths. "But I'm faster."

Hey, wait, I can feel the pull of my ability, May said. *Like I could when I was alive.*

Felix rubbed his forehead, eyeing the absurd amount of water she expected him to chug. "What are you talking about?"

"Felix, what's going on?" Arisa asked.

"Sorry, my sister's being a pain in the ass."

As Mason rose to his feet, a dark purple tail swished through the air behind him, ending in a tuft of lavender fur the same shade as the right half of his hair.

"Aw, that's kind of cute," Arisa said.

"Are you two going to do anything helpful?" Mason growled.

"Working on it!" Felix called. "May? What are we doing here?"

Here, let me just—I think I can do this for you!

"What, wait? What are you—?"

Felix was no longer in control of his body. Something threatened to pull him down into darkness, and it took all his focus to stay in his own head. *What the hell is going on?* He could hear the words, but his mouth didn't move.

"I'm killing this thing." This time his mouth did move, but it was May's voice that came out.

"Uh, is that normal?" Mason asked.

Arisa's eyes widened. A faint grin touched her lips. "No idea, but this is starting to get good."

Felix's hand picked up the water bottle, uncapped it, and held it to his mouth. May, who was apparently in control now, downed the entire thing in a shockingly quick amount of time.

The demon turned toward him and snorted. "Ready to fight now that you're hydrated?"

"Yes," May replied.

Felix's entire body turned to water.

Chapter Twelve
May's Possession

Felix's body, which was now entirely made of water, dropped to the floor and shot forward. He had no control over his movement. All he could do was hang on for the ride as May raced toward the demon.

When they reached the demon's feet, Felix's water form rose into a pillar, rapidly enveloping its skin. Every inch of the creature that he touched burned, letting off steam with a hiss. It howled in pain as the water spread, and within seconds, it had been swallowed completely. It only took another second for the demon to let out one last shriek and crumble into nothing.

Doors opened up and down the hallway. Demons emerged from the shadows. Eleven of them. These ones were smaller and wingless, but they raced toward Arisa, Mason, and Felix's body of water with alarming speed.

Relax, Felix, May said. *I got this.*

Their water arced through the air and struck the closest demon in the chest. It clutched its burning skin as it dropped onto its back. May wrapped the water around its neck until she'd burned a hole clean through.

Mason and Arisa plunged into the fight. Felix wasn't sure how exactly he was seeing the world around him, but he was dimly aware of Mason scrambling to pick up his dagger off the floor nearby, and Arisa picking up Helena's sword.

They two sliced at demons around them. After only a few blows, most demons dropped to the ground and stopped moving. May continued to burn up demons with water, moving between them at a speed that left Felix's head spinning. Not that he had a head anymore. Still, he was dizzy to the point of nausea.

It took a couple of minutes for them to kill all of the demons.

The water that was now Felix moved into a roughly human shape. Then, his body came back in the blink of an eye. He staggered backwards into the closest wall. His clothes were damp, and water dripped from his hair and slid down his skin.

Sorry, I'm a little out of practice, May said. *I usually come back completely dry.*

"You—you turned into water!" Arisa exclaimed.

Mason took a step back from Felix. "Holy water, at that."

"Wait, I drank holy water?" Felix held a hand to his throat.

Sort of, May said. *I need stone to channel my power, so most of our power in that water form came from the fact that the stone we were using has sigils on it that convert water into holy water.*

"Do you always have to drink water first?"

Not necessarily. But putting the stone in the water we drank first gave us a boost, since it takes time for the sigils to start working on the water form. The longer you leave the stone in beforehand, the better. Luckily those demons were pretty weak.

"So, if you turned into water using a regular stone, would you just be regular water?" Felix asked.

Yep.

"Who's he talking to?" Mason asked.

"My sister," Felix said. He explained May's ability as best as he could. She corrected him a few times, issued a snarky *You're welcome*, and left his mind.

"I think she wore herself out," Felix said. "I won't be able to do that again anytime soon."

"That's fine, we killed all of them." Arisa handed Helena's sword back to Felix. "It held up well."

"I still think you should strengthen it," Mason muttered.

"I'll look into it," Felix said. "So, what are you going to do now?"

Mason walked a ways down the hallway and looked up at the ceiling. "Well, I would call it a day, but I'd like to know what drew so many demons to one location."

"Yeah, this was bizarre," Arisa said. "Especially considering the other recent demon attacks in the area."

Something thudded against the ceiling overhead. Felix tensed. "What was that?"

"Maybe the building's settling," Arisa suggested.

"I'm not that lucky," Mason said. "I didn't sense any other demon magic, but—" His eyes widened. "Sh—"

The ceiling above him exploded. He raced toward Felix and Arisa. "Run!"

Felix darted through the closest doorway into a large, unfinished room. He glanced back as Arisa caught up. A cloud of dust filled the hallway behind them. "What happened to—?

A red demon erupted from the dust and grabbed Felix. Felix's feet lifted off the ground, and then he was sailing through the air. His back slammed into a wooden beam. He gasped as he sank to the concrete floor.

His vision blurred. The demon stalked toward him. More figures moved behind it.

"Arisa?" Felix tried weakly. The demon was a few feet away now. It lifted a clawed hand and summoned black flames.

Mason crashed into the demon. As they tumbled to the ground, Mason lifted his dagger and drove it into the demon's neck. The demon's fire went out. It choked as black blood spurted from the wound.

Felix pushed himself to his feet. "You said we killed all of them!"

"I didn't sense these ones until they were on top of us!" Mason glanced back with wide eyes. "I should have been able to feel them, even if they were hiding themselves. It doesn't make any sense!"

To Felix's relief, Arisa appeared at Mason's left. "There's at least ten more." She threw a frantic glance at the door. "I put up some protective sigils in the air, but—"

"At this rate, the demons will burn through them pretty quickly," Mason said. "Get ready to fight."

Felix's shoulders sagged. He was exhausted, and judging by the other's faces, they were too.

Arisa pulled her dagger from her bag. "Can Clementine help us?" Felix asked her.

She shook her head. "She won't do much damage to a demon. I've been meaning to strengthen the sigils on her knives, but I haven't had the chance."

"Who's Clementine?" Mason asked.

"I'll explain later." Arisa lifted her weapon. "Assuming we survive this."

Felix raised Helena's sword. If he weren't on the verge of collapse, he'd try hitting the demons with lightning to knock them down, but he couldn't imagine generating more than a few sparks now.

One by one, the paper planes hovering in the air in front of the door burst into different colors of flames. Red. Green. Blue. Yellow. The first few demons burst into the room and charged.

Blades swung. Felix cut clean through a demon's neck, taking himself by surprise. That had been smoother than expected. The demon's head hissed in pain as it hit the floor. Felix stepped forward to deliver another blow, but a second demon crashed into him. The sword slipped from his grasp. His head smacked against concrete.

The new demon pinned him to the floor with one hand. It lifted the other. Light glinted off its claws as it prepared to strike.

The blade of a sword burst from the demon's chest and came to a stop inches from Felix's face. A heartbeat later, the sword slid back out, and the demon collapsed to the ground next to him.

Archer barely looked at Felix as he decapitated the demon with his blade. Three more demons converged on him. Archer reached up a hand and pulled down his mask. With his other hand, he swung his sword through the air behind him. The demon it slashed staggered back, the skin around its wound burning away.

Felix pushed himself upright, eyes wide. He wanted to help Archer, but the thought of standing made him nauseous.

Archer didn't seem to need Felix's help, anyway. The second demon approached from the front and swung a hand at his face. The air in front of Archer's lips darkened, as if it were filled with smoke. The demon's skin burned as it passed through the cloud.

The demon grimaced in pain but kept moving. Archer took a step back to avoid its claws. The demon swung again, slower this time. It stumbled to the right. Swayed. Archer's sword cut through its body, leaving it in two halves on the concrete. With one swift motion, Archer sent the third demon falling to the floor next to it.

The demons attacking Mason and Arisa backed off and turned their focus to Archer, quickly realizing he was the biggest threat to them.

Archer ran to the nearest wall, jumped, and pushed himself off of it. The remaining demons followed. While he was in the air, Archer let go of his sword. The blade plunged into the head of the first demon to reach him. Meanwhile, he yanked the glove off his right hand, drew a dagger with his left, and slid the blade across his palm. Blood welled on the metal, turning from red to bright green in seconds.

Archer's boots slammed against the ground.

Another demon lunged at him. Archer ducked and swiped his dagger across its chest. The demon didn't slow. It grabbed Archer's wrist and pushed him backward into the wall. Archer twisted, broke free from its grasp, and plunged the blade into its back. The demon sank to the floor and desperately clawed at Archer's legs. Archer stepped away, grabbed his sword from the dead demon nearby, and lunged at the next one.

Felix watched in awe as Archer finished off the remaining demons. Mason and Arisa stood frozen nearby, equally stunned expressions on their faces.

After the last demon dropped, Archer started toward Mason with his sword raised. Arisa jumped in front of Mason. "Wait, don't kill him!"

Archer stopped but kept his sword up. "Why not? He's a demon."

"He's not!" Felix forced himself to stand up. "Well, he is, but he was only turned into a demon a few months ago." He gestured to

Mason. "Arisa and I didn't believe it either, but I used my dad's ability on his dagger and saw what happened to him. He came here to kill the other demons. The bad ones."

Laughter echoed around the room. Everyone's eyes moved to the demon Archer had attacked with his blood-soaked dagger. The demon was slumped against the wall, apparently unable to move.

"You may think he's good now, but he won't be like that forever," the demon said. "When he realizes he's not going to age, not going to die, that he's never going to be human again..." It wheezed. "Demon blood fills you with bloodlust. He won't be able to resist it forever."

Archer strolled over to the demon. "Care to explain what so many of you were doing here?"

The demon chuckled. Dark blood spilled from its mouth. "You can't kill me with this poison, no matter how much magic you put in it," it spat.

Archer slammed his boot against the demon's shoulder, knocking it flat on its back. "I'm not trying to kill you. Yet. And that poison will keep you paralyzed as long as I like." Archer leaned forward, putting more of his weight over the demon's shoulder. Something cracked.

"I'm not interested in answering your questions," the demon said. "But I do find that boy interesting."

"I know what happens to humans who are infected with demon blood," Archer said. "They don't turn into demons. They turn into mindless killers."

"Like zombies?" Felix asked.

"They're not rotting or dead. They're just monsters that won't stop until they're killed." Archer's gaze flickered briefly to Mason. "But they don't grow horns or tails or gain demonic abilities."

"Wait, follow-up question, are zombies real?"

Archer ignored the question, which Felix found unsettling.

"You've seen other humans turned demons?" Archer asked the demon. "Humans that didn't succumb to demon sickness?"

"Not with my own eyes," the demon replied. "But I'm not going to answer your questions just so that you can kill me."

"I figured as much." Archer lifted his sword. "Any last words before I send you back to hell?"

"If you want information, maybe we could make a deal." The demon attempted to lift an arm, but it only moved an inch off the ground before flopping back down. "Poison wielder. You are Archer Rosenbaum, aren't you? I have plenty to tell you about your dead friends, if you let me—"

In the blink of an eye, the sword passed through the demon's chest. It gasped one last time before falling quiet for good.

Archer turned around. "Where's Sebastian?"

Chapter Thirteen
Reluctant Agreement

Felix's head was still spinning. By the time he found the words to answer Archer's question, Arisa was already speaking.

"Uh, Sebastian got a message and had to check something out nearby," Arisa told Archer. "He didn't tell us to come here. We just wanted to see the building."

"And you thought coming inside was a good idea?" Archer asked. His stone-cold expression was far more terrifying than outright anger would have been.

"Well, no, not at first," Arisa stammered. "But then we met Mason."

Archer was quiet for a long moment. Then, he pointed to a spot in the middle of the room. "Stand right there, demon."

Mason folded his arms. "Why?"

"Because if you don't, I'll have no choice but to kill you."

"Fine," Mason hissed as he walked to where Archer was pointing. His tail swung behind him.

Archer dropped to one knee a few feet from Mason and began painting sigils on the floor with the green—blood? Poison? Both?—

staining his palm and fingers. "This is to keep you from running while I fetch my colleague."

"Wait, Archer, how did you know we were in here?" Felix asked. He was certainly grateful Archer had arrived to save them, but it was a miracle the man had shown up at all.

"I was here looking for signs of the demons outside. I felt Guardian energy appear on the other side of the building, but you had already gone inside by the time I circled around to the front," Archer explained. "Figured I should come in and investigate."

He drew one last sigil and rose to his full height. Then, walked to where his glove lay on the floor, picked it up, and slid it back on over his bleeding hand. Seeing Felix's concerned expression, he said, "The gloves have healing sigils. Now, are you two capable of staying put while I call Sebastian and make sure this building's completely clear of demons?"

"Is that a rhetorical question?" Arisa asked. Archer stared at her blankly until she sighed. "Yeah, we'll stay here."

Once Archer's footsteps had faded into the distance, Felix sank to the floor and leaned back against the wall. "I can't tell how pissed he is," he said. "He always looks like he wants to murder someone."

"Oh, so this is normal?" Mason asked.

Arisa cleared her throat. "Felix, we have a slight problem."

Felix looked at her. "What?"

"If your sister was able to take your body from you that easily, then that means Gideon probably can too." Arisa's expression hardened. "And he's a lot stronger than anyone in your family."

Felix's blood ran cold. He hadn't even considered that. Sure, he hadn't heard anything from Gideon since taking him in, but if Felix accidentally awakened him...

"Do you think we should keep it a secret?" Felix asked.

"I mean, the council will freak out if you tell them," Arisa said. "And it's not like that's going to help you any."

Felix rubbed the back of his neck. "I don't know. If there's a chance Gideon could possess me, maybe I should be locked up."

Mason folded his arms. "If that's grounds enough for your leaders to lock you up, then I'm definitely screwed."

"All we have to do is prove you're not a threat, and the council will have to let you go," Arisa said to Mason. She looked at Felix. "Right?"

"Have you ever actually been in a council meeting?" Felix asked her.

Arisa shook her head. "They didn't even invite me to the meeting where they decided to put me on probation."

"Ah. Well, they're not exactly the nicest group of people."

"Great," Mason muttered. "I don't have time for this. I'm supposed to be tracking down the guy who killed my parents."

Sebastian appeared in the doorway. "What do we have here?"

Mason jumped in surprise. His tail smacked into the barrier formed by Archer's sigils, and he hissed in pain. Felix winced.

"That was fast," Arisa said.

"I was already on my way in when Archer called," Sebastian said. "I felt a spike in demonic energy." He whistled as he took in the dead demons lying around the room. "Not bad."

Archer entered the room behind him, his mask still down around his neck. "Most of these were my kills, not the kids'."

"I'm well aware. It's a compliment." Sebastian rested a hand on his hip. "But the kids should be congratulated, too."

"For what, their disobedience?"

"They killed those demons out in the hallway, didn't they? That's impressive."

"It was reckless."

"I agree. They shouldn't have come in here. But what's done is done." Sebastian walked up to Mason. "So, you're the human demon?"

"I guess," Mason replied. "Demon witch is probably a better description, though."

Sebastian rubbed his boot against the floor, smearing the sigils Archer had drawn. Mason breathed a sigh of relief and stepped out of the circle.

"Sebastian," Archer warned.

"Oh, please. We can handle him if he tries anything." Sebastian leaned forward and squinted at Mason. "And you don't feel any urges to, say, murder me?"

"That should hardly be considered a qualification for demon sickness," Archer said. "Most people want to murder you."

"No, I haven't felt like killing anyone," Mason said, eyes narrowing. "I haven't hurt any humans. I'm killing the demons because they were attacking innocent people."

"Huh." Sebastian looked at Archer. "I mean, demon sickness doesn't usually give people horns."

"Exactly," Archer said. "He really seems to be a demon now. And a high-level one at that, given his mostly human appearance." To Mason, he asked, "Is this your most natural form, or are you actively altering it?"

"I'm not trying to alter it," Mason said. "But I usually don't have claws. They come out when I'm fighting. Same with the tail, sometimes."

"Your eyes turned purple, too," Felix chimed in.

Archer folded his arms. "I wonder if you could learn to control it."

Sebastian took a few steps backward, putting himself next to Archer. "You want to take him back to the castle?"

"The council will want to see this," Archer replied with a nod.

"You saw how they treated Felix. What do you think they'll do with someone like him?"

"I think any concerns they have are reasonable."

"He killed demons that would have gone after innocent people. Don't tell me you're going to let the council throw him in the dungeon."

Archer was quiet for a long moment, his expression calculating. "And what would you have us do with him instead?"

"He could help us."

Archer lifted his mask back up. "I'll vouch for his survival, but I can't make any promises about what the king will decide."

"His survival's not enough. I don't want him rotting in a cell." Sebastian waved a hand. "He seems to be a good fighter, for his age. If you have to argue that he should be allowed to work with us purely because he's useful, do that."

"Sebastian's right. He's really strong." Arisa moved to Mason's side.

Felix stood up and joined them, doing his best to ignore his body's aches. "He did take down most of the demons, before Archer showed up."

"So?" Arisa clasped her hands together. "Can we keep him?"

"He's a demon, not a pet," Archer said.

"First and foremost, I'm a witch," Mason snapped. "And I have my own problems to deal with. I'm not going with you people."

"We can't let a demon go free. Especially a case like this," Archer said sternly. "We've never seen anything like it before."

"No, he has a point," Sebastian countered. "We don't have jurisdiction over every magical being."

"I have a mission of my own." Mason's head turned toward the window. His eyes locked on the world outside. "Something was stolen from my family, and I'm going to find it and get it back. I made a promise."

"If you spend your whole life thinking you can do anything just because you promised, you'll be sorely disappointed," Archer said.

"Maybe we can help you," Sebastian suggested, lifting a hand. "We have a whole army of Guardians on our side. You work with us, we help you steal back your..." He waved his hand expectantly.

"Ironwood Wand," Mason said. He turned his gaze toward Sebastian and Archer again.

Archer shook his head. "You're not in a position to make those kinds of promises, Sebastian."

"And I don't need help from a bunch of wizards." Mason's eyes narrowed.

"Magicians," Arisa corrected.

"Really?" Sebastian asked. He folded his arms and lifted an eyebrow. "How much progress have you made on your own?"

"I know the name of the guy responsible. I've narrowed down his location to somewhere this side of Washington," Mason said.

"What's his name?"

"Ernest Abernathy."

Archer's eyes widened slightly. For him, it was a surprising amount of expression.

"Uh oh," Arisa said.

Sebastian blew out a breath of air. "Abernathy, eh?"

Mason frowned. "What, you guys know him?"

"Yeah, we know him," Sebastian replied. "He's a Bright Guardian. You don't have a prayer of getting that wand back, kid."

"I have to!" Mason exclaimed, gesturing angrily. "There has to be a way. That wand is dangerous. He killed my parents to keep his hands on it."

Sebastian and Archer exchanged a look.

Arisa folded her arms. "Couldn't you get it back yourself Sebastian? Just break into his house, blast him with some light magic, and take the wand!"

"It's not a matter of power," Sebastian said. "It's...politics."

Archer nodded. "Sebastian is right."

"I am?"

"We can't attack one of our own unless the king commands it," Archer continued. "But the fact that Abernathy has such a powerful weapon in his hands—a stolen one, at that matter—is cause for concern. And if he killed people for it..."

"Well, what do you think we should do, Archie?" Sebastian asked.

Archer was staring at Felix now. "I have a plan."

"You going to let us in on it?"

"No, because you won't like it. But it's the demon's only chance." Archer turned and walked toward the door. "I need to talk to Felix for a moment."

Felix looked to Sebastian, who shrugged. "Go ahead, I guess," Sebastian said.

Felix ran out into the hall after Archer. They walked to the end, out of earshot of the others. Archer came to a sudden stop and turned around. "Could you use your father's ability on Mason's dagger in front of the council?" he asked.

Felix barely stopped in time to avoid crashing into him. "Yeah, but—"

"Your father was able to manifest memories from an object and project them so that others could see," Archer said. "It was difficult, and he rarely did it, but it is possible. Can you show them that Mason was killing demons, and that he was a human who was transformed?"

"You want me to use an ability I barely understand in a way that even my dad with years of experience could barely do?" Felix asked.

"Yes."

Felix gulped, unable to break Archer's piercing gaze. "I'll, uh, do my best?"

"You'd better hope that your best is good enough, then." Archer passed him and walked back toward where the others waited. Felix hurried into the room behind him and moved to stand next to Arisa and Mason.

Archer faced Sebastian. "Believe it or not, I don't want to see him thrown in a cell, either."

"But you'll side with the king no matter what," Sebastian said plainly.

"So you'd better come up with a damn good argument for letting him live."

Arisa looked concerned, but Mason wasn't paying attention to the people discussing his fate. His head was tipped back so that he could examine the ceiling.

"Uh, Mason?" Felix waved a hand in front of his face. "You good?"

Mason's attention snapped back to the group. "I need to check something out on the floor above us," he announced.

"Care to elaborate?" Archer asked.

"It's just a hunch. It won't take long." Mason took a deep breath. "Look, trust me on this for five minutes, and I'll come with you to your stupid castle without any trouble. Promise."

"Fine," Archer said. "Don't try anything."

Mason led the group up a flight of stairs, down a hall, and into an office. The sight inside sent a chill down Felix's spine. A desk had been pushed to the middle of the room, and dozens of sigils—loopy, rounder ones like the kind on Mason's dagger—were carved into the wood. Candles burned in a circle around the desk, while various dried plants and gemstones were piled on top.

"This is what was luring in the demons," Mason said. "It's a weaker version of a summoning ritual. It won't bring any demons to this plane of existence, but it will draw them in if they were already nearby."

Kind of like what Arisa was planning, Felix realized. "But why would demons be drawn to these?"

"It's a magical pull. The stronger ones could resist it, but why turn down potential prey?" Mason lifted his dagger and carved a new line in the desk, cutting through the sigils. "This will disrupt it. I'll extinguish the candles, too."

"How far away would demons feel it?" Archer asked.

"Judging by this setup, I'd guess a fifty-mile radius?"

Sebastian whistled.

"That's insane," Arisa muttered.

Mason started blowing out candles, and the others joined him. Once the flames were out, Mason walked to the corner of the room, where the wallpaper was peeling. He ripped it back and placed a hand on the cracks running up and down the wall. "These offices are new. This damage doesn't make any sense. Unless..."

Sebastian lifted an eyebrow. "Unless?"

Mason turned around. "It's damage from a spell being cast in this room. I can't be sure what the spell was, but it could have been used to mask the demon's magical energy and make them harder to detect."

"Can you figure out anything else?" Archer asked. "Or should we leave?"

Mason glared at him. "That's all I have. You're welcome."

"You have to admit that was impressive," Sebastian said, shooting Archer a glance.

"Like I said." Mason lifted his chin. "I'm a witch first."

The five made their way out of the office building. By the time they stepped outside, Mason's tail and claws were gone. He pulled the hood of his sweatshirt up over his head to hide his horns.

The group returned to the abandoned store where Sebastian was still parked. Archer reluctantly left Mason in their hands, but not before confiscating his dagger and rattling off a string of threats directed at Sebastian.

"If you lose him, free him, or pull any ridiculous stunts, you'll never hear the end of it from the council." As Archer turned to walk away, he added, "You'll be lucky to keep your Guardian status. And I'll personally suggest you serve time in a cell."

Sebastian chuckled as he opened his door. "He's hilarious."

"We must have different definitions of that word," Mason muttered.

Arisa called shotgun, leaving Felix in the back with Mason. As Sebastian started the car, she asked, "Is Archer really just going to throw Mason in front of the council?"

Felix frowned. "I think he has something else planned. He was asking me about my dad's ability."

"Sorry, kid, but Archer's as cold as they come," Sebastian said. "He trusts the council to put the good of the Guardians above all else. And if they think Mason has any chance of putting the Brightlands in danger, they'll lock him up. Or worse."

"Let me guess, execute me?" Mason asked.

"Possibly."

"Great." Mason folded his arms and leaned back in his seat. "I'm headed to death or a prison sentence."

"I'm going to do everything in my power to make sure that doesn't happen," Sebastian said. "Promise."

Instead of responding, Mason turned his head to glare out the window.

"Where did you go earlier?" Felix asked Sebastian. "After we left the grocery store?"

"I got a message from another Guardian in the area asking for backup," Sebastian replied. "Another demon. Must have been one of the ones lured to the area by that spell."

Before Felix could question him further, Arisa sat up in her seat. "Wait, Sebastian, you said you're going to a party at Ernest Abernathy's tonight!"

"Yeah."

Mason's head turned forward, some of his aggravation melting away. "You are?"

Sebastian nodded. "I was going to steal food and eavesdrop, but given today's events, I suppose I should keep an eye out for that wand."

"Can you steal it back from him for me?" Mason asked.

"I'd have to find it first. I doubt keeps it out in the open," Sebastian said. "I'll learn what I can, but I can't risk getting caught.

If he accuses me of stealing and we wind up in front of the council, they'll take his word over mine."

"But Archer knows Ernest stole the wand from Mason's parents," Felix pointed out.

"Maybe he'd take our side, but I don't know if he even believes Mason's story fully." Sebastian's hands tightened around the wheel. "If there's one thing I know about Archer, it's to never count on him taking your side."

Chapter Fourteen
Mason Vs. The Council

The blade of Helena's sword stung Felix's skin. He drew a few drops of blood from his palm and held out his hand, focusing on the memory of his dad's voice and face and smile.

Dad materialized in front of him.

"It worked!" Felix sat down on his bed. "Dad, I need your help."

"With psychometry?" Dad asked.

"Sort of. I need you to use my ability for me in front of the council."

Dad frowned and moved to sit next to Felix. "Why do you need me to do it for you? You did a great job with that dagger."

"They're not going to believe my word alone. I have to project that memory in front of them so that I can prove Mason isn't a threat," Felix told him. "Archer said you used to be able to do that. I think you should just take over my body like May did and project the memory for me. Oh, and don't let the council realize you're the one in control."

Dad shook his head. "I don't think that's a good idea."

"Why not?"

"It's concerning that May was able to take control of you like that. Gideon is in here somewhere, too. Don't forget that." Dad sighed. "If he figures out the rest of us can possess your body, he's bound to give it a try, too."

"But I haven't awakened him," Felix protested.

"He may be powerful enough to break free and enter your mind anyway."

Felix was tired of learning new things to be afraid of. "Okay, maybe it's a risk," he said. "But I can't let the council lock Mason up. Or kill him!"

"When is this meeting?" Dad asked.

"Half an hour." The council had scrambled to set it up as soon as possible after Felix and the others returned from Everett. While Mason was taken to a holding cell, Felix had rushed up to his room to summon Dad.

"I'll sit in your head with you during the meeting, but I'm not going to take control of you," Dad said. "Projecting memories is difficult, but you can do it. I believe in you."

"I sure hope so." Felix leaned back on his hands. "Where are you guys, anyway? When you're not talking to me in my head?"

"We're inside of your soul."

"What's it like in there?" Felix asked.

"You should come see for yourself one of these days."

"How?"

"You'll learn. Or I'll teach you." Dad rested a hand on Felix's shoulder. "I can feel myself fading. Call me into your head when the meeting begins, okay?"

Felix nodded. Once Dad was gone, he paced back and forth until someone knocked at his door. It was Kendra.

"Ready?" she asked.

Felix grabbed his uniform jacket off his chair and shrugged it on. At Archer's suggestion, he'd swapped the plain shirt he was wearing earlier for a more formal teal button-up. "I guess."

They walked to the throne room in silence. When they were almost to the doors, Felix asked, "What do you think the council will decide?"

"Sorry, Felix. I have no idea what to expect. Archer told me what happened, but you and Arisa will need to tell your side of the story, too." Kendra nodded at the guards as she reached for the door handle. "But if it makes you feel any better, I doubt they'll execute him. We've never seen this happen before. They'll want to study him."

"That still doesn't sound great," Felix muttered.

"There's a slim chance they could let him live here on probation. Similar to you and Arisa. But I wouldn't get my hopes up."

They entered the throne room, which was packed with Guardians. Arisa was already inside, sitting next to Sebastian in the front row with Clementine on her lap. Kendra and Felix joined them.

"How are you feeling?" Arisa asked as Felix sat next to her.

Felix shifted in his seat. "Sore. Tired. Little bit of a headache."

"I meant about using your dad's power."

"Oh." Felix stared at the door to the king's chamber. "Let me get back to you on that."

The door swung open. Archer emerged and stepped aside, allowing King Atticus to pass and walk to his throne. While the rest of the crowd moved into the seats, the eight council members lined up.

Moments after the king sat down, the doors to the throne room opened again and six guards entered. Mason walked in the middle of them, his hands chained together in front of him. Felix caught a glimpse of some sigils carved into the metal. The guards escorted Mason to Archer before dispersing to stand along the wall.

Without further ado, Archer addressed the room. "Over the past week, Guardians have been searching for a demon responsible for terrorizing an office building. Four people died, and eight more were hospitalized." He paused. "This comes shortly after two demons killed three young adults in an abandoned grocery store."

Mason lowered his gaze to the floor.

"Despite this, Guardians who entered the office building were unable to locate the demon, even though that seemed to be the source of the demonic energy in the area," Archer continued. "I was in Everett investigating this, while Sebastian Armitage was in the area with his students to study the site where the previous demons were killed."

From there, Archer explained how he'd sensed Guardian energy arrive at the building during his investigation outside. By the time he'd realized Felix and Arisa were inside, they were caught up in their battle with the horde of demons.

"It's still unclear how so many demons escaped our detection," Archer said. "But the issue we're discussing right now is this particular demon." He gestured to Mason. Mason looked up and swept his eyes over the Guardians. His gaze met Felix's for a heartbeat before moving on.

"According to Mason, he was a human witch most of his life. After an accident, a demon with a rare ability transformed him in order to save his life." Archer lowered his hand. "As absurd as that story sounds, Felix Carver has decided to vouch for him, claiming he used his father's psychometry to confirm Mason's story."

Archer reached into his jacket and drew out Mason's dagger. He held it out toward Felix. With a shaky breath, Felix rose to his feet and crossed the room to meet him.

"Please don't screw this up," Mason muttered under his breath as Felix took the dagger from Archer.

Felix's hand tightened around the dagger. *Ready, Dad?*

You're the one doing this, Dad said, his voice encouraging. *Focus. Instead of letting the dagger's memory drag you in like before, you need to stand your ground and pull it out.*

Felix let Dad's ability awaken in his chest. The immediate pull of the dagger was overwhelming. The world went black. Mason appeared in front of him, sitting in his hospital bed.

You're going in, Dad warned.

Felix pulled himself back, and the throne room returned.

Keep your hold on the memory. Bring it with you.

The power in Felix's chest slammed against his ribcage, threatening to break free. *I can't control it,* he thought. His eyes stung.

Yes, you can. Trust yourself.

Felix took a deep breath, then let the power out. A shimmering projection of human Mason appeared in the middle of the room. Gasps and murmurs rolled through the crowd of Guardians.

Move the timeline forward, Dad told him. *Just like you did when you were inside the dagger.*

Felix regained his grasp on the magical energy that projected the past into the world. He pushed it forward, to the scene in the hospital where the demon nurse offered to save his life. After that, images of Mason killing demons danced around the center of the throne room. Felix pushed all the way up to the events of a few hours earlier, showing Mason fighting the first winged demon that they'd encountered.

Dad issued another warning. *Don't let them see May controlling you.*

Panic seized Felix at the reminder. The projection flickered, then disappeared entirely. He tried to bring it back, wanting to show Mason's explanation of how summoning magic had been used to lure in the demons, but the spark of energy in his chest was gone.

Felix collapsed to his knees, breathing hard.

"Not bad, kid," Archer said quietly. He reached down and took the dagger back. Louder, he said, "Go sit back down." He glanced at Mason. "You, too."

Felix returned to his seat next to Arisa. Kendra scooted further down so that Mason could sit on Arisa's other side.

Eliza Abernathy was the first to speak. "This is absurd!"

Mason's eyes narrowed as they fell on Eliza. He didn't say a word, but Felix could see his mind working.

"I agree." Archer faced Eliza. "But that doesn't change what we just saw."

Eliza shook her head. "Even if he's killed demons in the past, that doesn't mean we can trust him now. He could have done that to trick us."

Abraham Caldwell chimed in. "And for all we know, he could succumb to demon sickness at any moment. Perhaps the effect has only been delayed," he suggested. "Or, if he retains his intelligence, he could become even more dangerous."

"Mason had no desire to come here," Archer said. "And I fail to see why he would attempt to trick us when there was no way he could have known he'd run into us in the first place."

"Perhaps you're underestimating him."

King Atticus, who'd watched everything play out with an unreadable expression, finally spoke. "And what would you have us do with him, Abraham?"

"He's a demon," Abraham said. "The only choice we have is to execute him."

"He's a child," Michael Beck cut in.

"I'm sixteen," Mason snapped.

King Atticus held up a hand to forestall any further arguments. "Archer. What do you think we should do with Mason?"

"Mason's magical energy is indistinguishable from that of an ordinary demon," Archer said. "He's a promising fighter, but he doesn't have a solid grasp on his demonic abilities yet."

"Here we go," Sebastian muttered. He leaned toward the kids and lifted a hand to hide his mouth from the council. "Mason, if you have any idea how to wield hellfire, I'd get ready to pull that out. You might have a chance at escaping if you—"

"However," Archer continued, shooting Sebastian a brief but stern glance. "He was trained as a witch. He identified a ritual in the office building that was being used to attract demons to the area. He also believes a spell was used to hide the demons' energy from our senses."

"We don't know anything about witchcraft," Eliza protested. "He could be making that up."

"She has a point," Abraham added. "If it were possible to mask energy with a spell, why haven't we seen it before?"

"Well, if you were near a monster whose energy was being masked, I doubt you would have noticed," Archer replied coolly.

Sadia Malik spoke up. "We could have a local witch investigate the building and see if they can confirm what Mason said," she suggested.

King Atticus rose from his throne. "I'll put you in charge of handling that, Sadia."

Sadia adjusted her glasses and nodded.

"In the meantime, Mason will stay here," King Atticus added.

"Are you sure?" Abraham asked. "I think we all remember what happened last time we let a monster stay at the castle." His gaze flickered toward the audience in what Felix swore was Sebastian's direction.

"I don't believe him to be an immediate threat," the king said. "But I also don't want to let him go free until we have a better idea of what we're dealing with."

Mason jumped to his feet. The chains between his hands swung. "So I'm a prisoner?"

"You don't have to be. Prove yourself useful to us, and perhaps someday I'll be willing to place my trust in you," King Atticus told him. "And I'll allow you to leave the castle grounds if needed, as long as you're accompanied by Guardians. I could have you locked up in our dungeon, but I won't. For now."

Felix stood up and blurted, "You should let him train with us!"

Mason glanced at him. "What are you doing?" he hissed.

"Trying to help you," Felix shot back under his breath.

"Oh?" King Atticus turned his attention to Felix, and the council's gazes followed. "And why is that?"

"We—we worked well together fighting the demons," Felix stammered. "I know he's not technically a magician like the rest of us Guardians, but he could still help us fight."

King Atticus lifted an eyebrow. "Archer?"

"That would mean putting Sebastian in charge of training a demon," Archer said.

"You think that's a bad idea?"

"A terrible one."

"He seems to have done well training Felix, so far."

"Except for the part where he and Arisa ran into a demon-infested building," Archer reminded the king.

"Well, teaching discipline is a different skill than teaching magic. However, I think we can let Sebastian handle this matter, for now, provided you continue to supervise their training."

Archer nodded. "Of course, my king."

Sebastian rolled his eyes.

King Atticus's gaze returned to Mason. "You're surrounded by powerful Guardians who could kill you in the blink of an eye. And they will, if they believe you to be a threat."

"I'm not a threat," Mason said.

"Good. Prove it." King Atticus raised his voice. "I believe that resolves matters for now. This meeting is over."

Archer started toward where Felix and Mason were still standing. Arisa, Sebastian, and Kendra rose to their feet, and Kendra stretched out her arms. "If Hana and I leave now, we should still make our dinner reservations. I'll talk to you all later."

"You're not coming to Ernest's party?" Sebastian asked.

"Not tonight. Maybe we'll swing by for a few minutes after we eat, but it's out of our way."

Felix and Arisa waved goodbye to Kendra as she walked away. Archer reached them and stopped at Sebastian's side.

Felix turned to face him. "Thank you, Archer," he said. He elbowed Mason.

Mason shot Felix a glare. "Yeah, thanks for turning me into a prisoner."

"Better than dead," Arisa pointed out.

"Don't thank me," Archer said. "I gave the king my thoughts, and he made his choice."

"How about a group hug?" Sebastian suggested, holding out his arms. "Since you said so many nice things about Mason."

Archer took a step away from him. "I weighed the pros and cons of the possible outcomes and decided that letting Mason stay with us would be the best course of action, for the time being. Mason could be a valuable asset. But if he does anything questionable, there will be consequences."

Sebastian stepped forward and threw an arm around Archer's shoulder. Grinning at the kids, he said, "He won't admit, but I think Archie's not as mean as he acts."

"I could tell the king that I believe you encouraged the kids to go into that demon-infested building," Archer said. "That won't end well for you."

"Is it the arm thing, calling you 'Archie,' or insinuating that you're secretly a nice person?"

Archer ducked out of Sebastian's arm and took another step back. In the split second it took him to straighten up, a small knife had appeared in his hand.

Sebastian lifted his hand to his face and frowned at the scratch across his skin. "Ouch. Rude. Were you always so stabby?"

"No, but you weren't always so annoying." Archer lowered his voice. "Now, we do have another matter to discuss. I haven't told the king what Mason said about Ernest. Yet."

"Don't," Sebastian said.

"Why not?" Archer asked. "It's up to him to decide whether we question Ernest."

"You really think the king will investigate? Ernest is rich and powerful."

"The king cares about the safety of the Brightlands, not money."

"He needs money to run the Brightlands," Sebastian countered. "Mason's testimony won't be enough to put that jeopardy. We need solid proof."

Archer was quiet for a moment. "Fine. I'll hold off on bringing the matter up. For now."

"Really? So easily convinced?" Sebastian folded his arms and grinned. "Aw, are you mad at the king because he put me in charge of training Mason after you said it was a bad idea?"

"Of course not," Archer said. "I trust his judgement."

"Sure you do."

Archer turned to Mason. "That means you need to keep quiet about the matter, too."

"As long as you promise you'll help me get my wand back from him," Mason said. "And I'm leaving this damn place as soon as I get it back."

"We'll do what we can," Archer told him.

"Okay, well, I'm off," Sebastian said. "See you kids bright and early tomorrow for training."

Felix wasn't sure ten a.m. qualified as "bright and early," but he nodded.

"I suppose that means I'm showing Mason to his room," Archer said, followed by a small sigh. "Follow me."

"Bye, Mason." Felix waved. "See you tomorrow."

Mason huffed. "Can't wait," he said sarcastically as he followed Archer to the doors.

Felix and Arisa left the throne room behind them. "What do you think of Mason?" Felix asked Arisa once they were out of earshot.

"He seems cool, for a demon." Arisa shrugged. "I'm kind of excited to train with him. Can you imagine rolling up to fight monsters with a demon on our side?"

"You're not scared of him?"

"Scared?" Arisa asked with a laugh. "No. He's a bit of an asshole, but I don't really blame him, after what he's been through." She glanced at Felix. "Are you scared?"

"No, it's just..." Felix hesitated. "That demon at the office building sounded sure that Mason will turn evil eventually."

"Demons say a lot of things. Most of them are lies." Arisa fiddled with one of her bracelets. "I doubt we have to worry about him turning on us."

They reached the corner where their paths separated and said goodbye. As Felix rode the elevator up to his room, he couldn't quiet his mind. Bright Guardians were supposed to be good, but Ernest Abernathy had killed Mason's parents and stolen their wand. What did he want with a wand, anyway? Didn't he have his own magic?

Sebastian was on his way to one of the man's parties. Was Sebastian really only going for the food? Or was he friends with Ernest? Despite what Sebastian had said, Archer had defended Mason. Well, sort of. Enough to keep him alive and out of a cell.

Archer trusted the king, the king trusted his council, but the council was split. One of the council members was Ernest Abernathy's cousin. The king seemed to trust Felix and Mason and Arisa, but he likely trusted the Abernathys more. Sebastian didn't trust Archer, Archer didn't trust Sebastian. *And Archer trusts the king.*

The politics were enough to make Felix's head spin. Or maybe that was lingering dizziness from the fight with the demons. Regardless, he wanted to be able to count on Archer and Sebastian and Kendra and Hana. And Michael and Sadia, too, though he hadn't spoken to them much. And he wanted to believe the king and his council really would do what was best.

But if they couldn't trust each other, how could Felix possibly trust all of them?

Chapter Fifteen
The Living Curse

Mason refused to pick out a uniform, and Sebastian didn't care enough to force him. So, while Felix and Arisa prepared to train in their uniforms, Mason sat on the training yard dirt in dark jeans and a red sweatshirt. He'd hidden his horns under a new purple beanie. Felix wondered how many hats the guy owned. He only could have had so many belongings crammed into his backpack, right?

While Felix stretched his arms and Arisa cracked her knuckles, Mason picked up a rock off the ground and turned it over in his hand. "Give me one reason I shouldn't just leave and steal back the wand on my own."

"First, you'd never succeed on your own," Sebastian said, holding up a finger. "Ernest is strong, and his home is well-guarded." A second finger went up. "Two, you've been living on the run for a while. We're feeding and housing you for free."

"I was doing just fine," Mason muttered.

"Trust me, I'm doing everything I can to help. None of us want Ernest walking around with that wand any more than you do," Sebastian assured Mason. "If he really did steal it and kill your parents, the Bright Guardians aren't obligated to protect him, and we can take action. But the king would need to see proof, first."

Mason looked up at Felix. "Can't Felix use his power to prove Ernest stole the wand?"

"I'd have to get my hands on it, first," Felix replied. "Unless you have another item that was present when he stole it from your parents."

Mason sighed and shook his head.

"And Ernest isn't going to just admit to having it," Sebastian said. "I searched for it when I was at his house last night, but I didn't see any signs of it, or even sense its energy. He's hidden it well."

"Then what are we supposed to do now?" Mason asked.

"Nothing, yet. Ernest is throwing a bigger party in a few weeks to celebrate his cousin's birthday."

"Eliza's birthday?" Felix asked.

Sebastian shook his head. "Different cousin. Also on the council. He was one of the other guys who thought you should be locked up."

Felix sighed. "Of course he was. Sounds like Ernest has a lot of powerful family members."

"Yep." Sebastian's voice was surprisingly chipper. "But that's not something we should worry about. If we have solid evidence against Ernest, they won't be able to defend him without turning the rest of the Guardians against them." He waved a hand as he continued. "Anyway, what's important is that Ernest is throwing a birthday party, and way more Guardians will be there this time. That will make it easier for me to sneak around and figure out what the deal with the wand is."

"You should bring us," Mason said.

"Sorry. Students don't get invited to these things," Sebastian said. "Especially students on probation."

"I'm not a student!"

"According to the council, you are. Speaking of which, we should get started." Sebastian clapped his hands a couple of times. "Felix, let's start working with your fire today."

"Fire?" Felix repeated. He'd finally become comfortable enough with electricity to not feel a complete failure when he trained. He didn't like the idea of going back to screwing up every attempt at hitting a target.

Sebastian nodded. "I was originally going to take today to have you practice psychometry, but you're farther along with that than I expected," he said. "That's actually what I wanted you to try back at the grocery store. I was going to have you see if you could find the memory of the demon fight. But we'll save that for another time." He pointed a finger at the dirt and created a glowing rectangle. "Ready, Arisa?"

Arisa snapped her fingers. "Clementine, come on out."

Clementine climbed out of Arisa's open backpack. Mason was upright in a heartbeat, jumping back several feet. His claws burst from the tips of his fingers. "What the hell is that?"

"Relax, it's just a stuffed bear I animated with my ability."

Mason took a few cautious steps toward the bear. Once he'd apparently decided it wasn't a threat, he returned to where he'd been sitting. Knives slid out of Clementine's paws as she walked toward the rectangle.

"That's more terrifying than any demon I've ever seen," Mason muttered as he sank to the ground.

Felix entered the rectangle. "I don't want to burn Clementine."

"Don't worry, my magic makes her stronger than an ordinary stuffed animal," Arisa said. "You should be more worried about hurting yourself again."

"Or you," Felix added as he lifted his hands. Small, blue flames came to life in his palms. He swung at Arisa.

The scowl faded from Mason's face, replaced by something softer. He watched Felix and Arisa fight with what looked like genuine interest.

"Wrap your entire fist in fire!" Sebastian called as Felix dodged Arisa's sheathed dagger.

It took most of Felix's focus to keep the fire where he wanted it, making it harder for him to avoid Arisa's blows. He only managed to keep his fists wrapped in flames for a minute before he lost control. When the flames started crawling up his arms, he frantically shook them out.

Something flashed in Sebastian's eyes. "Okay, switch to lightning."

Happy to oblige, Felix let electricity crackle around his hands with renewed enthusiasm. He dodged another swing from Arisa and landed a soft blow against her shoulder. The electricity made her wince and stagger. Felix lifted his other hand to swing. If he could push her back a few more feet, he would win.

Something sharp grazed his ankle. Felix yelped in surprise and looked down. Clementine swung her other knife. As he took a step back to avoid it, he realized Clementine hadn't been planning to hit him at all. Arisa stuck out a foot behind him, and before Felix could stop himself, he was falling backwards.

Arisa gave him a push, and he landed outside the rectangle.

"Damn." Felix pushed himself up off the dirt.

Sebastian laughed. "Don't beat yourself up. Arisa's had way more practice." He turned. "Mason, you're up next. But I have a few quick questions."

"Of course you do," Mason grumbled as he rose to his feet.

"I assume now that you're a demon, you're stronger and faster?"

Mason nodded. "Stronger, faster, and I heal pretty fast."

"Well, that answers my second question."

"What about that scar in the middle of your forehead?" Felix asked.

"No idea what that's about," Mason said with a shrug. "I don't look in the mirror much, so I forget it's there most of the time."

"Felix, grab your sword," Sebastian instructed.

"Helena's sword?" Felix asked. "What if I accidentally hit Mason?"

"Keep it in its scabbard. The sigils won't hurt him if the metal doesn't make contact."

Felix and Mason started slow. His sword clashed against Mason's dagger over and over again, the collision a little stronger each time. Felix adjusted his grip and swung at Mason's head. Mason ducked and took a step back.

"Watch for the edge," Sebastian warned Mason.

Mason circled Felix, moving further into the rectangle. He lifted his dagger and started swinging faster, pushing Felix back a few feet. Felix swung at Mason's hands. He landed a blow that knocked the dagger from Mason's grasp. The weapon sailed through the air and landed outside of the box.

Felix smirked. He might actually be able to win this, despite Mason's strength and speed. He swung again. Mason's claws emerged. Mason swiped at Felix's face, but Felix blocked with the sword. Once Mason's hand passed, Felix shoved the weapon forward into Mason's chest.

Mason stumbled backward and lifted his hands. Blasts of purple fire burst from his palms.

"Whoa!" Felix jumped back. "What's that?"

"Ooh, hellfire!" Sebastian's face lit up. "Ever used it before?"

"Not very much," Mason replied. His hands closed into fists. "Or on purpose."

"Well, you should try controlling it." Sebastian gestured to Felix. "Try hitting Felix with a blast."

Felix's eyes widened. "Wait—!"

A beam of purple flame hit Felix square in the chest and knocked him off his feet. He landed on his back in the dirt. Outside of the rectangle. "Aw, come on!" he groaned. He sat up and examined the front of his shirt. There was a darker patch where the fire had hit him, but the blue material was still intact.

"See how tough the uniforms are?" Sebastian's arms folded. "You really should reconsider getting one, Mason."

Felix expected Mason to roll his eyes or turn down Sebastian's offer. Instead, he walked up to Felix, knelt down, and squinted at Felix's chest. "That is impressive," Mason said. "How much hellfire can this material resist?"

"Probably three times the amount you hit him with," Sebastian answered.

"So, my skin's not burned underneath?" Felix asked.

"No. You'll probably have a nasty bruise, though."

Felix sighed. "Great."

"Is the material sigil-enforced?" Mason asked.

Sebastian nodded. "Protective sigils. And healing sigils."

"Hm." Mason straightened up. "Not a bad fight though, Felix. But you do need some training with that sword."

"I know." Felix climbed to his feet. "Hana said she had time Monday morning."

"Hana?" Mason asked.

"Arisa's sister. She's the head librarian."

Mason's face lit up. "This place has a library?"

"You sound excited," Arisa said with a smirk. "Nerd."

Sebastian grinned. "Hey, anything to get him to like it here, right?"

Mason bent down to pick up the sword from the dirt next to Felix. He slid the blade out of the scabbard. "Can I put some better sigils on this?"

"Uh, sure?" Felix scratched his head. "You can do that?"

"I'm still a witch," Mason said. "And they won't hurt me if I wear gloves."

Felix glanced at Sebastian. "Seems like a good idea to me," Sebastian said. "But how are you doing to carve them in?"

Mason's expression darkened. "It'd be easy, if I still had my wand."

"Well, I wouldn't get your hopes up on getting that back anytime soon."

"No, not the Ironwood Wand," Mason said. "I had my own wand that my parents helped me make when I was a kid."

"What happened to it?" Felix asked.

"It was broken in the accident that almost killed me." Mason sighed and shoved his hands into his sweatshirt's pocket. "If it had only snapped in half, I might have been able to repair it, but it was reduced to splinters. And I haven't had time to make a new one, since I've been on the run as a demon."

"We can look into getting you another one," Sebastian said. "In the meantime, though, I want to see some more of that hellfire."

"I don't think I'm up for another fight right now." Felix glanced down at his chest again.

"No worries," Sebastian told him. "Mason and Arisa will have a quick match, and then we'll move on to target practice. You need to work on your fire, too."

The fight between Mason and Arisa was a close one. They both got the other within inches of the rectangle's edge several times, and Mason managed to knock Clementine out of the box before Arisa swept his legs and shoved him out.

After that came target practice, which was even harder with fire than lightning. Felix struggled to get the flames to do anything other than dance on his skin. Mason was slightly more successful, managing to shape his hellfire into a beam of flames, but his aim was far from precise. Any target smaller than Felix was a challenge. To make matters worse, Arisa decided to practice animating stones by making them roll around Felix and Mason's feet.

Despite the distractions, Felix finally unleashed a blast of blue fire from his palm. It didn't go anywhere close to the direction he wanted, but that didn't stop a grin from spreading across his face. "I did it!"

Sebastian gave him a thumbs up. "Nice job! I think you've both earned a break."

"What?" Felix whirled to face him. "But I'm just getting started!"

"You're going to wear yourself out. We'll come back to this later."

"Are we allowed to walk around outside the castle?" Mason asked.

Sebastian raised an eyebrow at the abrupt change of subject. "If a Guardian accompanies you, sure."

"Can we go now?" Mason glanced toward the door out of the training yard. "It doesn't have to be very long. I just want to take a look around. I didn't get much of a chance yesterday."

"Sure." Sebastian shrugged. "I've got time to kill."

Felix exchanged a confused look with Arisa. "Why do you want to?" Felix asked Mason. "There's not much out there, until you hit forest."

"I want to check out the view," Mason said sarcastically.

Sebastian didn't question it, though he had to know something was up. He slid his hands into his pockets and led the three inside and through the castle halls. They were almost to the front doors when a new set of footsteps sounded behind them.

"Where are you going?" Archer asked as he fell into pace next to Sebastian.

"Were you watching us train?" Sebastian asked.

"Of course."

"We're just taking a quick break to go on a walk around the castle."

"I'll join you, then," Archer said.

Sebastian raised an eyebrow. "I could handle him, if he tried anything."

"I don't doubt that."

They stepped outside. Sebastian paused. "Lead the way, Mason."

Felix and Arisa walked on either side of Mason as he headed west and up a hill. He stopped in the shade of a cluster of cherry trees at the top. After studying one for a moment, he reached up and ran a hand along one of its thinner branches.

"This is nice wood," Mason said.

"Is it?" Felix asked.

Mason's hand tightened around the branch. "Yes." A crack cut through the air as he snapped it off the tree.

"Hey," Archer said as he and Sebastian caught up. "What was that for?"

Mason studied the branch in his hands. "This should work. I made my old wand from the cherry tree in my backyard."

"Did you know he was planning this?" Archer asked, gaze flickering to Sebastian.

Sebastian lifted his hands. "How could I possibly have known? He didn't tell me." A smirk touched his lips. "What, you think letting the big scary demon have a wand is a bad idea?"

"It's fine," Archer muttered. "He's still outnumbered. But I would prefer if he didn't damage castle property."

"I bet it'll be worth it."

"We'll see. But that does remind me," Archer began. "Sadia was able to track down a witch last night and take them to the office building. They confirmed that an energy masking spell was used."

"Interesting." Sebastian lifted his fist and rested the side of his pointer finger against his chin. A hint of concern crept into his expression, though it seemed like he was trying to appear casual. "Why would someone want to do that?"

"I don't know, but if it happens again, it won't just be civilians at risk," Archer said. "Guardians could get themselves killed walking into a situation that's deadlier than they think."

Mason lifted his chin. "Once this wand is ready, I can do a lot more than just identify what spells were used. I might be able to amplify faint traces of magical energy. We could use it to follow the trail of whoever cast the masking spells."

"I hope you're right," Archer said. "For all of our sakes."

The five headed back down the hill toward the castle.

"How long will it take for the wand to be ready?" Felix asked Mason.

"Depends," Mason replied. "When's the next full moon?"

"One week from today," Sebastian said.

Arisa gave him a weird look. "You know that off the top of your head?"

"That's surprising," Archer muttered. "Considering he barely knows what day of the week it is, most of the time." After a moment, though, something else flashed across his expression, and he didn't make any further comments.

"If I can get the rest of the prep work done before then, I can use the full moon to conduct the activation ritual," Mason said.

When they returned to the castle, Archer and Sebastian left the three to their own devices. The two walked off together, speaking to each other in hushed tones.

"If Sebastian's serious, then something big is going on," Arisa said once they were gone. "And if he and Archer begin agreeing with each other, I'd be willing to believe it's the end of the world."

"Can you show me where this library is?" Mason asked. "I don't expect an extensive collection on witch magic, but I'd like to see if I can find anything useful."

"Oh, you definitely will," Arisa told him. She started down the hallway toward the library. "Our collection's huge. Guardians will pick up any book or artifact that's remotely magical and bring it to us. Usually, it gets filed away and no one ever looks at it again."

The three entered the library a few minutes later, and Arisa gave Mason and Felix a tour, pointing out various sections in a half-whisper. When they entered an aisle in the history department,

Mason ran a hand along the spines of the books to his right. He paused on a deep red one and slid it off the shelf.

"Ew." Mason held the book away from him and attempted to shake off the spider perched on top.

"Careful," Arisa said. "Don't kill it. I saw Eliza Abernathy step on one in the dining hall once, and Archer walked up to her and lectured her for twenty minutes."

"Why would he get mad at her for killing a spider?" Felix asked. Other than the one that had crawled into his bathroom vent his first day at the castle, Felix hadn't seen any spiders in his room. But they seemed to be common everywhere else in the castle.

"I don't know," Arisa said. "I tried getting close enough to eavesdrop, but Archer glared at me until I left."

"Well, Archer's not here." Mason swung the book at the nearest shelf in an attempt to crush the spider, but it took to the air on a thread and ascended into the shadows above them.

"What book is that?" Arisa asked.

"Oh, uh…" Mason glanced at the cover. "*A Brief History of Curses.* I've never read it, but I recognized the author. They wrote my first spellbook."

Arisa perked up. "Do you know a lot about curses?"

"A decent amount. Why?"

Arisa pointed to the bracelet on her right wrist. "This thing's cursed, and none of the Guardians have figured out how to break it yet. I figured a witch might know better than them."

"Cursed bracelets?" Mason asked. "Well, now I'm glad I didn't tell you I liked them."

"Don't worry, I complimented them when I met her," Felix said.

Mason leaned forward to take a better look. "What does the curse do, exactly? I'll need to know what kind it is before I can figure out how to break it."

"It made my ability stronger," Arisa said.

"And the side effects?"

Arisa hesitated. "Let's sit down at a table, and I'll explain."

Felix was surprised by how anxious Arisa seemed as they walked to a table. She'd explained the curse so casually when they met that he hadn't thought of it as that big of a deal.

"When I first put the bracelet on, I got a surge of power," Arisa explained. "And that's the last thing I remember before waking up in the medical wing with the counterbalance bracelet they made for me."

"How did they make the counterbalance?" Mason asked.

"Someone with a metal manipulation ability shaped it and carved magic nullification sigils along the inside. There was enough magical energy left over to make me more powerful than I was before I found the bracelet, but if I use too much power at once, the counterbalance starts to burn."

Mason's brow furrowed. "And what happened while you were out?"

This was clearly the part Arisa didn't want to talk about. She folded her arms and looked down at the table. "I animated all of the artifacts in the storage room upstairs and sent them on a rampage through the castle."

Felix's eyes widened.

"Some couldn't do much, but there were figurines and weapons that did a lot of damage," Arisa continued quietly. "Injured a lot of people, too. We're lucky no one died."

Mason's jaw tightened. "This is a living curse," he said. He held out an open hand. After a moment's pause, Arisa set her wrist in his hand so that he could examine the bracelet closer.

"What's a living curse?" Felix asked.

"A curse with a will of its own," Mason said. "Usually, it wants to cause as much destruction as possible." He ran a thumb along the orange jewel. "These are notoriously hard to break."

"But it's possible, right?" Arisa asked.

"Of course." Mason let go of her hand. "I'll do some research. I know a few places to start that your Guardians probably haven't thought of."

"Hypothetically, if Arisa cut off her hand, would that get rid of the curse?" Felix asked.

Mason picked up *A Brief History of Curses* and smacked Felix in the arm with it.

"Ow!" For a book that was supposed to be brief, it sure was heavy.

"It might work," Mason said. "Or it might kill her."

"All right, all right, it was just an idea." Felix rubbed his arm.

"The King's Council said they put me on probation because they were worried the curse would hurt me," Arisa said. "But I think they're actually afraid that the curse will take over again and I'll go on another rampage."

Mason chuckled.

"What's so funny?" Arisa demanded.

"Nothing," Mason said. "Just that your big, powerful council of Guardians is terrified of three teenagers."

Felix laughed, too. "He's right."

After a moment, Arisa smirked. "If they think we're a threat, then I guess we'd better train until we're as dangerous as they believe we are."

"As much as I don't want to be here, I would like to prove those smug assholes wrong," Mason said. "Maybe I'll stick around and kill all of their monsters for them."

Felix leaned back in his chair and smiled. Maybe, one day, they'd have a chance to prove themselves by fighting the Moonlit Army that Sebastian had mentioned. A cursed girl, a demon witch, and a boy carrying the ghost of one of their magicians.

Chapter Sixteen
Bad Necromance

Arisa and Mason sat on the grass early on Monday morning and watched Felix prepare for his first sword lesson with Hana.

"Are you guys sure you want to watch?" Felix asked as he drew the sword from its scabbard.

"I figured I could help you out with ASL while you talk to Hana," Arisa said.

Mason whittled away at his cherry branch with a knife. "I'm here to see how good you are."

"Not very," Felix muttered.

"Then this will be fun to watch."

Felix sighed. "Great. I love embarrassing myself in front of people. Real cool."

Hana, who stood a few feet away, waved a hand. "Are you ready?" she signed. Felix nodded. Hana corrected his grip on the sword and walked him through a few basic swinging motions. Then, she had him repeat them until he thought his arms were going to fall off.

Just when he thought he couldn't go any longer, Hana decided it was time for him to fight her.

"Don't worry, I'll move slow," Hana told him. After she was done signing, she extended her hand out in front of her. Her shadow wavered, and darkness pooled in her grasp to form a sword of pure black. She studied it for a moment. It shifted from a dangerous sharp-edged weapon into something much duller, as if it were made of pitch-black cardboard. Felix wanted to be offended, but he was mostly relieved.

Hana swung at him, and he lifted his blade to meet hers. She sped up gradually. Felix managed for the first couple of minutes, but after that, he found himself frequently getting whacked by Hana's weapon.

"Move faster, Felix!" Arisa called.

"I'm trying!" Felix ducked to avoid the next swing of the blade. "I'd like to see you do better!"

"You think I haven't taken sword lessons from my sister?"

Felix held his ground for another minute before a blow to his ankle knocked him onto his back.

"You don't suck as much as I thought you would," Mason said.

Felix lifted his gaze to where Mason and Arisa sat behind him. "Gee, thanks."

"Good start," Hana signed, her expression encouraging. "Get back up and let's try again."

They worked for another half an hour. After that, it was time for Felix, Arisa, and Mason's session with Sebastian. Today, he'd asked them to meet in a classroom on the third floor instead of in the training yard.

Felix waved goodbye to Hana and followed the other two back into the castle.

"I'm just glad we're not doing much physical training today," Felix said as they approached the classroom. The muscles in his arms were getting sorer by the minute. "But I'm probably going to suck at tennis tonight anyway."

"Tennis?" Mason asked.

"You know, where you hit a ball back and forth across a net with rackets?"

"I know what tennis is, dumbass. *Where* are you playing tennis?"

"My hometown. Kendra's taking me tonight so I can hang out with a friend of mine."

"Ooh, Mister Popular over here," Arisa said. She opened the classroom door and groaned. "This is the mold room."

Felix followed her in and recognized the space from their tour. "I didn't realize they actually used this room."

Mason eyed the patch of mold in the back corner as he entered. "Lovely."

The three dragged chairs from the wall to the front of the room and sat down in front of the whiteboard.

Sebastian threw open the door a minute later and strolled in. There was a large bandage on the side of his face, and a couple of bruises on the other. "Felix, I have an answer to your question. Garlic salt will make both ghosts and vampires very angry at you." He paused. "Damn. This is the mold room."

"Why are we in here, then?" Mason asked.

"I asked what classroom I could use, and the school administrator sent me to this one." Sebastian shrugged off his jacket and tossed it onto a nearby chair. "It's fine, we'll just stay away from that corner. All we're doing is reviewing sigils."

Felix glanced back at the dark spot. "Why not burn it away with fire?"

"Somebody tried that. It came back the next day."

"Is your face okay?" Arisa asked.

"Oh, yeah, it'll be good as new by this evening." Sebastian picked up a blue marker and began drawing widely spaced symbols along the bottom edge of the whiteboard, each made up of layers of geometric shapes. "Now, who all knows how sigils work?"

Arisa and Mason both raised their hands. Felix slouched in his chair.

"Go ahead, Arisa." Sebastian moved to the right to continue his line of sigils up the side of the board.

"They channel magical energy into a force powerful enough to expel spirits and demons," Arisa said. "They can also generate barriers—wards—that keep out certain magical energy signatures."

"Among other things." Sebastian took a step back from the board. "Arisa's one of the best at sigils," he said as he turned around. "Even better than some of the adults around here."

Arisa folded her arms. "That's because they get so used to using their abilities that they get sloppy."

"And what do these ones do?" Sebastian gestured to the board with his marker. "Mason?"

"They look like magic nullification sigils," Mason said. "I'm guessing that's so you can draw sigils in the middle of the board that won't actually do anything."

"Correct."

"They're a bit messy, though."

Sebastian lifted an eyebrow. "You think?"

"Some of your shapes aren't as symmetrical as they could be." Mason shrugged. "They'll work, but they could be stronger. Draw too much in the middle and you'll break through them."

Sebastian tossed him the marker. "Fix them."

Mason walked up to the board. He rubbed away lines with his finger and drew new ones in. After a few moments of consideration, he erased some of Sebastian's sigils entirely and replaced them with rounder, loopier ones. "The sigils you Guardians use are fine, but they're all hard edges. I'm guessing that's for strength, but it also means that when they break, they break hard."

"So, our weapons would explode less if we used different sigils?" Sebastian asked.

Felix shot an anxious glance at Helena's sword. Was it going to blow up on him one of these days?

Mason nodded. "You might need to replace them more frequently, but they'd lose their magic gradually, instead of shattering all at once." He stepped back from the board and, apparently satisfied with his work, handed the marker back to Sebastian.

"Well, it will take a lot of convincing to get the old geezers to change the way they draw sigils. But if you want to show us a thing or two, I'd appreciate it." Sebastian returned to the board. "Today, though, we'll start by teaching Felix a couple of simple banishing ones."

Sebastian drew a row of sigils on the board and had Felix come up to copy them. Felix mimicked the symbols with a fair amount of accuracy. After he'd copied the row a few times, he stepped back. "Is that good?" he asked.

"That's great," Sebastian said. "Now all you have to do is memorize them."

"Oh no."

After running through a few more examples of sigils, Sebastian dismissed the three. "Let's call it good for now and reconvene after lunch for a little target practice," he told them. "But Felix, I want you especially to practice drawing these. Ask those other two if you need help. And try not to blow anything up."

"Sure," Felix said, unable to hide his apprehension as Arisa and Mason started toward the door.

Sebastian picked up the eraser next to the board. "You'll get it, Felix." He started wiping away the symbols in the middle. "I wasn't always good at this stuff, you know. All you need is to figure out a way to study that works for you."

Felix hesitated. "Thanks. I'll try."

He spent his free time up until lunch attempting to memorize sigils. It went about as poorly as he expected. Target practice was more encouraging, though. Most of the bolts of electricity he fired off hit the bottles Sebastian had lined up. That was, until Sebastian told him to back up ten feet and try again. All Felix could manage in response was a groan.

He had never been more relieved to get into a car as he was when Kendra took him to meet Jace that evening. It would be nice to do something he was actually good at, Felix thought as he turned his tennis racket over in his hand.

Kendra pulled up along the curb when they arrived. "Text me if you need anything," she said as Felix climbed out. "I'll stay close."

"Thanks." He closed the door and turned to face Maple Point High School. The light of the setting sun cast long shadows across the grass. It was a familiar sight, but after the past week, it felt like a completely different world.

Felix walked around back to the tennis courts. Jace was already waiting, bouncing a ball on his racket as he paced back and forth next to the net. A grin crossed his face when he saw Felix. "Ready to lose?" he called.

Felix laughed. "Lucky for you, my arms are sore. You might actually have a chance at winning."

Jace served, and Felix dove to return the ball. Despite how much his body ached, he did pretty well. Jace got an early lead, though, and Felix couldn't quite catch back up.

As Jace prepared to serve again, he asked, "So, how's this new school of yours?"

"It's...big." Felix adjusted his grip on his racket. "And really fancy."

"Sounds like a private school."

"Yeah, I guess it kind of is."

They hit the ball back and forth a few more times before the ball sailed past Felix's racket and bounced off the ground just inside the court. He groaned.

"I heard some weird stuff happened at your house. I mean, around your...family." Jace cleared his throat. "I totally understand if you don't want to talk about it, but they were never really clear about what happened in the news."

"It's...complicated," was all Felix could manage. How much could he say without revealing that he'd gotten caught up in a world of monster-hunting magicians? His mouth opened, but he didn't get a chance to add anything else. A crash came from the bushes at the edge of the school's property, not more than twenty feet behind Felix. He froze. "Did you hear that?"

Jace nodded and leaned to the left to peer into the bushes behind Felix. "A raccoon, maybe?"

Felix's heart skipped a beat. He glanced back, realizing how dark it had gotten. The only significant light came from the posts along the edge of the school's property line. "It sounded bigger than that." He swallowed his fear and approached the source of the sound, reminding himself that he had magic now. Whatever it was couldn't possibly be stronger than him, right? His hand moved toward where Mom's ring rested against his chest.

Something exploded from the bushes and crashed into Felix. His back slammed against the ground hard enough to send pain shooting through his entire body. A weight pressed down on his chest, forcing the air from his lungs.

There was a crack, and Felix's attacker fell to the ground in a heap. Jace stood over Felix, clutching his racket. "What the hell is that?" Jace exclaimed, his voice shaking.

Felix sat up. He was pretty sure the thing lying next to him used to be a deer, but now it was barely more than a skeleton held together with shredded pieces of tissue. Slowly but surely, it climbed back to its feet.

"Run," Felix choked as he jumped to his feet. "Jace, run!" He grabbed his friend's arm and dragged him toward the front of the school. His other fist tightened at his side. Should he reveal his magic to Jace and torch the thing? He glanced back. No, it was limping, now. They could probably outrun it—

"Uh, Felix?" Jace stopped, causing Felix to stumble. As Felix righted himself, he turned his attention forward. His blood turned to ice.

A line of creatures stalked toward them. Some were mostly bone, while others had retained considerable amounts of rotting flesh. Felix noted a couple more deer, rabbits, something that had to be a bear skeleton, a smaller creature that might have been a fox—

"What are they?" Jace asked. "Zombies? Is the zombie apocalypse starting?"

"I think they're being animated." Felix lifted a hand and aimed his palm toward the approaching beasts. He realized with a jolt that some of them were human skeletons. The cemetery was nearby, he realized.

He pushed that unpleasant thought aside. At least none of the human skeletons were recognizable as much more than bones. He looked to the left, toward the woods next to the school. "That way. Let's go."

"What do you mean animated?"

"I'll explain later. Right now, we need to run!"

These skeletons were faster than the first deer had been. Felix threw a glance back as he and Jace raced across the grass. If he didn't do something, their pursuers would catch up before the two of them reached the tree line. He stopped and turned around.

Jace slowed. "Felix?"

"Hang on." Felix lifted his hands.

Blue lightning jumped from his fingers and lit up the night. Bolts of electricity struck a few of the closest skeletons. The unpleasant scent of burning flesh filled the air.

"Keep going, some might get back up!" Felix gave Jace a push as he ran by.

"What was that?" Jace exclaimed. Felix didn't answer. Jace caught up with him. "Are you sure they're not zombies?"

This time, Felix managed a response through his heavy breathing. "I'm pretty sure they're not infectious! They're just being animated with magic."

"Okay, then what are they?"

They crashed through the tree line. "I don't know," Felix said. "But it won't matter what they're called if we're dead!"

They ran for another minute before Felix dared to slow down. He looked back. The skeletons were nowhere to be seen, but branches snapped and leaves rustled nearby.

"Since when have you been able to shoot lightning from your hands?" Jace asked.

"Since my family became ghosts. Long story." Felix stopped and cupped his hands around his mouth. "Hello? Kendra?" he yelled. "Can you hear me?" Maybe he should have tried to lead Jace back toward the street. But now he wasn't sure which direction that was.

Felix started to reach for his phone, but Jace grabbed his arm, distracting him. Felix turned his head as a tall, lanky figure stepped into view, face hidden in shadow by the hood of his white coat.

The figure chuckled. "Felix Carver."

"Dude, when did your life turn into a wizard quest?" Jace whispered.

"I'm not a wizard. I'm a magician." Felix lifted his hand and let it catch fire. The blue light offered a glimpse of the dozen or so pale scars cutting across the man's tan face, but it didn't reach his eyes. "Are you the one controlling those zombies?" Felix demanded, sounding braver than he felt.

"They're not zombies." The man sounded offended. "My ability is necromancy. They're undead."

"What's the difference?" Jace asked.

"I'm guessing if they bite you, you won't turn into one," Felix replied.

"Correct," the man said. "Though, there's more to it than that—"

Felix cut him off. "What do you want with us?"

"I don't give a damn about this human child." The man gestured to Jace. "I'm looking for a friend of mine. Gideon Pollock. Maybe you could bring him out for me?"

A friend of Gideon's? Had this guy been part of the Uprising? "You'll never see him again," Felix spat, eyes narrowing.

"I highly doubt that. I can sense his energy."

Felix's confidence wavered. "You can?"

The man laughed. "Oh, yes." He lifted a hand. "Along with that coward family of yours."

The rage that flooded Felix's body in that moment drowned out his body's aches. And his fear. Fire blazed to life around his fists. Lightning danced across his skin. Vines erupted from the earth beneath the man's feet and wrapped around his ankles.

The man reached into his coat and drew out a scythe. Sigils carved into the handle glowed briefly as the weapon grew in size. When he swung, the blade easily sliced through the vines.

With a sigh, the man said, "I guess I'll just have to drag Gideon out of you myself."

Skeletons, animal and human, emerged from the undergrowth around them, coming from all directions. Jace yelped and ducked as a half-rotted bird swooped down from the air and slashed at his head with his talons.

Felix tried to hit the bird with a blast of fire, but it flew out of the way with surprising speed, for an undead thing. Before Felix could try again, the jaws of a wolf sank into his calf. He cried out in pain and dropped to his other knee. His jaw clenched. He lifted his hand and blasted the wolf with all of the fire he could muster. Its bones collapsed motionless into the dirt.

The ground trembled. Felix thought it might be from Ezra's power for a moment, but the sensation of his brother's ability was gone.

"Damn it," the man hissed. "Not her."

Hundreds of beetles emerged from the dirt around them. Jace yelped and dropped to the ground next to Felix. "Zombie beetles!"

"No, these are alive." Felix searched the trees around them, but there was no sign of Kendra.

The beetles quickly overwhelmed the undead attackers. The man turned and ran, disappearing into the night's shadows before Felix could even try to stop him.

"Your leg's bleeding," Jace warned as Felix climbed to his feet.

"Yeah." Felix took off his hoodie and tied it around his calf as tight as he could. He turned in a slow circle. Some of the undead were still struggling against the beetles, but the rest had been reduced to unmoving piles of bones.

A swarm of bees descended from above. When the swarm dispersed, Kendra stood just a few feet away from Felix and Jace.

"Whoa!" Felix took a surprised step back. "How did you do that?"

"I temporarily transferred my essence into a swarm of insects to transport myself," Kendra said. "It takes a lot of energy. Now, come on, we need to get out of here."

"Shouldn't we chase that necromancer?" Felix asked.

"The best thing to do now is to get you and Jace to safety."

Jace jogged at Felix's right as Kendra led the way through the trees. "Hey, uh, what just happened? Why can your teacher turn into bees?"

"I'll explain once we're out of the woods," Felix told him.

Streetlights appeared through the trees up ahead. The three emerged through a gap in the fence surrounding the woods and stepped onto the sidewalk.

"Jace, did you drive here?" Felix asked.

Jace shook his head. "I walked."

"Let me give you a ride home, then," Kendra said. "I don't think he would go after you, but I'd rather not risk it."

As they walked to Kendra's car, Felix tried to summarize the past week and a half to Jace. "Turns out my family was part of this magical organization that fights monsters, and I had this secret ability to absorb ghosts into my blood and use their magic, and now I'm learning how to use my powers so I can—"

"Get revenge?" Jace tried.

"Well, the guy who killed them is dead," Felix said. "And I'm carrying his ghost around, too. But apparently, he was working for someone, so I guess I'm trying to stop them. And kill monsters along the way."

"Who?"

"I don't know. No one's told me much about them yet." Felix stopped next to Kendra's car and rubbed the back of his neck. "But I guess I'm dangerous to be around now."

As they got into the car, Kendra sighed. "I'm afraid you're right, Felix. We didn't expect Gideon's friends would be able to track you down so easily." Her expression darkened. "It's concerning that they already know about your ability."

Jace moved his gaze back and forth between them. "Does that mean we can't hang out anymore?"

Kendra started the car. "I'll talk to the other Guardians and see if there's anything we can do. But I'm afraid you may need to hold off for the time being."

On the drive to Jace's house, he and Felix managed to have one last normal conversation. Jace talked about stuff that had happened at school over the past week, and Felix described his new room and how good the dining hall food was.

When they reached Jace's house, Felix walked Jace up to the front door, said goodbye, and watched the door close behind his friend. He stood on the porch for a long moment before returning to Kendra's car.

"Did the necromancer talk to you?" Kendra asked as Felix buckled his seat belt.

Felix nodded. "He said he was looking for Gideon." He leaned against the window. "You mentioned they were friends. I'm guessing he's part of the Moonlit Army, too?"

"Where'd you hear that name?"

Oops. "Someone mentioned it," Felix said vaguely.

"Sebastian?"

Felix sighed. "Yeah."

"I don't know how much I'm allowed to tell you," Kendra said. "Most students these days are too young to remember much about the Uprising, and we wait until they graduate to give them the full story."

"Why?"

"The council decided it wasn't relevant to their abilities to kill monsters."

"Do you agree?"

Kendra spoke carefully. "You saw today that the Moonlit Army is far from done fighting us. They won't rest until they've completed their mission. And if the students don't know that they're out there, it could put them in danger."

"And what is their mission?" Felix asked.

"Their leader wants to rule the Brightlands herself. And expand them into the rest of the world."

Herself. Felix perked up a little at the crumb of new information. "Can you tell me more about her?"

"If the council hears that you even know the name of her army, they won't be happy." Kendra's hands tightened around the wheel. "Still, I don't think they have much of a choice but to tell you about her sooner rather than later. If she knows you have Gideon's soul, it's inevitable that she's going to make herself known to you. He was closer to her than anyone else."

"What would be the point of coming after me, though?" Felix asked. "He's dead."

"She might want revenge," Kendra said. "Or..."

After a moment of silence, Felix prompted, "Or what?"

"Well, as long as his soul's still around—she might try to put it back into a body. Maybe even his, if she can find enough magic to restore it. Or figure out if he can use yours permanently." Kendra shook her head. "I'm sorry, this is just speculation. I shouldn't be saying this. I'll tell the King's Council what happened today. Maybe they'll change their stance on telling you kids about the Uprising." Her tone suggested she wasn't confident she'd be able to persuade them.

Felix nodded anyway. "Okay." Though he let the conversation end there, something she said nagged at him.

Souls can be put back into bodies?

Chapter Seventeen
Jack's Gang

"You fought zombies?" Mason asked at breakfast the next morning.

"Not zombies, apparently." Felix pressed his hands to the back of his head and leaned back in his chair. "But yeah, I torched some undead."

"Could you maybe try torching my toast?" Arisa held up a piece of bread. "I think the toaster's broken again." Clementine, who sat on Arisa's shoulder, folded her tiny bear arms.

"Can't they fix it with magic?" Mason asked.

Felix took the piece of bread from Arisa, but she was barely paying attention. "No one uses that kind of magic around here," she explained. "We've got our abilities, and we've got sigils for healing, killing, and keeping out monsters. That's about it."

Blue fire consumed the piece of bread. As quickly as it appeared, Felix extinguished it. Arisa stared at the blackened bread left in his hand.

"You used too much," Mason said. He reached toward Felix's tray. "Here, hand me a piece."

Felix swatted Mason's hand away. "Use your own bread!"

"Fine." Mason picked up the bread off the tray in front of him and held it a few inches above his palm. Purple hellfire came to life in his hand.

"It's bread, not a marshmallow," Felix said.

"If it works, it works." Mason closed his fist, putting out the fire. Felix had to admit, his toast looked pretty good. He lowered his gaze back to the burnt bread in front of him.

"Sure, but now some Guardians are giving you dirty looks." Arisa's gaze darted around the room.

Mason shrugged and held out the piece of toast to her. "Isn't it good if they see me use my powers for nonviolent purposes?"

"I guess." Arisa accepted the toast.

"That's not all that happened last night." Felix glanced around the dining hall and lowered his voice. "Kendra started telling me about the leader of the Guardian Uprising."

Arisa's eyes went wide. "Really?"

"What's that?" Mason asked.

"Us students aren't supposed to know about it," Arisa explained to him. "I barely know anything besides the name. I was nine when it happened."

"Sebastian mentioned that the Guardians who left afterward have started calling themselves the Moonlit Army," Felix said.

Arisa snorted. "Army? That's a little ambitious. I don't think there were *that* many of them." She bit off a piece of her toast.

"What *do* we know about them?" Mason asked.

"Not much, besides that," Felix said. "Kendra wouldn't even tell me the leader's name. All I know is that Gideon and this necromancer guy work for her."

"We could try asking Sebastian about it," Arisa suggested. "If anyone were going to give us secret information, it would be him."

"Sebastian did start telling me about their leader my second day here, but he didn't seem interested in saying much," Felix said. "He said he was trying not to overwhelm me. Now that I think about it, though, he was acting a little dodgy."

"Wasn't his family involved in the Uprising?" Arisa asked. "That could have something to do with it."

"Change the subject," Mason muttered. "Sebastian's walking this way."

A few seconds later, Sebastian stopped next to their table. "Whatcha kids talking about?"

"Uh, tennis," Felix blurted, at the same moment Arisa said, "Zombies." Mason buried his face in one of his hands.

"Great." Sebastian's gaze moved to the black toast on Felix's tray. "Are you going to eat that?"

Felix gave him a weird look. "Uh, no?"

Sebastian picked up the burnt piece of bread. "I have good news. I got permission to take you on another field trip." He took a bite.

"Really? After the last one ended so badly?" Felix asked.

"Hm?" Sebastian swallowed. "What are you talking about? That was a complete success." He gestured at Mason. "We got Mason, didn't we?"

"Ha, that's right." Arisa playfully punched Mason in the arm. "Good times, right?"

"Anyway, you'll want to bring anything silver that you own," Sebastian said as Mason pulled *A Brief History of Curses* from his bag, opened it to a random page, and held it up in front of his face.

"Silver?" Arisa asked, eyes widening. "You mean—"

"Werewolves," Mason muttered.

"Bingo." Sebastian snapped his fingers. "I'll bring silver weapons for you all, but the more we have, the better."

"Are werewolves easier to fight than demons?" Felix asked.

"Generally, they aren't as powerful," Sebastian said. "But don't let your guard down. Now, believe it or not, most werewolves aren't actually bloodthirsty monsters who go on rampages once a month. As long as they only hunt wild animals and stay away from urban areas during their transformation, we let them mind their own business.

"Unfortunately, there have been strings of killings during the full moon over the past several months," Sebastian continued. "All taking place within a five-mile radius of a town called Cold Creek."

"That's pretty far north, isn't it?" Felix asked, recognizing the name.

Sebastian nodded. "The drive's a few hours. And since the moon's full enough to induce transformation for three nights, we're going to stay in a motel in town, so pack for that. We'll leave Friday morning."

Arisa's brow furrowed. "This sounds like a real mission, not a field trip."

"It would be, if I were planning to have you engage with the wolves directly. I'll show you how to track them, but you won't be fighting them. Unless they attack you first."

"Does this mean we'll get to see you fight?" Felix asked.

Sebastian lifted an eyebrow. "You saw me fight Archer at training."

"I mean a real fight! Kendra said you're one of the most powerful Guardians." Felix had barely seen Sebastian use his ability.

"Well, if this trip goes as planned, it won't come to that," Sebastian said.

"Oh, this is why you knew the full moon was coming up when Mason asked, isn't it?" Arisa asked.

"Believe it or not, I am usually aware of the current moon phase," Sebastian said. "But on that note, how's the wand coming, Mason?"

Mason lowered his book. "I finished carving it. Now I just have to bond it to my blood, say a simple purification spell, and bury it in the earth during the full moon. It should be ready to go when we get back from the trip."

"Great!"

"It's passable," Mason said with an annoyed expression. "I wasn't able to add anything to the wood to amplify it's power, and I don't have many spell ingredients, so it won't be very strong. But it will work until I get the Ironwood Wand back."

"Hey, as long as it does anything at all, I'll be impressed," Sebastian said. "I'll see you all in a little while for training." He waved and walked away.

Mason sighed. "How long do we have to run around chasing monsters before we can do something important?"

Arisa yawned and tapped a napkin. It twisted itself into the shape of a swan. "Speak for yourself. I haven't done anything close to this interesting since I was put on probation."

"Saving people is important, isn't it?" Felix asked.

"Of course it is," Mason said. "But we have no idea what Ernest Abernathy is planning to do with the wand. He could hurt way more people than a pack of werewolves."

"Maybe we can use this trip to get information from Sebastian about Ernest," Felix suggested. "Or the Moonlit Army leader."

Arisa's face lit up. She glanced at Clementine. "You know, since Ernest is a Guardian, we might be able to find information on him in the library."

"Like his records?" Felix asked.

"We won't be able to access anyone's personal records," Arisa said. "They're locked. Students can't get into them. But a lot of mission reports are open access. We could search those and see if he's mentioned anywhere."

"Sounds like it's worth a shot," Mason said with a shug.

They finished breakfast and headed toward the library. Arisa led them to a shortcut through the central courtyard.

That ended up being a mistake.

As they passed the foot of the Silver Paladin statue, Jack Caldwell called out to them. "Look out, Arisa, there's a demon behind you!"

Arisa stopped and glared at him, fists tightening at her sides. "Hilarious," she spat sarcastically. "What, you gonna quit the academy to become a comedian?"

"Who are these assholes?" Mason asked as Jack and his three friends sauntered over to them.

Jack stuck out his hand. "Jack Caldwell. And my friends are Noah and Clara Wallace—" He nodded to the blonde boy and girl. "And Rose McAvoy." Rose's head tipped to the side as she sized up Mason, her brown curls swaying.

Mason stared blankly at Jack's hand.

Jack looked to Felix. "Does he not understand human manners?"

Felix jabbed a finger in the air in front of Jack's face. "He was human until a few months ago, dumbass."

Mason held an arm out in front of Felix. "Don't bother," he said. "He's just trying to rile us up. Let's go."

Mason only made it a few steps before Jack stepped into his path. Jack laughed. "It's a shame you're all on probation. I'd love to face you in combat."

"Real shame." Mason stepped to the right. Jack followed.

"What, you don't want to know if you could beat me?" Jack asked.

"I already know the answer to that question."

"I'd like to see for myself."

"Of course you would," Mason said. "It's not enough for you to be strong. You need other people to see you win."

Anger briefly flashed across Jack's face. Then, he forced a cold smile and shook his head. "I think you're just scared."

"Oh, yeah. I'm terrified," Mason deadpanned. "Please leave me alone before I start crying from fear."

Jack sighed. "Clara?" He gestured toward Arisa.

Clara lifted her chin. Her braid swung behind her. After a heartbeat of silence, Arisa cried out in pain and dropped to her knees. Clementine slipped from her shoulder and thudded against the ground.

Students wandering the courtyard around the two groups stopped and looked their way. Some whispered to each other. Alarm flashed through Felix as he realized there weren't any adults nearby.

Felix dropped to the ground next to Arisa. "Arisa? Are you okay?"

"What are you doing?" Mason demanded, stepping toward Clara.

Arisa pressed her hands to her stomach, face twisted in a grimace. "Don't," she managed between ragged breaths. She lifted her chin. "Clara can sense pain. And cause it. Nothing's actually hurting me."

Clara turned toward Felix. "You've got some injuries," she said plainly.

All at once, every sore spot on Felix's body burned. He gasped and doubled over. Clara's empty expression gave way to a wince, but it vanished when Jack rested a hand on her shoulder and laughed. Her face flushed.

Felix forced himself to his feet, lifted a hand, and tried to summon electricity. Nothing happened.

"Don't bother," Jack said. "Noah can negate magic."

Felix pushed harder. The faintest bit of magic sparked in his chest, and he latched onto it. The lightning that appeared between his fingers was weak, but it was enough for him to grab Noah's wrists and deliver a shock.

"Looks like I'm stronger than you," Felix told Noah through gritted teeth, his body still screaming in pain.

"Noah!" Clara exclaimed as Noah gasped.

Felix's head snapped toward her. "Let go of Arisa."

Clara's shoulders sagged. Arisa leapt to her feet and lunged at her. Jack pulled Clara out of the way, and Arisa stumbled past them.

"Enough," Mason snapped.

Everyone else ignored him. Felix pushed Noah backwards and whirled around. Rose swung a fist at his face. He ducked and tried to sweep her feet with his leg, but his foot passed right through her. He lost his balance and landed hard on the concrete path.

Arisa tried to attack Clara again. Clara sent her back to the ground with a yelp of pain. Felix lifted a hand but couldn't summon the strength to overcome Noah's ability again.

"Come on, Mason, you're not going to help your friends?" Jack slid his hands in his pockets and nodded at Rose. In one swift motion, she elbowed Mason in the side and knocked him to the ground.

"Why are you so desperate to prove you can beat me?" Mason exclaimed, glaring at Jack. "Because I'm a demon?"

Jack ran a hand through his black hair. Laughed. "I'm not desperate. I haven't lost a fight in three years."

"You haven't lifted a finger. You're making your friends do all the work."

"Until you actually put the effort in, this fight is beneath me."

Mason extended a hand toward Jack, black claws appearing at the ends of his fingers.

"Don't," Archer warned.

The seven kids swung their heads toward the man who'd appeared behind Mason. Noah's hold on their magic disappeared. Arisa's shoulders sagged in relief. Jack was the only person who didn't have the sense to look even a little guilty.

"What's going on here?" Archer asked. "Did you three forget that you're banned from combat with other students?"

Were fights like this normal among non-probation students? Felix glanced around the courtyard again.

"He started it!" Arisa pointed at Jack.

Archer's gaze flickered to Jack, and Felix couldn't believe the boy didn't immediately wilt under it.

"We were just discussing our abilities," Jack said with a shrug. "I wanted to see theirs in action."

"Don't you have a class on the third floor in a few minutes?" Archer asked.

"Am I in trouble?"

Archer was quiet for a moment. "Get to class," he ordered.

Jack walked by Felix, Mason, and Arisa with a smug grin. "Let me know when you're ready for a rematch."

"I'd hardly call this a match in the first place," Mason replied, keeping his tone even.

Jack ignored him. Noah, Clara, and Rose threw nervous glances at Archer as they hurried past him and followed Jack out of the courtyard.

"You're just going to let him get away with this?" Arisa asked. "He and his friends attacked us first."

"I didn't see the start of the fight," Archer said.

"You don't believe me?"

"I didn't say that. But I can't do anything about something I didn't witness." Archer shot an annoyed look at a group of students who'd been inching slowly closer. They scurried off. "Consider yourself lucky I don't have your trip with Sebastian cancelled. And stay away from those four if they're going to cause problems. Understand?"

The three climbed to their feet. Clementine ran up to Arisa, and Arisa picked her up and set her on her shoulder.

Archer wasn't done. "If Mason used his hellfire against another student, he'd be in the dungeons in a heartbeat."

Mason glanced at his hand. "Archer has a point. Unfortunately."

"I still don't think it's fair." Arisa folded her arms.

Felix agreed, but he couldn't bring himself to argue the matter any further. "Come on, guys. Let's just get back to what we were doing."

"Where are you three going now?" Archer asked.

"Library," Mason told him.

"Funny. I'm going there too."

"Yeah, I bet," Arisa said under her breath.

It probably wasn't a coincidence, but there was no point protesting. Archer followed closely behind the three as they walked to the library. Thankfully, he split off from them as soon as they entered, headed in a completely different direction than the one Arisa led them in.

The three gathered around a computer at a desk in a dim corner of the second floor. Arisa clicked and typed and clicked again while Mason watched intently and Felix spun in circles in his chair.

"Here!" Arisa pointed at the screen. "These are all of the mission reports involving Ernest Abernathy. All the ones we can access, anyway."

Mason groaned as Arisa scrolled down the list. "This isn't going to help at all. I need to know where he lives."

"We can't access that information—"

A shadow cast by a nearby bookshelf shifted, and Hana emerged from the darkness. Felix and Mason jumped in surprise. Hana signed something to Arisa with a confused expression.

"She wants to know what we're doing," Arisa muttered. She signed something back, and Felix actually understood the gist of it. "Reading old mission reports. For educational purposes." Arisa paused, then added, "Technically, we're not breaking any rules."

Hana lifted an eyebrow and a hand. "Technically?"

While Arisa and Hana continued their conversation, Felix's gaze darted between them and Mason, who had leaned forward to peer at something on the screen. He grabbed the mouse and began clicking.

Hana walked back into the shadow she'd emerged from. Before Felix could ask Arisa what just happened, she reappeared carrying a massive black binder.

Felix glanced back at Mason and found his chair empty.

"Hana didn't actually care about what we were doing," Arisa said, drawing Felix's attention back to her. Hana was gone now, too. Arisa let the binder drop onto the desk with a thud. "She just wanted to dump this on me. I have wedding planning to work on during the trip."

"Oh, fun!" Felix exclaimed.

"What, you want to take over for me?"

Mason returned, waving around a few pieces of paper. "Where did you go?" Felix asked as he sat down.

"Printer." Mason set the papers on the desk. "I saw something that looked interesting. It might be nothing, but—"

Felix picked up the top sheet. "It's a mission report." He frowned. "To kill...werewolves?"

"That sounds pretty standard," Arisa said as she opened the binder.

"Yeah, but Ernest was the only survivor," Mason said. "He and a small team of Guardians went to take on a pack, and he was the only one who returned."

Arisa looked up, surprised. "Even if it was an entire pack, they shouldn't have been that dangerous."

"Wait, this is near where we're going," Felix realized. "Sebastian wouldn't take us on a mission to track wolves that killed a bunch of Guardians, right?"

Mason slid aside one of the papers and pointed to the bottom page. "Ernest claims here that they did kill all of the wolves. He was just the only one who made it out without fatal injuries." He shrugged. "And it's miles away from Cold Creek. Location's probably a coincidence. But I want to know what happened here."

"Yeah, werewolves aren't hard to fight," Arisa said. "There's magic in their bodies, but they can't wield it. They just have accelerated healing and brute strength."

"So, it's not weird that there's another killer pack of wolves in the same area?" Felix asked.

Mason and Arisa shared a look. "This is a heavily forested area," Mason said. "It's a good place for wolves. It's not really surprising that a new pack would move in after the old one was killed."

"And even though most wolves don't hurt people, it's not super rare for them to kill, either," Arisa added. "Unfortunately."

"Staying out of trouble?" Archer asked from behind them.

The three jumped and yelped in surprise. As Mason slid the mission report papers aside, Arisa rolled in her chair to reveal the open binder in front of her. "Yeah, just, um, doing some wedding planning," she stammered.

Archer leaned forward and studied the printout of flower arrangements. He pointed at one. Voice as dead as usual, he said, "You should go with this one."

"You think that one looks best?" Felix asked.

"No, but those flowers repel malicious spirits." Archer stepped back from the desk and walked away without another word.

"He is without a doubt the most terrifying man I've ever met," Felix said. "And that's including the necromancer." He shook his head. "I can't believe Jack's not scared of him. I know his dad's on the council, but Archer's the King's Hand."

"I don't think Jack's had to deal with Archer much," Arisa said. "Archer makes sure training runs smoothly, but he doesn't get involved in student affairs directly. Well, except us. But that's because of the probation thing."

"One thing's for sure," Felix said. "First chance we get, the three of us are going to kick Jack's ass."

"Agreed," Arisa said.

"Honestly, he'd hate it so much more if we ignored him. If we avoid fighting him, he won't get the satisfaction of—" Mason paused. "Nah, scratch that. I'm going to punch him in the face."

Felix laughed. "That's the spirit."

Chapter Eighteen
Cold Creek, Colder Pool

Friday seemed to sneak up on Felix, leaving him to pack his things last-minute the morning of the field trip. He, Arisa, and Mason were out front of the castle with their bags by ten a.m., and Sebastian's car waited along the road just twenty feet from the front doors. Sebastian himself showed up five minutes after the trio with a suitcase, two duffel bags, and a backpack.

"That looks like a lot," Mason commented.

"It's mostly weapons," Sebastian replied. He somehow managed to carry all of the luggage without looking awkward or strained as he walked to his car. "Oh, and board games."

"Won't we be busy with the wolves?" Felix asked.

Sebastian kicked the back of his car. The trunk popped open. "We'll have some time to kill during the day."

The group loaded up their bags and climbed into the vehicle. Felix half expected Archer to pop out of nowhere again, but he didn't show.

Felix and Arisa passed the time by looking for Volkswagen Beetles and punching Mason when they spotted them. Mason took it well, not looking up once from the spellbook he'd found in the library a couple days earlier. He'd finally picked out a uniform, and today he wore it with a shirt the same shade of dark purple as the horns hidden under his maroon beanie.

When they arrived at Cold Creek Motel, Sebastian left the three of them to unload the luggage while he checked in. He returned a couple of minutes later with three room keys.

Sebastian held out the key cards. "Here's Arisa's, this one's for Felix and Mason—"

Mason grabbed the key before Felix could.

"—and this one's mine," Sebastian finished.

"You paid for three rooms?" Felix asked.

"It's an extremely cheap motel. Which reminds me, keep an eye out for bed bugs. I won't hesitate to set everything on fire to stop them from coming home with us." Sebastian plucked a stray hair off his jacket. "I have some very nice pillowcases, and I'd hate to have to throw them out."

"Is there at least a pool?" Arisa asked. "I brought my swimsuit."

Felix glanced at her. "You did?"

"You didn't?"

"There is a pool." Sebastian gathered up his bags. "You can check it out now, if you'd like. We won't leave to track the wolves until after a late dinner. In the meantime, I have some Guardian business to deal with, so you three are on your own."

"What kind of Guardian business?" Arisa asked as Sebastian led them to their rooms.

"Boring stuff. Guardian emails, Guardian phone calls, possibly a trip to get some Guardian snacks."

Felix adjusted the bag hanging off his shoulder. "You're really leaving us alone after we walked into a demon-infested building on our last field trip?"

"As far as I'm aware, there are no demon-infested buildings around here. Just don't summon anything, okay?" Sebastian opened the door to his room. "I'll come get you kids around seven."

After they dropped their bags in their rooms, Arisa pestered Felix and Mason until they agreed to accompany her to the indoor pool. Mason brought along a stack of books, while Felix brought a silver sword to practice with.

The sword's weight was different from Helena's, making Felix's already subpar sword wielding skills even worse. He tried to work through his frustration and be patient with himself, as Hana constantly reminded him during training, but patience wasn't one of his strong suits.

"Good thing this place is empty," Arisa commented as Felix paced along the edge of the pool, swinging the sword back and forth.

"Pretty sure it's because that water is freezing," Mason said. He sat on a pool chair pushed into a corner as far from the water as possible.

"You barely touched it before running off into that corner." Arisa rolled her eyes. "It's not that bad once you get used to it."

"I'll stay over here, thanks."

Felix turned the sword in his hands and cut through the air. "Do you guys think it's weird that I haven't interacted with Gideon since I took in his ghost?"

Arisa rested her arms on the edge of the pool. "Isn't that a good thing?"

"I guess. I just wonder if he's aware of anything that's happened." Felix swung again.

Mason looked up from his book. "Are you completely sure you have him?"

Felix paused. "Pretty sure. I mean, there was the same flash of light I saw with the rest of my family. Kendra and Archer saw it happen." He moved to swing again, but his hands slipped, and he lost his hold on the sword. Without thinking, he reached out to catch it. The blade grazed his palm.

Mason tensed. Arisa's eyes widened.

Felix flinched at the sting but forced himself to take a deep breath. He held up his hand. "It's fine. Just a scratch." He bent down and picked up the weapon by the hilt. A few drops of blood stained the ground as his hand brushed over it.

"Maybe you should practice with the scabbard on for a little longer," Arisa suggested politely. "Or stick to your powers tonight."

"I won't be able to kill a wolf with my powers!" Felix wiped the last of the remaining blood off on the sleeve of his jacket.

"You could if you were strong enough," Arisa told him. "Silver's the easiest way to kill wolves, but it's not the only way. You just have to beat their regenerative abilities."

"Do you think I'm strong enough to kill one with my powers alone?" Felix asked.

"Uh..."

"No," Mason said.

Felix's grip tightened around the sword in frustration. How was Helena so good at this? Stupid question. She'd had her sword for as long as he could remember—

A figure appeared next to him. "Your technique is better, but you lose focus quickly," Helena said. "Here, you need to adjust your grip."

Mason nearly fell out of his chair in surprise. Arisa yelped. "A real ghost!"

"You've never seen a ghost before?" Felix asked as Helena repositioned his hands.

"Well, I have, but only weak ones that barely show themselves." Arisa leaned forward and looked Helena up and down. "Which one are you?"

"This is Helena," Felix said. "She's the one with lightning."

Helena looked around the pool while Felix attempted another swing of the sword. "Where are we?"

"Cold Creek. We're going after some werewolves," Felix told her.

"Ooh, fun!" Helena rested a hand on her hip. "Reminds me of my first real mission. I think I was fourteen."

"What? Seriously?"

Helena smiled. "It was just a banshee. Nothing too scary. Mom and Dad are going to be excited for you, though. May might be jealous. She always wanted to fight a werewolf."

"It's not technically a mission," Arisa said. "Since we're all on probation. Our teacher's just showing us how to track werewolves."

Helena turned. "You're Hana Tamura's sister, right?"

Arisa nodded. "Arisa."

Helena's attention shifted to Mason. "And you are?"

"Mason Briggs," Mason answered. "Not technically a magician."

Helena stared at him for a long moment. "Right. You're the demon my dad mentioned."

"I'm also a witch."

"So, still no sign of Gideon?" Felix asked, changing the subject.

Helena's expression darkened. "We haven't...seen him. But we can sense him in your soul."

"That doesn't sound great."

"I still don't think he's aware of what's going on," Helena said. "And I think a lot of your energy is subconsciously going into suppressing him."

"Oh, good," Felix said.

"It's good that you've been able to keep him under, but it also means you're wasting a lot of energy that you could otherwise be channeling into your magic."

"It's not like I really have any other choice though, right?"

Helena sighed. "I guess not." Her form flickered and came back paler. "Looks like I'm going. Stay safe tonight, okay? And don't forget to drink a lot of water. May usually downed three bottles before a mission."

"Okay, okay, I will." Felix watched his sister fade. "Love you!"

"Love you, too."

He, Arisa, and Mason hung out at the pool for another hour or so before heading to Felix and Mason's room to try some board games. That didn't exactly go well.

"Arisa's animating the dice to make them roll in her favor," Mason announced after a several-hour long losing streak.

"Am not!" Arisa folded her arms. "You're just jealous that I'm so good at these games."

"Monopoly isn't a game of skill. It's a game of luck."

"Yeah, I'm good at being lucky!"

A knock came from the door. Felix got up and opened it while Arisa and Mason continued their argument.

Sebastian peered past Felix into the room. "Uh, you kids ready?"

"Also, Clementine can't be on your team if she's going to peek at the community chest cards!" Mason exclaimed.

"Yeah, we're ready," Felix said.

Arisa rose to her feet, picked up Clementine, and set the bear on her bed. "Guard the place while we're gone, all right?"

Sebastian handed out a few more silver weapons as they walked to his car. "Remember, you're not supposed to go after the wolves," he said as he handed Mason a dagger. "This is strictly for self-defense. Arisa, hold on to this silver net. We're probably going to need it."

Felix ran a hand along the strap holding the silver sword behind him. Sebastian had given him a couple of knives, too, but if they wound up in a fight, he was sure he'd fall back on his powers first.

Arisa shoved the net Sebastian had given her into the small bag at her side. "Where are we going?"

"We'll grab dinner, then drive to a trailhead a few minutes from here once it gets dark," Sebastian said. "Most of the documented kills happened in the same part of the forest, not far from the trail."

"Do a lot of people go hiking at night around here?" Felix asked.

"When it's warm, sure. There's also some camping sites nearby, but they were mostly empty when I checked them out earlier. The full moon pattern's becoming hard to ignore, even if the deaths have publicly been blamed on bears."

They stopped at a small diner to eat, and dinner gave Felix the perfect amount of time to get nervous. When he'd been attacked by Gideon's ghost and the poltergeist and demons and the undead, there had been no time to think. Now, it was hard not to imagine wolves jumping out of the shadows and sinking their claws into him.

"You don't have any problems eating normal food, do you?" Sebastian asked as Mason picked up the sandwich he ordered.

"It tastes different," Mason said. "But I don't have any issues eating it."

"Different?"

"Not as good as it used to."

"Hm."

"What do demons usually eat?" Felix asked.

"They don't have to eat," Sebastian said. "But they can use possession to feed on a human's life force for energy. They also enjoy the taste of flesh and blood, even if they don't need it to survive. It probably increases their power."

"Oh." Felix shuddered.

"I have no desire to do any of that," Mason said. He took a bite of his sandwich.

The sun wasn't quite gone when they left the restaurant, so they wandered around the town's few shops for a little while before getting back in the car and driving to the trailhead. After they parked and climbed out of the car, Sebastian drew a dagger and led the way into the forest.

"Based on the number of kills, it's probably a small pack," Sebastian said. "I'm betting about ten wolves."

"So, what's the plan from here, exactly?" Felix asked.

"We need to be sure what we're dealing with first. Especially after...recent events. Our goal is to locate the wolves without them noticing us, and we'll follow them as long as we can. If they get close to anyone, of course, I'll intervene immediately." Sebastian twirled his dagger around in his hand a few times. "Ideally, I'd like to catch one and interrogate it."

They walked for ten minutes before Sebastian had them stop and try sensing the werewolves' energy. The air was definitely heavy with something, but Felix couldn't pinpoint a source.

"It's all over the place," Mason said, echoing Felix's thoughts.

"Felix? You feel anything?" Sebastian asked.

Felix nodded. "I think so. But I don't know how to tell which direction to go."

"The most recent traces of energy are coming from that way." Sebastian turned and faced the trees to the north. Beyond the trail.

"How can you tell what's more recent?" Arisa asked.

"Practice," Sebastian answered. "That's the only real way to tell apart fresh and stale magic. Take a second to see if you can tell a difference between the two directions, then follow me."

Felix thought he could sense a slight difference between the magic behind them and ahead of them, but he wasn't positive. He wondered dimly just how *much* practice it would take to get the hang of it as he pushed through the undergrowth with the others. Sebastian lit the way with a small orb of light, enough to help them avoid tripping, but not so much that they would draw attention from anything that might want to hurt them.

Felix wasn't sure how long they walked, but at some point, he looked up and was startled by the bright moon hanging above them. Not long after that, a howl sounded in the distance. Felix's heart skipped a beat. A second, closer howl answered a moment later.

"I don't like how close to town that sounded," Sebastian muttered.

"I don't like how close to *us* that sounded." Felix scanned the shadows around them. A third howl sounded, this one much farther. The group waited in silence for a minute longer, but the sky remained quiet.

"The pack has split," Sebastian said. "They're looking for prey. When one finds something, they'll howl again to signal to the others. This is our chance to catch one alone."

The four moved forward again and didn't make it more than twenty feet before emerging in a clearing.

"Careful," Sebastian said as they crossed to the center. "This makes us an obvious target, and the wolves have great senses. Plus, one has been stalking us for the past ten minutes."

"What?" Felix yelped.

In the blink of an eye, Arisa had a dagger in each hand. Hellfire burned in Mason's open palm. Felix scrambled to draw his sword.

"Relax. I'll be the one they attack first." Sebastian turned around and raised his voice. "You're somewhere over here, aren't you?"

A low growl emanated from the darkness. Felix, Arisa, and Mason moved closer together. Sebastian stood between them and the monster waiting in the shadows. Felix's heart skipped a beat.

A figure burst from the black. A flash of dark fur flew through the air toward Sebastian.

The werewolf was massive. Much bigger than Felix expected, much bigger than an ordinary wolf. It had almost reached Sebastian when he lifted his arm and swung his fist into the wolf's chest. There was a flash of light, and the wolf sailed backwards through the air. It slammed into the ground with a strangled yelp.

"Damn." Sebastian shook out his hand. "You're weaker than I expected."

The wolf was back on its feet in an instant. "Sebastian Armitage," he snarled in a voice that was surprisingly human, albeit a bit raspy. "It's my lucky day." He tipped his head back and opened his mouth.

Before the wolf could howl, Sebastian lifted his hand and fired off a thin beam of light that pierced the beast's neck. "Arisa, the net!"

Arisa yanked the net from her bag and raced toward Sebastian and the wolf. Felix and Mason followed. As they approached, the hole that the light had left in the wolf's throat closed up on its own. The only sign the wound had been there at all was the blood splattered across the dirt.

The wolf let out a low growl. Sebastian jumped back, and the wolf's jaws snapped at the air where he'd been standing. Sebastian unzipped his jacket and reached a hand inside. Arisa, meanwhile, threw the net onto the ground.

"I'm not stupid enough to walk into that." The wolf turned and launched himself at Arisa with outstretched claws. She pointed a dagger at him, and he twisted to avoid the silver blade, hitting the ground a few feet away. Before he could try attacking again, a blast of purple hellfire struck the ground at his feet. He hissed in pain and jumped back.

"Get him in the net," Mason said, turning his head to meet Felix's gaze. Felix nodded. Together, they circled the wolf, firing off blue and purple fireballs in an attempt to herd it toward the net. Most of the attacks missed, but they came quickly enough to keep the wolf distracted.

"This won't work," the wolf growled, his head turning toward the net that was now only a few feet away. He ducked to avoid the next few fireballs and took a step in the opposite direction.

"Close enough," Arisa said. The net lifted off the ground and flew at the wolf, wrapping around his body in seconds. The air hissed, and it took a moment for Felix to realize it wasn't the wolf making the sound, but his burning skin.

Sebastian's hand lowered to his side. "That was great!"

The wolf's mouth opened, presumably to make another attempt at a howl. Arisa clenched her fist. The net wrapped tight around his jaw and forced it shut. More burns appeared across the wolf's face.

Felix grimaced. "That looks like it really hurts."

"This is nothing compared to what they put their victims through," Sebastian said. "Let's get him out of here. When he turns back into a human in the morning, we'll start asking questions."

They dragged the wolf back to the trailhead, careful to avoid his claws. Thankfully, a few adjustments of the net from Arisa stopped the wolf from struggling for long. When the group reached the car, it took all four of them to lift him into the trunk.

"Is this really the best way to do this?" Mason asked.

"If you have a better idea, I'd love to hear it." Sebastian slammed the door shut. "Just hope we don't get pulled over."

They drove in silence for a minute before Felix asked, "Why do some wolves avoid people and others hunt them? Can they control it?"

"Wolves have no control over their transformation, but they don't have to hurt people," Sebastian said. "They have new instincts and abilities, but they retain their memories and intelligence. I'll admit it's not easy, though. The first few transformations are rough and confusing. Especially if you were turned and not born a wolf." After a moment, he added, "At least, that's what I've heard."

"Still," Arisa said. "They are in control. It's not hard to go after wildlife, instead."

Sebastian nodded. "As to why they would choose to hunt people, the reasons vary. Some family lines of werewolves think they have a right to take human lives. Others just think it's more fun."

The car was quiet after that, until they parked at the motel.

"Let's take the wolf to my room," Sebastian said as he climbed out. He circled around the car to the back.

Felix stepped out of the car and scanned the parking lot. It was late, and there was no sign of anyone else nearby, but... "What if someone sees?"

Sebastian lifted the trunk door. "It's okay. The motel's pet friendly."

The werewolf didn't put up a fight, but he did let himself fall limp. It was a lot of dead weight to carry, and by the time they dumped him on the floor in Sebastian's room, Felix's breathing was ragged.

"There are still other wolves out there," Sebastian said. "I'm going to head back out and make sure they don't kill anyone. You kids get some rest, and we'll reconvene in the morning to deal with him." He nodded at the wolf, who glared at him through the gaps in the net.

"Are you sure it's okay to leave him here alone?" Felix asked.

"There's no way he's getting out of the silver," Sebastian replied. "But I'll add a circle of trapping sigils on the floor just in case. You kids have nothing to worry about."

Felix had a lot of things to worry about, but he was more than happy to take a giant, bloodthirsty werewolf off his list of concerns.

Chapter Nineteen
Interrogation

After taking one look at the motel's breakfast of burnt eggs and undercooked pancakes, Felix, Arisa, and Mason resorted to buying snacks from the vending machine outside the building.

As Felix slid the last of his quarters into the machine, he glanced at Arisa. "Hey, you know how you animated the net last night?"

Arisa broke off a piece of her chocolate bar. "Yeah?"

"Do you think you could animate a rug and turn it into a flying carpet?"

"Why would I do that?"

"To help me fulfill a childhood dream?" Felix punched in the code for a bag of chips.

"Hm. It would take a lot of energy. Might be too much for the counterbalance." She popped the piece of chocolate into her mouth.

The door to Sebastian's room opened. He leaned against the door frame and folded his arms. "Ready to talk to the wolf?" he called to them.

"Hang on!" Felix turned back to the vending machine. "My chips are stuck."

"Just buy another bag," Mason said.

Felix slid a hand into his pocket. "I'm out of money."

"Hold on." Sebastian walked over to them, pulling out his wallet. He slid a bill into the machine and typed in the code for the chips. The four of them watched as a second bag slid forward and failed to knock down the first.

"It's fine. I'll just starve," Felix said.

Sebastian pushed his sleeves up to his elbows and grabbed the sides of the machine. "Not on my watch."

"Be careful," Arisa said. "Vending machines kill more people than sharks."

"I think you're thinking of coconuts," Felix told her.

"No, I'm definitely thinking of vending machines."

"Pretty sure you're both right," Mason muttered.

Sebastian rocked the vending machine back and forth a couple of times. When that failed to dislodge the chips, he took a step back and slammed his foot into the front of the machine. A crack ran up the front of the glass. Bags of food and bottled drinks rained down inside the machine.

"Yeah!" Arisa cheered and pumped a fist in the air. Felix eagerly dove forward to collect his chips. Mason pulled the hood of his sweatshirt over his face and backed away from them.

Sebastian grabbed everything else that had fallen, somehow managing to balance it all with one arm.

"We don't need all of that," Mason said.

"Never leave evidence at a crime scene." Sebastian held up a bag and shook it. "You sure you don't want any of this?"

Mason reluctantly moved closer. After eyeing his options for a few moments, he snatched a few bags of candy and a bottle of soda.

Arisa lifted an eyebrow. "That's a lot of sugar."

"It's one of the few things that still tastes really good," Mason said. Claws extended from the tips of his fingers as he tore open a bag of caramels. "In fact, I think it might taste even better than when I was human."

"Well, we should get started." Sebastian turned around. "I think we've kept our wolf waiting long enough."

The four filed into the motel room. The werewolf was still wrapped up in the silver net, but he'd transformed into a tall, muscled man with messy dark hair hanging around his face. Welts cut across his pale skin where the net had touched it.

"All right." Sebastian pulled a chair over from the desk and sat down. "Let's start with your name." He leaned back and crossed his legs. Felix, Arisa, and Mason lined up behind him.

"So, we're finally talking." The man glared up at Sebastian. "Torture me all you want. I'm not giving you anything."

"Unfortunately, there won't be any torture. Either you talk, or I kill you." Sebastian grabbed a dagger off the desk next to him. "And then we hunt down your pack and kill them, too."

The man barked out a cold laugh. "What, that's it? You haven't seen me kill anyone. Hardly seems fair to give me a death sentence without evidence."

"You want a trial? That could be arranged. But the King's Council is far crueler to monsters than I am. You won't find any friends there." Sebastian leaned forward. "Besides, I tracked down last month's victims at the cemetery. There was still magical energy lingering around their graves, and you're giving off the same energy."

"The whole pack has the same energy. You can't prove I specifically killed anyone."

"Your whole pack has *similar* energy signatures. There's a subtle difference you can detect if you're as smart and talented as I am." Sebastian gestured with his dagger. "And even if your signature weren't on any of the bodies—which it was—that would still mean someone in your pack was killing people. If you associate with them, you're supporting monsters."

Felix took a bite of one of his chips. A crunching sound filled the room. The man in the net shot him a death glare.

"What?" Felix asked through a mouth full of chip.

"These are future Guardians?" The man snorted. "The Moonlit Army is going to destroy your precious Brightlands."

A dark expression flickered across Sebastian's face. "Why do you know that name?" he asked.

"Whispers of the Moonlit Army are spreading among us *monsters*," the man said with a sneer, heavily emphasizing that last word. "It's not just your old Guardian friends that you'll have to face when the time comes." He sniffed and lifted his chin. "You killed some of my pack. I can smell their blood on you."

"Rude. I did shower," Sebastian said. "But yes, I killed all the wolves that I pulled off the group of dumbass teenagers who thought camping last night was a good idea."

The man's face twisted in pain, but he pushed it away after a moment. "Did they survive?"

"The teenagers? They're in the hospital, but I think they'll pull through." Sebastian lifted an eyebrow. "I do have to give your pack credit. You're a smart little group."

"Little?" The man chuckled.

Sebastian continued. "Smarter than any other pack I've dealt with. And bigger. Faster. Stronger." His hand tightened around the dagger's handle as he pointed it at the man. "Except you. You suck."

"The rest of them will rip you and those pathetic children to shreds," the man spat.

Felix winced.

Sebastian lowered the dagger. "Oh, no, don't be fooled by my praise. Your pack of monsters is no match for me."

The man rolled his eyes. "Killing your kind is in a werewolf's blood. Lions kill zebras, snakes kill mice, spiders kill flies. You want to stand in the way of nature?"

"And yet most werewolves stick to hunting animals. I've even met a few who don't hunt at all while they're transformed. Hell of an appetite after, though. Have you ever seen someone eat ten burgers in one sitting?"

"You're annoying."

"Yes, I've been told that," Sebastian said. "But don't act as if you're something entirely unhuman. Werewolves are still capable of sympathy for innocent lives."

"What if wolves could only survive off human flesh?" the man asked. "Would you still call us monsters for doing what we needed to survive?"

"That's not the world we live in, and I'm not a fan of hypotheticals. I'll leave that one to philosophers." After a moment, Sebastian let out a cold laugh. "You're stalling, aren't you?"

"Am not."

"You think your pack's going to come rescue you?"

The man was quiet for a few seconds. Then, he lifted his gaze to the ceiling. "Maybe they won't find me before you kill me. But they will find you eventually." He chuckled. "They've been waiting for you."

Sebastian lifted an eyebrow. "Waiting for me? I'm flattered, really, but I can't imagine what a pack of werewolves would want with me. How did you even know I'd be assigned to deal with you?"

"I believe the plan was to just keep killing Bright Guardians until you showed up," the man said. "As to what we want with you, well, you'll find out soon enough."

After a moment of silence, Sebastian rose to his feet. "Kids, let's go outside."

A light drizzle had started in the parking lot. Sebastian's gaze flickered up to the gray clouds overhead. "Hopefully, this clears up by tonight." He turned his attention back to Felix, Arisa, and Mason. "It's not easy to kill a monster with a human face. You three aren't ready for that."

Felix expected the others to protest, but their only response was to nod.

"With some of their pack members missing, the rest of the wolves are going to be ready for a big fight," Sebastian continued. "I'll deal with this guy. You kids relax until tonight."

The three left Sebastian and headed to Felix and Mason's room. As they entered, Mason spoke. "That werewolf said their plan was to 'keep killing Guardians' until Sebastian showed up."

Felix nodded. "Sounds like they've already killed some."

"Exactly," Mason said. "Maybe they're the same wolves that killed the Guardians on Ernest Abernathy's mission, after all."

"But Ernest said he and his team killed all of them."

Arisa sat down at the desk and rested her chin on her hand. "Maybe he was wrong, and there were more wolves than he thought. But..." She trailed off and glanced at Mason.

"We already know he's bad news," Mason said with a nod. "It's not a stretch to assume he lied."

"You think he was lucky and got away while everyone else was killed?" Felix asked.

"Maybe," Mason muttered. "Or..."

"Or what?"

"I don't know. Never mind."

They played board games until Mason got tired of losing, flipped through TV channels until they were hungry, and grabbed food at a taco place across the street. The afternoon dragged by even slower than the morning. Mason flipped back and forth through his books. Arisa taught Felix a few card games and kicked his ass at all of them.

Finally, Felix won a round of rummy. He cheered loud enough to startle Mason, who jumped and knocked one of Felix's empty water bottles off the desk.

Arisa scowled. "I'm hungry. Let's go bug Sebastian for dinner."

Felix was disappointed to cut his potential winning streak short, but he followed Arisa and Mason out of the room and to Sebastian's door. Arisa knocked.

No response.

"Hello?" Felix called. "Sebastian?" Still, no reply came.

"Wait, I have an idea." Arisa rested a hand on the door. "Alright, buddy, could you open up for me?"

The door handle twisted itself, and the door swung open. The three entered Sebastian's room and found it empty. No Sebastian, no wolf. Arisa moved to his desk, where a folder holding a stack of papers lay open.

"What are you doing?" Felix asked.

Arisa picked up a sheet of paper. "Just taking a look."

"I don't know if going through his stuff is a good idea." Felix glanced at Mason, who shrugged.

"Why would I care?" Mason asked.

Arisa picked up a second paper. Her eyes widened. "Hey, this is stuff on Ernest!" She held it up. "It's the same mission report we found." Mason hurried over to take a look for himself.

"Sebastian is looking into Ernest," Felix said as he joined them. "That's good. Maybe that's why we're really here."

"Why not tell us then?" Mason asked as he took the paper from Arisa.

"Tell you what?" Sebastian stepped through the open doorway. The door smacked into him, sending him stumbling forward. "What the—Did you bring my door to life?"

"Oops." Arisa held up a hand. "I forgot to un-animate it."

"What are you all doing in here?" Sebastian asked.

"Uh, looking for food?" Felix tried.

It was no use. Mason held up the mission report. "Have you found more information on Ernest Abernathy?"

Sebastian shrugged off his jacket as he walked to the desk. "I don't have anything concrete, yet. Just a few theories." Specks of blood stained his shirt, and there was a tear in his right sleeve.

"Do you think Ernest lied about what happened on his werewolf mission?" Mason asked.

"It's certainly a possibility." Sebastian draped his jacket over the back of the desk chair.

Mason flung his hands in the air. "We should just steal the wand back already!" he exclaimed. "Ernest won't be able to do anything about it without admitting he stole it in the first place."

"It's not that simple," Sebastian said. "Even if we get in and out fast enough to avoid getting caught, he'll pick up on our magical energy. Especially mine, given the amount of power I have."

"Then just tell me where he lives and let me go by myself! I know I can do it," Mason insisted. "I've been trying to figure out that energy masking spell that was used at the office building, and I think I can replicate it—"

"I have considered it, believe me," Sebastian cut him off. "But if you were caught, the council would consider you an enemy. And for a demon, that means certain death."

"I'll run," Mason said. "I can get far away fast. I'm good at it."

"And go on your own again?" Felix asked. Mason didn't answer.

"At the very least, you should give me a chance to study his house more at the next party," Sebastian said. "Let me get a better idea of his security. He's bound to have wards in place. You won't be able to get through those."

"I guess," Mason muttered. He set the page from the mission report back on the desk, and Felix noticed that his claws had emerged during the argument.

Sebastian folded his arms. "Now, we still have a pack of werewolves to kill."

"What about dinner?" Arisa asked.

Sebastian paused. "Good point. Okay, dinner, then wolves."

Chapter Twenty
Blood Moon

A few hours later, a wolf howl cut through the night air. The group of four came to a halt in the middle of the dark forest. Their gazes darted around the shadows.

"They're definitely nearby," Sebastian said. "I can feel them, but—" He frowned as a second howl sounded, this one more distant. "Why go that way?" he murmured.

"Should we follow?" Arisa asked.

"I'm going to take a look real quick. You three get back-to-back," Sebastian ordered. "Weapons up. I'll be right back."

Felix's heart pounded an unsteady rhythm in his chest as the minutes passed. He tried to keep his breathing even. Tried not to imagine teeth tearing into his skin. He whirled around when a rustling came from the undergrowth behind him, opposite from the direction Sebastian had gone.

Wolf eyes glinted in the darkness.

"Run!"

Felix wasn't sure who said it. All he knew was that a heartbeat later, his feet were pounding against the ground and his lungs were struggling for air.

"Why aren't we fighting?" Arisa asked between breaths.

"I'm sensing ten wolves," Mason said. "We need to find Sebastian—"

They stumbled into a clearing.

"Get to cover!" Mason shouted, but it was too late. Wolves emerged from the trees on all sides. Fifteen of them, forcing Felix and the others toward the center. The wolves formed a loose circle around the three.

A voice spoke from the shadows. "So, these are the three lost causes Sebastian has decided to train?"

Felix whirled around as the man behind the voice stepped into the light of the full moon. He was old. Fifties, probably. His gray hair and beard were a few shades darker than the pale shirt under his suit jacket. He studied the three through a pair of glasses with gold frames.

"It's him!" Mason lunged forward. Two wolves immediately sprang on him. Mason jumped out of the path of the first, only to get slammed into the ground by the second.

"Mason!" Felix and Arisa shouted at the same time.

The wolf pressed its paw to Mason's chest, keeping him pinned to the ground. The man's expression was emotionless as he watched. "It's him," Mason gasped again. "Ernest Abernathy." He grimaced in pain.

"You idiot!" Arisa hissed to Ernest. "We'll tell the council about this, and you'll be put on trial."

Ernest flashed her a smile. "I'm from a prominent Bright Guardian family. I have two cousins on the council, and I've led countless successful missions. Atticus Brightland won't throw me in a cell. And he certainly won't side with three kids on probation over me. The Guardians would riot." He looked to the wolves. "Besides, you're going to die here."

"Wait!" Mason exclaimed.

Ernest lifted an eyebrow. The wolf pinning Mason lifted its paw but didn't back away from him as he sat up.

"What do you want with a witch's wand?" Mason demanded. "You're a magician."

"Oh, this?" Ernest reached into suit jacket and drew out a wand that was over a foot in length. Black lines swirled through its red wood.

Mason exposed sharp fangs with a low snarl. "What are you planning?"

"Why would I tell you that?"

Felix raised his hands and reached for his lightning. Before he could unleash it, Ernest pointed the wand at him. An invisible force paralyzed him. Arisa froze next to him.

"Really, it's a shame Guardians didn't try utilizing these sooner." Ernest examined the wand. "There's so much more to the world than our innate magic."

"That doesn't belong to you!" Mason hissed.

"Oh, and you think you deserve it? You're a demon. It's only a matter of time before you become one of the monsters you hunt." Ernest gestured to Felix and Arisa. "Your friends will probably have to kill you."

"That's never going to happen!"

The wolf next to Mason swiped at him. Mason yelped in pain and staggered sideways, three deep gashes in the side of his face.

Felix pushed harder against the magic holding him in place, desperately willing any of his abilities to work. The pressure on him increased in response.

"Don't bother," Ernest said. "This wand is more powerful than you three combined."

Felix glared at him. There had to be a way to break through the spell. Or distract Ernest so that Mason could break it.

"You're really going to kill us?" Mason asked, a hand pressed to the side of his face. "You'll leave your magical energy on us. That will be proof enough for the council."

"Oh, I'm not going to kill you," Ernest said. "The wolves are."

Why were these werewolves obeying Ernest? Felix's mind went back to the interrogation with the wolf they'd caught, desperately searching for some piece of information that might help. Anything.

His eyes widened.

Felix couldn't move his limbs, but he could open his mouth. "Wait! Don't you want to talk to Gideon?"

Ernest glanced at him. "Why would I care about Gideon?"

"The wolves work for you," Felix said. "And the wolf we interrogated mentioned the Moonlit Army. You must be working for their leader, too."

"So, what? You're trying to bargain for your friends' lives with Gideon?" Ernest asked, lifting an eyebrow. "I'm a businessman. I know a bluff when I see one."

Felix braced himself for the pain and bit down hard on the inside of his mouth. "That necromancer seemed real determined to get him back," he said as the coppery taste of blood hit his tongue. "Are you sure your boss won't be mad if you kill me, and Gideon disappears forever?"

"No one knows what happens if you die," Ernest said. "But if Gideon's not powerful enough to stick around on Earth without you as a vessel, he's no good to us anyway."

Felix spat his blood out onto the dirt.

Disgust flashed on Ernest's face. "Enough stalling."

"I agree," Felix said.

May appeared at Felix's left, and Ezra on his right. Before Ernest could react, May vanished and reappeared next to him. She swung a fist at his face. Her hand passed right through him.

"May!" Felix exclaimed.

"Sorry, but you haven't exactly given us a lot of time to practice being ghosts!" May swung again. This time, she hit Ernest and sent him flying backwards.

Mason used the distraction to jump to his feet and start running. Wolves lunged forward with alarming speed to chase him, but he flung out a hand and blasted them with a wave of hellfire.

Ernest sat up, still clutching the wand. Mason crashed into him. They rolled into a tree trunk. Mason wrestled the wand from Ernest's grasp and pointed it toward Felix and Arisa. "Release!" he yelled.

The pressure on Felix disappeared, allowing him to stagger forward. Arisa was already drawing her daggers and charging at Ernest. Ernest lifted a leg and kicked Mason in the stomach, sending him crashing to the dirt. While Mason lay on his back, gasping for air, Ernest turned toward Arisa.

Felix drew his silver sword and ran after her but only made it a few steps. Wolves leapt into his path to cut him off. These were the ones Mason had torched, but despite their crispy appearance, they moved just fine. New fur sprouted from their skin as it healed from the hellfire burns.

Felix turned his head. "Ezra?"

Ezra watched the wolves approach with wide eyes. His hands trembled. "I've never fought this many of anything before."

"You're a ghost!" Felix exclaimed. "You're not in any danger!"

"But you are!"

"Come on, Ezra. They're just werewolves, right?"

Ezra took a step back. "They're healing pretty fast for werewolves," he said.

"They are?"

May appeared on Felix's other side. "It takes so much focus to hit anything," she complained. "Aren't we supposed to be able to move stuff telekinetically? How does that work?"

"I don't know, but we don't have time for you to figure out your ghost powers right now," Felix told her. "Maybe you should possess me again. Does holy water hurt wolves?"

"Nope." May scowled. "I hate to admit it, but Ezra's ability would be best here."

"I haven't practiced that much." Felix glanced at Ezra. "Ezra, I need you to help me."

The first of the circling wolves lunged at Felix. He swung the sword and left a deep gash across its chest. It lashed out with its claws. Felix jumped back, but they still managed to tear open a hole near the bottom of his pant leg.

Felix risked a glance beyond the wolves. Arisa circled Ernest, brandishing her daggers. Paper planes looped through the air around them. The Ironwood Wand lay in the dirt nearby. Mason kept throwing desperate glances at it, but another group of wolves kept him occupied.

"Ezra, possess me!" Felix exclaimed.

Ezra shook his head. "That sounds like a really, really, really—"

"—really bad idea," Felix finished with him. "Yeah, I know. Just do it for a minute, okay? We can't let Ernest get away with the wand. May, try to keep as many wolves busy as you can." He hesitated. "You're not going to disappear, are you?"

"Given that bleeding gash on your leg, I think we'll be okay a little longer," May replied.

Felix glanced down. "Uh, that won't turn me into a werewolf, will it?" he asked.

May shook her head. "They have to bite you."

"Good." Felix lifted his chin. "Let's do this. Ezra?"

"How do I possess you?" Ezra asked.

"Just get in his head and reach for your ability," May told him.

"I don't like how easy you made that sound," Felix muttered.

Ezra disappeared from view, and Felix felt his brother's presence enter his mind. *Ready?* Ezra asked.

Ready, Felix confirmed.

One of Felix's hands lifted into the air in front of him, and Ezra's ability came to life. The ground rumbled. Thorny vines burst from the dirt and wrapped around the closest wolves, pulling them to the ground. As yelps and howls filled the air, Arisa turned and watched with wide eyes. Ernest dove past her and reached for the wand.

Ezra, the wand! Felix warned.

A cactus popped up from the dirt and bent over the wand to shield it from Ernest. Spines sank into his palm. He yanked his hand back with a hiss of pain, jaw clenching.

Felix experienced relief for approximately half a second. Then, Ernest sucked in a deep breath and shoved his hand under the cactus. Another growl of pain escaped his mouth, but when he raised his hand, he was holding the wand. He rose to his feet and ran for the edge of the clearing. Arisa gave chase, but she was lagging. Ernest was surprisingly fast for his age.

Ezra brought another vine up from the ground to grab Ernest's ankle. Ernest drew a knife from his side and sliced through the plant with ease.

Panic made Felix's heart quicken. He wasn't entirely sure if it was his panic or Ezra's. *Ezra!*

Ezra spoke through Felix's mouth. "What? Oh, no, what do I do?"

I don't know, just do something! Ernest was almost to the tree line.

"Got it." Ezra lifted Felix's trembling hands. "I'm going to grow a tree beneath him and trap him at the top."

Oh, cool! Felix exclaimed. *You can do that?*

"Well, theoretically. I've never actually succeeded before. But now's as good a time to try as any, right?"

What? Wait, no, now is NOT as a good a time as any—

Felix's protests were in vain. Ezra latched onto a patch of dirt a few feet in front of Ernest and pushed his magic into it. Branches erupted from the dirt as Ernest's foot hit the ground right in the center of Ezra's target. They wrapped around him and lifted him into the air, carried by a slender trunk. The tree reached fifteen feet in height before stopping.

"I did it!" Ezra exclaimed.

Felix's body swayed. *Dude, I'm going to pass out.*

Ezra's hold on his body slipped away, leaving Felix back in control. And in pain. The world spun as he pressed a hand to the side of his head.

Ernest yanked one of his arms back. The branch wrapping around it snapped in half. He used his freed hand to break off the branch pinning his other arm.

May appeared at Felix's right, but her form was flickering. "It was a nice try, but that tree's too weak and short to hold him," she said. "And he's got the wand."

Felix looked at her. "I'm still bleeding! Why are you flickering?"

"It's not just blood," May told him. "You're low on energy. Sorry."

She vanished.

Felix scanned the clearing. Mason was cutting down wolves that had broken free from the vines. Arisa stood over the body of a hopefully dead wolf, her dagger dripping with blood. Felix wanted to help, but when he took a step forward, he stumbled.

The wolves were mostly taken care of, Felix told himself. *Arisa and Mason can handle it.* He fell forward onto his hands and knees. Now all that was left was—

Ernest rolled and dropped from the tree. It looked like a rough landing, but he forced himself upright and pointed the wand at his leg.

Mason sprinted toward Ernest. Ernest held his fingers to his mouth and let out a low whistle. More wolves emerged from the shadows behind him.

"Better hope your teacher finds you before the wolves overwhelm you." Ernest backed into the trees and disappeared.

Chapter Twenty-One
The Light Magician

Felix staggered forward to where his silver sword lay in the dirt. His hand had just wrapped around the handle when the first wolf reached him.

Felix yanked his arm up and slashed the sword across the wolf's chest. It tumbled to the ground, but its outstretched claws grazed his arm as it went down. He cried out. The sword slipped from his hands.

Another wolf pounced on him, slamming him onto his back. He poured what little strength he had left into summoning electricity. The wolf's face twisted in pain as lightning raced across its fur. It only froze for a moment, though, before powering through and pushing a paw against Felix's chest. He gasped as claws sank into his skin.

Mason reached Felix and swiped at the wolf's side with his dagger. It yelped but kept its hold on Felix. Another wolf charged Mason, forcing him to jump out of the way.

Felix turned his head in time to see Arisa crash into the ground nearby. She rolled onto her side, her face away from him. "Arisa?" he called weakly. No answer.

The world tilted. The edges of Felix's vision darkened. He didn't have the strength to feel fear. All he wanted was to sink into the earth below and sleep.

"Felix!" Mason's voice was far away, as if he were yelling underwater. "Arisa!"

A blinding light flooded the clearing.

The wolf's weight disappeared. Felix forced his eyes open and lifted a hand to shield his face. The wolf stood next to him, head tipped back, snarling at something above them.

Sebastian hovered in the air over the clearing. The undersides of his boots shone with white light. His face was barely visible through the glow.

The wolf next to Felix jumped to a shocking height, jaws snapping at Sebastian's boots. Sebastian lifted a few more feet, and the wolf missed. The other wolves backed toward the trees, apparently deciding that one more opponent was too much. Sebastian's cold laughter echoed around the clearing.

"Too late," he said. "You were dead the moment you attacked my students."

A beam of light shot down from the sky and pierced the closest wolf's body. It silently toppled over next to Felix.

As Felix pushed himself up, he looked to the others. Mason stood over a white wolf, lifting his dagger to strike. The blood staining the wolf's fur indicated it had been struck by Sebastian's light, too. Mason finished it off with one quick swipe.

Arisa looked to be in worse shape, but she was climbing up off the ground. More bloody wolves lay around her. One started to move, and another beam of light struck it in the chest.

The wolf next to Felix twitched. He picked his sword up and prepared to finish it off, but his hands trembled too hard to get a good grip on the weapon. Even as the wolf rose to its feet, he couldn't bring himself to swing.

The wolf's mouth opened wide.

A figure dropped to the ground between them. Sebastian brandished a dagger in his hand as he rose to his full height. A cold smile touched his lips, but his eyes glinted with rage.

Felix briefly wondered how much of the blood staining Sebastian's clothes and skin was his. He had a slight limp as he moved forward, so he wasn't completely unharmed.

The wolf's jaw snapped shut. It turned and started to run, but a burst of light in the air in front of it blinded it. While it stumbled to the right, Sebastian drove his dagger into its back. His other hand reached into his jacket and drew out a second blade.

Felix turned around. Mason lay on the ground nearby with his eyes closed. Arisa knelt next to him.

Felix rushed over. "Is he okay?"

Mason's eyes shot open. "Am I okay? What about you?" He asked incredulously as he sat up. "Your shirt's soaked in blood."

"It's—" Felix glanced down. He was going to say it was mostly wolf blood, but there was no way that was true. It was hard to determine exactly which parts of him were injured, though. His entire body throbbed in pain. He lifted his gaze to Mason's face. The gashes that had been spilling blood earlier were only scabs now. "You look surprisingly good."

"Demonic healing," Mason said. He winced as he stood up. "Still hurts like hell, though. I'm not healing anywhere close to the rate those wolves were."

A growl came from somewhere near the group. Their heads all turned in unison as a gray wolf jumped at them. Sebastian collided with it mid-air and sent it crashing to the ground with a dagger in its side. Sebastian, meanwhile, twisted himself upright in time to land on his feet and slide across the dirt. He lifted an arm and wiped blood off his face.

The wolf climbed to its feet and limped forward, despite the silver dagger in its side.

"All right, everyone, listen up." Sebastian clapped his hands together and took a step back. "Silver is the easiest way to kill werewolves, in most situations, but it's not the only way."

The wolf's pace slowed, but it pressed forward, snarling, fangs bared.

"But if you have enough magic to completely obliterate them, they won't be able to heal themselves." Sebastian raised his right hand and turned the palm toward the wolf. "You might want to shield your eyes, though."

The wolf stopped. Its eyes widened, but if it wanted to run, it was too late.

The massive pillar of light that dropped from the sky completely swallowed the wolf. An eerie, high-pitched tone pierced the air.

When the light faded, a crater the size of a small car was left in the ground. Silence fell over the clearing. There was no sign of the wolf.

It took Felix a moment to realize his mouth was hanging open.

"Holy shit," Mason said.

Sebastian turned in a slow circle. "Don't be impressed yet," he said.

"Why not?" Arisa exclaimed.

"Because not all of these wolves are dead." Sebastian reached into his jacket. "And I've used a lot of magic already."

"How are they not dead?" Mason asked, stunned. "We cut them up with silver!"

"I think most of them would die from those wounds if we left them here, but I'm not taking any chances." Sebastian lifted his hand. Moonlight glinted off the gun in his hand. "Bullet to the head will guarantee they don't come back."

Sebastian walked around the clearing and fired off shots in rapid succession. The echo of the final shot hung in the air as he stared at the body of the last wolf. After a long moment, he looked up and walked to where Felix and the others waited.

"Silver bullets?" Felix guessed.

"Yep." Sebastian returned the weapon to his side. "I brought it for someone else, but they decided not to show." His gaze slid past Felix to the tree Ezra had raised. "Did you make that tree, Felix?"

It took Felix a moment to answer. "Uh, yeah, I did," he lied. Not wanting Sebastian to figure out Ezra had possessed him, he quickly changed the subject. "Why don't all Guardians carry around guns instead of knives?"

"Some do take silver bullets to fight wolves, or iron bullets if they're dealing with fae," Sebastian replied. "But sigils work against all monsters, and you can't fit many on a single bullet."

Mason surveyed the bodies. "I haven't fought many werewolves," he said. "But the ones I have encountered were nothing like this."

"Yeah, I got ambushed and figured out the truth halfway through my own battle with them." Sebastian tipped his head back and looked at the sky. At the moon staring down at them. "They're Supermoon Wolves."

"Impossible," Arisa said. "The Silver Paladin killed them all!"

"What's a Supermoon Wolf?" Mason asked.

"An extremely powerful pack of werewolves that attacked the Brightlands decades ago," Sebastian explained. "I thought they were all killed, too. But it seems a few survived, and we were lucky enough to meet them and their children."

He lowered his gaze and studied the three with surprising intensity. "I came back for you as soon as I realized what we'd walked into, but you were impossible to find for a few minutes. That same energy masking spell was used to hide you from me."

"It was Ernest Abernathy!" Mason's fists clenched. "He was here. And he had the wand!"

"Of course, he'd leave before I showed up," Sebastian muttered. "Coward." His brow furrowed. "Was that before the wolves attacked you?"

"Ernest was the one who told the wolves to kill us," Mason said. "They were obeying him."

"Unbelievable," Sebastian said. "Not that I don't believe you. I just can't imagine why this particular pack of wolves would agree to obey a Bright Guardian."

"Could it have been a spell?" Arisa asked.

"No way," Mason replied, shaking his head. "Mind controlling spells exist, but they require way more than just a wand. And they're a challenge even for witches who have trained their entire lives." He turned to stare off into the trees where Ernest disappeared. "It's terrible that he has the wand, but he'll only be able to perform basic spells. For now."

"If Ernest is the one casting the masking spells, maybe he did it in exchange for the werewolves' allegiance," Sebastian suggested. "In return for helping him, they get to lure in Guardians who are expecting an easy mission."

"Then we have to do something, now," Mason said. "Tell the council. We have proof!"

"You don't have proof. You have a story."

"Why wouldn't they believe us?" Felix asked.

"Because you're going up against Ernest Abernathy," Sebastian answered plainly.

"But you could vouch for us." Arisa folded her arms. "That would help, wouldn't it?"

Sebastian shook his head. "My word won't mean much to the council. In this case, it could make things worse for you."

"But you convinced them to let you train us," Mason protested.

"That's different. And even that was hard to swing. If anyone else was interested in dealing with you, they would've been put in charge instead." Sebastian held up a hand to stop further arguments. "Let's pick this up later. You three are about to collapse. Now, I believe I gave someone a light blue bag."

"I have it," Arisa said. She reached into her backpack.

"There are rolls of bandages with healing sigils in there," Sebastian said. "They won't perform miracles, but you can patch up the worst of your injuries so that you can make it back to the motel. We'll rest here until you've healed enough to start walking."

Felix sank to the ground, grateful he didn't have to stand on his shaking legs any longer. While he, Arisa and Mason helped each other bandage up their deeper wounds, Sebastian circled the clearing. Felix wasn't sure if he was double-checking that the wolves were dead or thinking about something else entirely.

Sebastian finally returned to where the three sat. "I have a lot to consider before we make any moves regarding Ernest," he said. "There was a lot at play tonight."

Mason grunted and nodded. Maybe he was okay with continuing to wait, or maybe he was just too tired to press the matter.

"Are we going back to the motel now?" Felix asked wearily. He wasn't sure he could walk all the way to the car.

"No, take some more time to rest. I'll keep watch. We'll leave when the sun comes back up." Sebastian's brow furrowed. "This wasn't supposed to be anywhere near this dangerous. If it were, the king never would have let me bring you. Hell, I wouldn't have wanted to bring you."

Felix laid back and stared up at the night sky. Mason joined him on the left, and Arisa on the right. Sebastian stood nearby, occasionally walking a few feet to a new position. Other than that, he was completely silent.

The pain that had settled into Felix's body gradually lessened. It didn't fade entirely, but he was able to relax enough to drift into a light sleep. When his eyes opened again, the first rays of dawn had found their way into the forest.

He sat up and yawned. Mason and Arisa were already standing, their attention on something at the other side of the clearing. Felix followed their gaze.

As sunlight spilled over them, the dead werewolves remained in their wolf form, save for one. Her fur melted away, and she transformed into a woman wearing torn jeans and a tank top. As she lifted her head, she reached up to grab at the knife in her shoulder but didn't have the strength to pull it out.

"Damn it." Sebastian took a few steps to a nearby wolf's body and yanked a dagger from its back. He approached the woman. "Any last words?"

She laughed. Blood spilled from her mouth. "Mira says hello."

Sebastian's expression didn't change, but his hand tightened around the dagger's handle. "Funny. Based on how our last interrogation went, I have a feeling she didn't want me knowing you're associated with her."

"We were supposed to beat you and drag you back to her."

"Yeah, I imagine so."

The woman shook her head. "You're stronger than she expected. But she'll learn from this. Next time, you won't be so lucky."

"I don't think she'd want me knowing this."

"Maybe." The woman spat more blood on the ground. "I just figured if I'm going to die anyway, it would be worth a shot to see if I could get to you. You have an interesting reputation."

"Well, you're going to have to do better than that," Sebastian told her. All expression had left his face.

"Fine." Her eyes shifted to Felix, and she grinned at him with teeth stained red. "He's going to die a very painful death for what he did to Gideon."

Sebastian's fingers twitched. "Anything else?"

"Oh, you want me to keep going?" the woman asked. "Anyone who sides with your king will die. Mira will save you for last, I'm sure. One by one, you can watch your friends either betray you or suffer a painful death. The harder you work to train these kids, the bigger the waste—"

Arisa lunged forward and plunged her dagger into the woman's chest. The woman slumped to the ground as Arisa stepped back. Breathing hard, she looked back at Sebastian. "What were you waiting for?"

"I thought we might get more information from her." Sebastian lowered his own weapon. "But there was no point. She was just trying to rile me up. Good job."

"She won't come back from that, right?" Mason asked.

"No. The blade's in her heart."

"Who's Mira?" Felix asked as he climbed to his feet.

Sebastian returned his dagger to his jacket. "The leader of the Moonlit Army."

"So, that's who Gideon worked for?" Did Felix finally have a name for the person who'd sent Gideon to kill his family?

"Yep," Sebastian said. "And, apparently, Ernest Abernathy."

Arisa's eyes narrowed. "So, not everyone who stayed after the Uprising is really on the king's side."

"Nope." Sebastian slid his hands into his pockets. "Looks like we've got some spies in our midst."

Chapter Twenty-Two
Employee of the Month

They stuck around in Cold Creek for the last night of the full moon so that Sebastian could make sure no remaining wolves killed anyone. He told the three the next morning that the night had been completely quiet.

Felix was grateful to hear that. But it didn't change the fact that he'd spent the night reliving the same nightmarish scenario over and over: one by one, the Supermoon Wolves killed everyone in Cold Creek, and he was powerless to stop them.

Sebastian also told the three not to tell another soul about the spies in the Brightlands. "We don't need anyone thinking we're onto them," he'd said. "It will only make them harder to identify."

By the time they returned to the Brightlands Monday afternoon, Sebastian was back to his usual cheery self. "You know what makes field trips better than missions?" he asked as they climbed the hill to the castle. "You three don't have to fill out mission reports."

"We also don't get credit for killing all those wolves," Arisa complained.

Getting credit for that nightmare was the last thing on Felix's mind. "All I care about right now is sleeping."

Mason split off from the group. He caught up to them at the entrance, brushing dirt off the wand he'd buried somewhere on castle property.

"Does it work?" Sebastian asked.

Mason lifted the wand. "Light," he said. A small orb of purple light appeared at the tip. A smile touched his lips.

"You just say words in English and it responds?" Felix asked. "I was expecting, I dunno, Latin?"

"For basic spells, it's not about the language, it's about intent," Mason replied. "Technically, you don't need to say anything at all, but verbal cues are helpful when adjusting to a new wand." Gaze darkening, he added, "Ernest seems to have gotten the hang of it. I didn't see his mouth move when he used the Ironwood Wand."

Sebastian gave them the next two days off of training in exchange for taking their weekend. Felix spent most of the first day in bed healing up from the fight. The morning after, Mason texted him and Arisa and asked them to meet in the library. And to bring their weapons. Now that his wand was ready, he could add extra sigils to their blades.

Felix found the way Mason carved sigils into the metal impressive, but Mason kept muttering about how slow his progress was as he got used to his new wand. He had to carve out each symbol with the tip of the wand, occasionally whispering words under his breath. Simple surgical gloves protected his hands from the sigils already in the metal.

"You're still doing it faster than we could," Arisa informed him after another complaint. "That wand works way better than traditional etching tools. The only one who could beat you would be a Guardian with a metal ability."

Mason grunted. Then, he changed the subject. "This spy stuff is all the more reason to break into Ernest's house as soon as possible," he said quietly as he looked over the work he'd done on Helena's sword. "On top of stealing back the wand he's using to hurt Guardians, we might be able to find out who else in this castle is reporting the Moonlit Army. Especially with Felix's psychometry."

"But how are we supposed to keep him from knowing we're in his house?" Felix asked.

"I know I can figure out the masking spell." Mason glanced at the stack of books next to him. "I'll need a few things, though."

"Okay, hold on," Arisa said. "I'm all for this—"

"You are?" Felix asked.

"Yes. But we still don't know where he lives."

"No, but Sebastian and the other Guardians do." Mason stared off into the distance. "There has to be some way to get that information."

Felix glanced at Arisa. "Okay, Mason wants the wand and revenge on the guy who killed his parents. And Ernest is working with the people responsible for my family's deaths, too," he said. "I'm willing to risk going after him. But, Arisa, are you sure you want to do this? You have the least to gain." *And the most to lose.*

"Yeah, Felix and I are new here," Mason said. "If the council turns on us and we lose our place, it won't be nearly as bad as you losing your home."

"That's exactly why I have to do this," Arisa replied. "I've spent my whole life here. I'm not going to let it fall into the hands of this Mira lady and her army." She lifted her chin. "Plus, Ernest robbed my friend and killed his parents, and Gideon killed my other friend's family. I'm not letting them get away with it."

The light glinted off something in the air in front of Felix. He reached out and swatted the thread of spider silk away from his face. "I know Hana would probably disapprove of us doing this, but do you think there's any chance she'd be willing to help?"

"I wouldn't risk asking," Arisa said. "Even if we convinced her that Ernest needs to be dealt with, she'd want us to stay out of it."

Felix nodded slowly. "Mason, you mentioned needing things for the spell?"

"My wand isn't anywhere near as powerful as the Ironwood Wand," Mason said. "If I want to hide all three of us, I'll need a few other things to boost the spell. A couple of crystals, ash, and bone shards from an animal. Only certain animals will work, and the ash has to have been formed by burning wood in a ritual." A faraway look entered his gaze. "We'll need to go to a witch shop to get those."

"Are witch shops common?" Arisa asked.

"Common enough. I know where a few are near Seattle, and I know how to find them anywhere else," Mason replied. "There's just one problem. Witch shops are warded. Now that I'm a demon, I won't be able to go inside. You two will need to pick up what I need."

"Will we need to sneak out?" Felix asked. "To go to a witch shop?"

"I don't think that will be hard." Arisa absentmindedly fiddled with one of her bracelets. "Most of the castle security is focused on keeping enemies out."

"Then how would we get back in?" Mason asked. "If a Guardian doesn't accompany me through the wards, I won't be able to get through."

"Then you could stay, and Felix and I will go."

"What if we waited for another field trip?" Felix suggested. He feared that if they screwed up trying to sneak out for witch supplies, they'd be so intensely supervised afterward that they wouldn't have a prayer of getting to Earnest's. "I bet we could convince Sebastian to let us stop for souvenirs somewhere."

"That might work," Arisa said. "Or I could come up with an excuse to get Hana to take me into town."

Mason leaned back in his chair. "Even if we get the supplies I need, we still need to find a way out of the castle and to Ernest's house."

Arisa pursed her lips. "Allegedly, there are secret tunnels that lead out of the castle underground. I think they connect to the interior passages somewhere." She sighed. "But they're probably guarded."

Interest flickered across Mason's face. "It could be worth taking a look, though."

"True." Arisa grinned. "It's been too long since I went exploring, anyway."

With most of the castle occupied with training and classes, and plenty of Guardians out on missions, they decided that now was as good a time as any to see if the tunnels offered any way out of the Brightlands. Arisa led them to a kitchen tucked away in the northeast corner of the first floor and through a false wall at the back of the pantry.

"How do you know about all of these secret doors?" Felix asked.

"I spent a lot of time exploring as a kid."

The tunnel they entered led them in a circle around the outer edge of the castle. Every door they passed led either up or deeper toward the center of the castle. Other than that, the place was all dust and cobwebs.

After their third loop through the tunnel, Arisa kicked the wall in frustration. "This is ridiculous!" she exclaimed. "I know I read somewhere that there's another layer of tunnels below us."

"Maybe they can only be accessed through the basement," Felix suggested.

Arisa shook her head. "I've searched the basement before. There's not much in there. I thought this tunnel would be the best place to search for a connection, but—"

"There's something below us," Mason interrupted.

"Huh?"

Mason pointed to the ground. "There's a faint level of magical energy coming from below." He walked past Felix and Arisa and continued down the tunnel. After exchanging confused glances, they followed him.

He stopped in the corner where the hallway they stood in met the next. "It's stronger here," he said. "There might be an opening nearby."

The three ran their hands along the walls and floor. After a couple minutes of searching, Felix found a loose piece of stone in the floor. "Here!" he called. Mason and Arisa moved to stand over him as he pulled at it. Nothing happened.

"Move back," Mason said. He pulled his wand from the pocket of his sweatshirt and pointed it at the stone. "Lift."

The stone lifted two inches before stopping with a click. A gap opened in the floor nearby, stretching from wall to wall. Arisa knelt next to it and pressed her hands to the edge of the rift. The section of floor slid forward with surprising ease, revealing a set of stairs that led down into darkness.

Mason illuminated the way with a purple glow at the tip of his wand. When the three stepped off the stairs into another hallway, the light reflected off something thin hanging from the ceiling. Felix frowned as they reached it.

"Is it string?" Arisa asked.

Felix tapped it. It was hard to pull his finger off. "It's sticky." As he stepped back, he realized he'd backed into more threads crisscrossing through the hallway. Where had those come from?

"Don't touch it, genius," Mason said. "It might be some kind of trap—"

Too late. Something invisible wrapped around Felix, pinning his arms to the side of his body. As he struggled against it, he realized it wasn't invisible at all. More threads wrapped around him. "I'm stuck," he said, panic creeping into his voice.

"Me too!" Arisa tried to yank her arm away from the web of strings she'd backed into, but it was no use. They thickened around her. Next to her, Mason faced a similar fate. One by one, they were all plucked off the ground and left hanging from the ceiling.

"We're going to die," Arisa groaned.

Mason rolled his eyes. "No, we're not."

Felix spun slowly, turning away from the others. "I can feel my blood draining into my head," he said.

"You're not even upside down!" Mason exclaimed.

"I'm sideways!"

"That's not the same!"

"No, he's right," Arisa said. "I feel it too. We're going to pass out, and then we're going to die."

"Do you think the spiders will eat us?" Felix asked as a black one crawled up the wall in front of him. Maybe his eyes were playing tricks on him, but he swore it was at least the size of a rat.

"Spiders don't eat people, right?" Arisa asked.

"I don't know, this one's really big."

Arisa's voice rose with alarm. "There's one here?"

"Would you two please calm down?" Hellfire engulfed Mason's body, burning away the threads. He dropped to the ground. "I swear, it's like you two share the same brain cell."

A woman's voice rang out farther down the corridor. "What are you three doing down here?" She spoke the words with a French accent.

Felix twisted his body in the air, trying to rotate himself so that he could see the source of the voice. Footsteps echoed through the tunnel as the woman approached.

She stopped just inside his field of view. She wore a black Guardian uniform with the jacket zipped all the way up to the high collar. Straight, dark red hair fell to her waist. She folded her arms and sized the three up.

"Who are you?" Mason asked.

Two more arms emerged from behind the woman's back. They weren't covered by sleeves, but she did wear black fingerless gloves on her second set of hands. She gestured with them as she spoke. "I'm Adrienne. Head of security. I'm responsible for everything that comes in and out of Bright Castle, so I'll ask you again: What are you three doing down here?"

"Uh, exploring?" Felix tried. He still couldn't quite believe what he was seeing.

"Yeah," Arisa said. "That."

They both looked at Mason, who shrugged. "I was looking for a bathroom."

Adrienne's second set of arms rested on her hips. "You three are the kids on probation, aren't you?"

"You know, we didn't technically do anything wrong," Felix said. "They should come up with a better word to use."

"Why did you come down here?" Adrienne pressed. "If you don't cooperate, I'll have no choice but to hand you over to the council."

"Seriously," Arisa said, her voice panicky again. "We were just exploring. No need to get the council involved."

"Real answer, please." One of Adrienne's hands moved to her pocket to pull out a phone. "The king always answers when I call." Her thumb hovered over the screen.

"We know that one of the Bright Guardians is secretly working for the Uprising," Felix blurted.

"Felix!" Mason hissed.

"Look, if we don't tell her, we're definitely screwed," Felix shot back. "If we do, we have like a fifty-fifty chance at getting out of this. Maybe."

"Your friend is right," Adrienne said.

"She is head of security," Arisa added reluctantly. "I think we can trust her."

Hopefully. Felix continued. "Ernest Abernathy is helping the Uprising, and he stole a powerful witch's wand. We have a plan to steal it back. We were looking for a way to sneak out of the castle when the time comes."

"And what was your plan from there?" Adrienne asked, gesturing with her phone. "You thought you'd be able to walk into a Guardian's house, steal a powerful artifact, and walk out?"

"It's a work in progress," Arisa said.

Adrienne's brow furrowed. "And you're certain he's with the Uprising?"

"Yeah," Felix replied. "He pretty much told us himself."

"And I have to get that wand back," Mason added. "It belonged to my parents. Ernest killed them for it!"

Adrienne's first set of arms unfolded. The webbing clinging to Felix released its grip. He dropped to the ground, and Arisa landed next to him.

The second set of arms disappeared as Adrienne turned around to face the opposite wall. An opening in the back of her jacket stretched from just below the collar to midway down her back, but there was no sign of the extra arms after they vanished.

"This is concerning," Adrienne said. "You haven't told anyone else?"

Felix brushed some stray pieces of webbing off his jacket. "We...were told not to."

"By your teacher, I assume? Armitage?" Adrienne glanced back over her shoulder.

"Everyone always guesses him," Felix muttered. "But yeah, he said if we went around talking about it, it could be harder to figure out who else is a spy."

"He is right about that." Adrienne paused. "Do you trust him?"

Felix thought back to the fight with the werewolves. To Sebastian, injured and bleeding, tearing them apart to save his students. "I trust him to keep us safe."

"And the other Guardians you've worked with?"

"I'm...not sure." Felix glanced at the others. Mason shrugged. Arisa looked lost in thought. "I want to," he said.

Adrienne turned back around. A thread of webbing descended from the ceiling, lowering a white mug into the air next to her. She grabbed the handle and took a sip. "Would any of you like tea?"

"I'm good," Felix said.

"I'll pass," Mason added.

Arisa shook her head. "No thank you."

Adrienne took another sip. "I follow most of what happens in the council. You don't see me at meetings, but I watch every one. If there are spies, they've been very good at conducting their business somewhere I don't have eyes." As if on cue, a large silver tarantula crawled onto her shoulder.

Felix restrained a shudder. "Are your abilities like Kendra's, but with spiders?" he asked.

"Kendra Ford?" Adrienne shrugged. "Sort of. We have parallel abilities. Like Sebastian and Hana Tamura. Or the members of your family who wield elements."

"So, you can do the same things with your power?"

"Parallel abilities can be shaped in wildly different ways. It all depends on the magician," Adrienne explained. "Sebastian and Hana fight with completely different techniques. The amount of power you build up as you grow and train also affects what you can do."

Mason cleared his throat. "Adrienne, if you care so much about castle security, you should let us go to Ernest's house," he said. "We have a plan. I'm working on a spell to mask our magical energy, and—"

"But you still don't know his location," Adrienne cut him off. "Or anything about his security. I imagine he'll have wards to prevent demons from setting foot on his property, let alone getting inside."

"There are ways to destroy wards. I'm a witch, too."

"Will you be able to do that without drawing attention to yourself?"

Mason's lack of response answered for him.

A third arm appeared and pressed its closed hand to Adrienne's chin. She thought for a moment. "I think we all assumed that everyone who wanted to overthrow King Atticus left with the Uprising. If he and his council believe otherwise, they've kept quiet about it."

"Did you really think everyone in the castle was an ally this entire time?" Mason asked.

"I can't say I put my blind trust in everyone," Adrienne replied. "But I have yet to see anything that leads me to be suspicious of any particular person."

Felix frowned. "But if you have eyes and ears everywhere, wouldn't you have overheard something between spies at some point?"

"They would undoubtedly be smart enough not to conduct that kind of business here at the castle. Most Guardians know what I'm capable of."

"Ernest has cousins on the council, doesn't he?" Mason asked. "Do you think they could be with the Uprising, too?"

"I've always been under the impression he values them more for their status, not out of deep love for his own family," Adrienne said. "There's no reason to assume the bond between them is strong. If he turns on the king, it's not a stretch to believe he'd turn on them, too." She shook her head. "This isn't something you kids should be concerning yourself with. There's nothing you can do."

"There has to be," Mason protested. "Ernest tried to kill us!"

"You'll be safe as long as you're in the castle. I'll keep an eye on you when you're not in your rooms, and I'll keep an eye out for any information on the Uprising." Adrienne dismissed them with a wave of her hand. "Now, get back to the surface, where you belong."

"Are you going to tell someone we were down here?" Felix asked.

"As long as you stay out of trouble, this will stay between us. For now."

Felix, Mason, and Arisa reluctantly trudged back up to the main halls of the castle. Mason's tail had appeared at some point, and it twitched behind him as he walked. Arisa jumped at every sound and distant voice.

"Now what?" Felix finally asked.

"I don't know," Arisa said. "But we'd better hope no one comes to drag us in front of the council."

"Adrienne said she wouldn't tell anyone."

"Sebastian told us not to tell anyone about Ernest for a reason. If she's actually on the Uprising's side, we could have just signed our own death sentences."

"If we hadn't, we'd be in trouble with the council right now, anyway."

"I don't think she's with the Uprising," Mason said confidently. He blew out a harsh breath of air. "But she's still an obstacle between us and getting to Ernest."

"Dude, one of her spiders might be listening right now," Felix reminded him.

"I'm not saying I'm going to try to sneak past her," Mason said, shooting him a glance. "I'm just saying that I'm getting real tired of people telling us not to worry about the guy who killed my parents!"

Felix winced. Was he supposed to be as angry about Gideon as Mason was with Ernest? To be fair, Gideon was dead—sort of—so Felix couldn't do much on that front.

But his leader was still out there, somewhere. And Felix had agreed to sit around and train to fight random monsters instead of going after her.

Chapter Twenty-Three
Party Planning

Heavy rain the next day forced Felix and the others to carry out training in an indoor gym on the fourth floor. Arisa's anxiety about getting into trouble had passed, but Mason was still on edge. His thoughts were clearly elsewhere as he and Felix ran through a few practice matches. Felix actually managed to beat him in the second one, but Mason came back more aggressive in the third.

"Whoa!" Felix jumped to the side to dodge one of Mason's fireballs. He barely stopped himself from stepping out of the box. "Uh, that one was pretty big."

"This is a waste of time," Mason stormed out of the rectangle, but Felix had a feeling he shouldn't count it as a victory. "I don't need to control my demon powers. I need to get the wand back and figure out how to turn myself back into a human."

Felix frowned. "I didn't realize you were trying to do that. Is that possible?"

"It might be, with the Ironwood Wand."

Arisa looked up from where she was playing a game of cards with Clementine. "We could try bothering Sebastian again when he gets back. Maybe if we tell him Mason's figured out the energy masking spell, he'll be more open to helping us break into Ernest's house before the party."

"I didn't want to tell him about the energy masking spell because I didn't want him knowing we were planning to sneak out." Mason sighed. "But I guess since we don't have a chance of getting past Adrienne, trying to convince him to take us might be our best bet. I don't like our odds, though."

The gym door opened and Sebastian entered, sliding his phone into his pocket. "Sorry, that call went longer than expected. How's it going in here?" He looked around the gym. "Arisa, I thought you were practicing those new banishing sigils Mason showed us."

Arisa held up one of the cards she was holding and pointed to the sigil she'd drawn on the back.

"Alrighty," Sebastian said. "Well, I have news. You all have permission to go to the student party."

"Student party?" Felix asked.

Arisa groaned. "Seb, do we really seem like the kind of kids who want to go to one of those parties?"

Felix frowned. "I want to go to a part—"

Mason clapped a hand over Felix's mouth and glowered at Sebastian. "What the hell is a student party?"

"Oh, they're pretty standard when a lot of Guardians are going off to an event," Sebastian explained. "Since so many parents and teachers will be at Abernathy's birthday, the students get to have the ballroom to throw their own party."

"They're not as fun as they sound," Arisa said, glowering. "There are still Guardians here at the castle supervising. It's basically a high school dance."

Sebastian shrugged. "Well, if you change your mind, you have permission to go."

"How about you take us to Ernest's party, instead?" Mason tried. "I have the energy masking spell figured out. We could move around his house without anyone being able to sense that we're there."

"I'm sure you could pull the spell off, but it's still too risky," Sebastian replied, shaking his head. "Ernest wants you dead, and if he catches you at the party, he'll find a way to make it happen."

"What if he tries something with the wand?" Mason asked. "He's not going to sit around with it forever. He obviously intends to use it against the Brightlands."

"That's probably true, but he's not going to do anything at a party where he's outnumbered by Guardians. The entire council is going to be there."

"What about the king?" Felix asked.

"Oh, no, the king never goes to things like this," Sebastian said. "He'll probably hang out in that gloomy office of his and come up with new ways to waste our tax money."

"Guardians pay taxes?"

"Well, I don't."

"Doesn't that technically count as treason here?" Arisa asked.

"Yeah, don't tell anyone I said that."

Felix couldn't have cared less about magical tax evasion. "Is Archer going to the party?"

"He is," Sebastian answered. "But I'm guessing he'll stand in a corner and glare at everyone the whole time. That's how it usually goes, anyway."

Mason had yet to give up on trying to convince Sebastian to take them. "There might be a lot of Guardians at the party, but any number of them could be spies. If Ernest has enough people on his side, he might decide to fight."

"Oh, he won't win," Sebastian said. "Not if I'm there."

"You sound confident."

"I have good reason to be. You still haven't really seen me fight."

"What are you talking about?" Felix asked. "We saw you fight those werewolves."

"That wasn't a fight, that was me killing a pack of werewolves."

"I don't know," Mason said skeptically. "The wolves did do some damage."

"They were Supermoon Wolves, and they took me by surprise." Sebastian's gaze moved to the window and the rain falling outside. "It won't happen again."

"Even if you can handle a fight with Ernest, why not let us help?" Arisa asked.

"You don't have enough experience to take on a Guardian."

"We fought demons!"

"Archer had to save you."

Mason folded his arms. "We did well against the wolves, considering how strong they were."

"Yeah, but we still would have died without Sebastian," Felix muttered.

"I trapped a poltergeist on my own," Arisa said.

"Oh yeah." Felix perked up a little at that reminder. "And I helped!"

"Not really."

Sebastian held up a hand. "Listen, you all have the potential to take on someone as powerful as Ernest Abernathy—"

Felix and Arisa's faces lit up. Even Mason's eyes widened a little.

"—someday," Sebastian finished. "Today is not that day, and I have a feeling two weeks from now won't be, either."

Mason's hands tightened at his sides. "Promise me you'll at least get the wand. This is your best chance, since he's inviting you in."

"I'll do my best. And if I fail, I won't rest until I've helped you get it back." Sebastian moved his hand to his chest. "Promise."

Mason looked skeptical. "How do I know I can trust you?"

"Even if you can't trust me, trust that the Bright Guardians as a whole will stop Ernest." Sebastian's expression darkened. "Turns out we're not the only victims of his energy masking spells. More and more Guardians have been reporting that their missions have turned out to be far more dangerous than they were supposed to."

"Has anyone died?" Felix asked.

"You don't need to worry about the details," Sebastian said. Felix had a feeling that meant the answer was yes.

"That's all the more reason to take action now," Mason said.

"It's all the more reason to be careful," Sebastian countered. "But I will put all of my focus at the party into finding the wand and coming up with a way to deal with Ernest."

"Fine," Mason said after a long moment. "We'll leave it to you. For now."

When they left the gym at the end of the training session, Felix fell into step at Mason's right. "So, it sounds like we're staying here during the party? I'm surprised you gave in, after all that."

"Me too," Arisa added.

Mason's gaze darted around the hallway. His voice dropped to barely more than a whisper. "I haven't given up yet," he said. "I don't know how we'll avoid the spiders or get to Ernest's, but I did realize one thing: the energy masking spell can hide us from Adrienne, too."

Chapter Twenty-Four
Soul Sweet Soul

In the week that followed, Mason didn't say a word about his plans to get the wand back from Ernest, despite his insistence that he wasn't giving up. Felix was dying to know what he was planning, but he had bigger things to worry about. Every time he felt he was really starting to master one of his family's abilities, Sebastian would throw a new challenge at him that made him feel like a beginner all over again.

It only added to his stress when Archer, Kendra, Hana, and a few Guardians Felix didn't know the names of showed up at a training session one afternoon. Archer insisted it wasn't an official assessment, simply a check on Felix's progress, but Felix still felt the way he did when he walked into a test he hadn't studied for.

"Ready?" Sebastian asked.

Right. Time to focus. Felix lifted his hands and adjusted his stance. "Ready."

Sebastian nodded at Arisa. "Go ahead."

"Remember, they'll be harder to destroy because they're imbued with magic," Arisa warned. The tiny garden statues

Sebastian had picked up at a hardware store came to life. A gnome, a plastic flamingo, and a stone rabbit launched themselves at Felix.

Felix torched the flamingo first. Its plastic body began to melt, but it continued its approach. Felix jumped out of its way and fired a blast of flame at the gnome. The fire barely left a mark. He switched to Helena's lightning and hit the gnome with a blast that completely shattered it.

A vine burst from the ground and wrapped around the flamingo. Thorns popped out and sank into the plastic. While the flamingo was pulled into the dirt, Felix turned in a circle, searching for the stone rabbit.

It tackled his calf with enough force to send him toppling over. He flung his hands up in front of his face as he landed on his back. The rabbit sprang at him with outstretched paws, aiming for his chest. Felix sent a burst of electricity at the rabbit to fling it backwards.

"You don't have much power behind your fire," Sebastian noted as Felix sat up.

"What do you mean?" Felix asked. "It's fire." The rabbit jumped at him again. He summoned a vine from the dirt. The vine wrapped around the rabbit and slammed it against the ground.

"It feels weaker than your other abilities. Like there's not as much energy going into it." Sebastian shrugged. "It's not that big of a deal. It will probably strengthen over time. Let's work on May's ability."

Felix groaned. "I hate using that one. When is it ever going to be useful?"

I saved your ass from those demons, remember? May chimed in.

"I don't like turning into water. And why would I do that when I can throw fire or lightning at something?"

"You might be in a situation where you have stone, but not metal," Sebastian said.

"Okay, slim chance, but sure." Felix climbed to his feet. "Water's still weaker, most of the time."

"You'd be surprised. Don't underestimate it. Especially holy water." Sebastian lifted his fists. "Here, give it a try against me in combat." Lowering his voice so that Archer and the other Guardians couldn't hear, he asked, "How much have you used it without May being in control?"

Felix couldn't keep his surprise off his face. "How did you—?" He hadn't told anyone besides Mason or Arisa about the possession thing, still terrified he'd be locked up.

"I suspected it could be a possibility from the start. You described using May's ability in the fight against the demons, but when we first tried it in training you could barely move," Sebastian replied. "Then there was that tree Ezra grew in the clearing with the wolves, which was far beyond anything else you did with his ability—"

"What's going on?" Archer asked.

Sebastian shot him a glance. "Just a moment." His eyes moved back to Felix. His hands lowered. "We often use more power in a life-or-death situation than we do in training, but that doesn't give us a miraculous level of control over our abilities."

"Okay, yeah," Felix conceded quietly. "May took over at the office building, and I asked Ezra to control me in the clearing."

"Did your dad project the memories in Mason's dagger for you at the council meeting, too?" Sebastian asked.

Felix shook his head. "I wanted him to, but he made me do it myself."

"Really?" Sebastian lifted an eyebrow. "That's impressive. Good job."

"Thanks."

"I'm glad he had you do it alone. You need to learn to control these abilities yourself." Sebastian's fists moved back up into the air. "Better to figure it out now while you're in training, and not in the middle of a fight with monsters that want you dead."

"Fine." Felix closed his eyes, took a deep breath, and...

Nothing.

Felix opened one eye. "May?"

Oh, what, you want my ability? I thought it was stupid.

"May, come on!"

Here's an idea: Let me use the ability, if you have such a problem with it. I'll totally kick Sebastian's ass.

Felix laughed. "No way."

I'm serious!

Felix replied in his head so that Sebastian couldn't hear him. *Fine. Do it. I'm going to laugh when you fail.*

Sure. I mean, it's your body. May's presence expanded from his mind to take over his entire body. Before Felix could adjust to his loss of control, he turned to water.

May whipped around the combat box with surprising speed. For a minute or so, Sebastian effortlessly dodged her as she twisted into a whip and attempted to strike him in the face. When he switched to delivering blows of his own, she avoided them with surprising ease. Until his hand cut up through the air from below and punched a hole through the center of the water mass.

Felix landed on his back, his form now solid. He was in control of his body again, but the air had been knocked from his lungs.

Sebastian dropped to one knee next to him. "Very impressive, but you weren't in control." He said, his voice low. "I'm not testing your sister's skill, I'm testing yours."

Felix felt May beam. *He thinks I'm impressive—*

Shut up, Felix shot back. *I'm the student here, not you.* He climbed to his feet. Quietly, he said, "I don't see why I can't just let her possess me in a fight—"

"It takes extra energy to maintain their presence, doesn't it?" Sebastian asked. "It's a waste of power you could otherwise be using to fuel your magic. Plus, we still have Gideon to worry about."

"All right. I'll try doing it myself." Felix took a deep breath and willed himself to melt back into a puddle of water. He tried lifting himself off the ground, but his new body refused to cooperate.

Hey, Felix, here's a tip, May said. *Stop trying to move the water like you would your body.*

Huh? Felix thought back.

You keep trying to move sections of water like they're arms and legs. They're not. You're one complete unit, so act like it.

Felix forced himself to relax. For a moment, he let himself feel every drop of water, taking it all in as one continuous mass.

He lifted himself into a shaky pillar. After a few seconds of struggling, he collapsed back into a puddle. He transformed back into his own body. How the hell did May zip through the air the way she did?

"That was great!" Sebastian said, despite the fact that Felix was lying on his back, drenched in water, and gasping for air.

"Really?" Felix wheezed as he sat up. "I didn't even come close to attacking you that time."

"Guardians who have the ability to transform into elements like that take a long time just to learn to control their body, let alone wield it in combat," Sebastian told him. "That pillar was a good start."

"What's he doing now?" Archer called. "That's nothing like how he was fighting a minute ago."

"We're, uh, trying a different technique," Sebastian replied.

Felix rested a hand against May's stone in his pocket.

Mason looked up from the book he was reading. "Does the amount of channeling material present affect his ability to wield an element?"

"Good question," Sebastian said. "No, more material doesn't increase the amount of magical energy he can draw from his body, though you do need a minimum amount of the material for the channeling to work."

"But there is a way to draw ambient magical energy to you through your channeling material, isn't there?" Arisa asked. "I swear one of my old teachers said they did that once."

"Yes, it's possible, but it takes years of experience to do right. And it's dangerous," Sebastian said. "Not recommended unless you're completely out options. It typically damages or breaks the channel material, and that can get explosive fast. Not to mention that you wouldn't be able to channel your ability if the material you're using is destroyed."

"Interesting." Mason glanced down at his book and turned the page. "There are similar principles with spellwork. You can generate more power, but it results in your ritual tools breaking."

Sebastian nodded. "Well, good job today, Felix."

Felix smiled as he stood up. "Thanks."

His sense of accomplishment was short-lived. Sebastian clapped a hand against his shoulder and added, "Keep this training up every day for a few years, and you'll make a great Guardian."

"Years?"

Sebastian ignored the despair in Felix's voice. "That's all for today," he announced. The Guardians who'd been watching dispersed. Felix moved to join Arisa and Mason as they headed inside. Dinner sounded like the best thing in the world right now.

Archer appeared at Felix's right and held out a hand to stop him from following the others through the door. "Sebastian's doing a fine job training you."

Felix swallowed. "Uh huh?"

"But I'd like to give you some advice of my own," Archer continued. "Meet me out in front of the castle after dinner."

It didn't sound like there was room to argue. Felix nodded. "Sure."

He caught up to a confused Mason and Arisa and explained. Their confusion turned to concern, and they debated what Archer might want with him as they headed toward the dining hall.

"There's probably only a fifty-fifty chance he's going to kill me, right?" Felix asked as they stepped into the dining hall line.

"He's not going to kill you," Arisa assured him.

"We don't know that," Mason muttered as he began loading his tray with nothing but desserts.

"If he does want to train you, though, you might get a little roughed up."

Felix groaned. "I'm already exhausted. All the time. I just want a nap."

Sleep would have to wait. Felix ate his food as slowly as possible, but when he spotted Archer standing at the dining hall entrance and scowling, he jumped to his feet and quickly dumped his tray. Archer vanished as quickly as he'd appeared, leaving Felix to wander to the front of the castle by himself.

"Your fire comes from your mother, correct?" Archer asked the moment Felix stepped outside.

Felix jumped. "Uh, yeah."

"Follow me."

They walked to the top of a nearby hill and stopped in the long shadows cast by the trees around them. The setting sun turned the sky a deep orange and cast a dramatic glow over the thick clouds passing by overhead.

"Is the sun...actually the sun?" Felix asked as he stared in its direction. "You know, since we're in a pocket dimension?"

"Yes. The sky overhead is essentially a portal to the real sky over Washington," Archer explained. He turned to face Felix. "You speak to your family regularly?"

Felix nodded.

"But you haven't had any interaction with Gideon?"

"There's still no sign of him, except that my family said they can sense his presence sometimes," Felix said. "I'm pretty sure as long as I don't tap into his power, he'll stay unconscious in my blood or soul or whatever."

Archer drew his sword, taking Felix by surprise. Felix hadn't even realized the weapon had been at Archer's back. "We're going to try something," Archer said. "Instead of pulling your family out of your soul, we're going to send you in."

"Huh?"

"With enough focus, it's possible for a Guardian to enter their own soul, similar to how you would a dream."

"Oh, I remember my dad saying something about that," Felix said. "But how do I do it?"

"The most common way is meditation—" Archer started.

"Yeah, I don't think I'd be very good at that."

Archer's eyes narrowed.

Felix winced. "Uh, but I mean, I guess I could try—"

"We're going to do something quicker." Archer peeled off one of his gloves. "I'm going to poison you."

"Wh—what?"

"It's completely safe. I can remove the poison at any time, and this one doesn't have any permanent effects." Archer rested the blade of his sword against his palm. "But it will induce a level of unconsciousness that will drive you into your soul."

"How long will I be in there?" Felix asked.

"I'll pull you back out in twenty minutes, no matter what. But time might pass differently for you in there."

Felix's brow furrowed. "And what exactly am I trying to do?"

"Assess your connections to your family's abilities. Particularly your mother's fire." Dark purple liquid welled on Archer's skin. "Hold out your arm."

Felix pulled up his sleeve and stuck his arm out. Archer placed his palm on Felix's wrist. "It will enter your blood through your skin," he explained. "It only needs a few seconds to take effect—"

Felix opened his eyes in a black void. He turned around. "Hello?"

Scenery materialized around him. Grass, a wooden fence, a patio, his house...he was in his backyard. He hadn't been out here since before the day Gideon attacked. He turned in a slow circle, taking it all in.

"Felix?"

Felix spun. His Mom stood at the back door. He blinked, hardly able to believe the sight. It only took a moment for him to unfreeze. "Mom!" He ran to her and threw his arms around her.

They lingered in the embrace for a moment before Mom pulled back. She smiled at Felix, but there was confusion in her gaze. "What are you doing in here?"

"I guess I'm here to talk to you." Felix rubbed the back of his neck. "About your fire ability."

"Let's sit down." Mom moved to the patio table and pulled out a chair.

Felix slid into the chair next to her. "Where is everyone else?"

"Inside the house, if they're conscious right now," Mom said. "It's not uncommon for the soul to take on the shape of someone's home."

"Can you go into your own soul?" Felix asked.

"I could when I was alive, but now my soul is all that I am." Mom rested a hand on Felix's. "How is your training going? I watch when I can, but I didn't see today's session."

"It went pretty well. But I'm having a hard time putting a lot of power into my fire," Felix told her. Now that he thought about it, he was pretty sure it had been stronger the first couple of times he'd used it than it was now. What had happened?

Mom frowned. "I don't know why that would be."

"Me neither." Felix looked down at the table. "I mean, it's not like you're keeping it from me on purpose like May was."

"What was May doing?" Her tone sharpened.

Felix glanced up. "Oh, uh, it was just for like a minute during training. It wasn't really that big of a deal—"

Mom turned her head back toward the house. "May Eleanor Carver, don't take your ability away from Felix, he needs it!"

May's voice called back faintly. "I didn't!"

"Yes you did!" Felix yelled back.

"Shut up!"

"There's more to controlling the fire than you think," Mom said, her attention moving back to Felix. "The thing about Helena's electricity is that once you let go of it, it dissipates. My fire can keep moving and spreading and burning. You have to be careful."

Something clicked. Felix's eyes widened. "I think you are holding back the fire. You're scared."

"I promise I'm not trying to keep it away from you," Mom told him. "And I am scared for you. But that's why I'm glad you can use our abilities to protect yourself."

"I don't think you're doing it on purpose," Felix replied. "Now that I know how magic feels, though, I think I lost some of my power after I burned myself and Arisa in training. I know I had full access to it when I first started." He pulled his hand from Mom's to stare at the spot where the burn had been. "I haven't thought about it much since it healed. But—"

"That did scare me," Mom murmured.

"You can't protect me from myself," Felix said. "I have to learn to control it at full strength."

Mom's shoulders sagged. "Okay. I'll try to relax my hold on the fire, and we'll see if that helps." She rose to her feet and gave Felix a sad smile. "You should try coming in here more often. It would be nice for us all to be together again."

Felix nodded. It took him a moment to speak. "I will," he promised. Rising to his feet, he added, "But before I go, we need to talk about...everything else."

Mom frowned. "Is everything okay?"

"I don't know what to do about anything!" Felix blurted. "Sebastian thinks there are Moonlit Army spies at the castle, and Ernest Abernathy wants us dead, and I don't know how to focus on learning to kill monsters when I have no idea who to trust."

Mom let out a heavy sigh and pulled Felix in for another hug. "I was hoping you'd have more time before you had to worry about all this," she told him. "We know bits and pieces of what's going on. We weren't very active Guardians, but we were aware of the growing concerns around the Uprising and their possible return."

Felix tightened his arms around her. "Why did Gideon kill you, then?"

"Because..." Mom hesitated. "We were guarding something that might powerful enough to defeat the Moonlit Army. It was supposed to be a secret, but we had to get help containing it, so there was always a chance that word would spread."

That sparked something in Felix's memory. May had said something...what was it? *We thought we'd have time to tell you what we were protecting.*

"What were you protecting?" Felix asked.

"It's safe, for now. You don't need to worry about it," Mom said quickly. "Gideon thought we were keeping it at the house, but he was wrong. It's somewhere his leader will never be able to find it."

Felix pulled back from her. His stinging eyes met hers. "Tell me!"

"It's too dangerous to give you that information right now." Mom placed a hand on Felix's shoulder and gave him a sad smile. "For now, you need to focus on becoming strong."

Felix wanted to plead for more information, to know what his family had died for, but then his house was gone and the yard was gone and Mom was fading into the darkness. His eyes opened.

"How do you feel?" Archer asked.

Felix was lying on his back in the grass, looking up at the darkening clouds. His senses gradually returned to him. "A little groggy," he said as he sat up. There was no pain, though, so he suspected Archer had caught him and laid him down gently rather than letting him fall.

Archer nodded. "That should pass in a few minutes."

"I talked to my mom." Felix rose to his feet. "I think I can do it now."

Archer lifted his sword and took a step back. "Let's see it, then."

Felix started by summoning a small fireball. It was a good thing he started small, because it came out three times the size he expected. Archer sidestepped and stuck out his sword to stop the fireball before it could scorch a tree. Then, he brought the sword in a slow arc toward Felix's face.

Felix threw up his hand and pressed it against the flat side of the blade, pushing it back, intending to summon electricity and send it down the blade at Archer. As his hand made contact with the metal, though, a heaviness washed over him. The weight of its memory. The last thing he saw was the evening sunlight shining off the red metal rose on the pommel. Darkness swallowed him.

In the void, a younger version of Archer stood in the distance. He had his black hair pulled up the same way he usually kept it, but there was no mask hiding his face. His sword hung at his back.

A familiar man stepped out of the darkness. "Ready to lose?" he asked. It was the necromancer, Felix realized. His face was free of scars, and he wore a Guardian uniform with a shirt the same bone white as his curls of hair. A rectangle took shape on the ground around them, not made from Sebastian's light, but from ordinary yellow spray paint.

Archer drew his sword from the scabbard on his back. "We'll see."

The memory changed. The sword cut through the chest of a different man in a Guardian's uniform. He dropped to the ground, and more bodies appeared around him, lying around Archer's feet. Before Felix could look at Archer's face, the scene shifted again.

A girl lay dead on the ground. Short auburn hair the same shade as King Atticus's fell over her face. Then she was upright, facing Archer, but she hovered in the air above him, her form semi-transparent.

The flashes came faster. Felix glimpsed a woman with long waves of silvery-white hair standing under a full moon in a tattered blue gown. A younger version of King Atticus lifting his crown to his head. Young Sebastian, laughing, suddenly standing right next to Archer—

Felix pulled himself free from the memory and staggered back, away from Archer.

"Is something wrong?" Archer asked.

It took a moment for Felix to recall what was happening in the present. He forced his mind to focus. "Yeah, I just...don't want to set anything on fire. I don't know if fighting out here by the trees is a good idea."

Archer lowered his weapon. "Okay. I don't want you throwing fire around if you're nervous. You can work on controlling it with Sebastian tomorrow." After a long moment, he added, "Good job."

Praise? From Archer? That was new. It was hard for Felix to appreciate it, though, being as rattled as he was.

Felix glanced back at the spot on the grass where he'd been laying. "So, I can go into my soul on my own?"

"Yes, but it takes a lot of practice. It's difficult even for experienced Guardians," Archer said. He started back toward the castle, and Felix followed. "It's usually used to deal with power blocks, like you just did, or to refine dangerous techniques in a safe environment."

Felix understood the gist of it, but he couldn't help but wonder how safe an environment his soul truly was.

What would Gideon be capable of if he awoke?

Chapter Twenty-Five
Third Time's the Charm

On a particularly hot evening the week before Ernest's party, Felix, Mason, and Arisa walked into the library. "Thank god Hana keeps this place cool," Arisa said. "I swear, it's like half the Guardians forget that fans exist."

Mason's gaze darted around the first floor. "Where is she, anyway?"

"Relax." Arisa stopped next to the front desk. "She's bound to be around here somewhere—"

Hana stepped out of a shadow and placed a hand on Arisa's shoulder. Arisa whirled around. "Hey, Hana," she signed.

"How are you three?" Hana asked.

Arisa was barely able to sign, "Good, you?" before Mason nudged her in the side. Arisa rolled her eyes. "Be patient," she said out loud, turning her head toward Mason so that Hana couldn't see her lips. "I'm trying to act casual."

Felix leaned toward Mason. "Arisa has a point. You won't get far if you make Hana suspicious."

"Fine," Mason muttered.

Arisa continued her conversation with Hana in ASL for a minute before asking the question Mason had been impatiently waiting for. "Can you take us into town? We wanted to pick up some stuff for the party."

Hana, fortunately, didn't ask for details. Unfortunately, she didn't say yes, either. "Sorry, I'm busy this week," she replied. "You should ask Kendra to take you on the way back from your next field trip."

"Next field trip?" Arisa repeated, clearly confused.

Hana frowned. "Kendra hasn't told you yet?"

Arisa shook her head.

"I don't know all of the details. You'll have to ask her," Hana told Arisa. "She's actually on her way here now."

"I didn't catch that last part," Mason said aloud. Arisa explained.

"Great." Mason grabbed Felix and Arisa's arms and pulled them toward a nearby table. "We'll just wait here."

Arisa turned back to sign something to Hana while Felix stumbled into a chair next to Mason.

"Do you think we can get Kendra to take us?" Felix asked Arisa as she sat down across from him.

"No idea," Arisa replied with a shrug. "But it's worth a shot."

Kendra arrived at the library five minutes later. She spent another ten at the front desk in animated conversation with Hana. Finally, Hana pointed toward the table where the three sat, and Kendra came their way, a book tucked under her arm.

"Ooh, what book is that?" Arisa asked.

"Oh, it's part of a series I'm rereading," Kendra said, holding it up. "When I was younger, I wanted an excuse to talk to one of the library assistants I thought was cute, so I picked these books at random and started checking them out." She examined the back cover. "Hana caught on pretty quickly, though, since I was checking them out in the wrong order."

Mason cleared his throat. "Hana said something about you taking us on a field trip?"

"Oh, sure, it's just a two-day trip. We leave Thursday." Kendra lowered the book. "We have to check out a house where a powerful spirit was exorcised and make sure the place is still clean. Sometimes they stick around after you kick them out of a person's body. It shouldn't be dangerous, though."

"That's what you guys said about our last two field trips," Felix said. "And I've almost died twice now."

"At least we'll get to stay in a hotel again," Arisa said. "That was fun."

Archer emerged from behind a nearby shelf, a stack of books in his arms. "Absolutely not."

"Unbelievable," Mason muttered.

Arisa turned in her chair to watch Archer approach. "Are you coming, too?"

"Yes. Kendra and I are usually mission partners." Archer dropped the books on the table. "You should read these books on exorcisms before we go."

Felix picked up the top book and studied the cover. "Seb didn't make us do readings before our field trips with him."

"Unfortunate."

"Wait, why isn't Sebastian taking us?" Arisa asked. "Is he coming, too?"

"He wasn't assigned to this mission," Archer said. "I was. And I wanted to bring you."

"*We* thought it would be an easy mission to bring you along on," Kendra added.

Felix glanced at Archer. "And you said we're not staying in a hotel?"

"No," Archer replied.

"Why not?"

"It's a waste of money, and we'd have to interact with more people. We're camping."

"The house is way up in the mountains, anyway," Kendra added.

Mason shot Arisa a pointed look.

"Oh." Arisa cleared her throat. "Kendra, do you think you could take us into town on the way back? We wanted to buy some stuff...for the, uh...student party."

Kendra frowned. "Well, I'm glad you've changed your minds about going. I guess I could help you pick out some—"

"Uh, well, I also had a gift idea," Arisa interrupted. "For the wedding. It needs to be a surprise, so you can't come with us." She fiddled with her cursed bracelet. "You can just drop us off and pick us up when we're done."

"Maybe it would be better if Archer took you, then."

"I don't have time for that," Archer said sternly. "Besides, we have those other kids to deal with, too."

"Other kids?" Felix asked, heart sinking. It was unlikely, but what if Archer was talking about—?

"When we asked the council for permission to bring you, Abraham Caldwell requested we take Jack and his friends, too."

"You still have until later this summer to get the gift," Kendra added. "Maybe we can try next week, okay?"

Arisa glanced at Mason. He sighed and leaned back in his chair. Arisa nodded at Kendra. "Okay."

Kendra returned to the front desk to resume her conversation with Hana, while Archer left the library.

"Sorry, Mason," Arisa said. "But I think we've tried everyone we had a chance at convincing to take us to a witch shop."

Mason's eyes narrowed as he watched the doors close behind Archer. "Yeah. Everyone we had a chance with."

"Forget that for a minute," Felix said. "We're going to be stuck on a two-day camping trip with Jack Caldwell and his stupid friends."

"Seriously!" Arisa flung her hands up in exasperation. "How can Archer tell us to avoid them and then turn around and take us camping with them?"

"Well, to be fair, it didn't sound like he wanted to bring them."

Mason rose to his feet. "Either way, they're coming," he said. "And as much as we all want to punch Jack in the face, we'll just have to try our best to not do that."

Felix's anxiety around dealing with Jack and the others was worse than his fear of whatever awaited them at the exorcism site. When Tuesday morning rolled around, he dragged himself down to breakfast to meet the others with a sizeable amount of reluctance.

He, Arisa, and Mason got to ride with Kendra, while Jack and his friends rode with Archer, which was a small upside. But soon as they reached the campsite, everything went downhill.

For starters, Felix, Arisa, and Mason somehow didn't have any tent assembling experience between the three of them.

"Have none of us seriously been camping before?" Arisa asked.

"I have, but my family always took an RV," Felix replied.

"That doesn't count as camping," Mason said with a roll of his eyes. "And my family always put up our tent with magic. You know, because we're witches?"

Arisa threw her hands in the air. "Then use magic to put it up!"

"It would take more than my shitty wand—"

Kendra walked by and lifted an eyebrow. Mason lowered his eyes and scowled. Arisa forced a smile and waved. Felix rubbed the back of his neck.

Jack and the others had gotten their tent up within minutes of arriving. Even though they only had one more person, their tent was nearly twice the size of the one Felix and the others were currently struggling with.

And then the rain started.

"We need to get this up," Arisa said, staring at the pile of tent on the ground between them. "The last thing I want is mud on Clementine's fur."

Mason lifted the hood of his sweatshirt over his head. "Really? *That's* the last thing you want?"

"Can't you animate the tent and make it put itself up?" Felix asked Arisa.

Arisa lifted her hand and immediately yelped in pain. "It's too big," she said, rubbing her wrist.

Kendra returned to where they stood, this time with Archer at her side. She lifted an eyebrow. "Maybe we need to add 'putting up a tent' to our lesson plans."

Archer didn't respond. He knelt on the ground and lifted a section of the tent. "This seam is torn," he said. He swept his gaze over the ground. "And you're missing a pole."

Kendra's brow furrowed. "Who grabbed these for us?"

"I don't know. Probably a council member." Archer stood up. "It's fine. Mine's the same size. They can use that one instead, and I'll stay outside tonight."

"Don't be ridiculous. It's raining."

"It's just water. I've spent the night in worse conditions," Archer replied. "I was planning on keeping watch, anyway." He spoke as if he were suggesting a walk in the park, not staying up all night in the rain.

Kendra frowned. "But—"

"Come on," Archer said, gesturing to Felix and the others. "You should get your sleeping bags in the tent before they get completely drenched."

Felix felt a twinge of guilt at the thought of forcing Archer to stay outside all night, but he wasn't about to say no to shelter. He and the others scrambled to gather up their bags and carry everything into the waiting tent.

The rain lessened as the evening went on. At sunset, Felix and the others took a break from reading and slipped outside to watch the forest around them turn red and gold.

Jack and the others were outside, too, kicking a soccer ball back and forth on the opposite side of the campsite. Kendra was nowhere to be seen, presumably in her tent. Archer sat at the edge of the site with his back to a tree and a large coffee thermos at his side.

"I'm not used to this," Felix said as Jack sent the ball sailing through the air between Clara and Rose. "I got along with pretty much everyone at my old school."

"Well, I am," Mason muttered.

"Before my curse thing, I wasn't that close to anyone at the castle," Arisa said with half-hearted shrug. "I lived there, but my parents sent me to a public school, and all my friends were there. But now I spend most of my time at the castle because everyone's so concerned about this." She held up a hand to flash her bracelet.

Felix moved his gaze from Jack's gang back to Archer. Though he was staring toward Felix and the others, there was a faraway look in his eyes.

"Great, they're coming this way," Mason muttered.

Jack, Rose, Clara, and Noah walked up with an array of expressions. Jack had his usual confidence, Rose kept her face free of emotion, Clara threw nervous glances at Jack, and Noah looked like he'd rather be anywhere else.

"Mason, you're not wearing your uniform," Jack said, mock disappointment in his voice.

"I'm wearing the shirt and jacket under my sweatshirt," Mason replied. "It's cold up here."

"What's the point if no one can see it?"

"What's the point of wearing it in the first place if there's no one around but us?"

Jack smirked. "It's about making us feel unified."

"I don't feel very unified with you right now, asshole."

Felix snickered. Arisa grinned.

Jack's eyes narrowed. He turned and waved his hand at Archer. "Archer!" he shouted. "These guys are complaining about the uniforms. Not very becoming of future Guardians."

That snapped Archer out of whatever thoughts he'd been having. His stern gaze shifted from Jack to Jack's friends to Felix and the others. Felix's heart skipped a beat. Getting in trouble now was the last thing they needed.

"We're a mile from an exorcism site after a string of unprecedented monster attacks have resulted in Guardians being injured and killed," Archer deadpanned. "I need you to understand that I have never cared less about anything in my life than whatever meaningless drama is happening between students who barely understand anything about the Brightlands."

Despite the fact that the last bit seemed to be directed at all of them, Felix grinned. Jack turned away from Archer, a scowl on his face.

"Seriously? That was your play?" Mason asked.

Jack leaned forward and jabbed a finger in Mason's face. "Don't forget that you three are on probation," he said, his voice low. "So stay out of my way tomorrow."

Felix frowned as Jack led his friends away. Before he could dwell on Jack's words for long, Arisa laughed. "That was hilarious, Mason," she said.

"Yeah." Felix chuckled. "You really know how to push his buttons."

A rare smile touched Mason's lips. "Thanks." He lowered his gaze. "But I usually don't snap as much as I have been. I feel bad that I've been so on edge lately."

Felix shrugged. "Hey, you've been through a lot."

"Yeah, we understand," Arisa added.

"You two have been through a lot, too." Mason shook his head. "Anyway, I just saw what an asshole that guy was being and figured I should do the opposite of that. Especially since if everything goes the way I'm hoping, I won't be here much longer."

"Right," Felix said, surprised at how much the words stung. He'd gotten used to having Mason around, as grouchy as the guy was.

Disappointment flashed across Arisa's face, too, but it faded quickly. "Well, I feel bad for Jack's friends." Grinning, she added,

"And I bet the four wouldn't last two seconds in a battle with Supermoon Wolves."

"Agreed," Mason said with a sly smile. "Anyway, I'm starving. Let's go eat the sandwiches we packed."

Felix threw one last glance at Archer before following the others into the tent. Archer appeared to be deep in thought again, his gaze fixed on a point somewhere in the trees.

Chapter Twenty-Six
Wrath and Wraith

The world was cold and damp and still mostly dark when Felix and the others were awoken the next morning. Archer stood next to the tent and started rattling off instructions before Felix was even sure he was no longer dreaming.

"—get the tents packed up before we start hiking," Archer was saying. "Make sure you seal up any containers of food."

Felix groggily unzipped the tent. "Could you repeat that?" he asked, trying to blink the sleep from his eyes. "Slower?"

"We don't have all day," Archer replied, his voice cold.

"We don't?" Mason mumbled a few feet away.

Archer was already walking away, likely off to shake Jack's tent awake with the same lecture. Felix dragged himself outside. It took a couple of minutes for Mason to follow. Arisa stumbled out last, Clementine under her arm.

Archer passed by again a moment later, carrying his bags to the car.

"What about breakfast?" Arisa called after him.

"You can eat snacks while we hike," he replied.

Kendra emerged from her tent, looking the most put-together of any of them. She joined Archer in cleaning the site up immediately. Felix and the others stumbled around, trying to help as much as they could, but they didn't contribute much. At least they weren't Jack's gang, who went back to kicking around their ball until Archer barked at them that it was time to go.

It didn't rain during the hike, but the previous night's storm left the trail muddy. Dark clouds in the sky kept visibility low even after the sun broke the horizon. Felix nearly slipped more times than he could count.

"If we're going to a house, why couldn't we just drive?" he asked after recovering from a particularly close call.

"The road to the house was taken out in a landslide earlier this year," Archer said. "This entire part of the forest was the family's property, and since they moved out after the exorcism, no one's bothered to repair the road."

The group finally trudged out of the forest into the yard around the house. It was three stories, rustic, and while it was already falling into disrepair, it had clearly been a nice place when it was occupied.

"See if you can sense any magical energy inside," Archer ordered. "All of you."

Felix stared at the house and focused. A minute passed, and he felt nothing.

Jack yawned. "There's nothing here."

Arisa shook her head. "I'm feeling something. It's not much, but it's definitely there."

"Arisa's right," Archer said. "What you're sensing is ambient energy left over from the exorcism. It will take a few more years to fade fully."

Jack shot Arisa a dirty look.

"This low a level of energy is hard to sense, even with experience," Kendra added. "But the rest of you should keep trying until you feel it."

"Mason." Archer glanced in Mason's direction. "Can you tell if an energy masking spell has been used here?"

Mason studied the house. "Not by sense alone," he replied. "I would have to find the site where the spell had been cast. Or cast another spell that will undo it if it's there. But my wand isn't strong enough for that."

Archer nodded. He turned to Kendra. "I'm not sensing anything active inside, but given everything that's happened recently, we should go in to confirm."

Jack folded his arms. His friends exchanged nervous looks.

"You kids stay out here," Kendra said. "We'll be right back." She waved a hand. Butterflies darted out of the trees and circled the air around the kids. The patterns on their wings shifted into sigils.

"Wait," Jack said. "Shouldn't we come, too?"

"We need to make sure it isn't dangerous, first," Archer told him.

"But wouldn't it be more dangerous to leave us out here alone?"

"If there are still spirits bound to the house, they won't be able to leave," Kendra said. "And I marked these butterflies with protective sigils just in case."

"Now, you're going to stand out here and concentrate until you're able to feel the magical energy coming from the building," Archer added. "All of you."

He and Kendra walked up to the ajar front door and entered the house. Felix was happy to stay back and try sensing the energy, but Jack had other plans.

"Let's go," he said the moment the two were out of sight. He started toward the house. Clara was the first to follow. After a moment's hesitation, Noah and Rose joined them.

"Where are you going?" Arisa called. "There's nothing in there!"

Jack ignored her. The four disappeared inside.

"What should we do?" Felix asked.

"Nothing," Mason said. "They'll get in trouble, and we won't." He glanced at one of the butterflies flitting near his face.

"Why would they go in? It doesn't make any sense." Arisa paced back and forth, fiddling with her bracelet as she walked. Clementine surveyed the area from her shoulder, head turning back and forth.

"Who cares?"

Felix folded his arms. "Jack has been acting weird. Almost like he knows something that we don't."

Mason rolled his eyes. "Again: who cares?"

He had a point. Felix went back to trying to sense energy, while Arisa continued pacing and Mason stared at the house with narrowed eyes.

A scream pierced the morning air.

"That sounded like Clara," Arisa said, eyes widening.

"What the hell did they do?" Mason muttered.

Felix stared at the house. His fists clenched. "We should go help."

Mason shook his head. "Archer and Kendra are in there. We should leave it to them."

"The scream sounded like it came from this side of the house. What if Kendra an Archer don't get there fast enough?"

"Yeah," Arisa added. "They're assholes, but we can't just let them get killed."

A heartbeat passed. Mason nodded. "Okay. Let's go."

They sprinted up to the building. Mason torched a window with hellfire as they approached, shattering the glass and creating an opening for them to jump through. When they landed inside, shouting reached their ears.

On the bright side, the fight was easy to locate.

Felix was the first to reach the door. He threw it open and found a large living room on the other side. Jack, Rose, and Noah were pressed up against the opposite wall. Clara lay on the floor next to them, eyes closed.

Hovering in the middle of the room was a pitch black, vaguely humanoid spirit. It was easily over seven feet in heigh, even with its lower half fading into black mist. Tattered pieces of fabric hung from its body and drifted weightlessly through the air.

The thing's head turned back to stare at Felix and the others as they entered. Its face was hidden in the shadow of the hood over its head, but it didn't seem to have any features besides a gaping mouth and two spots of red light where eyes should have been. It extended a hand toward them, revealing that its fingers ended in claws several inches in length.

"What is that?" Felix yelped.

"Wraith," Arisa answered. "You know how poltergeists are basically extra violent ghosts? These are even worse."

Mason lifted his fists and let them burn with hellfire. "They're not that much more violent. The real problem is that they'll drain your life force if you get too close. There's nothing left of them but bad memories and hopelessness, and that's what they feed on."

"Noted," Felix said. "How do we kill it?"

"Our magical fire will do the trick. Arisa, can you keep it distracted?"

"We're on it," Arisa said. Clementine jumped off her shoulder and charged forward. Arisa drew a deck of cards from her jacket as she ran in a different direction to circle the wraith.

Felix brought his own fire to the surface and moved forward with Mason. He hadn't had many opportunities to practice since talking to Mom, and he had no idea what the full extent of his power was now. Or how hard it would be to control.

The wraith drifted toward him. Playing cards spun through the air in front of it, cutting off its path with sigils. It swung its head toward Arisa.

Mason jumped in with a blast of hellfire. The wraith shrieked and backed up toward Jack's group, the edge of its shoulder fading into black smoke. Felix darted to the right and unleashed his own fire, hoping to drive the wraith away from the others. He hit with enough flame to wipe away half of the arm attached to the shoulder Mason had burned.

"Nice!" Mason shouted.

"I was aiming for its chest," Felix admitted.

Clementine darted by underneath the wraith, distracting it momentarily and allowing Mason a clear shot at the lower half of its form. An even louder shriek echoed through the room. Felix clapped his hands over his ears.

"It won't stop until it's completely destroyed!" Mason shouted.

The wraith swung its head toward Mason and raced through the air. When Mason lifted his hands to hit it again, it stopped and reversed, carrying itself out of the hellfire's path. Felix attempted to dive out of the way, but he wasn't fast enough. The wraith passed directly through him.

Felix's world fell apart at the edges. His vision blurred, and then he was staring down the Supermoon Wolves again. Then the necromancer. The demons. Gideon. His family's bodies. He sank to his knees, ready to give up here and now. What chance did he stand against these monsters? If he kept going with the Bright Guardians, he'd be dead in no time. May as well get it over with.

Something solid collided with him, knocking him back into reality. He and Mason slid across the floor together. As they came to a stop a few feet from the wall, Mason lifted a hand and torched the wraith behind him.

"Are you okay?" Mason asked, revealing his fangs. His eyes were wide, and his pupils had narrowed to slits. His irises glowed purple.

Felix nodded, heart racing.

"It's still got half its body!" Arisa yelled.

Mason climbed to his feet. "Can you keep going?"

Felix reached into the well of energy in his chest. "Yeah," he said as he stood up. "I've got a little more fight left."

"Let's hit it together." Mason turned around. "Arisa, send it our way! We need it close!"

Felix and Mason faced the wraith as it backed toward them, moving away from the protective sigils Arisa sent spinning through the air. Felix lifted his hand, but Mason held out his own to stop him. "Wait."

The wraith drew closer. And closer. Despair crept into Felix's chest. He breathed through it and held his ground.

"Now!" Mason yelled.

Blue and purple fire mixed together in front of them. The beam of flames engulfed the wraith. It let out a deafening shriek. Felix gritted his teeth and forced his fire to keep pouring out.

The shriek cut off abruptly. Felix's shoulders sagged as he let go of the fire and watched it dissipate. With the wraith gone, the room looked lighter.

Mason didn't pause for even a second. He stormed over to Jack, grabbed him by the front of his shirt with clawed hands, and lifted him into the air. "What the hell were you thinking?" he snarled.

"You—you really are a demon," Jack stammered.

Felix jogged over and knelt down next to Clara, who hadn't moved. "Is she—?"

"She's fine," Noah said, though his voice was strained. "I was able to negate the wraith's power long enough for us to pull her away before it could sap much of her energy. But she did pass out." His hand shifted, and Felix noticed he was turning over a coin in his fingers. His channeling material, maybe?

Arisa's eyes were on the ceiling as she walked over, Clementine perched on her shoulder. "Damn. You guys did a number on that paint."

Felix glanced up and took in the scorch marks on the ceiling.

Mason let go of Jack. Jack grunted as he hit the floor. "Seriously," Mason said. "Why did you come in here just to freeze up?"

Jack's only response was a glare. Mason turned to Rose. "You wanna give me any answers?"

Rose rubbed her arm and looked at the floor.

"We need to get Clara out of here," Noah said. "She's still unconscious."

"He's right, Mason," Arisa said. "Let's get outside. Let Archer and Kendra deal with Jack."

"Fine." Mason's gaze flickered to Felix. "You're bleeding."

"Huh?" Felix held a hand to the side of his face and found blood.

"Here." Mason reached into his sweatshirt and pulled out his wand. He pointed at Felix and muttered, "Heal." A wave of energy swept over Felix's skin, wiping away the gash. The stinging faded in seconds.

"Can—" Noah looked terrified of drawing Mason's attention. "Can you help her?" He glanced down at Clara.

"I can try. This wand's not much, so it will depend on how much energy that thing sapped from her." Mason pointed the wand at her. "Wake."

After a moment of tense silence, Clara's eyes fluttered open.

The seven of them made their way back outside through the window Mason had broken. As they watched Jack climb through last, Archer and Kendra came around the corner.

"We told you to wait—" Archer started.

Kendra cut him off, eyes wide. "What happened? Are you okay?"

"What do you mean 'what happened?'" Felix asked. "Did you not hear the fight?"

"We didn't hear anything. There was a minor spirit on the other side of the house we dealt with, but it wasn't much trouble," Archer said. His gaze darted between them. "What happened over here?"

Jack opened his mouth. "We went in—"

"You went in," Mason cut him off. "We followed when you all started screaming for help."

"That's not—"

Clara had apparently regained enough strength to punch Jack in the arm. "They're right, moron. We'd be dead if it weren't for them."

Jack shut his mouth and let Mason finish explaining what had happened.

When the explanation was finished, Archer shook his head. "It's like every mindless monster in the state is suddenly interested in tricking us and attacking our students."

Jack's gaze moved to the ground. He had a guilty expression on his face, for what could have very well been the first time in his life.

"Let's go," Archer said. He led the way toward the trees without checking to make sure the others followed.

Mason hurried to catch up to him. After exchanging a quick glance, Felix and Arisa followed.

"I found a spell in a book that could be used to undo the energy masking spell," Mason said as the two caught up to him and Archer. "It requires more power than my wand has, so I would need extra supplies. But if I were able to use it, we could know what we're walking into next time."

Archer thought for a moment. "If you're right, and this pattern keeps up, we may not be able to continue without a spell like that." He looked at Mason. "What do you need?"

With a brief summary of what the spell required, Mason was able to convince Archer—the last person any of them would have expected—to take the three to a witch shop.

Chapter Twenty-Seven
Hunger

"I didn't technically lie to him," Mason said as he handed Felix his list of supplies. "You will be getting supplies that would allow me to undo a masking spell. But I'll also be able to cast my own masking spell on us." His eyes glinted. "Which will allow us to enter Ernest's house undetected."

Arisa peered over Felix's shoulder to look at the list. "Right. All we need after that is an address, transportation, and a way to get you through protection wards."

"One thing at a time." Mason lifted his gaze to the sign hanging above the store. "I came here a couple of times on trips with my parents." He sighed. "I wish I could go in again."

"There's really no way they'd let you in?" Felix asked.

Mason shook his head. "It's fine. Just go get the supplies so we can get back to the castle." He threw a quick glance back at where Archer waited across the street, glowering at every passerby who gave him a second glance. "Thankfully, I don't think any of the Guardians know enough about spellcasting to question us."

Felix and Arisa had to pester some of the store employees for help, but they were able to find everything and check out in about ten minutes. When they handed the bag to Mason outside the store, he dug through it with a concerned expression on his face.

"Did we get it all right?" Felix asked.

Relief crossed Mason's face as he lowered the bag. He looked up. "Perfect. Thank you."

They returned to Bright Castle in a considerably better mood than when they'd left. They were one step closer to breaking into Ernest's house, they'd beaten the wraith without too much injury, and Jack Caldwell had been humbled. Jack's weird behavior still nagged at Felix, but he decided to chalk it up to the guy's obsession with winning fights.

The good day ended with Felix waking up in the middle of the night in a cold sweat.

He sat up, a hand pressed to his forehead. He couldn't remember what his dream had been. He could only remember being paralyzed while something drew closer and closer.

His stomach growled. No way was he going to make it to morning without a snack. He climbed out of bed and grabbed his shoes. Kendra had mentioned a nearby kitchen on his first day, but he couldn't remember which floor it was on. The only kitchen he knew how to reach off the top of his head was one that Arisa had shown him, through one of the secret passages.

Using his phone's flashlight, Felix entered the passages through a door hidden near his room and made his way to the kitchen, where he snagged a couple of rolls and a yogurt. On his way back, as he passed an exit into one of the main hallways, the sound of a door slamming made him freeze.

He frowned. Wasn't this part of the castle residential? Who was awake at this hour? Felix crept toward the door that he was pretty sure opened behind a tapestry. He dared to turn the handle and push it open an inch.

The tapestry in front of the door was hung from the ceiling rather than attached to the wall, leaving a small gap between it and the door. Felix peered down the hall toward the source of the sound.

Jack Caldwell stood in front of the door that must have been the one slammed shut. He glared at it for nearly a minute before turning and storming off.

Felix waited for Jack to disappear around the corner at the end of the hall. Once he was sure Jack was gone, he slipped through the door and out from under the tapestry. He tiptoed up to the door and rested a hand on it.

Everything but the door faded away. Jack reappeared next to Felix, materializing from nothing. As Felix took a step back, Jack moved forward to knock on the door. When a minute passed without a response, he knocked again, harder.

The door swung open. Abraham Caldwell stood on the other side. "What are you doing?" he demanded. "Your mother and I are sleeping."

"I can't sleep," Jack said, no sign of his usual confidence. In fact, he sounded scared. "I'm having nightmares about the wraith."

"You're fine. The healer said none of you would suffer any permanent effects."

"But—" Jack's jaw clenched. "I haven't seen you since I got back. We need to talk about—"

"There's nothing to talk about."

"I need another chance! I promise, I'll beat anything you give me."

"I can't cash in another favor, Jack. That was your only chance to get close to something that powerful." Abraham rubbed his forehead. "I'm going back to bed. I suggest you do, too, since you'll need to train twice as hard tomorrow."

The door slammed shut. Felix resurfaced and backed away from it, alone again in the empty hallway.

Awesome. As if things weren't already complicated enough.

The next morning, Felix opened his curtains and spotted Mason and Arisa sitting on the castle lawn far below his window. He quickly got dressed and raced down to meet them.

"What are you guys doing?" Felix called as he approached.

"You're up earlier than usual." Arisa looked up from the notebook in front of her. She'd scribbled loopy sigils all over the page in pen.

"I knew they existed, but I wasn't sure I'd be able to find them," Mason said. He held up a dark red book. "But I did last night. They're sigils that can be used to break wards. We'll use them to get me into Ernest's house."

Felix sat down next to Arisa. "It's that easy?" he asked as he watched her draw another sigil.

"No," Mason said. "They take a lot of energy. We'll have to draw them in advance over the next few days." Glancing at Arisa, he added, "She's just practicing."

"And why are you guys all the way out here?" Felix asked.

"We're hiding from spiders." Mason swept his gaze across the grass around them. "I wouldn't be surprised if Adrienne keeps some out here, too, but it's easier to pinpoint their magical energy in an open space."

"Well, I have news, too," Felix said. He explained what he'd seen the night before.

"So, Jack did know there was a wraith inside," Mason said, brow furrowing. "But why would he want to fight one?"

"No idea," Felix replied. "But whatever the reason, he failed, and his dad's not giving him another chance."

"Sounds like his dad can't give him another chance." Arisa tapped her pen against her notebook. "I wonder what he meant by that 'cashing in a favor' thing."

Mason perked up. "Hey Felix, do you think it would be possible to use your psychometry to get Ernest's address?"

Felix blew out a breath of air. "I mean, maybe, but I have no way of knowing what objects in the castle could hold a memory involving his house."

"We'll just have to go with plan B," Arisa said.

Mason lifted an eyebrow. "I wasn't aware we had a plan B."

"I came up with it while talking to my parents this morning," Arisa said. "Turns out my uncle in Oregon needed emergency surgery last night, so they're flying down this afternoon to help take care of his kids."

"So, they're not going to the party?" Felix asked.

"Nope."

Mason frowned. "How does that help us?"

"Kendra and Hana are driving them to the airport as we speak," Arisa said. She smirked. "Which means their car is here, just waiting to be driven. All I have to do is grab the keys from their apartment."

"And how will we find Ernest's house?" Felix asked.

"We'll just have to follow the other Guardians when they leave." Arisa shrugged. "My parent's car is plain, and a lot of people will be driving off."

"But someone like Hana or Kendra would recognize it."

"The Guardians will have to space themselves out as they leave the pocket dimension and enter the main road," Arisa explained.

"We can wait for anyone who would notice us to leave first, and then we'll follow someone else out."

Mason nodded, though his expression was reluctant. "I guess that will work. I'd prefer to know where we're going beforehand, though."

"At this point, we have to take what we can get," Arisa said. "I'm surprised we've made it this far."

Chapter Twenty-Eight
The Two-Time Party Crashers

In the days leading up to the party, Felix trained as hard as he could, hoping he'd feel more confident when the time came to sneak off to Ernest's house. His aim with his fire was still far from perfect, but he was hitting more and more of his targets. Attempting to control his water body still felt like a lost cause, though, and he was only halfway decent with Ezra's plants.

Time ran out, as it tended to all too often for him. He left the last training session of the day—the last one before Ernest's party—clenching and unclenching his fist, hoping what he did know would be good enough.

"I'll see you kids tomorrow morning," Sebastian said as he waved goodbye. "We'll discuss what I learn at Ernest's then."

The three ate dinner quickly. Afterwards, Felix and Mason went to the library to wait for Guardians to begin leaving. Arisa joined them after grabbing her parents' car keys from their room.

Kendra and Hana were among the first to head out.

"Be safe," Arisa signed to Hana as she passed. Hana looked a little confused, but she smiled and nodded.

After another ten minutes passed, Mason rose to his feet. "All right, enough waiting. Let's go."

Arisa picked up Clementine and placed the bear in her backpack. Felix grabbed Helena's sword from under the table and double checked that May's stone was in his pocket.

His heart quickened when they entered the hallway. It wasn't Guardians that had him anxious, but the dozens of students headed to the ballroom for whatever lame party had been thrown together for them. At least, Felix hoped it was lame. He'd hate to miss out on a fun party. Especially to risk his life.

Jack Caldwell walked by, saying something that made Clara laugh at his side. Noah and Rose were smiling, too, though Noah's expression fell when he noticed Felix watching.

"I need to talk to Jack," Felix said.

"Ew, why?" Arisa asked.

Mason shook his head. "We need to go."

"We still have time." Felix met Mason's gaze. "Please. Trust me. I think everything that happened is connected to Ernest. I'm just not entirely sure how."

"What if it's not?" Mason asked. "Or what if he won't talk?"

"I promise we'll leave in ten minutes, no matter what. Okay?"

Mason sighed and nodded. "Okay."

Felix turned to Arisa. "You ready?"

"To crash their dumb party?" Arisa grinned. "Always."

Mason looked down at his sweatshirt, dark jeans, and sneakers. "I'm not changing."

Felix and Arisa were dressed just as casually. Felix's green hoodie had a juice stain on the sleeve from breakfast that morning. Arisa's jeans were full of holes that Felix was pretty sure hadn't been there when she'd bought them.

"Good," Arisa said. "I wanna kill their vibes as hard as we can."

The three followed the crowd to the ballroom. Massive speakers had been dragged in to blast pop music. Strobe lights moved over the room, offering glimpses of white streamers and the disco ball hanging from the ceiling. It was a surprising change of pace from the fantasy aesthetic the ballroom had when it was empty.

Felix scanned the room and quickly realized how pointless searching was. They didn't have a prayer of finding Jack in this dimly lit party.

"Knowing him, he'll come right to us if we make ourselves obvious." Mason nodded toward the dessert table nearby, which was illuminated by a pink spotlight.

They approached the table. Arisa picked up a cupcake. "How long do you think it'll take him?" she asked before taking a bite.

"Hm." Felix glanced back at the crowd. "Probably a few minutes."

Arisa swallowed. "No way," she shot back. "He'll be here in a minute, tops."

Mason wrapped a cookie in a napkin and shoved it into his pocket. "He has to notice us first."

"Yeah, but I swear he has some kind of radar for us."

By Felix's count, it took about seventy-six seconds for Jack to emerge from the crowd and stroll toward them at an uncomfortably fast walking pace. "You guys are here? Why are you dressed like that?" He asked as he looked them over. His gaze darted to Felix. "Is that your sword behind you?"

"We're stealing your food," Arisa said through a mouthful of cupcake.

"Uh, we are technically allowed to be here," Felix added.

Mason added a donut to the growing collection of food in his sweatshirt. "Don't worry, we won't be staying long." He met Felix's eye and nodded.

Felix returned the nod before turning back to Jack. "I wanted to apologize."

Arisa choked on the food in her mouth.

"I know how it feels to walk into a trap and get taken by surprise," Felix continued while Mason grabbed Arisa a glass of punch from the other end of the table. "You must have been terrified when the wraith showed up."

"I'm not an idiot. I knew the wraith was there!" Jack snapped. His eyes immediately widened. He glanced around, checking if anyone had heard him.

Felix reached out and grabbed Jack's wrist while he was distracted. "How?"

Jack glared at him. "As if I'd tell you."

Felix yanked the wooden ring off Jack's finger before Jack could stop him. "Then I'll just find the memory myself."

Jack reached for the ring, but Felix held it back out of reach. "Give that back!" Jack grabbed at it again and missed.

"Watch it." Arisa pointed her half empty glass of punch toward Jack. "I will spill this all over you," she warned. "I'm not afraid of getting any on my shirt."

Jack's shoulders sagged. He sighed. "I don't know all the details, okay? My dad just told me that the house would seem empty, but if I went inside, there would be a spirit for me to fight." He hesitated. "He said something about an energy masking spell."

"And why did you need to fight a spirit?" Arisa asked. "You've been on a ton of successful missions, haven't you?"

"Yeah, as a student," Jack replied bitterly. "I haven't killed much myself. Nothing more powerful than the world's weakest demon." He rolled his eyes. "Dad told me if I wanted to move up in the world, I needed to prove I was capable of more. And then he told me he had this—this *opportunity* for me. And I blew it."

"Why can't you just try again?" Felix asked.

"I guess it was hard to set up. The guy who arranged it won't do it again for us, unless my dad earns another favor from him."

Mason folded his arms. "Does this guy happen to be Ernest Abernathy?"

Alarm flashed across Jack's face. "Hey, that wasn't my fault! I didn't make those kids summon the poltergeist. They were lying!"

"Poltergeist?" Felix glanced at Arisa. "The one we ran into during my tour of the castle?"

"Yeah. I—I'm the one who told them how to summon it into the castle," Jack admitted. "They told Archer I forced them to do it, but I didn't. I just...suggested it."

"I'm sure you were very polite," Mason said sarcastically.

"Wait, what does that have to do with Ernest?" Felix asked.

"I knew how to do it because I overheard Ernest telling another Guardian about it," Jack said. "He said he was concerned about castle security because he knew of this way to summon certain spirits without triggering the wards."

Felix frowned. "And Ernest was the guy who set up the wraith for you?"

"I don't know. Maybe. My dad never told me."

"I bet it was," Mason said. "Ernest isn't stupid enough to let a random kid eavesdrop on him. You overheard the bit about summoning and convinced some other kids to try it, proving it would work. That was the favor that made Ernest help your dad in return."

"Mason, you're a genius!" Felix exclaimed.

"I was...tricked?" Jack asked. The hurt in his expression took Felix by surprise. "But why?"

"Yeah, the poltergeist was easy to banish." Arisa took a sip of the punch she'd threatened Jack with. "What was the point of summoning it in the first place?

"Maybe it was a test," Mason suggested. "A way for Ernest to find out whether it would actually work without getting himself in trouble."

"A test for what?" Felix asked.

"Good question."

"Can I have my ring back now?" Jack asked.

"Oh. Right." Felix held it out. Jack snatched it back with a little more aggression than Felix thought necessary and slid it back on his finger.

"Now, are you three morons done crashing our party?" Jack asked.

"Wow. Right back to being an asshole," Mason muttered.

Arisa snickered. Jack shot her a glare that managed to be even sharper than usual. "What's so funny?"

"There's a spider on your shoulder."

Jack's gaze flickered to his shoulder. He yelped in surprise and swatted at the spider, but it jumped out of the way first.

The spider landed on the floor and scurried toward Felix. As he took an instinctive step back, a second spider emerged from under the table behind him and joined the first.

"Why are all of these spiders...?" Felix trailed off as he looked up. "Oh my god."

"What?" Jack asked. His head tipped back, and Felix's heart skipped a beat.

Thankfully, the spiders spread out before Jack's eyes found the shape they'd made. "Oh. Gross." He turned around. "I'm going to go tell someone. Maybe one of the Guardians can torch them."

Felix lowered his gaze as Jack walked off. "Did you two see what was on the ceiling?"

"The arrow? Yeah, I did." Mason shoved one more wrapped desert into his hoodie. "Let's go."

They left the ballroom and found more spiders waiting on the ceiling outside. The spiders led the three through the castle, forming arrows and dispersing as they moved. The three entered the hidden passages through a door hidden behind a painting and descended to the lower tunnels through a loose grate in the floor.

"Hello? Adrienne?" Felix called as they walked.

No response. Spiders scurried past Felix's feet and formed a new arrow on the floor. He held back a shudder as he looked to where they were pointing. Adrienne's mug lay on its side.

"What happened?" Mason asked as Felix moved to pick it up.

Felix's hand tightened around the handle. A memory pulled at him. He let it take him under.

Adrienne sat cross-legged, perched in the center of a web with the mug in one of her four hands. Threads stretching out in every direction around her, filling the tunnel. She sipped from the mug. A thread to her right trembled.

She downed the last of the tea and crept along the webbing, mug still clutched in her hand. Felix followed her through the memory as she turned a corner. She paused. Waited.

The entire web shook. A new thread pulled Adrienne into the air. As her feet and hands touched the ceiling, an invisible force shredded the web beneath her.

"Show yourself," Adrienne demanded.

Shrieking laughter echoed around the tunnel.

"Fine." Adrienne extended one of her free hands. Spiders dropped from the ceiling, carrying extra webbing to her. The white threads wrapped together and took on the shape of a staff. Adrienne jumped to the ground and swung at the air.

The mug slipped from her hand, and the memory ended. Felix snapped back to the present.

"What is it?" Arisa asked. "What did you see?"

"Follow me!" Felix was running before the words finished leaving his mouth.

They raced through the tunnels until Mason slowed, holding up a hand. "I'm sensing energy. Some kind of spirit."

"Poltergeist," Arisa said.

Mason's gaze hardened. "Lots of them."

"Lots of them?" Felix's blood went cold.

Arisa snapped her fingers. "We can handle this." Her backpack unzipped itself. Clementine jumped out, knives at the ready.

"With enough sigils, we could banish them all at once," Mason said, glancing at Arisa.

"Leave that to me."

"Guess we're keeping them busy, then?" Felix asked. He met Mason's gaze.

Mason nodded. "Yep."

The three pushed forward and took the next corner at full speed. Adrienne stood in the middle of the next corridor, a white staff in all six of her extended arms. Spirits swooped through the air around her. The tunnel trembled. Lights flickered overhead.

Adrienne swung at a poltergeist as it passed within a few feet of her. It hissed and vanished into thin air as her staff passed through it, only to reappear a moment later. She took a few steps forward to swing again, making it obvious that her right leg was injured.

Mason and Felix raced toward her. Mason hit every poltergeist in their path with hellfire, while Felix blasted others nearby with electricity to keep them from getting closer. Arisa sent paper stars spinning through the air to form a circle of protection around Adrienne. They refolded into planes as the three reached her.

Felix and the others stumbled into the safe circle. Arisa moved to the edge with Clementine on her shoulder, allowing the bear to jump into the air and swipe at passing poltergeists with her knives. Arisa raised out a dagger of her own, ready to strike anything that got too close. Mason walked to the other side and sent fireballs shooting through the air.

"Do those hurt them?" Felix asked Adrienne, nodding at one of the staffs she held out.

"Yes." Adrienne turned it so that he could see the spider clinging to the side with red sigils marking its back. "I've been holding up all right so far," she said. "But this just a fraction of the ones that were summoned."

Arisa looked at Adrienne over her shoulder. "Who summoned them? And how?"

"I don't know about the who, but I found the supplies for a summoning ritual in a nearby tunnel," Adrienne answered.

"We should check it out. I could see who summoned them—" Felix started.

"We don't have time for that now," Mason said, throwing a quick glance back. "I'm guessing you called us down here for a reason?"

"Yes. I knew I wouldn't be able to fight much longer." Adrienne pressed one of her hands to her side. "I've lost a lot of blood, and they've kept me too busy to do anything about it."

"Why call us?" Arisa asked. "Why not other Guardians?"

Adrienne's expression darkened. "Because you're the only ones I can trust right now."

Spiders came scuttling across the floor and made their way up Adrienne's body. She lowered her arms and allowed the spiders to wrap webbing around the places where her uniform had torn to expose bleeding skin.

Felix tried to hide his instinctive disgust at seeing so many spiders. "Will that heal you?"

"It will help, but it won't heal me instantly." Adrienne watched the spiders wrap their silk around her torso. The white turned red in seconds as blood pooled under the webs.

"So, now what?"

"This hallway isn't it," Adrienne said. "There are more poltergeists all around the castle perimeter."

"Why summon them down here instead of inside?" Arisa asked. "We know it's possible."

"I don't know," Adrienne tipped her head back. Three more eyes opened in her forehead, all entirely the same shade of red as her hair. "But I've been monitoring the castle as much as I can. None of the poltergeists have tried to move inside."

"That's because they don't need to go inside," Mason realized. "I think they're here to prevent anyone from leaving after the party guests. Once everyone leaves, they'll move up to the castle yard."

"Poltergeists don't have the same intelligence as demons or werewolves," Arisa said. "I don't see how someone could be giving them orders."

"If the summoning ritual was done properly, they could be kept confined to a certain area," Mason replied. "And time increments could be incorporated. But the how isn't important. If they're only here to make sure no one leaves—"

"Then something must be going down at Ernest's party," Felix finished.

Arisa's eyes went wide. "We have to warn them." She pulled out her phone. "There's no service down here. Let's get back upstairs—"

"We don't know for sure who we can trust," Mason said. "The last thing we want to do is let Ernest know we're onto him."

"We can trust my sister!"

"I'm not saying I don't believe that. I just don't know if texting anyone at the party is a good idea."

"What, you think just showing up would be better?" Felix asked.

"We could assess what's happening and go from there," Mason replied, folding his arms.

"He has a point."

They all turned to stare at Adrienne.

"You agree with me?" Mason asked, surprised.

Adrienne nodded. "Arisa, can you expand the sigil circle?"

"A little, but the barrier will weaken," Arisa warned. "Some of the stronger ones might be able to get through."

"I just need another foot of space."

Arisa nodded. She lifted her chin, and the paper planes widened their perimeter.

"What are you going to do?" Felix asked Adrienne.

Adrienne's extra eyes closed. She lifted an eyebrow. "You were already planning to go to Ernest's house tonight, weren't you?"

"Were you going to stop us?" Mason asked.

"I was, until all of this happened." Two sets of arms folded into Adrienne's back, leaving only her original pair. "I would go myself, but I'm too weak to travel that far. I'll fight my way to the upper passages and keep an eye on things from there. We still can't be sure the poltergeists won't move on to attacking people inside."

Felix's brow furrowed. "What should we do, then?"

"I'm afraid I don't know the answer to that," Adrienne replied. "I've never been one for strategy. My job is to keep things out."

"How are we supposed to get to Ernest's house, though?" Mason asked. "Maybe there will still be people leaving that we can follow if we hurry, but—"

"You won't be going by car," Adrienne interrupted. "There's no time for that."

Arisa frowned. "What's faster than a car?"

"This."

More spiders emerged from gaps in the walls and converged on them. Felix, Mason, and Arisa backed to the edges of the sigil circle as the arachnids swarmed the center. Within seconds, they merged together to form one massive black tarantula.

Adrienne patted the spider's back. "He can cut through forests where there aren't roads."

"And he knows the way to Ernest's house?" Mason asked, unfazed by the eight-legged beast in front of them.

"He knows what I know," Adrienne replied. "You should arrive in about twenty minutes."

"We have to spend twenty minutes on the back of a giant spider?" Arisa exclaimed.

"Just close your eyes and pretend it's a horse." Mason was already climbing onto the spider's back.

"Horses are scary, too!"

Felix used his shaking hands to pull himself up onto the spider behind Mason. With a reluctant sigh, Arisa followed. Clementine climbed back into her backpack, and the zipper closed itself up.

"You aren't responsible for the mistakes of other Guardians." Adrienne spoke with the sincerest expression Felix had seen on her. "Right now, you may be able to help us. But no one will blame you if you can't save everyone."

"Are you sure you'll be okay?" Felix asked.

Adrienne nodded, but her hand was pressed to her side again, and most of the webbing wrapped around her limbs had turned a dark red.

"Go," Adrienne commanded.

The spider shot forward.

Chapter Twenty-Nine
Ernest Abernathy's Stupidly Large Mansion

The spider carried the three with surprising speed. They had to fend off a few poltergeists on their way to the surface, but once they were out of the tunnels and off castle grounds, it was an easy ride to Ernest's house.

Well, easy was relative. Felix's hoodie was not enough to shield him from the chill of racing through the night, and the ride was bouncy as hell, but at least monsters weren't trying to kill them. Yet.

It felt like much longer than twenty minutes before the spider slowed. It stopped at the edge of the forest they'd traveled through and waited for them to climb off. Moments after Felix's feet hit the ground, the spider scurried back the way they'd come.

"So much for a ride back," Mason said.

"Let's worry about that later." Felix moved to the tree line and peered through to the other side.

A disgustingly extravagant mansion sat at the center of a sprawling green lawn. The long driveway leading up to the front was packed with cars. Felix could just make out figures moving in the warm glow spilling from the front windows.

"As far as I can tell, no one's screaming or dying," he said.

"Good. Let's look for the wand." Mason cautiously raised a hand to the air at the edge of the lawn. Nothing happened. "Maybe the wards are closer to the house. Let's circle around and approach from the back. I'll get the masking spell ready."

Before they crossed the backyard, Mason dug the supplies from the witch shop out of his bag and laid them in a careful formation. The crystals formed a triangle, and Mason had each member of the group stand at one of the three points. He piled the bone fragments in the middle, sprinkled ash over them, and muttered a few words under his breath as he pointed the wand at the setup.

"I used the crystals as an anchor point," Mason said once he was finished. "Hold onto yours, and it will keep your energy hidden."

Felix picked up his crystal and slid it into his pocket. He and the others stepped out of the cover of the forest and started across the lawn.

They made it all the way to the house without running into any barriers.

"It doesn't make any sense," Mason muttered. "There's no way Ernest would leave his house open to monsters, even if he does have some obeying his orders. He's not stupid enough to leave himself vulnerable, right?"

Arisa tried the handle to the back door they'd stopped in front of. "Can I animate the door to unlock it?" she asked.

"As long as you un-animate it when you're done," Mason told her. "Once we're inside, avoid using magic as much as possible."

The door clicked and swung open. Mason entered without hesitation. Arisa followed. Felix had to take a deep breath to steel himself before crossing over the threshold into Ernest's house. Arisa waved her hand, and the door eased shut behind them.

"What do we do now?" Felix asked, his voice barely above a whisper.

"We should look for Hana," Arisa said. "Or Kendra."

"We should try to find the wand." Mason's eyes scanned the quiet hall ahead of them. "Once we have it, we'll have the upper hand if Ernest tries anything."

"I guess," Arisa muttered.

"Plus, once someone sees us, it's over," Felix said. "No more element of surprise."

Mason nodded. "As long as we stay away from the rooms where the party guests are, we can sneak around and see what's happening before we do anything stupid."

"Investigate now, do something stupid later," Arisa said. "Got it."

Mason sighed. "Let's go."

The distant sound of party chatter drifted around them as they moved silently through the house. Felix was terrified of touching any of the expensive-looking decor. Expensive paintings, expensive tapestries, expensive glass statues. He wondered if the occasional plant they passed was expensive, too.

The thought brought Ezra into his mind long enough to confirm. *Yes. Yes they are.*

The sound of conversation grew louder, making Felix's heart quicken. Mason pressed forward anyway, leading the group to a staircase. They moved up to a hall that led into a walkway hanging over the open first floor. The volume of the party increased dramatically as the three neared the start of the walkway.

"No one sounds upset," Felix whispered.

Mason dropped to the ground at the edge of the shadows and peered down at the party through the gaps in the railing. Felix moved as close to him as he dared and watched the Guardians below. They all wore their formal suits, and most carried drinks or small plates of dessert in their hands. Felix found himself nervous for the white and gold rug directly below them.

"Any sign of the wand?" Arisa asked under her breath.

"No, but I can see Ernest," Mason replied. "He's talking to some other Guardians."

"So, he's busy," Felix said.

Mason nodded. "Let's keep looking."

They backed up and moved into a different hallway that took them toward the back of the house.

"Where do we start?" Felix asked. "This place is huge."

"The wand will emit a powerful energy signature," Mason said. "It may be hard to narrow down with all of the Guardians around, but that's going to be the best way to track it."

"What if Ernest masked it?" Arisa asked.

"A wand can't cast a spell on itself, and no other wand would be powerful enough to hide it." Mason stopped. They'd reached an intersection. The hallway split off in three directions. "This guy's house sucks," he said. "Let's split up."

"Are you sure that's a good idea?" Felix said.

"We'll find the wand faster," Mason replied. "And one person has a better chance at avoiding getting caught than a group of three. Easier to hide if someone comes up."

Felix sighed. "Makes sense."

"First person to find the wand can send a text."

Mason went right, and Arisa went left, leaving Felix to continue straight down the hall. As he checked the rooms he passed, he quickly realized that the upper levels of Ernest's house were populated with taxidermy animals. Mounted deer heads, stuffed birds on shelves, even glass cases with predators standing at their full height.

What kind of guy kept all this around? Apparently, not only was Ernest a monster hunter, but a regular hunter as well. Though, Felix had a hard time believing it was legal to kill most of what he was seeing.

Felix paused in an office and sighed. Enough stalling. He doubted he'd be able to pick up the wand's energy, but he had to try. He closed his eyes.

All at once, magic overwhelmed him. There was a steady pulse of magical energy all around, and it was particularly strong in the direction of the party. Felix stumbled into a desk, knocking off a book and two pairs of glasses as he tried to get his bearings.

In the opposite direction of the party, not much farther down the hall, was a single point of particularly powerful energy.

Felix tried to push the energy out of his senses so that he could think, but it didn't work. "Someone help," he gasped.

The energy faded. Felix blinked.

This is why your teachers said you're supposed to take it slow, Mom said. *Trying to turn on your senses with that much energy around was a bad idea.*

At least I know which way to go now, Felix thought. He stepped back out of the office, trying to remember the exact place he'd sensed the power. It was somewhere up ahead, but it could have been on either side of the hallway.

Felix, get out of here while you can, Mom urged. *It isn't safe.*

Felix tried doors near the end of the hall and found a bathroom, storage closets, another office, and a few bedrooms that must have been guest rooms, judging by how little they were furnished. After that, the hall split to the left and the right.

Felix ventured a few feet down the hall to the right and encountered a locked door. Secured with a keypad, not a keyhole. He rested a hand on the keypad. The memory of Ernest appeared, and Felix carefully watched him type in the code. Once he disappeared, Felix stepped forward and repeated the numbers.

The door unlocked. Felix pushed it open. There, in a glass case in the middle of the room, was the Ironwood Wand.

And a demon standing on either side.

Felix tossed his backpack aside and drew Helena's sword. In a heartbeat, the two demons were attacking. The one on the left was tall and thin, with bright yellow skin, while the one on the right was shorter with skin a deep shade of orange. The yellow one flung up a hand and let out a blast of golden hellfire. The orange one charged at Felix with outstretched claws.

Felix dove to the left to dodge the fire. As he straightened up, he swung the sword blindly in the direction of the orange demon. The demon caught the blade in its hands. Dark blood welled on the metal, turning to steam as it slid across the sigils.

"Go get Ernest," it hissed to the yellow one.

Uh oh. Felix shifted his weight, yanked the blade free from the demon's grasp and swung at its legs. It jumped back.

The yellow demon darted behind Felix. He spun around and managed to slash open its arm, but it kept running. Felix tried to follow. The orange demon grabbed his shoulder and threw him to the ground. As the door clicked shut behind the yellow demon, the orange one moved to stand over him. Its hands burned with white hellfire.

Felix rolled out of the way as the demon lunged. He swung the moment he was back on his feet and landed a blow across its chest as it whirled around. The flesh burned around the gash, but it quickly began stitching itself together at the ends.

"You're not strong enough to kill me," the demon growled. "I'm healing faster than you can do damage."

Felix lunged and aimed for its neck. A clawed hand flew up to meet the blade. He sliced right through it. The demon twisted and used Felix's momentum to send him stumbling into the wall. Claws raked across his back, deep enough to draw blood.

Felix blindly jabbed the sword backwards. A hiss of pain came from the demon's direction. He spun around and brought the blade down on its head. It reached up to pull the sword free, but its arm only made it halfway before going limp and dropping to its side. A moment later, the demon collapsed. Silvery white blood pooled on the wood floor.

Felix grabbed the sword's handle and yanked it free. He wasn't positive that the demon was completely dead, but he just needed to grab the wand and get out.

A beep came from the door behind him. Someone else had typed the code into the keypad. He had seconds.

Felix backed into the corner to the right of the door, set the sword on the ground, and dropped into a puddle.

Ernest Abernathy entered the room. "What the hell happened?"

The yellow demon followed him in. "Some kid got in here."

"Where is he now?"

"Not sure," the demon replied. The wound on its arm was still spilling blood. Only the edges had closed up. "He might have left. Can you sense him?"

"No, but that doesn't mean much these days. Hard to believe he'd leave without the wand, though." Ernest crossed the room and nudged the orange demon with his foot. "This one's dead."

The yellow demon's expression didn't change. "He was a tough kid."

"Well, no matter. If he's still here somewhere, he's not getting out." Ernest lifted the lid of the wand's case and took it out. "I can't risk letting him and his friends live any longer."

"Do you want me to stay in here?"

"No. Join your friends hiding on the first floor. I didn't want to start a fight so soon, but we may not have a choice."

Ernest walked out of the room. The demon followed. As soon as the door closed behind them, Felix shifted back to his regular body and stumbled to where his backpack lay on the floor. The gashes across his back screamed in pain as he bent over. He found the Guardian uniform jacket he'd shoved in the bag and swapped it for his hoodie.

Next, he grabbed his phone and typed out a message to the others. *Found wand room. Ernest took it. Demons here too.*

Felix moved to the door and inched it open, heart hammering. Distant footsteps indicated the direction Ernest was going. He followed to the closest intersection.

Felix peered around the corner at the same moment Arisa and Mason appeared at the other end of the hall. Ernest stopped halfway between them, the yellow demon still at his side.

Mason had his fists up in a heartbeat, blazing with hellfire. "That wand belongs to my family. Hand it over."

"Take care of the knockoff demon and his friend," Ernest ordered, sliding the wand into his suit jacket. He grabbed the handle of a door to his right. "I don't have time for this."

The yellow demon charged forward as Ernest stepped through the door. Felix sprinted after the demon, lifting the sword. In the same moment that Mason torched its face with hellfire, Felix left a deep slash across its back.

The demon rolled out of Felix's and Mason's reach and jumped at Arisa. With a sweep of her arm, Arisa sent an army of paper planes shooting toward it. The force of the sigils forced the demon backward. Clementine, who'd escaped Arisa's backpack at some point, sliced at the demon's ankle as she ran by. The demon howled in pain and dropped to the ground.

"Damn, those sigils you added are powerful," Arisa said. She stepped forward and swiped at the demon's face with her dagger.

Mason lifted his hand and unleashed another blast of hellfire, leaving the demon either dead or close to it. "Follow Ernest!"

There was another hallway on the other side the door Ernest had gone through, leading back in the direction of the party. As Felix, Mason, and Arisa ran, the sound of chatter and laughter and clinking glasses grew louder.

Felix eyed some of the taxidermy they were passing. "Arisa, you should animate these and send them after Ernest."

"Yeah," Mason added. "I saw a giant bear standing around somewhere. I'd like to see him fight that off."

"I don't know how well that would work," Arisa said. "They're bigger than what I usually animate, and it's harder to manipulate things that were once living. The will of the former inhabitant is left behind. Necromancy requires a different kind of magical energy than—"

"There he is!" Mason hissed, cutting her off.

The three slowed. They'd returned to the walkway. Ernest stood with his hands on the railing, watching the party below. His head turned toward the group as they approached, a cold smile crossing his face. "You just walked into your own execution."

Felix froze. "What?"

Ernest's hand slid into his suit jacket. He drew the wand long enough to flick it toward them before hiding it again. Something pulled Felix, Mason, and Arisa forward. Felix tried to resist, but it was no use. He stumbled into the light.

"Guardians," Ernest shouted, drawing the room's attention. "I hate to interrupt the celebration, but I'm afraid we have a small problem." Light reflected off his glasses as he swept his gaze over the crowd below. "These three broke into my home a little while ago, and they've caused quite a bit of damage already. I think something needs to be done here."

"You know exactly why!" Mason exclaimed. "You killed my parents and stole their wand, and I'm here to get it back!"

Ernest put on an air of confusion. "I have no idea what you're talking about."

Felix peered over the railing as the Guardians below erupted into conversation. He desperately searched for a familiar face, but there was no sign of Kendra, Hana, Sebastian, or Archer.

Ernest lifted a hand. The crowd quieted. "All of the council members are here, aren't they?" he asked. "Perhaps we should have an emergency meeting to determine their fate."

"You can't do that without the king!" Arisa protested.

"I'm sure he would understand."

"Ernest is lying, and I can prove it!" Mason pointed at Ernest and looked out at the crowd. "This house is full of demons who are following his orders."

A woman in the crowd laughed. Eliza Abernathy. "That's absurd!" she shouted.

Mason shot her a glare. "Of course, you'd defend him. You're his cousin!"

"My blood doesn't matter. If there were demons in this house, we'd be able to sense it." Eliza glanced at the Guardians around her. "None of us here sense any demons, do we?"

"She's right," a man added. "The only magical energy here is coming from us Guardians."

"I'd say it was a nice try, but that was a rather pathetic lie—" Ernest began.

Mason's hand slid behind him, into his bag. "Hold on! Some of you have seen with your own eyes that monster energy can be hidden. Ernest cast a masking spell on the demons here. And he's the one who's been casting masking spells at monster sites, too."

"You really expect us to believe a Guardian would do that?" The question came from Abraham Caldwell. "We don't do spells."

"Think!" Mason snapped at him. "You didn't notice any protective wards around his property when you came in, did you? It's because he let demons in!"

Uncertain glances flickered across the Guardians' faces. Most of them must not have considered checking.

Mason carefully slid the bag from the witch's shop out of his backpack. Felix inched forward to shield it from Ernest's view.

Sadia Malik stepped forward. "We could check that, easily. We'll send someone outside while we hold the kids here—"

Ernest cut her off. "Don't bother. I don't have wards up, but that's because the sigils wore down and needed to be redrawn. I figured tonight would be the best night to do that, with so many Guardians here." He looked to the three, his calm expression finally giving away to annoyance. "Besides, if I had only taken them down to let demons in, why wouldn't I have put them back up after to prevent anything else from entering?"

Felix frowned. That was a good point—why *not* put them back up? Ernest must have known Mason would try coming for the wand eventually.

"Cover me if he tries anything," Mason whispered. He straightened up and lifted his wand that he'd pulled from his bag. His other hand hung in a tight fist at his side. "Are you done defending yourself, Ernest?"

Ernest glared at him. "You'd better watch yourself if you want a chance at living, demon—"

"You already stated you wanted us dead. Several times," Mason said. "Maybe Felix can show the council that at your trial. I'm sure the Ironwood Wand has lots of interesting memories." He stepped aside, revealing the crystals and bones he'd arranged on the floor behind him. He opened his left hand, allowing ash to rain down on the floor.

"What are you doing?" Ernest stepped forward. Felix drew his sword and pointed it at Ernest's face. Hopefully, whatever Mason had planned worked. Otherwise, he was *definitely* going to be in trouble for this.

Mason pointed his wand at the spell ingredients. "Unmask." A wave of magical energy rippled through the air. Felix grimaced as it passed through him, turning his stomach.

Fury took over Ernest's expression. "You—"

"Ernest, this place is infested with demons!" Down below, Michael Beck stepped onto a chair. His voice carried over the crowd. "I'd ask for an explanation, but it seems that Mason was right."

"And the entire council is here to witness it." Sadia moved to stand next to Michael. "The king will—"

Laughter cut her off. Abraham Caldwell shook his head. "We? There is no we, Sadia. The days of the King's Council are over."

Sadia whirled to face him. "What?"

"You've left me with no choice." Ernest pulled the Ironwood Wand from his jacket. He pointed it toward Felix, Arisa, and Mason.

Felix tried to back up. The wand's power latched onto him. With a flick of his wrist, Ernest sent Felix flying over the railing and into the party below.

Chapter Thirty
The Second Uprising

The ground raced toward Felix. Only one way to make it through this uninjured. He sucked in a deep breath and let his body melt into water.

The landing was disorienting. Felix hit the floor and was dimly aware of confused shouting around him. His panic brought him back together. He reassembled himself and shifted back into a person.

"Felix?" Kendra burst forward, shoving Guardians aside as she ran toward him. "What are you doing here? What—?"

Arisa was flung through the air next. Felix looked up and frantically racked his brain, trying to figure out which ability he could use to save her—

Threads of pure black reached out from shadows around the room to form a net beneath Arisa. She was lowered safely to the ground, and Hana emerged from the crowd to grab her.

Kendra glanced back. "I have to get back to Hana. I was relaying everything that happened to her—"

Mason crashed into a table of food nearby, snapping it in half.

"Mason!" Felix rushed to the table.

Mason staggered to his feet. "I'm fine," he muttered, brushing crumbs of food off his sweatshirt. "Focus on Ernest!"

Ernest, still on the walkway above, raised the Ironwood Wand. "You've had eight years to prepare for this, and what have you done? Keep to the same old regime and hope we wouldn't try again?"

"It doesn't matter how powerful that wand is," Sadia said. "You're outnumbered."

"I'm not as outnumbered as you think," Ernest replied. "We're almost evenly split into Guardians and the Moonlit Army." He paused. "Or, we would be, if it weren't for the demons on my side."

Something dropped from the shadows beneath the high ceiling. The figure that had been perched on one of the horizontal beams overhead hit the railing and used it to launch themselves at Ernest. Light glinted off a blade as it swung through the air.

And hit a barrier.

Archer bounced off the invisible wall. He flipped backwards and managed a surprisingly graceful landing on the railing.

Demons appeared at either side of the walkway. Ernest lifted a hand to stop them. "Not yet."

A few hissed and snarled, but they stayed put.

"You think I wouldn't cast a shield, Archer?" Ernest asked.

Archer's eyes narrowed. "You figured out how to use a witch's wand rather quickly."

"I taught myself some basics. Enough to handle a bunch of magicians."

"Not satisfied with your own ability?"

"It serves me well enough." Ernest pointed the wand at Archer. "But why settle?"

Archer jumped. The railing shattered beneath him. He landed on top of the barrier shielding Abernathy, raised his sword, and brought the tip down to a point in the air above Ernest. The invisible barrier apparently burst, allowing Archer to drop to the ground behind Ernest.

"Whatever magical energy that wand uses, I can sense its weak points." Archer lifted his sword in front of Ernest's neck. The blade grazed his skin. But one of the demons shot hellfire at Archer, forcing him to jump out of the way. More demons inched forward, eager to fight.

Archer lifted his sword to try again. Ernest pointed the wand his way, flinging him backwards through the air. Archer went over the railing, twisted himself in the air, and dropped onto the top of a display cabinet on the first floor.

Arisa ran to where Felix and Mason stood.

"What do we do?" Felix asked.

Mason started running. "Get the damn wand!"

Felix and Arisa followed. They made it ten feet. A whip of light cut through the air and slammed into all three of them, knocking them to the ground.

"Sorry, kids, but I think you should sit this one out." Sebastian rose into the air, carried by the light energy under his shoes. He folded his arms. "Really, Ernest? I thought maybe you'd stolen the wand as some kind of trophy, like all those stuffed animals you keep around. Why the hell are you joining the Uprising?"

"The Brightland Era is coming to an end," Ernest said plainly. "Most of the family's died off. More and more Guardians are leaving active duty. They're losing faith in their council to make the right decisions." A thin smile touched his lips. "I would think you of all people would understand that."

Sebastian laughed. "Sure, but I don't exactly like your methods. Or should I say Mira's methods? Is following her orders really better for you than following the king's?"

"At Bright Castle, I'm just another Guardian. On the other side, I command an army of my own. And with the Ironwood Wand, I'll wield even more power. Perhaps as much as Mira herself."

"What, because you can cast a few masking spells?" Sebastian raised an eyebrow. "That won't do you any good in a real battle."

"War isn't only won through battles," Ernest said. "How many Guardians have died on recent missions, walking into my death traps?"

Sebastian's expression shifted. Became cold. "You're responsible for every masking spell cast over the past few weeks, then?"

"Of course. Who else could have done it?"

"That means you almost got those kids killed *multiple* times." Sebastian lifted an arm and pointed a finger at Ernest. "So now, I'm going to kill you." A glowing orb formed at his fingertips.

"He needs to stand trial!" Archer shouted.

"Fine." Sebastian's mouth turned up in a cold smile. "I'll just rough him up a bit, then."

Ernest flicked the wand. The entire first floor of the mansion plunged into darkness. Even Sebastian's light went out.

Ernest's voice cut through the black. "Your days are numbered, Sebastian. You made your decision years ago, and Mira's not one for forgiveness."

After a moment of darkness and gasps and murmurs, a small orb of light appeared in the air, illuminating Sebastian's face and throwing rainbows across his hair. "Come on, Ernest, you know I can generate my own light." He pushed the light forward so that Ernest was visible, too.

"I also know you only have so much energy saved up," Ernest said. "Sooner or later, you'll run out. I just have to keep you from accessing any other light sources, and then I'll kill you."

"Hmm." Sebastian rubbed his chin. "You'd have to catch me first. You know, I think that would be a very interesting fight. Might even be a challenge! But I don't think I'll bother. Hana Tamura is here, after all."

"Tamura?" Ernest's voice was incredulous. "She spends her days in the library, not on missions. She may be able to manipulate darkness, but I'd hardly consider her a threat."

"Would you like to say that to her face?" Sebastian asked. "Because I think you're about to get your chance."

"Huh?"

Hana appeared at the edge of the light on the walkway. A staff of pure black took shape in her hands. She swung, sending it cracking against Ernest's skull.

Ernest staggered sideways, a hand pressed to the side of his head. Blood trickled down the side of his face. He lifted his other hand and snapped his fingers. "It's time!"

That was all the demons needed. They surged forward and scrambled over the railing, more than happy to throw themselves into battle against the Guardians below.

Sebastian dropped to the ground next to Felix, Mason, and Arisa. The orb hovering above his palm cast cold light over their faces. "Follow me."

"What? Where are we going?" Arisa asked.

"Outside."

"But the demons—" Felix started.

"The other Guardians will handle them."

"But the wand—" Mason tried.

"Leave that to us, too. It's too dangerous for you in here." Sebastian squinted at them. "How are you here in the first place?"

"Long story," Felix said. "Adrienne helped us."

"You met Adrienne Farrow?"

A demon launched itself at Sebastian's face. He obliterated it with a beam of light in the blink of an eye. "You three hold hands," he ordered. "It'll be safest if we keep ourselves in the dark for now."

Mason opened his mouth to protest, but Arisa grabbed his hand. She grabbed Felix with her other. Sebastian extinguished his light.

Now, the only thing visible in the dark was colorful blasts of hellfire.

Sebastian grabbed Felix's arm and pulled him forward. Arisa and Mason trailed behind. Felix tried to figure out which way they were going, but he'd lost all sense of direction. They left the battle behind and entered quieter hallways.

Occasionally, Sebastian would fire off a beam of light at a demon that got too close. Other than that, the four were completely in the dark. Whatever spell Ernest had cast on the first floor prevented light from even breaching the windows.

A door opened ahead, and they stumbled into the night air and the light of the moon and stars. Felix breathed a sigh of relief before he realized they hadn't actually left the house. They were in a courtyard.

"Seriously? He has a courtyard?" Mason exclaimed.

Arisa frowned as she let go of Felix and Mason's hands. "How are we not outside?"

"Sorry. My sense of direction is terrible," Sebastian said. "I'll just fly up and figure out the fastest way out—"

A figure slammed into him, sending him flying. He landed on his feet and slid backwards across the concrete, carving out the ground and sending a spray of rubble into the air. As he rose to his full height, the light faded from the bottom of his shoes. "Not saying that wasn't deserved, but what was that for, exactly?"

Archer drew his sword and pointed it at Sebastian. "What are those three doing here?"

"I'd like to know the same thing."

"You expect me to believe you're not responsible?" Archer flew forward with surprising speed. Sebastian stepped back to dodge the sword, but Archer switched directions and wound up on the other side of Sebastian with his blade in front of his neck. "I know you wanted them at that office building with the demons."

Sebastian looked rather calm for someone with a blade to their throat. "I would never put them in a situation I didn't think they could handle."

"You're not exactly denying it."

Annoyance flickered across Sebastian's face. "May I remind you that said building wasn't supposed to be full of demons?" He lifted his hands. "Archer, I care about these kids. I never would have let them walk into that if I'd known about the masking spell."

"And Sebastian's not responsible for us being here now," Felix added, taking a step forward. "Adrienne Farrow is the one who sent us here."

Archer slowly lowered the blade. "Why would she do that?"

"She would have come herself, but she was injured. Someone summoned poltergeists around the castle property," Felix quickly explained. "And she wasn't sure who to trust inside the castle."

Sebastian's eyes narrowed. His gaze shifted to his left, toward a window leading inside. "Do you think Ernest wanted them here?"

"He does want them dead," Archer replied.

"He didn't have to kill them here, though."

A crash came from the other side of a nearby wall. Sebastian sighed. "We have bigger problems to deal with right now," he said. "The battle is spreading across the house. Let's get the kids out of here and—"

A glass door shattered above them. Ernest stepped onto a balcony, looking worse for wear than he had earlier. He wordlessly held up the wand. The courtyard plunged into darkness.

A hand grabbed Felix's wrist. "Now's our chance," Mason whispered. "Ernest can't see under a darkness spell, either."

"Felix? Mason?" Arisa's voice came from Felix's left. Felix reached out blindly and found her arm. The three stumbled together toward the door on the other side of the courtyard.

A light orb appeared nearby, not quite bright enough to reach them. "Kids?" Sebastian called.

"Better not make yourself a target, Sebastian!" Ernest shouted. "I've got ten demons that'll be on you in seconds."

Felix slowed and threw a glance back over his shoulder.

Sebastian sighed. With a flick of his wrist, he expanded the orb enough to illuminate a large circle around him and Archer. "All right, I've got some time before I run out of light. Let's do this."

Archer lifted his sword. "Can you keep up?"

"What kind of question is that?" Sebastian asked.

"I did get a blade in front of your throat."

"Maybe I let you." Sebastian lifted an eyebrow. Archer rolled his eyes.

Mason grabbed Felix's arm and pulled him forward. "Come on," he said, his voice low.

"We should help—" Felix started.

"They can handle demons. We need to get the wand," Mason said. "That's the fastest way to end this."

Chapter Thirty-One
Fangs

Felix, Mason, and Arisa made their way up to the second floor, outside of Ernest's spell of darkness. Light spilled in through the windows, and lamps in the rooms along the hall cast a soft glow.

When the sound of hushed voices became audible ahead of them, the group slowed and pressed themselves against the wall to their right. Mason took the lead, and Felix found himself at the back of the line as they crept toward the intersection looming ahead.

"—asked her for backup," Ernest was saying. "They should arrive soon. This wasn't the plan, but if we do enough damage tonight, taking Bright Castle later will be easy."

"What if they don't arrive in time?" Eliza hissed in reply. "If we lose our advantage—"

"It's too late to change course," Ernest told her. "We can only move forward. Now get back to the fight."

A new voice spoke. "Trust in Mira."

Felix frowned. The man sounded familiar.

"Hugo's right," Ernest said. "We'll return to her, and she'll come up with a new strategy."

Footsteps faded into the distance. A hand grabbed Felix's shoulder, making him jump. He whirled around.

"Sorry." It was Michael Beck. "Didn't mean to scare you. Everyone from the Uprising is trying to find you. We need to get you out of here."

"Not without the wand," Mason said, eyes narrowing as he turned to look at Michael.

Michael's gaze flickered to Mason. "I understand. Okay, how about this? You go grab the wand and meet us outside." He pulled Felix toward him.

"No way, we're not splitting again," Arisa said.

Felix hesitated. He pulled his arm from Michael's grasp. "I appreciate it, but we need to get the wand. We can handle it."

Desperation crept into Michael's voice. "Felix, please. You're going to get yourself killed."

Uneasiness raised the hair on the back of Felix's neck. Without thinking, he took a step back.

A second copy of Michael materialized from nothing. The second Michael grabbed Arisa, drew a dagger, and held it to her neck.

Felix's heart stopped. "Arisa!"

Mason raised his fists, but two more copies of Michael appeared behind him and grabbed him. One pressed a dagger to the side of his face. Sigils in the blade glowed. Mason shouted in pain as his skin burned.

"I mean it when I say I don't want to hurt any of you," the original Michael said. "Unlike Ernest, I'm trying to avoid casualties. But they're inevitable when you're at war."

"You're—you can't be with the Uprising," Felix stammered. "You didn't know the demons were here, and you didn't join the other council traitors—"

"I thought it would be unwise to blow my cover so quickly." Michael took a step toward Felix. "Seems I was right."

"Why?" Felix asked, mirroring the motion with another step back. "What the hell are you all fighting for, anyway, if not to just take power from the king?"

"The king is wrong. About Guardians, about monsters, about how to run his sad excuse for a kingdom. The Moonlit Army will save far more innocent people than the Bright Guardians ever did."

Arisa glared at Michael. "How can you possibly say you care about innocent people when the Uprising killed so many Guardians? Do you have any idea how many died because of Ernest's masking spells?"

"The Guardians know what they signed up for," Michael replied, eyes still on Felix. "This is all for the greater good. Now, Felix, your best chance is to come with me." Another step forward. "Ernest wants you dead, but I'm willing to keep you alive. I believe you have something we need."

"What are you talking about?" Felix asked. His hand inched toward his sword.

"I think you do."

Felix froze. "You—that's why you helped buy my house, isn't it?"

Michael gave him a sad smile. "Don't get me wrong, I did feel awful about what happened. Your family didn't have to die. Gideon always was so violent..."

"Felix, what does he mean?" Mason cut in. "What does this have to do with your house?"

Felix shook his head. "Whatever my family was protecting, it isn't there."

That sent a look of surprise across Michael's face. "Where is it?"

"I don't know! They never told me about any of this!"

"Well, they're still with you, aren't they?" One of Michael's hands clenched into a fist. "We can get the weapon's location from them."

Another copy of Michael appeared and grabbed Felix's arm. Felix yanked his sword free with his other hand and swung. The blade cut clean through the copy's chest, and as blood began spurting from the wound, the copy vanished into thin air.

Arisa gasped in pain as the dagger at her neck touched her skin. Clementine jumped from her backpack and jammed a knife into the head of the copy holding her. The copy disappeared as quickly as the first Michael had. Mason's entire body erupted into hellfire, burning away the copies holding him.

Felix lunged at the real Michael and jammed the hilt of the sword into his forehead. Michael staggered backward. Another copy appeared, but Arisa cut through it easily. Mason caught up on Felix's right and slashed at Michael with his claws.

Felix shoved his foot into Michael's chest, knocking him onto his back. He raised his sword and aimed the tip at Michael's heart. Michael looked up at Felix with wild eyes. Blood trickled from the gashes Mason had left across his face.

Felix couldn't bring himself to bring the blade down. He adjusted the angle, readied himself to hit Michael with the flat side instead—

"Felix!" Mason shouted in warning.

"Michael!" Ernest stepped into the hallway. "What the hell are you doing?"

"Capturing Felix." Michael's breathing was ragged as he sat up, eyeing the tip of the sword's blade.

"He and his friends have beaten you," Ernest said. "This is why I wanted him killed."

"He's more valuable alive."

"And I'm ordering him dead."

Michael lifted his hands in the air as he slowly rose to his feet. Felix moved the sword, keeping it inches from Michael's face. "You command the monster army," Michael said. "You don't command the rest of us."

"Mira didn't ask us to keep him alive," Ernest replied.

"And what about Gideon?"

"Gideon's dead! Felix has access to all of his family's abilities, and he's already proven to be a challenge. Keeping him alive isn't worth the risk." Ernest's eyes narrowed. "Even if there's a slim chance of getting Gideon back."

Michael fell silent. To Felix's surprise, he didn't bring up the location of this supposed weapon. Did Ernest not know about it? Did Michael not want him to know?

"Surely you didn't care about Gideon that much," Ernest said. "Do you feel bad for the kid? That's pathetic." He raised the Ironwood Wand.

Mason held up his own wand. "Counter!"

A blast of energy rolled through the hallway. Mason staggered backwards. "My wand's not powerful enough to hold him off for long," he hissed through gritted teeth.

Ernest sighed. "It's disappointing that you still need verbal cues as a crutch. I thought you were raised by witches." He pointed the wand again. "I've only had this for a few months."

Mason lifted his own wand, ready to unleash another counterattack.

"Fine," Ernest said. "Let's try something new." He lifted an eyebrow. "Pierce." A thin beam of translucent energy burst from the wand's tip.

"No!" Michael took a step forward and shoved Felix out of the way. The beam entered his chest and emerged from his back, continuing on to blast a hole in the wall behind him.

As fast as it had appeared, the energy vanished. Michael swayed. He pressed a hand to his chest. When he pulled it away a moment later, blood dripped to the floor.

Michael collapsed.

Felix dropped to the ground next to him, barely understanding what had just happened. "Michael?"

"Felix," Michael gasped. Blood spilled from his mouth. "Listen to me, you have to—"

"Fool." Ernest's voice boomed, halting Michael's attempt to choke anything else out. "He always was too soft for the Moonlit Army."

Mason's hand tightened around his wand. "Null!" he shouted.

Ernest stumbled back a few steps. He shook out the hand holding the Ironwood Wand and glared at Mason. "Not bad, but you must know it won't last."

"I'd say we've got about five minutes." Mason returned his wand to his side. "That spell negated the Ironwood Wand's power. We just have to get it back before it wears off."

Felix looked at Michael. The man's dead eyes were fixed on the ceiling. An overwhelming wave of shock washed over him, and he realized it wasn't entirely his own emotions. His family's souls had entered his mind.

I can't believe Michael was with them all along. Ezra sounded shattered.

The rest of Felix's family were equally broken. Their pain clawed its way into Felix's chest, weighed down his heart with a heavy ache.

I was so sure we could trust him, Dad said.

Mom's voice followed. *Not now. Felix needs help.*

Felix forced himself up onto his shaking legs. Mason and Arisa charged at Ernest. Mind completely blank, Felix forced himself to follow, not sure what would happen when they reached him.

Ernest sighed and lifted a hand, his palm facing toward them. A blast of wind sent the three flying.

Felix was the first to hit the wall at the end of the hallway. He sank to the ground with a sharp gasp. Mason landed to his right, and Arisa to his left.

"He's manipulating air," Arisa managed between ragged breaths.

Felix's mind found its way back to him. He took another sharp breath. "What's his channeling material?"

"No idea."

Mason was already back on his feet. Felix and Arisa rose on either side of him, only for another current of wind to blast open the door to their right and send the three stumbling down the next hallway.

More doors swung open and slammed shut around them. Air rushed in and out of nearby rooms. Felix, Mason, and Arisa were pushed to the end of the hall and around the next corner. They were back at the walkway.

The moment the air's pressure alleviated, Mason started racing back the way they came. Felix and Arisa, still dazed from being violently tossed around, lingered behind him.

Ernest emerged from a hall branching to the left, hands raised. He sent another blast of wind down the hall. Mason unleashed hellfire to push back.

Felix found his senses. As Mason's fire faded, he lifted Helena's sword and charged forward, summoning lightning to dance up and down the blade. Arisa followed.

Felix started swinging the moment he was in range of Ernest. Each blow was knocked off target by a powerful gust of air. He tried to strike while Ernest was distracted by Mason's fireballs and Arisa's daggers, but the man was impossible to hit.

You gotta adjust your aim, Helena said.

My aim isn't the problem! Felix tightened his grip. *He's knocking me off course.*

That's exactly the problem! Don't aim where you want to hit, or he's going to move you.

Felix sucked in a deep breath. *If I'm not going to hit anything, he won't move me.*

Only if you aim too far off course. Find the balance.

Felix swung again. And missed. The blade passed through the air two feet to Ernest's right.

Ernest turned on him. "Losing steam, kid?" There was a crack running up the right lens of his glasses.

Felix focused on Ernest's shoulder. If he went for it, Ernest would push the blade up. Instead, Felix aimed for the air above his target and brought the blade forward.

Ernest pushed back with the air, but he didn't push very hard, expecting the blow to miss anyway. Felix twisted the blade and redirected his motion.

Metal met skin. A gash formed where Ernest's neck met his shoulder, just deep enough to draw blood.

Thanks, Helena! Felix thought. *You know, your sword's pretty great.*

Oh, come on, Felix, Helena replied. *It's your sword now.*

Felix grinned.

Ernest's hand shot forward and wrapped around Mom's ring. Felix hadn't realized it slipped out from under his shirt. The chain snapped. Light glinted off the ring as it sailed through the air and over the walkway railing behind him.

"No!" Felix tore his gaze from Ernest to follow the ring.

Mason reached toward him. "Felix, look out—!"

Ernest's fist struck the side of Felix's face. Felix crashed into the wall at his right. His sword slipped from his grasp. He stumbled with one hand on the wall, until the wall disappeared and his hands were brushing over the walkway's railing instead.

Ernest stormed toward him. "I think spending all that time with Sebastian made you cocky. You may outnumber me, but I have far more experience than you. Far more than you'll ever get, now." He grabbed Felix by the front of his jacket and lifted him. Felix tipped backward. His heart slammed in his chest as he found himself staring at the shroud of darkness below.

Behind Ernest, Mason and Arisa moved to attack again. A door swung open behind them. A demon lunged.

That was the last thing Felix saw before Ernest pushed him over the railing and into the black.

Felix had the sense to turn himself into water before he hit the ground. He frantically glanced around as he returned to his human form and sat up. Ernest's darkness spell must have been fading, because while it was still dim, he could make out the outlines of overturned furniture around him.

There was no sign of life, though. Where had all of the Guardians gone? Shouting echoed in the distance, coming from the direction of the front lawn. Maybe they'd dragged the fight out there to get out of the darkness.

Felix climbed to his feet. He needed to get back to Mason and Arisa. He ran in what he hoped was the direction of the stairs.

Ernest's foot hit the bottom step as Felix reached them. The Ironwood Wand was apparently still out of commission, because he resorted to immediately swinging at Felix with his fists. Felix staggered backwards, ducking and dodging and using most of his remaining focus just to avoid getting hit.

He had to retaliate. Now or never. He dropped into water, twisted into a whip, and—

Ernest hit him with a blast of wind.

Felix's water form sprayed the floor. His mind went completely blank, and it took him a moment to pull himself back together mentally. He felt awful. Shattered.

May, he thought dimly. *May help me!*

May slipped into his fractured mind. *You can do this. You're still in control of every drop.*

"You're out of abilities," Ernest gloated. "No dirt, no metal, water's useless against me. And I don't think seeing the past is going to do you any good here."

The scattered drops of Felix began moving. Slowly but surely, he reorganized himself.

Ernest lifted a hand. "I will admit, you fared pretty well. It's a shame the Guardians got you on their side. Mira might have been willing to take you in."

Felix returned to his human form. Mostly. His lower right arm was still water. Droplets lifted themselves off the floor and congregated in the air as he climbed to his feet. "Oh, sure, Mira sounds great. I'd love to help her out."

His gaze shifted up to the walkway. There was no sign of Mason or Arisa. No sound of fighting, either. His heart was running out of control in his chest.

Ernest glared at him. "You should try being respectful to people stronger than you. I've been a Guardian for decades, and I—"

Felix swung the upper half of his arm. The water twisted into a sphere and smacked Ernest in the face. While Ernest choked and gasped for air, Felix pulled the water back in to reform his real arm. Then, he moved in to throw a real punch.

Ernest caught his fist. Felix gasped in pain as Ernest twisted his arm.

"All right. I'm sick of this." Ernest lifted the Ironwood Wand and pointed it downward. May's stone lifted itself out of Felix's pocket and dropped to the ground. Felix reached out with his free arm to try to grab it, but another flick of the wand sent him stumbling back.

"Hm. Not back to full power yet. But we're getting there." Ernest took aim again.

Felix was thrown into a table. It tipped over, and he tumbled to the ground. He barely had time to get back on his feet before the next blow of magic sent him crashing through a door. The blast that followed was even stronger. It threw Felix the entire length of the hallway he'd entered.

Blood trickled from his nose as he sat up. It was dizzying just to be upright. Still, he climbed to his feet and watched a blurry Ernest stroll down the hall toward him.

"Why do you keep getting back up?" Ernest demanded. The wand lifted again.

Felix flew through an open doorway to his right and hit glass. It shattered around him. He squeezed his eyes shut and flung up his hands to shield his face as he crashed to the floor with the shards.

He opened his eyes. Blood stained his hands.

Felix threw a glance back to see what he'd collided with. A taxidermy bear nearly ten feet in height glared down at him, mouth open wide to show off its sharp teeth. Its display case lay in fragments on the floor.

"Impressive, right?" Ernest asked as he entered the room. "My best hunt, so far. The only species bigger than a Kodiak bear is a polar bear." He laughed. "I'll have to add one of those to my collection one day, too."

All Felix could think to say was, "Isn't that illegal?"

Ernest flicked the wand. The bear leaned forward. Slowly, at first, then it was falling too fast for Felix to process. Fangs and claws rushed toward him. He ducked and rolled to the right, but he wasn't fast enough to completely escape. His legs wound up pinned under the bear's weight.

Felix groaned and lifted his head.

"If you know what's good for you, you'll stay down this time," Ernest said. "Play nice and maybe I'll let you live after all."

Felix's blood spread across the floor in front of him. The air shimmered. One by one, his family appeared.

"Felix, you did your best," Mom said. She dropped to one knee next to him and rested a hand on his shoulder. "Let the other Guardians handle him."

"I'm not done," Felix mumbled.

"What was that?" Ernest asked. "Are you begging your family to save you? With you being so weak, I doubt they'll have the energy to hurt me." He spread his arms wide. "But they're welcome to try."

Felix pushed himself up onto his arms. "I'm not done yet," he repeated, louder.

"Hit me, then," Ernest challenged. "Lightning? Fire? You have nothing."

Felix looked to the others. Helena shook her head. "You are done, Felix. You barely have the strength to keep us standing here."

"You have nothing you can use to channel any of our abilities," Ezra added. "It's okay."

"Yeah, don't do anything stupid." May folded her arms. "Stupider than you already have, anyway."

Felix's gaze moved to the right, to the bear's mouth, to the fangs hovering inches from his face. "I said I'm not done yet."

The ghosts flickered out. Dad reappeared a moment later, standing closer to Felix in the pool of blood. "Felix, it's okay." He knelt down between Felix and the bear's head. "Sometimes there's nothing you can do."

"I know."

Dad smiled at him, eyes shining.

Felix took a deep breath. "But there is something I can do." He reached through Dad's translucent form into the bear's mouth.

Ernest took a step forward. "What—?"

Felix focused on his family, on drawing them back out of his blood. "Distract him!"

May and Ezra reappeared. May raised her hands, and the shelves around the room rattled. Ezra lifted his chin, and the light bulb above Ernest exploded. Glass rained down on him.

Helena materialized next to Felix as he wrested a fang out of the bear's mouth. "Felix, you have no way of knowing what will happen if you do this," she warned. "If you lose control, you're handing yourself over to the Uprising!"

"Then I won't lose control." Felix gritted his teeth. "I wasn't prepared when May first did it, but I'm prepared now." He looked up at her. "I can do this."

"I hope you're right."

Ernest stumbled into a nearby shelf, grabbed a glass bottle, and smashed it against the wall. A spray of salt clouded the air. The ghosts of the Carvers vanished.

"I'll kill you," Ernest snarled. "You've given me no other choice."

Felix's hand tightened around the fang. "Then I guess I have no choice, either."

Something lay dormant deep in Felix's soul, and the longer the fang rested against his skin, the more restless it grew.

Felix let the last ability in his blood take over.

Chapter Thirty-Two
The Sixth Ghost

The power Felix had in the Kodiak bear's body was overwhelming. He chased Ernest through the halls of the mansion, momentarily forgetting everything but the unbelievable strength and speed he had now. His exhaustion and even his pain had fallen to the back of his mind.

Ernest looked back over his shoulder and lifted the Ironwood Wand. That was a mistake. With one swipe of his paw, Felix knocked the wand aside. As it clattered against the ground, some part of him thought he should grab it, but then Ernest was running again and that was all he could focus on.

Felix took the next corner too quickly and slammed into the wall hard enough to send a painting tumbling to the floor. He pushed forward, driving Ernest through an archway into a room. A dead end. He had Ernest cornered.

Ernest unleashed a blast of wind, but it wasn't strong enough to move Felix. He was losing strength.

Footsteps sounded from the direction of the doorway. Ernest glared past Felix at the newcomer. "Took you long enough."

The distraction caused Felix to lose his hold on the bear form. He shrank back into a human as he whirled around. A jolt of fear shot through him.

The necromancer stopped in the middle of the room and laughed. "We meet again." He wore the same long white coat he had the night he attacked Felix and Jace, but the hood was down to expose his short curls of white hair.

"You," Felix hissed.

"Actually, the name's Hugo Underwood."

"Enough, Hugo," Ernest snapped. "I want the boy dead."

Hugo clicked his tongue. "If you wanted him dead, you should have done a better job. I'm not killing him as long as Gideon's still in there."

"If we take him alive, we'll regret it."

Cold laughter echoed around the room. "Ernest, you think too small. We don't need to kill him to stop him from being a threat." A wicked grin crossed Hugo's face. "He doesn't need his legs and arms to live, now does he?"

Ernest lifted an eyebrow. "Fine. He's all yours. I have to go find the wand, anyway."

"No!" Felix flung out an arm. A bear arm, covered in brown fur and ending in sharp claws. He tried to reshape the rest of his body to match, but his form remained firmly human.

Hugo chuckled. "Oh, I have the perfect match for you." He turned and assessed the room's decor. "Taxidermy animals are harder to animate. All that stuffing puts them in this strange gray area between dead and inanimate. But I think I can—"

Ernest's hands twitched at his sides. "Just shut up and do your job so I can get out of here!"

Two peacocks perched atop bookshelves took to the air and swooped at Felix. Felix knocked them aside with his bear hand and raced toward Hugo.

"What's with all these scars?" Felix asked as he slashed at Hugo's face.

Hugo ducked. "Bit rude to ask about that."

"Bit rude to try to kill me." Felix swung and missed again.

Hugo laughed. "These scars are a gift from your friend Archer. One of these days, I'll have to repay the favor."

Ernest attempted to run past Felix. Felix's other arm took on the bear's form as he jumped into Ernest's path. He grabbed the man's shoulders, and the two stumbled a few steps while Felix let his claws sink into skin. He picked Ernest up and threw him into the closest wall.

Hugo, meanwhile, brought a small bobcat to life and sent it after Felix. It pounced on him and knocked him on his back. The remaining few animals in the room joined the fray as Felix struggled to fight it off.

Through the pain of claws digging into his skin, Felix shouted, "Is this all you've got?" Besides the bobcat, his only enemies were some smaller birds and a rabbit.

"Don't worry, there's more on the way," Hugo replied. Crashes echoed through the hall behind him.

The Kodiak bear that Felix had stolen a fang from burst into the room.

Felix threw the bobcat off of him and returned fully to his bear form. His arm swung as the stuffed bear reached him. The first blow landed, but his excitement was short-lived. The bear lashed out with its claws and left light scratches in Felix's shoulder.

He quickly realized that had the advantage. Like the zombies—er, undead—this animal only had what remained of it. Skin and teeth and claws. Felix had bones and muscle and a massive bear's heart pounding in his chest.

That advantage diminished as Hugo's army grew. An antelope stumbled into the room, followed by a cougar and a dingo and several geese. Individually, they didn't do much harm, but enough of them jumped on Felix at the same time to knock him down. His skin stung as teeth and claws and beaks tore at him.

Just as Felix managed to rip himself free and get back on all fours, a new voice spoke in his head.

You could die here.

Felix froze. The other bear slammed a paw into his chest and sent him staggering.

Laughter, the same laughter from his nightmares about the day his family died, reverberated through his mind. *Seriously, kid,* Gideon said. *Admit you've screwed up and let me take over.*

I'm not stupid. Felix let out a low growl. *If I let you in, you're never giving my body back.* He threw himself at the bear and pinned it against the ground.

Of course not! I'm not giving you anything but an opportunity to live. I'll take your body and your family to the Moonlit Army. Gideon laughed. *Of course, if you're not going to hand yourself over willingly, I'll just put up a real fight. You're tired, and—*

"No!" Felix dropped back into his human form. The three geese flying his way crashed into the wall above him.

Ernest and Hugo had slipped out of the room. *The wand.* Felix needed to get the wand before they did. He sprinted out of the room. The swarm of undead animals followed, but they were thankfully slower than he was.

Once Felix was clear of the doorway, he transformed back into the Kodiak bear. He caught up to Ernest and Hugo easily, though part of his mind—what little he could cling to in the bear form—was occupied pushing back against Gideon. So far, at least, Gideon's "real fight" didn't take much focus to hold off.

Ernest and Hugo dove out of the way when Felix caught up. He slid past them, his claws scraping the floor. What had he come this way for?

Right. The wand. He spotted it lying on the floor near the end of the hall. He transformed back into a human and stumbled to an abrupt stop next to it. He picked it up. When he turned around, Ernest and Hugo were back on their feet, cautiously approaching.

"How hard is this thing to use, anyway?" Felix asked, examining it. Mason had just said simple words, and Ernest was able to use it without saying a thing.

"Felix, don't be stupid. That thing's dangerous." Ernest reached out a hand. "Hand it over, and we can discuss saving you and your friends from any more trouble."

Felix snorted. "Yeah, right." He pointed it at Ernest. "Uh, let's see, uh, how about—"

"You idiot, don't—"

"Float."

The magical energy that exploded from the wand knocked Felix onto his ass. It also launched Ernest and Hugo into the air. They slammed into the ceiling and drifted down a few feet, where they hovered.

Felix climbed to his feet. He leaned against the wall, trying to hide his pain from Ernest. The landing had sent it shooting through his bones. Every ache he'd ever felt had returned with a vengeance.

"That hurt pretty bad, didn't it?" Ernest spat. "The Ironwood Wand isn't a toy."

Felix pointed the wand at him as a warning, but he wasn't sure he could bring himself to use it again. Glaring up at Ernest, he said, "How about you tell me how you managed to get so many monsters on your side. Why are demons and spirits helping you fight the Guardians?"

"You really expect me to answer your questions?"

"Fine. I'll just—" Felix's hand tightened down the wand. Gideon's presence had crawled back into his mind and was fighting for control, with more ferocity this time. Felix swallowed. "I'll just leave the interrogation to the other Guardians."

"Assuming they're still alive," Ernest said.

"Felix, you seem to be forgetting my own allies." Hugo's amused tone was an odd contrast to Ernest's boiling anger. "You have about two seconds."

"Huh?" Felix lowered his gaze. Oh, right, the animals—

The first goose collided with him, violently flapping its wings. The wand slipped from his hand and rolled away. Ernest and Hugo dropped to the ground.

"Hugo, take your army outside and make sure the battle's under control out there," Ernest ordered. He had a grimace on his face as he staggered to his feet, but kept his voice strong as he added, "I've got Felix."

Felix chucked the goose into the nearest wall and raced for the wand. Ernest reached it first, but Felix got his hands around it, too, as Ernest raised it into the air. Felix stomped on Ernest's foot and attempted to yank the wand free. Ernest's jaw clenched as he pulled back.

Give it up, Felix, Gideon said, his voice singsong.

"Shut up!" Felix snapped.

Confusion flickered across Ernest's expression. It was quickly replaced by a thin smile. "You're fighting him, aren't you?"

"I don't know what you mean." Felix stopped struggling for a few moments before jerking the wand toward him, hoping to take Ernest by surprise. It didn't work.

"Maybe Hugo was right," Ernest said. "Give up the wand, boy."

"I'm not letting go." Felix's grip tightened.

"Give it up," Ernest pressed. "Unless you want to risk losing your battle with Gideon."

"I've got him under control," Felix insisted.

"Really? Why not shift back into the bear, then?"

Felix lifted his gaze, and his heart soared. A smile touched his lips. "I don't need to."

Ernest frowned. "What?"

The gold and white rug swooped down from the air above. Mason looked like he was going to be sick. Arisa, on the other hand, was having the time of her life. She pumped a fist in the air and cheered as the rug she'd animated carried her right over Ernest's head.

Ernest used the distraction to push Felix away with a blast of air. Felix lost his hold on the wand. Terror paralyzed him as Ernest took aim.

Mason reached down and grabbed Felix by the collar of his jacket. The rug shot up vertically, carrying Felix out of the wand's range. With Mason's help, he pulled himself up onto the top of the rug.

"He's still got the wand—" Felix warned.

He barely got the words out before Mason slid off the carpet, hit the ground, and pointed his own wand at Ernest. They stared each other down.

"This wand is no good to you, demon," Ernest said.

"You have a problem with me being a demon?" Mason asked. "You employ demons yourself."

"'Employing' being the key word. They know their place. They wouldn't dare call themselves Guardians. Or witches." Ernest took a step forward. "Do you really think your parents would have wanted you to do this?"

Mason roared and charged forward. Hellfire swallowed him, starting at his hands and spreading until it covered his horns and boots and the tuft of fur at the end of his tail. The flames licked the wand in his hand, inching up toward the tip.

His wand exploded in a shower of purple sparks.

"See?" Ernest said as he sidestepped Mason. "You resort to demonic violence instead of using your head. And now your wand is gone." He took aim with the Ironwood Wand.

"We have to help him!" Felix exclaimed as Mason narrowly dodged whatever spell Ernest had fired off. "Lower the rug!"

"I'm thinking!" Arisa looked to Felix. "What ability are you going to attack with?"

Felix hesitated. "I—I don't have anything on me, except..."

"Except what?"

Felix pulled the bear fang from his pocket and held it up.

Arisa's eyes widened. "Felix, what did you do?"

"It's going to be fine, I—"

An explosion of hellfire beneath them knocked the rug off balance. They plummeted toward the floor. Arisa grabbed the front of the rug and pulled them up just before they hit the ground.

"Leave Ernest to me," Arisa said.

"Are you sure?" Felix asked. "Animating the rug must have been—"

"I'm sure!" Arisa hissed. She immediately winced. "Sorry. I've got this."

Glass animal figurines jumped off the shelves below. Arisa laughed as they converged on Ernest. "Take that, old man!"

While Ernest attempted to pry the figurines off himself, Arisa lowered the rug. Mason ran toward them, holding up the Ironwood Wand. "Let's get out of here!" he shouted. He jumped and rolled onto the rug. Felix grabbed him to stop him from falling off the other side.

The rug lifted into the air and shot forward.

Felix glanced at Arisa's hand and realized that the skin under her counterbalance bracelet was badly burned. "Arisa, your wrist!"

Mason leaned forward. His eyes widened. "Here, let me heal—"

"It's fine." Arisa's jaw clenched. "Let's get out of here, first."

A crash came from behind them. Felix glanced back and groaned. "He's chasing us!"

"What?" Arisa yelped. "How fast?"

"Pretty fast! He's flying with his air magic!" Felix turned his attention forward. "Turn left up ahead. That should take us outside."

The rug swerved. They rounded the corner with alarming speed.

"Windows!" Mason warned.

Arisa veered toward the wall, bringing them toward a shelf. "Grab something off the top of that to smash the window!"

Felix leaned over and stretched out a hand. He snagged a bronze rabbit statue. His gaze lifted to the approaching window. Closer, closer, closer...

"Now!" Arisa yelled.

Felix threw the statue. The window exploded in a shower of glass, and they burst out of the mansion into the night.

Chapter Thirty-Three
Inner Demons

The lawn was a mess. Bodies were scattered across the grass. Most weren't human, but there were a few here and there wore Guardian suits. Felix wondered how many were with the Moonlit Army and how many were on their side.

The carpet dropped a few feet. Felix's stomach lurched.

Arisa hissed. "I'm running out of—"

They hit the ground before she could finish. Felix bounced off the rug and rolled across the grass, spinning hard and fast. Even after he stopped moving, the world continued to spin. He forced himself up and immediately regretted it as bile threatened to jump into his throat.

Mason was back on his feet in a heartbeat. "Where is everyone else?"

Felix followed the sound of distant shouting to the tree line. Flashes of color cut through the darkness beyond.

Ernest flew out of the window they'd shattered and landed on the grass in front of them. The right lens of his glasses was even more fractured now, on the verge of shattering.

Mason pointed the Ironwood Wand at him. "One more step and I'll blow your limbs off."

"You can't do that." Ernest held up his hands. "You can't bluff with me. My senses are still too tuned to the wand."

Mason's eyes narrowed.

"Wait, why can't you blow his limbs off?" Arisa asked as she stood. "That sounds like a great idea."

"In theory, I could," Mason said. "But he and I can sense that the wand's energy is...fracturing. He used it a lot already tonight, and I'm an opposing force to Ernest, which the wand can pick up on. It needs to adjust to me. If I tried something too violent on Ernest right away, it would probably backfire." He glared at Ernest.

"How long does it need?" Felix asked.

"Not long for basic spells, but I wouldn't trust it with anything big, tonight." After a moment, Mason chuckled. "It doesn't matter. I am a demon after all, right?" He tossed the wand toward Felix, and Felix barely caught it.

A circle of purple hellfire sprang up around Abernathy.

"What's your plan?" Ernest asked. "You can try keeping me here as long as you can, but either you'll run out of steam and the fire will die, or it will get out of control and hurt your friends."

"I just need to hold you until backup arrives." Mason looked to Arisa and Felix. "Could one of you get to the battle and find someone who can help us?"

"Don't bother. You forget who I am." Ernest blasted the fire in front of him with his air. That side of the circle flickered, but the flames held and strengthened after a moment. Ernest gritted his teeth and tried a stronger gust. More cracks ran through his glasses.

Mason charged forward through the fire, claws emerging. He grabbed Ernest and lifted him into the air.

The scar across Mason's forehead was…opening. Something black shone underneath, reflecting the light of the hellfire. "My parents spent their lives protecting the wand from people like you!" Mason shouted.

"And now what?" Ernest hissed in reply. "You've got me. You've got the wand back. What are you going to do now? Your parents are dead, and you've been cursed to the life of a demon."

The fire burned brighter around him and Mason. Still, Ernest persisted. "You haven't even begun to grasp the hell you've made for yourself."

Demons erupted from the tree line. No, not just demons. The grass rippled as three wraiths took shape in the air. The battle was here.

"Aren't demons supposed to be rare?" Felix asked, his shoulders sagging.

Arisa looked ready to sink into the ground beneath her. "Yes. Yes they are."

Wind whipped through the air, finally extinguishing the circle of hellfire. Ernest raised his voice. "Help me!" he yelled to the approaching demons. "I need to get the wand back—"

Mason threw him against the ground. He stomped on Ernest's shoulder and leaned forward, tail twitching behind him. "How do you still have so much energy?"

The first demons raced right past Felix and Arisa to swarm Mason, forcing him to turn away from Ernest. Claws tore at his skin and clothes. He blasted the monsters back a few feet with hellfire.

One of the demons laughed. "That stung a little." It lunged again.

While Mason dealt with the demons, Ernest jumped to his feet and ran toward Felix. It took Felix a moment to remember he was holding the wand. He tried to get up to run away, but his legs refused to cooperate. As Ernest drew closer and moonlight glinted off his cracking glasses, Felix remembered something Sebastian had told them.

Arisa stepped in front of Felix and lifted her fists. A blast of wind knocked her into the air.

"Arisa!" Felix's head snapped to the right. He watched her slam into the ground ten feet away. Groaning in pain, she rolled onto her back.

Ernest had almost reached Felix when Mason grabbed his collar and threw him onto his back.

"Mason!" Felix exclaimed. "Remember what Sebastian said about channeling ambient magic?"

Mason reached down and yanked Ernest's glasses off his face. "Got it," he snarled. He snapped them in half, shattering the lenses completely, and threw the frames far out of Ernest's reach. "You need glass to use your ability, don't you?"

Some of the demons lying on the ground behind him stirred. "They're not all dead," Felix warned.

Arisa staggered over and dropped to the ground next to Felix. "And there's more on the way." She looked up, and Felix followed her gaze. The three wraiths circled overhead. How long until they attacked, too?

A shadow darted across the lawn, zipping past the next wave of approaching demons before stopping in the air above Felix, Arisa, and Mason. The patch of shadow took on a human shape and transformed into Hana, still dressed in her completely black suit. As she dropped to the ground, a sword formed in her hands, so black it looked like an opening into the void.

Hana moved into battle with ease. Her blade sank into the chest of the closest demon, and it sank lifelessly to the ground. Threads of darkness hovered in the air around her, forming a spherical net. The moment any demon passed through the net, Hana was swinging at them and slicing them open.

Just as Felix thought Hana was going to be overwhelmed, a swarm of bees emerged from the forest and raced to her side. The swarm turned into Kendra, who already had her daggers in hand as she fell seamlessly into action at Hana's side.

While those two fended off demons, Mason dragged Ernest to where Felix and Arisa sat. He let go of Ernest's jacket, leaving the man to slump against the ground with a grunt. Mason lifted his foot and brought it down on Ernest's chest.

Whatever had been happening with the scar on Mason's forehead was over. It had returned to its usual appearance as a simple horizontal line.

"Are you two okay?" Mason asked.

"No," Felix answered.

"Absolutely not," Arisa added.

Mason turned to watch Hana and Kendra. The demons he'd fought moments earlier had torn his sweatshirt and the shirt underneath to shreds, revealing stretches of bloodstained skin visible beneath. He shifted his weight onto the leg pressed to Ernest's chest. Ernest gasped as something cracked. He coughed. Blood sprayed the front of his shirt.

"We took care of that wave," Hana signed as she and Kendra joined the three. "But there are some demons left in the forest." Her gaze darted up. "And those wraiths overhead."

"Your swords can kill demons?" Felix asked. He threw a quick glance at Arisa to make sure he'd signed the question right. She nodded.

"I build sigils into the blade when I construct it," Hana replied. "They're hard to see." As she lowered her hand, she looked toward the tree line.

Felix turned to Kendra. "Where are Sebastian and Archer?" he asked aloud. "And the rest of the Guardians?"

"Making their way back," Kendra answered. Her voice was hoarse. "We killed the demons in Abernathy's house, but more approached from the forest. The battle wound up moving that way."

"That explains why he left the wards down," Mason said. "He had backup." He glared down at the man pinned beneath him.

"Something's moving over there," Arisa warned, her eyes on the trees.

Archer trudged out of the shadows, sword in hand, mask down, blood splattered across his skin and tattered suit. When he reached the group, his attention was focused on Mason. "You still with us?" Archer asked as he looked him up and down.

"What's that supposed to mean?" Mason replied.

"Just wanted to make sure you weren't overcome with bloodlust."

"He's fine," Felix insisted.

Archer was quiet for a long moment before nodding. "Good job getting Ernest."

Mason scowled, but responded with a curt, "Thanks."

The clouds hanging overhead in the night sky emitted a sudden glow, drawing everyone's gazes upward. One by one, beams of light cut through the air and touched down somewhere in the forest. Each was accompanied by a high-pitched whine.

Dead silence followed.

Sebastian descended from the sky, his eyes glowing as bright as the circular platform beneath his shoes. His face was completely devoid of emotion as he touched down in front of the group. He'd ditched his suit jacket and pushed the sleeves of his shirt halfway up his arms. Sizeable patches of blood stained the otherwise blue fabric.

His head tipped back, and he lifted his hand. A blade of light formed in the air and went spinning up toward the wraiths. It sliced through each one and turned them to clouds of smoke.

"Shame I was busy fighting Guardians most of the battle. They're the real challenge." The glow faded from Sebastian's eyes. His blank expression gave way to concern. "What happened to you kids?"

"We got Ernest and the wand," Mason said.

Felix half-heartedly waved the wand. "Yay us!"

"Did you get all of the demons?" Archer asked.

"Not quite," Sebastian said. "Those bastards are fast. But there's only a few left, and—"

Hugo burst from the trees, his army of taxidermy animals trailing behind. He stopped after a few feet and stared at the group. His gaze darted from Kendra to Hana to Sebastian and finally to Archer.

He turned around and ran back into the darkness.

Archer moved to follow. Sebastian grabbed his shoulder to stop him. "We've lost enough tonight already."

"I'm not letting him get away again!" Archer's voice carried more emotion than Felix had ever heard in it.

"Archer," Sebastian said firmly. "The kids."

Archer glanced back. Mason, despite his unwavering confidence, was bleeding heavily. Felix and Arisa still sat on the ground. Arisa rubbed her wrist where the counterbalance bracelet had burned her. The hand Felix held the Ironwood Wand with trembled violently.

"Fine." Archer turned his head. His eyes met Sebastian's. "You said there were some demons left?"

Sebastian stared back at Archer for a long moment. "Yes," he finally replied. "But there are still Guardians on our side out there, too. They might take care of the rest."

"Still, we should be prepared." Kendra turned and signed something to Hana a little too quickly for Felix to follow.

"What about the Guardians who joined the Uprising?" Arisa asked. "Or the Moonlit Army, or whatever?"

Sebastian folded his arms. "Most of the traitors ran off once the demon army began dwindling."

"Cowards," Archer muttered.

"Mason," Felix said, his voice weak. He shrugged off the backpack that had miraculously clung to him through everything. "You should grab my hoodie from my bag."

"You sure?" Mason glanced at Felix. "I don't want to ruin it with my blood."

"It's fine. It's already torn and stained," Felix told him. "It's a little big on me, so it should fit you."

Mason slowly stepped back from Ernest. Archer moved into position next to him and aimed his blade at the man's throat while Mason dug Felix's hoodie out of the bag, stood up, and peeled off the tattered remains of his sweatshirt and shirt.

Arisa's eyes widened. "Hey, Mason, have you always had those scars on your back?"

"What scars?" Mason tried to peer at them over his shoulder.

"There's two big ones," Felix told him, eyeing the slightly angled lines cutting through Mason's skin. "Uh, vertical? Or is that horizontal—?" He always mixed those two up.

"They're almost vertical," Arisa said. "But they look like the one on your forehead."

"Hm." Mason pulled on Felix's hoodie and zipped it up. "Weird."

"That's all you have to say?"

"That's, like, the least weird thing that's happened to me since I turned into a demon."

Hana raised a hand. The group fell silent. She signed something to Kendra, who frowned.

"I sense it too," Kendra both spoke and signed.

"What's happening?" Felix asked.

Kendra glanced at him, worry in her expression. "Hana and I just picked up on an increase in magical energy," she told him.

"Me too." Archer's brow furrowed. "But—"

Arisa groaned. "If one more thing comes out of that forest, I'm going to cry."

"It's not coming from the forest," Mason said. "It's coming from..." He trailed off, and then he was looking at Felix too. Felix shifted uncomfortably.

"We've got demons," Sebastian warned. "Coming toward the tree line. About twenty left. Guardians are chasing them, but the demons are faster."

"But—" Mason started.

Felix's legs moved beneath him, pushing himself to his feet. His mouth opened beyond his control.

Gideon's voice came out.

"I'm afraid you have a bigger problem right now."

Chapter Thirty-Four
Mirabelle

Gideon laughed through Felix's mouth. "Felix picked the nastiest beast in Abernathy's collection." Magic surged through Felix's chest as they transformed into the Kodiak bear.

"Ah. That is a nice choice," Sebastian said.

Archer lifted his sword. "Bad for us."

Panic overtook Felix at the sight of Archer's blade pointed his way, enough for him to pull himself back into a human form. "Wait! Don't kill me!"

"We aren't going to hurt you, Felix." Sebastian held up his hands. "But Gideon—"

Ernest laughed from where he lay on the ground. "Gideon's going to free me, and we're going to kill you."

Felix's head snapped toward Ernest. Gideon spoke. "Really? After you were so ready to kill him and send me to whatever's next?"

"I didn't think you were coming back!" Ernest protested. "Besides, I've done so much for you. Hell, how many of my hunting trophies did I let you raid for parts?"

"It's going to take a lot more than that—" Gideon started.

Archer grabbed the back of Felix's jacket and held his blade to the side of his face. Felix wrestled control back from Gideon and shoved him down, out of his mind. "I've got him under control!"

"No, you don't."

Felix's jaw clenched. He couldn't bring himself to protest. Gideon was already clawing his way back up.

"Listen, Felix." Sebastian's voice was calm, though there was genuine distress at its edges. He took a cautious step forward. "Let us take you back to the castle and put you somewhere Gideon won't be able to hurt anyone. Just long enough for us to sort us out. I know you're strong enough to beat him, but right now you're exhausted."

Felix dropped to his knees. Archer's blade followed, keeping within a few inches of his face.

Arisa watched with wide eyes. "Don't hurt him!"

"We'd all be dead without him," Mason added.

"That means nothing if Gideon takes control," Archer said. "Felix, Gideon's much stronger than you."

The demons Sebastian had warned them about entered the lawn and started toward them. They were slow, injured, but persistent. They'd reach Felix and the others in a minute, tops.

"I'm in control," Felix insisted. "Archer, you can go fight."

"I'm not leaving your side," Archer replied. Felix wasn't sure if that was supposed to be reassuring or threatening. Probably the latter.

"Sebastian?" Kendra asked. "Do you have enough energy left to handle the demons?"

Sebastian pressed his hands together and cracked his knuckles. "I think so. But Archer might have to carry me back to the castle."

"I'm not carrying you anywhere."

Felix took a deep breath. His fingers dug into the dirt.

Dirt.

How could he have forgotten?

Felix chuckled. "Sorry, Ezra," he said under his breath.

"What was that?" Archer asked.

Ezra must have heard him. His presence slid into Felix's head. *Me and the others were busy trying to pull Gideon back. Otherwise, I would have reminded you.*

"Nah, that's on me. I think I neglected your abilities a bit." Felix paused. "And your cactus. How often should I be watering it again?"

A new presence slammed into Felix. *Enough talk. I've almost got you, kid,* Gideon hissed.

"Sebastian, we have to do something," Archer said. "Felix is losing."

"Do you or do you not want me to handle these demons?" Sebastian asked. He gestured toward the demons that were halfway to them.

Felix looked up. "Look, Archer is right. Gideon is stronger than me alone. But I'm not alone." He pushed himself to his feet. "My family and I have Gideon outnumbered."

I've got you, Felix, Ezra said.

Felix let go and allowed Ezra to take control. *The others are here too, aren't they?* he asked.

Ezra spoke aloud with Felix's mouth. "They're going to drag Gideon back down into your soul and keep him there as long as they can. I'll join them once I'm done here." He raised Felix's hands. "Lawns like this are awful for the environment. Let's try a little biodiversity."

If Felix could use his mouth, he would have grinned. *Okay, nerd.*

Vines burst from the ground at the demons' feet as they ran, grabbing them and slamming them against the earth. After one last glance at Felix, Archer darted forward, sword spinning in his hand.

Sebastian stepped back. "I'll watch Ernest," he said to Kendra. "You two go."

Kendra nodded, grabbed Hana's hand, and pulled her forward. They joined Archer in cutting down the demons Ezra's vines pinned to the ground.

Can we try the tree thing again? Felix asked.

"I think it would kill you if I tried that right now," Ezra told him.

What about what Ernest did to summon more energy? By fracturing his channeling material? There's plenty of dirt around!

"That's an advanced technique and it takes a lot of practice," Ezra said. "Again, I'd like to avoid killing you."

Some of the more distant demons managed to avoid Ezra's vines. While Kendra and Hana killed the rest that were trapped against the earth, the last few darted past them and continued their approach toward Felix and the others.

Felix was back in control of his body. He dropped back to his knees, dimly thinking he was going to be bruised to hell and back tomorrow.

That's all I got, Ezra said. *Good luck.* He vanished, leaving Felix's mind empty.

Archer, who'd stayed close, rejoined the group. "You didn't get all of them," he warned.

"Yeah, I'm done," Felix said. "Sorry."

"No worries. We'll take it from here," Sebastian said. "And by that, I mean that I'll take it from here."

"No need for overkill," Archer told him. "There's five left."

"Six, actually, but I'll leave that guy trying to sneak up on us to you."

While Archer walked off, Sebastian lifted his hands and wiggled his fingers, grinning at the approaching demons. "Any last words?"

The demons slowed. "Sebastian Armitage," one of them hissed. "Your death approaches—"

"Boring!" Beams of light burst from Sebastian's palms. The first carved a hole through the head of the demon that tried to speak. The second ripped through another's chest. He fired off two more through the next two demon's abdomens.

"I don't suppose you'll be any more interesting," Sebastian said to the last one.

The green demon let its leathery wings stretch out to its sides.

"Oh, fun!" Sebastian blasted a hole in each wing. While the demon howled in pain, he unleashed a final beam to pierce its neck.

Archer returned and threw the sixth demon down on the ground in front of Sebastian. Blood spilled from a gaping wound in its chest. "We've got one more incoming, according to this one." Gaze lifting to Sebastian's, he added, "She wants to talk to you."

Apparently, that was all Sebastian needed to know who Archer was talking about. He sighed and walked up to the demon. Kendra and Hana returned and stopped next to Archer.

"Another demon coming?" Arisa asked.

"No," Archer replied. "Something worse."

The demon tried to scramble to its feet, but Sebastian knocked it back to the ground with one solid kick. He rested his foot on its chest and spoke.

"Why are you helping her?" Sebastian asked. "Mira and the Brightlands don't see eye to eye, but she's still interested in killing monsters like you, last I heard."

"Oh, no, not at all." The demon's tone was frantic. "Mira's on our side now."

"I find that hard to believe."

"Ask her yourself, then. She's one of us. And she could be all of us."

Sebastian's expression darkened. He held a hand over the demon's face.

"No, wait, please—"

The ray of light obliterated the demon's head entirely. Afterward, the air echoed with a faint trace of the odd tone that accompanied the light.

Archer walked between the bodies of the demons Sebastian had killed. With each swing of his sword, he cut off another head.

"What, you don't like my work?" Sebastian asked as he turned around.

"I'm making sure they don't regenerate," Archer replied.

"These are weak ones," Sebastian said with a dismissive wave of his hand. "Not the big nasty guys that can stitch their heads back to their necks—oh, here she is."

Something moved at the edge of the lawn.

"I'm getting real sick of watching monsters walk out of that forest," Mason muttered.

Arisa let out an exasperated sigh. "Right?"

Felix frowned as the massive wolf approached, silver fur glinting in the light of the moon that was definitely not full. "A werewolf? How is that possible?"

"I don't know, but we can kill a werewolf," Arisa said. "Easy."

Sebastian held up a hand. "Not this one. Not when we're this exhausted. And if she's brave enough to walk up to us alone, more of her army must be nearby." He threw a quick glance up at the sky.

The wolf stopped twenty feet in front of Sebastian.

"Why are you here?" Sebastian called to her. "Battle's over. The traitors ran off and the monsters are dead."

The wolf tipped her head back and laughed. "I just wanted to say hello before I left."

Sebastian folded his arms. "You always had a way with words, but how the hell did you get all of these monsters on your side? You swore you'd destroy them."

"I was wrong when I was young." The wolf's head cocked to the side. "But now I can see my path forward."

"You don't care about protecting people anymore?"

"Oh, I do, but there are far better ways to do it than dancing around under the council's rules."

"Is this—Mira?" Felix whispered. Kendra nodded.

"The thing about monsters is that they're hungry," Mira continued. "As long as you keep them occupied with food, they'll do whatever you want."

Sebastian's eyes narrowed. "Do I want to know what you're feeding them with?"

Mira responded with cold laughter. "I know it doesn't seem like it from your pathetically small perspective," she said. "But everything I'm doing will save human lives in the long run."

"Too many people are going to get killed in your fight for power," Sebastian told her. "Far more than you could ever hope to save by changing a few rules." He sighed. "I know the council hurt you, but this isn't—"

"Oh, I don't give a damn about what the council did to me anymore. This is so much bigger than that," Mira said. "In a way, though, I'm grateful. If they hadn't acted the way they did, I never would have had my eyes opened." She turned around. "We'll meet again soon, Seb."

"Wait, Mira!" Ernest shouted. "Help me—"

"Sorry, Ernest." Mira looked back. "But this is your own fault. I'm not risking my life to save you here."

A frantic expression overtook Ernest's face. "Gideon possessed the boy. Only for a minute, but he spoke."

Mira's gaze shifted. Her cold, blue eyes moved to Felix. A chill ran down his spine.

"Why did Gideon kill the Carvers?" Ernest asked.

"Gideon had his job, just as you had yours," Mira replied. "And now you're done."

"Wait—!"

Sebastian moved his foot to Ernest's neck and pressed down, cutting him off. "Shut up, old man."

Mira walked toward the edge of the lawn.

"Shouldn't we go after her?" Mason asked.

Sebastian shook his head. "We're all drained. And—" He glanced up again as a flock of bats raced by overhead. "—the only reason she's leaving is because she knows a fight right now would be close. It's not worth the risk. For either of us."

Halfway to the tree line, Mira looked back one last time. "Goodbye, brother." She flashed sharp teeth as her lips drew back in an expression that could have been a grin or a snarl.

"Brother?" Felix nearly choked on the word.

The wolf sprinted into the shadows and vanished.

"Well, you've met the leader of the Moonlit Army," Sebastian said, watching her go with a distant look in his eyes. "Mirabelle Armitage. My sister."

Chapter Thirty-Five
King's Orders

This time around, the king waited for Felix to be healed before calling him and the others in front of the council.

Well, mostly healed. Only three days after the fight at Ernest's mansion, Felix was far from full strength. Bandages were wrapped around the worst of his wounds, he felt nauseous when he moved too fast, and he was still taking pain medication for his various aches. The Ironwood Wand could have helped considerably, but it was still recalibrating from the battle.

Of the hundred or so Guardians at Ernest's party, forty-five had been a part of the Second Uprising. No one was certain how many of the traitors had been killed, but ten had died on the Brightlands' side. A small fraction of the roughly three hundred total active Guardians there had been before the party— approximately two hundred of which lived at the castle, Felix had learned—but a painful blow nonetheless.

The goal of the party had clearly been to wipe out a fourth of the Brightlands' forces, between killing the loyal ones and the rest turning traitor. With the number of active Guardians down to about three hundred, it was hard to say their plan had been a complete failure.

Felix stopped in front of the doors to the throne room. Kendra, who'd accompanied him, nodded to the guards as they stepped aside to let the two in.

"Where are Mason and Arisa?" Felix asked as they entered.

"On their way," Kendra replied. "Hana's bringing Arisa, and I think Sebastian went to get Mason."

King Atticus was already on his throne. Archer knelt in front of him, speaking too quietly for anyone else to hear. The remaining four council members stood in their positions on either side of the throne. Ernest's two cousins—Eliza and the man the birthday party had been for, whose name slipped Felix's mind—along with Abraham Caldwell and Michael Beck were gone. As far as Felix knew, Michael was the only one who'd died.

"Do you know what's going to happen to Jack Caldwell?" Felix asked as he and Kendra sat down. Not only had Abraham run off with the Moonlit Army, but his wife had disappeared, too.

"He'll remain here as a student."

"They're letting him stay? What if he's on his parents' side?"

"They can't prove he was involved. And he seemed pretty upset when he found out what happened," Kendra said. "But we'll keep a close eye on him."

Arisa, Hana, Mason, and Sebastian arrived in the minutes that followed. A few more Guardians came in behind them, the final one being a bandaged and limping Adrienne Farrow, walking with the help of a white cane.

King Atticus rose to his feet. Archer stood and moved to stand at his right.

"I am ending the probation of Felix Carver, Arisa Tamura, and Mason Briggs," King Atticus announced.

That was it? No testimony? No debate among council members? Felix glanced at Archer, but he only wore his usual scowl.

"They still have special circumstances around their status as students, but it's time they moved on to real missions and classes with their fellow Guardians-in-training," the king continued. "Given recent events, it's important that we all be prepared for challenges unlike any we've ever seen. The Moonlit Army's goals are not much clearer than they were eight years ago, but it seems that Mirabelle Armitage may have an agenda beyond simply overthrowing the Brightlands and taking my throne. We need to be alert as we move forward with our usual missions."

The king dismissed the meeting with nothing more of a wave of his hand before retreating to his office.

Felix, Arisa, and Mason exchanged confused glances. Felix jumped to his feet and started toward Archer, but Adrienne beat him there.

"The perimeter is secure as of this morning," Adrienne told Archer. "No more poltergeists lingering around."

"Good," Archer replied.

"Hi, Adrienne," Felix said as he reached them. "Glad to see you alive."

"Thank you. I should be fully healed in a couple of weeks." Adrienne gave him a faint smile. "I heard about the battle with Ernest. Very impressive, for kids your age."

"Thank you for trusting us enough to send us."

Adrienne adjusted her grip on her cane. "I'm just grateful it all worked out. Except for the ritual supplies. I'm afraid the poltergeists kept me busy long enough for someone to come and collect them."

"And it's still unclear why they were summoned in the first place," Archer added. "There's a chance our suspicions are correct, and they were to prevent backup from reaching Ernest's. But we're still not completely positive whether he would have started a fight if you three hadn't shown up."

"You think whoever summoned them is still here at the castle?" Felix asked.

"Possibly. A lot of traitors left us, but it's more than likely that a few spies have decided to hang around."

"They're like flies," Adrienne said with a wave of her hand. "Pests. But I'll catch them eventually." She nodded goodbye to Archer and left to join a group of Guardians gathered nearby in hushed conversation.

"So, that's it?" Felix asked. "We're all off probation?"

Archer lifted an eyebrow. "That is what the king said, isn't it?"

"But Arisa's still cursed, and Mason's still a demon, and I'm..." Felix glanced around and lowered his voice. "What about Gideon?"

"Gideon fought his way to the surface when you were weak and injured," Archer said. "And you haven't heard a word from him since the battle." His eyes narrowed. "Correct?"

Felix nodded quickly. "I talked to my family this morning. They were able to keep him under control until I had the strength to try forcing him back into unconsciousness myself. We're pretty sure it worked."

Arisa and Mason joined them. Sebastian, Hana, and Kendra followed close behind.

"So, Archer," Sebastian said. "How much of this probation decision was your idea, and how much was the king's?" His question was completely serious, with no hint of the snark he usually liked to throw Archer's way.

"That's between me and the king," Archer said.

"What if Gideon comes back?" Felix persisted.

"Then you'll fight him back down." Archer swept his gaze over Felix, Mason, and Arisa. "After what I saw at Ernest's, I believe you three are capable of managing the burdens you're bearing." His expression managed to harden even further. "Of course, if Felix were overtaken by Gideon, if Arisa succumbed to her curse, if Mason turned into a monster...I would do whatever it takes to protect the Brightlands."

"Wow, what a nice thing to say," Sebastian said. He clapped his hands together. "On that happy note, Archer, you said you had something you wanted to discuss with the six of us?"

"Yes. Kendra, since you're the most proficient, can you relay this to Hana for me? I have to talk fast."

"Ready when you are," Kendra told him.

"Keep watch for any eavesdroppers, too."

Kendra nodded.

"There are questions we have to answer regarding the events that led up to the battle," Archer said. "To begin with, I'd like to know how Ernest assembled so many demons. They're supposed to be rare."

"The only time I've heard of anywhere near that many demons working together was when the old Brightlands were attacked," Sebastian said.

"It's concerning." Archer sighed. "Additionally, we only saw Ernest command werewolves, demons, and some spirits. I want to know if he succeeded at recruiting anything else for the Moonlit Army. And how."

"And you're, what, putting us in charge of finding all this out?" Arisa asked.

"In charge? Heavens no. I'm asking you to help me in any way you can," Archer replied. "Every Guardian is going to be on the lookout for information on the Moonlit Army, but you're the only ones I feel remotely confident placing my trust in." He lifted his gaze and swept it across the room behind them. "I certainly wouldn't put children in charge of doing anything dangerous. However, you are resourceful, and we could use your minds."

"We're teenagers, not children," Mason muttered.

Archer ignored the comment. "For instance, Mason, I'd like you to perform that unmasking spell at potential monster sites. Ernest still could have some death traps waiting for us."

"Sure," Mason said. "Should be easy now, with the Ironwood Wand."

Felix glanced at him. "I thought you were ditching us once you got it back."

"And let you all get yourselves killed?" Mason scoffed. "Besides, it's my responsibility to undo all of the damage Ernest did with the wand." His eyes lowered to the floor as he added, "And your library's cool."

"Good. We'll be stronger with you on our side," Archer said.

Kendra chuckled and lifted an eyebrow. "I'm surprised you're bringing Sebastian into this little club." She signed as she spoke.

"I'm offended, but I agree with you," Sebastian said.

"Yes." Archer's gaze flickered to Sebastian. "Let's hope I don't regret it."

"So, we're like a team now?" Felix asked.

Arisa lit up. "Can we come up with a team name?"

"That's not necessary," Archer said.

"Too late. I'm coming up with a name."

"I'm happy to help," Sebastian said, folding his arms. "But isn't this what the council is for?"

"We just lost half the council," Archer said. "I'm being cautious."

"Sure."

"What's that supposed to mean?"

"Nothing." Sebastian dropped his arms to his sides and smirked. "Now, do you have anything else to say, King's Hand, or can I go get food?"

"Go," Archer told him with a sigh.

Kendra and Hana left after Sebastian. Mason and Arisa walked away, too, but Felix hung back. He had one last question.

"Did you fight Hugo during the battle?" he asked.

"I only saw him briefly before he ran off," Archer replied. "Did you fight him?"

"Yeah. He sent those stuffed animals after me for a few minutes." Felix hesitated. "I think he wants revenge on you or something. Those scars you gave him looked pretty bad."

"He deserved worse than that."

"What did he do?"

Archer didn't respond.

"Ah, sorry, never mind." Felix rubbed the back of his neck. "Thanks again."

"For what?"

"For saving our lives. And not killing me, I guess." Felix took a step back. "Hopefully you made the right choice."

"I think I did." Archer stared at him for a long moment. "But only time will tell."

When Felix stepped out of the throne room, Sebastian was waiting, leaning against the wall by the doors. He flipped a quarter into the air. "How precise would you say you are with the psychometry thing?" he asked as he caught it.

Felix blinked. "Huh?"

"Well, you've been able to find big events in an object's history. Important stuff you're looking for." Sebastian flipped the coin again. "But say you wanted to find something that happened at a certain time. Could you do that?"

Felix watched it spin and land in Sebastian's palm. "Uh, I haven't tried. But probably?"

Sebastian tossed the coin to him. Felix barely caught it. "Morning after the battle at Ernest's," Sebastian said. "Around eight a.m." He stepped away from the wall and walked away.

Felix hurried to his room. When he arrived, he set the quarter on his desk and opened one of the drawers. He sifted through the junk the drawer had accumulated until he found Gideon's necklace that he'd hidden away. He laid the necklace out next to the quarter.

He stared at them, mind racing, for a couple of minutes before picking up the quarter and closing his eyes. He slid into the object's memory.

Sebastian walked by, the only person in the void besides Felix. This was today, at the council meeting. Felix pushed back along the timeline.

"Need some help?" Dad asked as he formed at Felix's side.

"Uh, yeah," Felix replied. "How do I get to a specific time? I can feel the pull of certain events, but I don't know when they take place."

"That's hard. It will get easier with practice, though." Dad thought for a moment. "Think about where you were at the time. What were you doing? How far away does it feel?"

Felix frowned. The morning after the battle, he'd slept in until noon. Maybe that would be close enough to push along the timeline to whatever event Sebastian wanted him to see.

The void shifted around Felix. Walls rose and fell. Sebastian disappeared and reappeared and disappeared again.

Archer became visible, standing on a balcony that ordinarily overlooked the central courtyard. But in here, there was nothing below him but darkness. Sebastian slid the quarter into his pocket and approached him.

"How's Adrienne doing?" Sebastian asked as he rested his hands on the railing next to Archer.

"Fine. Still recovering," Archer answered. "Until she's back on her feet, we have extra Guardians assigned to the tunnels."

"Why do you think she encouraged the kids to go? She could have come alone." Sebastian tapped his fingers against the railing. "Or found some other way to warn us, if she really was too injured."

Archer scowled. "I don't know."

Sebastian glanced back over his shoulder. "You think they left a few spies behind?"

"Are you trying to imply that Adrienne—?"

"No," Sebastian cut him off and turned his gaze to the side of Archer's face. "I'm just trying to put together the pieces. A lot happened."

Archer stayed quiet.

"If we can't trust each other," Sebastian said. "I don't think we're going to win this."

After a long moment, Archer asked, "Do you mean the Guardians, or the two of us, specifically?"

When Sebastian didn't answer right away, Archer met his eyes. "If you really mean that, you have to find some way to get over what happened."

Sebastian let out a cold laugh. "What you did to me, you mean?" He stepped back from the railing and turned around.

Felix frowned.

"Wait." Archer turned away from the railing. "I asked Adrienne about the kids, and why she sent them to the party."

"Oh." Sebastian paused. "Why didn't you tell me that a minute ago?"

"I was still thinking it over," Archer replied. "Adrienne said that she had a meeting with a king a few days earlier. The topic of the three came up." He hesitated. "The king mentioned that he was impressed with how they'd fared on their field trips, despite the way the tables turned on them."

"And?"

"I don't know. Maybe that pushed Adrienne to trust that they could handle Ernest."

"I think there's something else."

Archer was quiet for a long moment. "The king told me that he suspected the werewolves at Cold Creek were related to the Supermoon Wolves when he sent you."

Something flickered across Sebastian's face. Confusion? Anger? "He didn't tell me that."

"He wasn't certain," Archer said.

"He could have warned me."

"Regardless, he was impressed with the three of them."

Sebastian stared for a long moment. "You're saying that you think the king wanted the kids at Ernest's."

"I'm saying it's a possibility."

"You must think he had a good reason, then."

Archer didn't answer. He turned around. His hands moved to the railing.

"If you think it's because he wanted them to get killed, then I disagree," Archer said after a moment. "If he wanted them dead, he could have ordered them executed."

"I'm not arguing there," Sebastian said.

"We have to tread very carefully." Archer's eyes closed. "Everyone thinks they know what's best for the Brightlands."

"But it's easy to get caught up fighting each other instead of monsters." Sebastian's gaze flickered to something in the distance. "And more and more Guardians are leaving active duty."

"But most of those who remain have still sworn their loyalty to the king."

"Including you?"

"Of course." Archer's hands tightened around the railing's edge.

Under his breath, Sebastian muttered, "That's what I'm afraid of."

Sebastian, Archer, and the balcony faded into the black. Felix returned to his body standing next to his desk.

"Why would Sebastian show me that?" Felix asked, staring at the quarter in his hand. "It sounds like he..." Sebastian wouldn't actually turn on the king, would he? He was clearly opposed to whatever Mira had planned with the Moonlit Army, but he didn't exactly seem eager to follow the king's orders, either.

You brought Gideon's necklace out, Dad noted.

Felix sat the quarter down and reached out a hand to gingerly touch the necklace. "Dad, it has to be full of memories involving the

Moonlit Army. Maybe I could learn something that could help us defeat them."

You're right, Dad said. *But you need to be careful. It's easy to get lost in memories. Especially painful ones.*

"I'll start slow." Felix's hand moved to brush the fang. Like when he'd touched Archer's sword, he was hit with flashes. The same woman with silver hair that he'd seen in Archer's sword. The view of his house from the rose bushes. A raccoon darting across his driveway, growing taller, taking on the form of a man—

Felix yanked his hand back. He grimaced. "I don't want to be scared of him," he said. "I know I can control him, but I also have to accept that he's here."

Dad was quiet for a moment. *You think you can use his ability without him taking control.*

"Maybe," Felix said quietly. "Do you?"

I don't know. Dad was far from confident. That should have been enough to deter Felix. But...

"I know May was able to hold her ability back from me, so Gideon must be able to do the same. But I might be able to take it back on my own." Felix's hand wrapped around the necklace's chain. He lifted it into the air. "And I was able to fight back when he tried to possess me. Maybe, with enough practice, I could have complete control over his ability *and* his soul."

Just trying will be dangerous.

"I know."

There was a beat of silence.

Felix, you know my journal? Dad asked.

Felix nodded. He pulled open the top drawer of the desk. He'd given the book an occasional glance to try and decipher the text, to no avail. Dad had never offered any help, and Felix had gotten too wrapped up in training to give it much thought.

I think it's time you took a closer look at it.

Felix frowned. "But I can't read it."

You don't need to be able to read it. Everything I wrote is just notes and dates, Dad said. *The real story is in its memory.*

Before Felix could think much about what that meant, there was a knock at his door.

We'll talk later, Dad said. His presence vanished.

Felix opened the door to find Mason and Arisa waiting on the other side.

"We're celebrating our freedom from probation," Arisa said. "I convinced Hana and Kendra to take us to the beach."

"We're going to go steal food from the kitchen to take with us," Mason added. "You in?"

Felix grinned. "Of course I'm in."

Magic could wait.

Thank you for reading
A DROP OF HAUNTED BLOOD

To get updates and find out how you can be the first to read
new books, find me at:

www.rorynorth.com

If you enjoyed the story, please help support this indie author!
Tell a friend, leave reviews, request the book at your local
library, and talk about it on social media! #hauntedblood

More by Rory North:

Villain Complex: After defeating the city's biggest hero, supervillain Julian Godfrey finds himself in over his head when he attempts to train the woman who took on the hero's powers as part of an elaborate scheme.

Van Terra: Cyborg thief Jasper Van Terra is after revenge. Escaped lab experiment Grace Alvarez might be just what she needs.

Plague Saint: In a frozen city in the distant future, Winter Pierce kills the hospital's Plague Saint to save her mother after discovering his corruption. When she steals his identity, she quickly finds herself tangled up in a government conspiracy.

Be the first to know about new stories and upcoming releases! Sign up for my newsletter at:

rorynorth.com/starchatter